GRACE

GRACE

MICHAEL STEWART

THE ATLANTIC MONTHLY PRESS
NEW YORK
•

This is for Martine
and for Amelia, our daughter

***

ACKNOWLEDGEMENTS

Especial thanks are due to: Dr John Coggle, Head of Radiation
Biology, St Bartholomew's Hospital Medical College, London; 'Friends
of the Earth'; Dr David Geaney, Department of Clinical Psychiatry,
Littlemore Hospital, Oxford; 'Greenpeace'; Dr Richard Lindenbaum,
Department of Medical Genetics, Churchill Hospital, Oxford; Father
Herbert McCabe, Blackfriars Priory, Oxford; the Nuclear Industry
Radiation Waste Executive (NIREX), London; and, above all, to Dr
Oliver Sacks.

***

First published in Great Britain in 1989 by William Collins Sons & Co. Ltd.

First Atlantic Monthly Press edition, August 1989

Printed in the United States of America

Library of Congress Cataloging-in-Publication Data

Stewart, Michael, 1946–
    Grace.
    "First published in Great Britain in 1989
by William Collins Sons and Co., Ltd."—T.p.
verso.
    I. Title.
PR6069.T464G7   1989   823'.914   89-6860
ISBN 0-87113-305-9

The Atlantic Monthly Press
19 Union Square West
New York, NY 10003

FIRST PRINTING

Receive into Thy hands, O Lord, the soul of this Thy servant Matthew . . .

The murmur of the priest's voice, lowered in prayer, lapped gently against Matthew's ebbing consciousness. The soft, rhythmic hiss and click of the respirator grew muffled, distant. The tall doctor in the white coat seemed to be gradually receding into the background blur. Matthew wanted to let go. The waves were coming more insistently now, tugging at him, plucking him off the shore with their relentless undertow, washing him into the limitless ocean.

The pain and the panic was gone. Nothing hurt any longer. He no longer felt frightened. Everything seemed very simple, very necessary, very obvious. Slowly an extraordinary sense of lightness began to fill him – first his chest, then his head and limbs and finally the rot-riddled cave of his stomach. His whole body seemed gradually to be shedding its weight. But for the bedclothes tucking him in and the tubes and drips guying him down, he would unstick from the bed and rise gently upwards and away.

Eternal peace and life everlasting . . . continued the voice from further off.

His gaze came to rest upon the small statue of Our Lady standing on the bedside table. Shafts of sunlight radiated out from behind her image like spokes of white fire. Her face, cast in half-shadow, was smiling. One hand gestured towards her heart, the other, outstretched, was beckoning him. '*Come unto me,*' she was silently saying.

The light grew ever more intense, now shimmering in fast pulses, bathing the holy form in wondrous radiance. It

9

became brighter and more brilliant, brighter than the sun and yet somehow not blinding, swelling all the time and expanding so that it filled the room, the world, the whole universe. The eyes smiled comfort, the halo hinted reassurance, the arms promised safe haven. *'Come unto me.'* Yes, he was coming.

Far away, voices muttered, *Amen*.

Up, up he gently rose into the air. For a moment, looking down, he glimpsed his own body lying on the bed, pale yet peaceful, surrounded by figures in white. And then suddenly he was floating quite free. Floating into the smiling eyes and the beckoning embrace, into the shimmering, all-suffusing light.

Matthew Francis Holmwood died on 6th March 1981 at the Royal Hospital, Gloucester. He was twelve. He had been admitted three weeks before, complaining of severe stomach pains. His blood count was catastrophically low and, despite frequent transfusions, it continued to fall. In a last-ditch effort to save him, he was given a bone marrow transplant. The donor was his twin sister, Grace. The graft failed to improve his condition, and two days later he died. The cause of death, as certified by the consultant on the case, Dr Leonard Grigson, was gastro-intestinal failure, aggravated by pneumonia.

Five years previously, Alec, Matthew's father, an active man in his early thirties, had died of a heart attack while playing tennis. This second bereavement left Grace alone in the family with her mother, Laura.

I

One

A young girl runs laughing across a forest
clearing, her eyes blazing, her pony-tail flying. Flurries of frost dance in the sunlight
at her heels. 'Wait for me!' she cries. She
collapses against a small, low door hanging
from one hinge, and fights to regain her
breath.

Inside, it's dark, damp. A narrow shaft,
hacked out of the rock, falls sharply away
out of sight. Torchlight picks out broken
wooden pit-props, standing askew beneath
a half-fallen roof. The earth is red and
sticky. Flecks of minerals glint from the
hewn seams. The beam of light whips back.
The girl is now crawling in through the
tight passage, profiled against the light outside. She slithers past a twisted prop, slips
and falls, gashing her hand on a rock . . .

The sunlight behind the figure grows
dazzlingly, incredibly bright, until it engulfs
everything, exploding in one brilliant,
searing starburst . . .

*

Grace jolted awake. She fumbled frantically for the bedside
table and switched on the lamp. Nothing. She blinked. Still
nothing! Her whole field of vision was blotted out by a
bright blue disc, as though she'd been staring full into the
sun. She rubbed her eyes hard. Had she suddenly gone *blind*?

Gradually she began slowly to make out the familiar objects in her room, one by one – the lamp with its scorched plastic shade, the alarm clock at ten past five, the brass bedstead glinting in the light and, beyond, the desk piled untidily with books and half-finished homework, standing beneath a cork pin-board plastered with her photographs – of Mum in her studio, of Leo on holiday together, and, of course, always of Matthew.

She felt hot yet shivery. Her throat was dry, but she felt too uneasy to go downstairs for a drink. She lay back and stared up at the ceiling.

She'd often had dreams about Matthew since his death, but never one quite like this. Never one so vivid, so absolutely real, so exactly how it had been at the time, and yet, somehow, so . . . odd. That girl was *her*. Uncanny, she thought, to see yourself in a dream. From someone else's point of view, too. She remembered clearly that day when she'd gone exploring the disused mine with Matthew, the day before he'd fallen ill. It was almost as if, for a strange moment, she'd shared his thoughts again, as they'd used to. Dreamed *his* dream.

She felt the familiar gnawing ache. How badly she still missed him! They'd been so close, like a single coin with two faces. They'd often exchange a secret smile, knowing they were thinking the same thing; sometimes they held whole conversations in their minds without speaking a word. Some people, she knew, had found their closeness touching, others rather disturbing. But all that had ended five years ago. Pray as she might, she'd never received the merest hint of any communication from him since.

Until now?

'Don't be so absurd!' she told herself severely. Dreams were illogical, meaningless and incoherent: that was what Leo said. No-one had yet explained why we dreamed, let alone what our dreams meant. They were *sur*real, not real; they bore the same relation to reality as a limp watch in a Dali painting bore to time. She mustn't fall prey to these subversive inner voices whispering panic at five in the morning.

Growing calmer after a while, she got out of bed and wrapped her dressing-gown round her. She stole down the gallery past the spare room, past her mother's bedroom and into Matthew's old room. Slipping in between the fusty blankets lying folded on the bed, she curled up in a tight ball, with her knees tucked up at her chin, and within moments she was fast asleep.

*

Laura glanced at the wall clock above the fridge as she put away the breakfast cereal. Eight-forty. She had better hurry: she hated being late for Mass. She looked across the kitchen to the back porch where Grace stood in her hacking jacket, her fair hair pinned up, tugging on a pair of muddy riding boots. Beyond the half-open door, a thick autumnal mist stretched across the lawn in a low, undulating band, blotting out the apple trees and giving the great yellowing chestnut beyond the appearance of floating on cloud. The mist concealed the river that bordered the garden, too, so that only the line of the poplar trees and the perpetual sound of water rushing down the abandoned wooden race gave any hint that this house was, or at least had been in an earlier generation, a mill.

Laura caught her daughter's eye. 'I really don't think . . .' she began.

'It's all right, Mother.'

'How can you ride if you can't even see the ground?'

'I'll muck out till it clears.' Grace stood up. 'I'd rather.'

Laura reached for her coat and checked automatically in the pocket for her missal. *I'd rather muck out stables than go to church*. She felt a familiar twinge of disappointment. Well, tomorrow was Sunday, and Grace would be coming along then. The girl was only seventeen, after all; she would come back to her faith. People always returned in the end to the influences that shaped the first years of their life.

'Ready, then?'

As she turned, she saw the girl give a sudden, violent flinch and throw up her hand to shield her eyes.

'Are you all right, darling?'

Grace blinked and rubbed her eyes.

'Just saw a funny flash.' She laughed oddly.

With a stab of alarm, Laura searched her daughter's long oval face; her lightly freckled cheeks were ashen and her grey-blue eyes were drawn. *Oh God*, was her instant thought. *Is all that starting again?*

'I'll call Leonard,' she said, moving to the phone.

'No, don't. Nothing's the matter. Something just flashed. The sun, I expect.' There was no sun. 'Anyway,' she added in a bravely provocative tone, 'after last night I thought Leo was banished.'

'Grace . . .'

'Come on, Mother, we do live in a rather open-plan place.' She gave a conspiratorial smile. 'I think you're very hard on him. You like him, don't you? So do I. Well, then.'

Laura took the car keys from their hook.

'If it's your migraines again, darling . . .'

'Stop worrying. I'm perfectly fine. Promise.'

'You shouldn't be riding. I'll call Ralph and say you're not feeling well.' She paused; she knew that stubborn look on her daughter's face. She sighed. 'Well, I suppose you're old enough to know what you're doing. But do take care.'

'Hurry up, Mother, or you'll be late. Just drop me at the end of the stables drive.'

Laura reached into the larder for a pot of cherry jam she'd made.

'Here, give this to Benedict for Mary. But warn her to watch out for stones.'

As she handed the jam to Grace, she recalled fleetingly the terrible time just after Matthew died when Mary, their cleaning-lady, had suddenly gone blind. Benedict, Mary's son, had long had a crush on Grace. He was a nice enough lad, but he'd never get much beyond a stable-hand.

'Do come on,' said Grace, taking the jar.

She grabbed her riding hat and crop and led the way out into the misty morning. She skipped down the mossy stone path that led along the side of the house, past the Virginia creeper spreading like a crimson flame along the wall, and slipped through the small iron gate set in the tall yew hedge and flanked by two stone mushrooms. As they reached the green Volvo estate car parked on the gravel at the front, she turned to her mother with a teasing smile.

'You could do worse, you know,' she said. 'After all, he's already one of the family. He virtually lives here. I'm sure Father Gregory could put in a good word with the powers upstairs.' She affected a sigh. 'Well, I suppose you're old enough to know what you're doing.'

*

Laura dropped Grace at the manor stables and headed east out of Coledean village along the five-mile road that wound through the misty woodland to the small town of Abbotsbury. Here, the convent where Grace went to school offered the only Catholic church for miles around, now that the small chapel at Coledean had been closed down in a diocesan rationalization plan. She felt anxious and disturbed. Earlier that morning she'd found Grace asleep in Matthew's bed — she hadn't awakened her, but merely shut the door quietly and woken her with a call from the foot of the stairs — and she couldn't help wondering if Grace's sleepwalking habit was coming back again. And then there'd been that strange moment in the kitchen . . . She bit her lip. It was ominously reminiscent of what had happened after Matthew died. Hadn't they left all that behind, for good?

Grace had gone to pieces after the tragedy, coming, as it had, on top of her father's death. Her faith, hitherto so strong and simple, was shaken to the foundations. She'd openly voiced her doubt. 'God's ways aren't mysterious,' she'd once cried, 'but murderous!' Laura recalled the anguish she'd felt, watching the young girl's belief falter and her hope dwindle. Usually so outgoing and sociable, she'd grown withdrawn, lost in a world of her own. She'd developed migraines, lost weight alarmingly and seemed robbed of all her zest and vitality. Gradually and painfully, however, mostly due to Leonard's unflagging care, she had returned to life. If there were still times when she slipped back into an earlier mood – going for long walks alone, moping about the house without speaking, shutting herself in her room for hours on end – these were far outweighed by those when she was a normal, lively, loving, considerate, if often a wilful and infuriating, teenage girl. Leonard had nursed her back to life with all the care and love of a father, but he'd always warned of a possible relapse. Was this it?

'Holy Mary, Mother of God, grant my child Grace peace of heart,' she muttered.

Soon she came to the run-down slate quarry that marked the boundary of Abbotsbury town. She slowed down as she reached the first streets of miners' cottages with their walls whitewashed, windows curtained and gardens husbanded with all the pride of hard and bitter poverty. As she passed one of the town's Methodist chapels, people were arriving for a wedding. Her thoughts went back to Grace's remark: *You could do worse.* She smiled. Worldly-wise though she thought herself, Grace was innocent, even ingenuous, for seventeen. She'd lived all her life in Coledean, a rural village on the edge of the Forest of Dean, deep in the west of England. She had plenty of friends at school, but while her classmates were dating boyfriends, she was exercising horses or messing around in the darkroom or going on wildlife rambles with Leonard. She knew all the principles of life and love – she'd been largely brought up in adult company – but her practical experience was narrow. Was she too cloistered in that museum of a mill, living alone with her mother among all their memories and memorabilia? Did she lack a *father*?

She sighed. Couldn't things stay easy and uncommitted? Why did there always have to be that sexual undercurrent waiting to break out, as it had last night? She'd met Leonard when Matthew went into hospital: he was the consultant on

20

the case. He was so kind and caring towards her throughout that terrible time. Only later did she stop to ask herself how much his kindness owed to duty and how much to desire. Perhaps she'd been wrong to let him grow so close; she should have foreseen it sooner and not encouraged him. Above all, she should have controlled her own feelings for him. There had been that one time . . . it was shortly after Matthew died, and she'd been in desperate need of comfort and reassurance. But human frailty was no excuse, and ever since, for all her penances, that act had lain heavily on her conscience. Leonard, a confirmed atheist, simply could not understand. It drove him to exasperation. Divorced with two grown-up children, he could accept that marriage, according to her religious convictions, was virtually impossible, but why not a liaison *outside* marriage, he kept asking, a normal love affair between two normal adults? There were times, such as the previous night, when she was sorely tempted. Was she right to go on tormenting herself, and him? And what about Grace and *her* needs?

She accelerated as the spire of the wrought-iron gates of the convent came into view. Her soul, confused and troubled, yearned to be unburdened. She'd go to confession that morning.

*

After lunch, Grace shut herself in the study and struggled with her art essay, but her mind kept wandering back to her dream. She glanced distractedly around the low, oak-beamed room. Dad's old books – on film and sport and especially on architecture – lay in their places on the shelves, as they had done those ten years past. The walls were still hung with his diplomas and photos of the mill, before, during and after restoration. This room had formerly been the granary, and a primitive internal hoist in the corner, returned to working order but serving no practical purpose any more, connected with the box-room upstairs. She turned away. This was still Dad's room; he was present in every inch of it.

She was wrestling with a critique on Van Gogh when her mother came in. She looked very businesslike in her dog-tooth suit with her short-cropped, greying hair and her portfolio under her arm. Saturday or not, she was off to see a publisher. Slaving to pay the school fees.

'I'm away now,' she said. 'Back around six.'

Grace rubbed her eyes behind her glasses. 'Let's see, Mother,' she said.

'It's only a rough.'

'Don't be so modest.'

Her mother brought over the portfolio and took out a cover illustration for a children's book of myths. Grace studied the work. It was exquisitely done.

'It's wonderful,' she said.

'It'll pay a bill or two.' As her mother slipped the artwork back, she caught sight of her essay. 'Well, we can't all be Van Goghs,' she said with a self-deprecating smile.

Grace shot her a brief glance. It was sad to be so brilliant and yet ashamed of being commercial.

'Well, *I* think it's great,' she said.

'You're very sweet.' She leaned forward and switched on the reading light. 'Don't strain your eyes, darling. It's about time for your check-up, isn't it? Remind me to fix an appointment. Well, I must dash. Wish me luck.'

'You don't need luck, Mother. Truly.'

*

Grace sprawled uncomfortably across the desktop, leaning on her elbow and chewing her pen. She looked up into the naked bulb staring out at her from under the glass lampshade. Momentarily blinded, she turned back to her essay. A bright blue-fringed disc masked the centre of the page. She shivered. That was just how it had been when waking from her dream in the early hours of that morning. Same again, too, when getting ready to go riding. Was it her eyes? She took off her glasses and rubbed them hard. Perhaps Mum was right about having them checked. Her eyesight had never been perfect, but she'd only ever needed glasses for reading. The specialist had said migraines had nothing to do with eyes, but maybe he'd been wrong. Leo always said, *Never trust the experts.* Could this be a different kind of migraine, a kind that *did* have to do with her eyes, a kind that sent you blind? Mary had once told her what going blind was like. She'd said it was just like the way a lightbulb burnt unnaturally bright before suddenly going *pop*.

Abruptly she got up and went to the kitchen to pour herself a glass of orange-juice. Too troubled to return to work, she prowled restlessly around the large, open-plan living-room that formed the heart of the house. This old mill had been her home all her life, and it remained as it always had, stamped indelibly with the spirit of happier days. Before she was born, Dad had chanced upon it, lying derelict and abandoned; he'd fallen in love with it, bought it and set about designing it into a dream home. Now it wore the homely patina of age and use. The structure centred around a tall, light living-room that rose to the roof beams, with the walls stripped to the stone. Above, on three sides, ran an oak gallery built of old church fittings, from which the bedrooms led off. The floor was flagged in York stone and carpeted with faded rugs, and the whole was furnished with worn old leather chairs, lamps with threadbare tasselled silk shades and highly polished early English oak tables and chests. Only the sofa was relatively new – a gift from Leo after Matthew died.

She remembered her childhood as one long, sunny idyll. As Dad had to spend the week up in London and Mum's own career was beginning to take off, she and Matthew were left alone together for long stretches of the day. It was the happiest period of her life. Then, just as she had started at the convent school, Dad died. For weeks after, she would crawl into Matthew's bed and they'd cry themselves to sleep. Mum had to work extra hard to make ends meet and she spent more and more time away from home, and Mary came in more often to help. But Matthew was always there, and nothing else mattered. Then, five years later, it was his turn . . .

She gripped the stair-post. How, after so long, could she still feel as bad as ever? Didn't wounds ever heal? Just as she thought she'd got onto an even keel, some memory would lash back at her.

She stared out of the tall west window. Out there lay the fields and woods they'd so often explored. Somewhere, too, beyond that far ridge was the wilderness with the small disused iron mine which they'd explored that last happy, sunny afternoon. She turned away. In all the years since, she'd avoided that strange, abandoned place. She'd never even felt tempted to return. Certainly she'd dreamt about it, but never so vividly, with such frightening precision and clarity. After so long, how could it appear so fresh? She tried to picture the scene, but her memory gradually began to fade, as if it had used itself up. Had there actually been a grassy clearing in front? And a small, low door hanging from one hinge? Was the mine-shaft really that narrow passage hacked out of the rock, with twisted pit-props and a half-collapsed roof and flecks of minerals glinting from the seams?

Was this a dream at all, or a memory?

*

A light breeze had sprung up, carrying a hint of rain on its chill edge. Behind, in the east, the sky was darkening. She pedalled faster. She should turn back or she'd get drenched. But she carried on. She had to know.

A mile into the forest, she turned off the narrow road and, leaving her bicycle, followed a sandy track that curled gently around the contour of the slopes, wooded with spruce and silver birch. Soon the going grew rougher. She tripped over the naked sinews of tree-roots and slipped on the mulch of fallen leaves. The sun faltered for a moment, then abruptly went in, dulling the rich gold foliage to base metal. The wind rose a degree, numbing her fingers. After a while, the track divided and she took the upper path, which gradually grew flatter and broadened into a grassy ride. Ahead, round a gentle bend, lay the clearing.

As she approached, she slowed her pace. An eerie stillness gripped the forest. Barely the smallest movement rustled the undergrowth, scarcely a leaf or a blade of grass stirred. A new track led into the clearing from the side, with tyre ruts gouged deep into the earth, well overgrown with long wiry grass. The ruts led in a direct line across the clearing to the entrance to the mine, itself a small, low channel dug directly into the side of the hill. In place of the old wooden door with its broken hinge, stood a stout metal grille, chained and padlocked and bedded firmly in a concrete footing. Fixed crookedly to the bars and streaked by several years of rain and rust hung a sign, PRIVATE: KEEP OUT. With the light failing, she couldn't see beyond into the mine itself. Nervously, she stepped forward. As she reached the entrance, overgrown with roots and ivy, she peered in through the grille. No more than a few feet inside, a solid wall, built of roughly mortared breeze blocks, completely blocked the passage.

The mine had been sealed off.

With mounting unease, she headed back across the clearing. As she went, she became aware of a strange, metallic taste in her mouth. Her head had begun to throb. She'd reached the other side when she cast a glance behind her.

She stopped dead.

The mine was . . . glowing. A strange light hovered over the entrance. No, the light came from somewhere between, from the middle of the clearing. As she watched, spellbound yet curiously unafraid, the light grew rapidly brighter and more brilliant, brighter than the sun and yet somehow not blinding, shimmering in fast pulses and radiating like spokes of white fire, until it seemed to fill the clearing, the forest around, the entire world from sky to earth. She had the sensation of growing weightless, unsticking gradually from the ground and rising gently up into the air until she was floating quite free. Floating in rapture into the shimmering, all-suffusing light.

Two

Laura stood at the chopping-board, preparing supper. Her hands worked fast, automatically, but her mind was else-where. Distantly she was aware of the six o'clock time signal on the radio and she reached to switch it off; she couldn't face more news of hijacks and famines. She glanced up at the window and caught a glimpse of her own reflection in the dark panes. A sudden squall of rain lashed ferociously at the glass. Grace had gone off without her anorak. On her bicycle.

By seven she was seriously worried. She called Ralph Cottrell up at the manor in case she'd gone back to the stables. She phoned several friends in the village, too, in case she'd stopped to take shelter, but no-one had seen her. She felt a flush of annoyance; couldn't the child at least have phoned? Then she rebuked herself. This was no child but a girl of seventeen. Then she thought back to that morning, and began chopping more determinedly.

She had finished the vegetables and was garnishing the roast when another gust of rain slashed the window-pane. A sudden picture flashed across her mind: a girl on her bicycle, in the driving rain and the failing light, a truck steaming round a bend in the narrow road, headlights pick-ing out the lone cyclist, suddenly on top of her, swerving, braking, too late . . . She pushed the roasting-tray aside and wiped her hands. She had to *do* something. With sudden decisiveness, she reached for her oiled anorak, slipped into her wellingtons and headed out into the squall. Grace was most likely at Mary Nolan's, though it wasn't her day for going over to read to her.

Hurrying along the stone path in the light thrown from the windows, she had reached the towering black wall of the yew hedge when she realized she'd left her car keys in her bag. As she turned back, a movement across the lawn caught her eye. She stopped and strained to see in the sheeting rain. Gradually a figure detached itself from the far bushes. For a moment she stood frozen to the spot, fascinated, as Grace sauntered dreamily forward into the centre of the lawn, then stopped and bent to pick something off the ground.

'Grace!' she called, rushing over.

The girl looked up, and smiled a strange, other-worldly smile. Her long fair hair was knotted and straggly, rain streamed down her cheeks and her clothes were soaked through to the skin, but she hardly seemed to notice. She held out a large, speckled chestnut leaf.

'Beautiful, isn't it?' she said.

'For God's sake, are you out of your mind?' She gripped her arm; it was limp, unresisting. 'Come inside at once!' She marched her back towards the house. As they reached the back porch she caught again the enigmatic half-smile on her face, and hesitated. 'Are you really all right?'

The large grey-blue eyes were radiant.

'Wonderful.'

*

Laura reached across the table for the supper plates but Grace jumped up at once and began stacking, continuing her argument with Leonard as she carried them over to the sink. Laura smiled to herself: the two were always disputing something or other. Pehaps it was because they were so alike. This time they were bickering about a proposal to cull the Forest deer. It was good to see her so happy and cheerful. She'd been like that all evening. Extraordinary.

'Rubbish, Leo,' Grace was protesting. 'Foxes have got nothing to do with it.'

Leonard tilted his chair back on two legs and stretched

his long body. An inch further, and the chair would break. It wouldn't be the first.

'More foxes means fewer deer,' he said. 'Statistics show . . .'

'Statistics show anything you like, Leo. They just call it a cull to make it sound respectable. It's a *kill*. Killing for sport. Disgusting.'

'Hang on, Duchess,' he pleaded, using a favourite play on her name, 'culling *protects* the herd. It's the lesser of two evils.'

'Still evil. You've just admitted it.'

Leonard laughed, conceding the point. He leaned to his side. 'Laura,' he said smoothly, 'you're very quiet.'

'Leave Mum alone,' intervened Grace, returning for the dishes. 'She's not in the mood for playing games. Coffee?'

'Thanks,' he replied, smiling. 'Actually, I can't stay late. I said I'd drop in on someone. A patient,' he added quickly.

'He's fibbing, Mum,' she said. 'Consultants work nine to five. He's *visiting* someone.'

'My cleaning-lady, if you don't mind. Well, her husband, to be exact. He suffers from terrible migraines.'

Laura glanced at Grace, expecting a cheeky riposte, but her face had suddenly gone solemn and a thoughtful frown puckered her brow. She toyed with her coffee-spoon, keeping her eyes lowered. There was a moment's silence.

'I've got a friend at school who has bad migraines,' she began quietly.

'Commoner than you think,' he responded, sipping his coffee. 'Rest and dark, that's the only cure.'

Laura nodded. 'Remember when you used to have them, darling?'

'But my friend's are different,' Grace went on, her voice growing troubled.

Leonard's smile had faded.

'Different?' he echoed.

'Yes. Everything apparently goes brilliantly bright. Just like Mary said happened just before she went blind.'

He fixed her with a suspicious, penetrating stare. When he spoke his easy tone didn't match his expression.

'With migraines you often see funny lights. Whorls, zigzags, blotches, all kinds of things. Some people get whole firework displays.'

Grace's frown had deepened further.

'It's more like a light . . . coming out of nowhere . . . just appearing there in front of you . . . and getting brighter and brighter. Or so she says,' she added hastily.

'Your friend,' he enquired gently, 'does she have these often?'

Grace looked up. A light blush had spread across her cheeks, and in her palm lay the coffee-spoon, bent out of shape.

'Just once so far, I think.'

'She hasn't been sniffing or smoking anything she shouldn't?'

'No. Positive.'

His expression relaxed.

'Well, I'm sure there's nothing to worry about. All the same, I think she should tell her doctor. Or someone she can trust.' A pointed silence fell between them. He glanced at the clock on the wall and, swallowing back his coffee, rose to his feet. 'Laura, you must forgive me, I have to be going. Thanks for a delicious supper. I'm afraid I'm leaving you both with the washing-up.'

Laura rose, too. His departure was uncomfortably sudden, but no doubt he meant to avoid things being more uncomfortable later.

'Must you go so soon?' She could see he was determined. 'Well, then, let me see you out.'

She led the way through the large open living-room and into the hallway beyond, where she handed him his coat. Outside, the rain had stopped, and a large, wall-eyed moon glowered intermittently from behind restless clouds. Pausing on the doorstep, she took a deep breath of the dank night air. Standing an arm's reach away, he turned up his collar and shot her a puzzled glance.

'What was all *that* about?'

'She's been strange all day.'

'Strange? How?'

'Oh, it's nothing. Just Grace.'

He hesitated, uncertain. She scrutinized his face: was there something *really* serious going on? But he reached out and squeezed her arm reassuringly.

'Call if you need me, Laura,' he said. 'At least I'm good for that,' he added with an ironic smile.

He drew her forward and gave her a brief, brotherly kiss, then turned away. For a moment he hesitated again and his brow knitted in a frown, then with a shrug he strode across the gravel to the silver Jaguar parked by the studio outhouse.

As she watched the tall, lean figure step into the car, she felt the urge to run after him and clasp him tightly, so as to make him tell her that everything was all right. But she held back; he'd only misunderstand. She was confused, too. Was it just because he was backing off? And now he was going to be away for a few days at a conference somewhere. But at once she felt a pang of alarm: she had to feel he was *there* . . . in *case* . . . Not too close, but not too far either. Then she checked herself. This whole business was quite absurd. She was leading them on some adolescent dance of advance and retreat, pursuit and flight, in which they never actually met and touched. Had her timidity reduced them to that?

For a moment she stood on the doorstep, watching the car's tail-lights disappear down the winding drive, then abruptly she turned and went back indoors. Outside the study she paused and glanced through the door at the books lining the walls. Perhaps she'd take some Gerard Manley Hopkins up to bed. She needed something to set her mind and heart at peace.

*

Grace heard her mother's bedroom door finally close. She waited, listening carefully. Apart from the cracking of beams and boards as the heating went off, the house was quite silent. She felt strangely excited, almost elated. The mood alarmed her. What was happening? What did it all *mean?* Slipping on her dressing-gown, she tiptoed along the gallery and down the broad oak staircase. She had to find out.

The moon had risen in the sky, casting shallow panels of light at the base of the tall window and leaving the inner reaches of the room in thick shadow. She felt her way along the furniture until she reached the study. Closing the door quietly behind her, she switched on the light. In the corner behind the desk stood the small library of medical textbooks Mum had bought during Matthew's illness in a desperate attempt to understand what was wrong. Between a book on chemotherapy and another on neurophysiological disorders, she came upon an old, well-thumbed prayer book. How sad, she thought, to have to rely at the final stand on the comfort of religious superstition. And yet both had failed him.

She then found Dr Oliver Sacks' classic study, *Migraine*, and took it to the light.

'Symptoms,' she read: 'pulsating, splitting, throbbing headache; nausea, vomiting; listlessness, photophobia, hypersensitivity to sound and movement . . .' Hang on, she thought; that's not me. But there was such a thing as 'migraine equivalent' – a migraine without the headache. Very well. 'A migraine can be thought of as an epileptic seizure in very slow motion,' she read on. 'EEGs show seizure-type spike formations, starting deep in the brain stem, projecting upwards onto the cerebral cortex, then downwards and to the sides to the plexuses of the body . . .' Oh Christ, she thought: had that been an epileptic fit that afternoon? How could she tell? She remembered the amazing light but very little of what happened afterwards until she was back home.

She went on, growing more anxious. She read about hallucinations, or 'auras', common in classical migraines. There, just as Leo had described, people often saw brilliant stars, sparks, flashes, sometimes in simple geometric forms, sometimes swarming randomly, white or coloured, 'shimmering undulations, like looking through watered silk; moiré patterns, lattices, tessellated motifs, boiling silently . . .' This was more like it. 'Most scotomata take the form of brilliant luminosity near the fixation-point, from where it expands and moves slowly towards the edge of the visual field, assuming the shape of a giant crescent or horseshoe. Its subjective brightness is blinding.' Exactly. 'Characteristically, these auras come on suddenly, from no-where; their effect is overwhelming; they give the sense of the effect being "forced" into the mind; they last only a few minutes, and they convey a sense of stillness, timelessness, leading to elaborate illusory images or dreamlike states . . .'

She closed the book quietly. That was it. Oh, God. They'd come back. Worse than ever.

Slowly she traced her steps upstairs. For a while, she stared out of her bedroom window into the moonlit garden. It could mean brain damage. A cerebral tumour, like Mary Nolan had had. You didn't have to feel pain to know something was wrong; the book had said that irresistible euphoria could be a sign, too. She shivered. Yes, she had been feeling dangerously well all day.

She switched on the bedside light and cast her eye slowly around her room. On the back of the door hung the Fifties overcoat she'd picked up at a jumble sale, and the walls were covered with posters of wildlife and art exhibitions. She glanced over the photographs on the pin-board, at the one of Matthew and herself, dressed up alike for a school play and quite indistinguishable, and at another of herself alone, taken by Leo that summer in the farmhouse they'd rented in the Dordogne, standing on tiptoes in a freezing rock-pool. She looked at the books jammed haphazardly in the shelves and the stack of tape-cassettes scattered on the table, at the zany plastic clock on the mantelpiece with devil's-tail hands her mother so abhorred and the large felt frog she'd once made Matthew, croaking silently at the foot of her bed, and she thought to herself, *Will I ever see these things again?*

Quickly she climbed into bed and lay staring at his photo

on the bedside table until gradually she felt herself dropping off. Perhaps she'd dream about him and, for a brief while, they'd be reunited and laugh and play together as they'd used to. She reached to switch off the light, then stopped. Tonight she'd sleep with it on.

*

Leonard jammed the typescript of his speech into his bulging briefcase and forced the locks shut, then gave a final glance over his desk. One o'clock in the morning and tomorrow was a long day – a full stint at the hospital, then a long drive to Brighton in time for the oncology conference reception. His own paper was scheduled for the following afternoon. Sometimes he wished he'd stuck with paediatrics; there, at least he'd dealt with the whole range of children's ailments, whereas now, as a cancer expert, he felt his field was narrow and over-specialized. It was a good five years since he'd made the switch.

He thought back to the evening. Grace hadn't fooled him, of course. He'd played it down to Laura, but the alarm bells had started ringing. Old Mary Nolan had complained of migraines just before she'd developed the tumour, barely a month after Matthew died. The drugs he'd prescribed had contained it, but at the cost of sending her blind. And now Grace was having migraines. Were his worst fears coming true?

His eye lingered briefly on the large photo frame that stood swamped by textbooks, medical journals and un-answered correspondence. He held it under the desk lamp and studied the jumbled collage of photos and snaps. Vanessa and Mark, at fourteen and twelve, frozen in time as the children he really remembered, when he'd been their only father and they his only family. Angie, too, smiling proof that the marriage had once been happy. And, between them, his other, newer family, Laura and Grace. Laura, six years older than Angie – three years older than himself, too – with her short dark hair and wry, twisted smile. Laura, so strong

33

and capable and independent, yet so vulnerable and, for all her faith, so fearful. And Grace, standing with her arm protectively around her mother. So fearless, so beautiful. His Duchess.

He snapped open his briefcase. Throwing out a thick file of notes, he slipped the photo frame in its place. He couldn't face travelling alone.

Three

'Mother,' said Grace as she put on her school coat, 'you look terrible.' Twice in the early hours of the past few nights, feeling too restless to sleep, she'd looked across the garden to see lights burning in the studio outhouse. Mum had a deadline to meet. 'It's a wonderful day. I'll cycle to school. Save you a good hour, there and back.'

'No, darling, I don't think it's wise, not just now,' replied her mother. 'Anyway, you've got late swimming, haven't you, and it'll be dark.'

'Wait till I've got my driver's licence.'

'We won't be able to afford a second car. You know that.'

'Leo's offered to lend me the money. I'll work in the holidays to pay it off.'

'Absolutely not. I don't want us to be indebted to Leonard any more than we are already.' She reached for her coat and car keys. 'Besides, I enjoy the trip. Makes a natural break.'

'It's your coffee-and-chat morning with Father Gregory, isn't it? That's half the day blown.'

'Don't talk like that about Father Gregory. He's a very busy man, and it's good of him to spare the time to visit at all. Anyway, he can't make it today.'

'Well, I'm sorry to be such a trouble, that's all.'

'Don't be silly, darling.' She gave her arm a brief, tender squeeze, then turned to the door. 'Ready?'

Grace picked up her school case and followed. It really wasn't fair to her mother when she had so much work. She had to find a way, somehow, to be less of a burden.

*

The swimming-pool was hot and the air heavy with chlorine. Small knots of Sisters and pupils sat in the banked stalls. The relay race was next on the schedule. Grace slipped off her towel and joined the other sixth-formers, standing in their teams at the deep end. She took up the second place, behind her friend Emily. Sister Thomas gave the signal.

'On your marks . . . get set . . . *go!*'

With a ragged splash, four swimmers hit the water. Cries of encouragement broke sporadically from the onlookers. Sister Thomas, stop-watch in hand, hurried abreast of the swimmers at a fast walking pace. Grace stepped forward and curled her toes eagerly over the edge. She felt a strange excitement taking hold of her. In her lane, Emily was now labouring down the return length, giving ground with every stroke. First one, then the second and the third swimmer touched the end and the next in line dived off. Finally Grace took a deep breath, and dived in.

She was an arrow, a fish, a dart, slicing through the water with exhilarating ease. She'd never swum so fast, so effortlessly. She was without weight, just an edge shearing through the water. Above her the roof lights flashed as she rolled this way, below her the water bubbled as she rolled that way. Already she could see the far end and the water growing lighter as the pool grew shallower. She was on the heels of the third girl as she took the turn with her best flip-over and, kicking hard, shot herself back down the pool. Suddenly the water seemed to be growing brighter – it couldn't be, it was getting deeper! – it was becoming luminous, iridescent, she was swimming in pure light, in a sheet of brilliant white, ahead and below, growing ever more intense, shimmering now in fast pulses, expanding to fill the whole pool and beyond . . .

Terrified, dazzled, she gulped in a mouthful of water. Choking, she gasped for air and drew in a lungful of water. A frenzy of panic gripped her. She jerked upwards, but that only seemed to take her deeper. Which way *was* upwards? She lashed about, thrashing, kicking, fighting, screaming, choking, gasping in more water still, her windpipe scorching, her lungs burning, her head exploding . . . she was suffocating in water, drowning in light . . .

Suddenly, a brilliant flash.

Matthew!

She saw him, clear as life. Pale. Peaceful. Dressed all in white and surrounded by whiteness.

A fleeting second later, the image was gone, absorbed into the shimmering light. But even as she clawed in terror for air, the blazing light all about her gradually, ineluctably, began to turn dark. White pearl turning to black pearl. Silver turning to lead. A bright blue-fringed disc remained, lingered briefly, and then it, too, was abruptly snuffed out and total night fell.

*

Laura saw the doctor off and poured herself a drink. She went round the living-room, turning on all the lights. Upstairs, Grace was asleep, lightly sedated. Laura sat down in her chair by the fire, but got up a moment later and paced the room, unable to settle.

All Dr Stimpson had been able to offer was questions. Had she had any fainting fits recently? Was she having her period? Had she shown signs of *absences* – little day-dreaming trances that might suggest *petit mal* epileptic fits? But surely, Laura had protested, you don't get seizures when the body is exerting itself under stress. The doctor had merely shaken his head, equally puzzled. He'd taken blood and urine samples, but his bet was that 'the thing was hormonal'. He'd told her to avoid giving Grace cheese and cured meats and left a prescription for Deseril tablets, one gram to be taken three times a day. She'd checked in her *Home Guide to Medicines*: Deseril was a regular prophylactic against migraines. The man had simply no idea. She bit her lip. Hadn't she been through all that before, with Matthew? If the doctors didn't know, *who did*?

Her hand shook as she sipped her drink. She'd arrived to

collect Grace in the normal way, to be told by Sister Thomas that there'd been a slight 'incident'. She'd raced up into the sick-room and found her daughter lying there on the bed like a corpse, her face grey, her lips bloodless and behind half-open slits her eyes rolled back to the whites. Hormonal? She frowned. That really wasn't good enough.

*

Dr Tom Welland glanced at the clock on the lab wall and swore softly. Seven-fifty: he'd never make it through the Bath city traffic to the cinema in time, and that would set off another domestic row. Shutting down the computer terminal, he hurriedly locked away the tissue cultures in their lead-lined cabinet and checked the banks of dials monitoring activity in the small isolation chamber at the far end of the room. All seemed fine. A quick glance through the thick glass inspection panel in the concrete housing confirmed that at least the nutrient was circulating properly. Five years was a long time to store neural tissue and hope to regenerate it intact – but that, of course, was precisely what the experiment was designed to test. Four days before, he'd registered a blip on the differentiometer, suggesting the tissue was taking up oxygen, and just that afternoon he'd given it another gentle prod and got the same result. Only time would tell, however, if this was just an aberration or the first glimmering spark of life returning.

He flicked on the red *No Entry* light and set the alarm, then he slipped quickly out into the corridor and double-locked the door behind him. The scrub-room door briefly held him up – they were always changing the damned combinations – but within a few moments he had torn off his protective gloves and overshoes, dumped them in the disposal drum for low-level wastes and was scrubbing meticulously his hands, arms and face. Finally, retrieving his jacket and coat from his locker, he made his way down the empty corridors, through two further sets of security doors, each marked with the yellow and black hazard symbol, and down three flight of stairs to the ground floor, where he bade goodnight to the dozing security guard on the reception desk and headed out through the falling dusk and the spotting rain towards the car-park.

*

Father Gregory's rich and ready laugh from downstairs woke Grace from her doze. Morning sunshine flooded in through the open curtains, throwing weird rhomboid shapes across the ceiling. A moment later, she heard the priest's familiar, flat footfall on the staircase. She shut her eyes quickly, feigning sleep. Once, Father Gregory had been everything to her; he'd been her guide and friend, and she'd trusted him utterly. Now he made her feel uncomfortable, tampering with her thoughts and peering into her soul. She wished she could love him still as simply and unconditionally as she had, but she couldn't. Not after all Leo had made her see and question.

The door opened. She sensed the florid, tousled-haired priest in the doorway, watching her closely. She could picture, too, that look in his eyes, sympathetic yet suspicious, so familiar to her from hours spent in his lodge-house over scones and scriptures. He had always singled her out from the others at the convent school. She must be a disappointment.

Suddenly the thought struck her that this must be exactly what going blind would be like, and abruptly she opened her eyes. She blinked, assuming a look of surprise. The priest sat down on the end of her bed. His black jacket gave off a musty, aromatic smell that reminded her of the vestry.

He winked.

'The trick,' he smiled, 'is to breathe slower on the intake.'

'Ah, it's you, Father,' she responded. 'Thou from whom no secrets are hid.'

'Don't be profane, Grace.' He took her hand and fixed her with a look of deep concern. 'I heard what happened. How do you feel?'

'A bit doped-up, but okay.' She braved a smile. 'Dr

Stimpson says it's hormonal. That's because he doesn't know.'

'Your mother's very worried.'

'I wish she wouldn't be so *anxious* all the time. Imagining the worst is bound to provoke it happening.'

'That's superstition!'

'No, seriously. Leo says there are Indian tribes who never get cancer because they don't have a *word* for it. In the Beginning was the Word, right, Father?'

'There's always some tribe that can prove anything you want.'

'But I thought that was how prayer worked. Using the power of faith to make things happen.' She gave her sweetest smile. 'Like voodoo.'

Father Gregory shifted uncomfortably.

'Grace,' he said with a frown, 'your mother needs love and understanding. It distresses her to hear you talk like this.'

'Of course I love her!' she retorted with sudden exasperation. 'And I think I understand her pretty well. It's just that she reduces everything – all right, she *raises* everything – to God.'

'God *is* everything. Everywhere.'

She was about to demand where God was when people had accidents or got ill and died, but she checked herself. 'I'm sorry, Father,' she said simply.

The priest held her under his keen scrutiny.

'There's something troubling you, isn't there?'

She nodded, chastened.

'Father, I'm . . . afraid.'

'Tell me.'

She hesitated; shouldn't she work it out for herself? But how could she? Impossible, yet she'd *seen* Matthew with her own eyes. How would anyone, even Leo with all his cleverness, explain that?

'Father,' she began hesitantly, 'is it possible to communicate with someone who is dead? To *see* them?'

40

His frown deepened. 'Well, Grace,' he replied, 'you know the Church's teaching on that.'

'But what do *you* believe, Father?'

'Come on, what's really on your mind?' He paused as she didn't reply. 'All right, then. The short answer is no. The Church regards spirit mediums and people claiming to speak to the dead as heretical. Of course, we can pray for intercession on behalf of the dead, but once a soul is called to the Lord, it's in the spiritual domain, so to speak. Beyond our mortal reach.'

'Always?'

'Any exception would be a miracle.' He searched her face. 'Has this got something to do with what happened yesterday?'

'No. Just had a funny dream, that's all.' She held his eye. 'Thanks, Father. I feel a lot better.'

He rose and patted her arm uncertainly.

'Come and see me as soon as you're up. Take care of yourself and remember what I said about your mother. And don't forget to say your prayers. You'll find that'll comfort you.' He smiled. 'You may call it voodoo, but the difference is that it's true. God be with you, Grace.'

'And with you, Father.'

*

Laying a tray for Grace's lunch, Laura heard the priest coming slowly down the stairs. With her back to the door, she looked up and caught his reflection in the mirror on the wall. He wore a thoughtful frown. She turned to face him. He brightened at once.

'How did she seem to you, Father?' she asked.

'I remember,' he replied almost wistfully, 'when you brought the twins to be baptized, Laura. Alike as two peas in a pod! I nearly mixed them up.' He chuckled, then his expression saddened. 'It's a wonderful thing, a searching mind. But a burden, too.'

'She'll find her own peace, in time.'

He reached for his coat.

'Let's pray she will,' he said despairingly.

'Father, where's your faith?' she smiled in reproof.

'Everyone has doubts, Laura.'

'Not you.'

'Doubt is the *test* of faith. It keeps the spiritual muscles in tone. Mind you,' he admitted, 'plenty of people seek a sign. Something to say they're on the right track. That their work hasn't gone unnoticed. Plenty of people. Even in the ministry.'

She held his eye as she handed him his coat and scarf. She knew he was referring to himself.

'The act itself is the reward, Father,' she said quietly. 'The ultimate test is humility. Not seeking signs, but just trusting.'

The priest's face slowly softened into a grin.

'I should have said that myself.'

'You once did, Father.'

He laughed. 'That's what I love about this place, Laura. Everywhere else I visit, it's all about Mrs So-and-so who's got a poorly leg and can't do the flowers this week, or Mr Whatsit who's taken a carnal shine to his secretary. In this house, it's altogether different. I end up discussing doctrine with you and spiritualism with your daughter. What's more, you make the best cup of coffee in the parish. Stimulating, in every respect. *That*'s the reward.' At the door, he turned. 'And *stop worrying*, Laura. She's a beautiful girl and she'll be perfectly fine.'

'I know. I'll try.'

'God bless you, Laura.'

'And you, Father.'

She saw the priest out to his white Mini and stood on the front doorstep in the chill morning sunshine as he drove off in a wandering path down the drive. She stayed there for a moment, staring at the lawn and the long white shadows in frost thrown by the poplars, and thinking, *What was that about spiritualism?* It was all very well for Father Gregory to say Grace would be perfectly fine and there was nothing to be achieved by worrying.

*

''Bye, Duchess.'

''Bye, Leo.'

Grace replaced the receiver and, turning back to the percolator, poured out two cups and placed them on a tray along with a plate of biscuits. She put on her yellow tracksuit and tied her hair back in a pony-tail, and she'd never felt better in her life. She took the tray and hurried out of the back door into the crisp mid-morning sunshine and followed the stone path in the lee of the house, along the tall yew hedge and through the small iron gate to the studio outhouse. With a tap on the door, she let herself in.

Her mother looked up from her drawing table and frowned.

'You shouldn't be up,' she said.

'It's Friday,' replied Grace, laying the tray down on top of a light-box. 'I can't stay in bed for ever.'

'Dr Stimpson said specifically . . .'

'Dr Stimpson hasn't a clue. I don't need rest, I'm not ill. Here, I brought you some coffee.' She peered over her mother's shoulder as she put the cup down. On a sheet of Kodatrace, taped to the drawing-board over a jacket illustration, she was carefully sketching a layout. Underneath, the figure of Orpheus bent over his lyre was just discernible. 'Will you have it finished in time?'

'I think so, just.' As she reached for a felt-pen, her mother cast her a long, hard look. 'I could easily get a courier to bike it over.'

'Don't be silly, Mother. Nothing's going to *happen*. Anyway, I'll be going to Mary's later.'

'You're not thinking of going out!'

'Mum, I can't let her down. She looks forward to it all week. Don't *worry*.'

A moment's silence fell. Grace sauntered round the large,

airy studio. In the background, an early opera played softly on the tape recorder. Order and harmony reigned in this room. Tubes of paint lay neatly lined up in their boxes, oils here, acrylics there, watercolours to the side. Pots holding brushes, ink-pens, crayons, pastels and charcoal stood in tidy rows on the shelves, and a large map-chest behind the door stored the paper, each drawer clearly marked to distinguish graph from tracing paper, oil board from layout block, pure rag watercolour paper from smooth cartridge.

'Who was that on the phone?' asked her mother, engrossed again in her work.

'Leo.' She caught her looking up sharply. 'It's okay. I just said I'd fainted. Well, I had to say something. He wondered why I was off school. Still, it'll stop him coming rampaging all over the place like a bull in a china shop.'

'We should be very grateful to Leonard. He's a dear man.'

'Like the sofa. That was pretty dear. An arm and a leg, I should think.' She grinned. 'What do we need next? New curtains? Carpets? I think it's time we redecorated the living-room.'

'Grace!'

They exchanged a glance and simultaneously dissolved into laughter. Leo had been so kind and concerned when they'd been at their lowest ebb. From the very start, he'd made their well-being his business. The very day Matthew died – they'd barely known him three weeks – he'd astonished them by coming over with a bunch of travel agents' brochures and virtually insisted they went off on a holiday. He'd even driven them to the airport himself and met them when they came back a fortnight later. In the meantime he'd had the whole house spring-cleaned. They'd found Matthew's room completely redecorated, his bed and desk replaced and even his clothes thoughtfully removed. The sofa in the living-room, a dreadful dog-chewed leather object with the stuffing bursting out but nonetheless wonderfully comfortable, had been taken away and its place taken by a smart new three-seater, sent down by special delivery from

Maples in London. He'd wanted them to come back to a new, fresh home in which to make a new, fresh start. He'd adamantly refused to take a penny in repayment. Actually, Mum had been a little shocked at the time – it was rather an intrusion. And she was upset about Matthew's room, but she hadn't shown it, for he'd meant well. How he'd found a key to get in, though, always lingered in her mind as a mystery. Mary hadn't given him one: she remembered once asking her.

She went back and stood looking over her mother's shoulder as she peeled back the overlay to reveal the illustration beneath. It showed Orpheus in the underworld with his lyre; in the background, dressed in pale green, stood Eurydice, while all around spread a dreamlike mist.

'Not sure about the green,' she muttered. 'Why not gold?'

'Green is for hope. At least in Goethe's colour theory.' Her mother began rubbing out the pencilled key-marks in the margin. 'Think it'll do?'

'It's magic,' she replied quietly.

'I'm not sure it's quite that, darling.'

But Grace couldn't drag her gaze away. The closer she looked, the more she felt drawn into the strange, mystical world of the painting. It seemed so alluring, so hypnotic and somehow so . . . familiar.

'Mum?' she began after a pause. 'Is it just a metaphor, or do you think he actually *saw* her?'

'Orpheus? It's just a myth. A fable.'

'I mean, they must have believed it was possible, crossing the Styx and all that. Seeing and talking to someone who was dead. Or is it just supposed to be a dream?'

'It's fantasy. Pure imagination.' She began gathering her pens and pencils together, then stopped and threw her a curious glance. 'Maybe the idea *started* as someone's dream.'

'After Dad died,' Grace went on hesitantly, 'did you ever dream about him?'

'You can't spend fifteen years with someone you love and say goodbye just like that.'

'Did you *see* him, then?'

'Darling, what is all this? I don't believe in ghosts, if that's what you mean.' Her laugh died short and a puzzled frown flashed across her face. 'Your father's body is in his grave. His soul is with God. If I ever were to see him, in bodily form, I'd know it was a projection of my thoughts, a creation of my mind. He'd exist in *here*,' she tapped her forehead, 'not out there.'

'Suppose he came in the door right now and just stood there and you *knew* he was real.'

'Then I'd be a head case.' She smiled and rose. 'Unless you saw him, too.'

'And then?'

'We'd both be head cases.' She glanced at the clock. 'Hey, look at the time!' She laid a hand on her arm. 'We'll talk about it tonight. All right?'

*

Leonard excused himself from the group at his lunch table and went over to the notice-board set up on an easel at the door of the grand hotel dining-room. He hated conferences: the food was over-rich, the papers over-long and the drinking hours over-late. Still, only the afternoon session left to go now. He checked the schedule and looked at his watch. Hell, he'd pack it in. He had all he wanted. His paper on radiotherapy in the management of tumours had been well received, he'd made contact with everyone necessary and he'd already received invitations to lecture at two American medical schools and a university in France. But, most of all, he'd learned about a new drug being developed by a Dr Williamson at London University that could represent a breakthrough in the treatment of malignant tumours. Called cytosuppressin, it had been only proven in tests on animals so far and permission had not yet been granted for clinical trials. It worked by directly shrinking the abnormal tissue; its operation seemed highly localized and there were no apparent side-effects. His thoughts flashed to

46

Grace. If validated in time, it could be the answer to his prayer.

He stood for a moment longer, weighing up the decision. If he checked out now, he'd miss the Friday rush on the London Orbital. He could even surprise Laura for tea and give her the tickets for *Tosca* he'd bought as a peace offering. He had resolved to let things remain as they were, to return to being just fond companions, sharing a love of music, enjoying their few common friends and providing company for each other on holidays and at dinner parties and business evenings. But even as this resolution went through his mind, his stomach rebelled. Companionship be damned! A man, a woman, *everyone* needed someone to love, to care for, to cherish. The only life we had was here on this earth, and the only love we had to enjoy was the love we made for ourselves. Only by loving fully could we be complete human beings. What, then, of an incomplete love? A companionable, affectionate, caring love, but one lacking its vital consummation?

But then, there was Grace. He thought back to his phone call that morning. She'd *fainted*? And been off school for two days as a result? Oh, *Christ*. Not yet! With sudden resolve, he headed down the thickly carpeted corridor and across the marble and gilt hall to the reception desk. He'd pay the bill and get on the road.

*

Grace made herself a ham sandwich for lunch but tossed it away after one bite. She left her glass of apple-juice untouched. She took out the hoover, meaning to clean the house before her mother got back, but gave up after a minute. She opened one of the books Sister Bertram had called by and left for her, a commentary on *Hamlet*, but she couldn't get beyond the words to their meaning. For a while she stared out of the tall window at the lawn speckled with leaves, at the far chestnut tree and row of poplars, all ankle-deep in their moultings, but for her eyes the scene was a stage back-drop, a vista without depth. She turned on the television, then switched it off again, knowing without looking at it that it wasn't what she sought. Eventually, she sat down on the sofa and, hugging her knees under her chin, fixed her sightless gaze on the gesso peeling off the mirror frame above the mantel.

'*Suppose . . . you knew he was real?' 'I'd be a head case.*' She shivered. One, it wasn't an epileptic fit: you didn't *see* things then. Two, it wasn't migraine after all: you might hallucinate, but not about *real* things, *real* people. So, what *was* it? Could it be the prelude not to blindness but to madness? Yes, these were *mad-attacks*. They came without any warning, just a brief, funny metallic taste in her mouth, impossible to place, a sort of *purple* flavour. That was all. Then the onslaught, the irresistible brightening, until everything exploded in a total, dazzling white-out. When might they strike again? What if she were riding? Or cycling? Would she ever be able to drive? Would she be housebound for ever, and even if allowed out, then always chaperoned, watched over, guarded? Would she ever be *herself* again?

But the real question was more frightening still. Did it exist in *here* – she touched her forehead as her mother had done – or out *there*? How could she find out? Where should she start?

By going back to where it had begun.

Rising slowly, she went into the kitchen and slipped on her anorak and wellingtons. As she was leaving, she turned back and reached into a drawer for a piece of paper. She'd better leave a note, in case Mum came back early and was worried. Then she hurried out to the shed where she kept her bicycle.

*

Leonard drove the final few miles slowly, relishing the twisting country lanes after the speed and dullness of the motorways. The dashboard clock read a few minutes to four; he'd made good time. On the seat beside him lay flowers for Laura and a second-hand copy of Clive Bell's *Art* for Grace.

As he passed through the small village of Coledean with its stunted stone cottages and single meagre pub, its slate-grey Methodist chapel and its ironstone Baptist church opposite, suspicious stares returned his greeting smiles. Over the past five years he'd got to know most of the people by sight and many by name, and yet still he was a stranger – in Forest language, a *foreigner*. How must it be for Laura and Grace, separated by deep differences of class and creed and kind? He'd always been trying to persuade them to move. And not only for those reasons, either.

He frowned as he swung left off the road and followed the winding gravel drive that led to the old mill house. Why couldn't he ever rid himself of those thoughts, those worries? Why did Grace only have to mention migraines or faint at school and he was driven into a panic of dread? Everything had been fine so far. Why shouldn't everything *remain* fine? He knew well enough why. Because you could only really tell the long-term effects in the long term, and five years wasn't long enough.

As he pulled up, he noticed Laura's Volvo was gone. Good, he thought; he'd have Grace to himself. Picking up his gifts, he slipped through the small iron gate that led into the garden and hurried round to the back door. He rang. There was no reply. Perhaps she was upstairs, in bed. He let himself in with the key they always left under a slate and halted on the threshold inside.

'Grace?' No answering call. 'Yo ho! Anyone at home?'

The house was silent. As he stepped inside and laid the flowers and book on the table, his eye fell upon a note in Grace's handwriting.

Gone for a ramble up by Dent's Cross, it read. *See you later. Hope it went well. Tons of love, G.*

Dent's Cross, he muttered to himself. Why there? On all their walks together, they'd tacitly avoided that place. He laid the flowers and book on the table and looked around the room, wondering what to do. As he glanced about him, he felt a twinge of sadness. He was forty, with his home broken and his family dispersed. Would he ever have a proper home again, a place to which he'd come back and find a note left for him? Suddenly he felt ashamed, an impostor. This was not his family! He had none; he'd do well to remember it and not try and play pretend.

Abruptly he turned and retraced his steps outside to his car.

*

At the end of the drive, he hesitated. Why Dent's Cross? He'd better take no chances. Instead of turning left towards Abbotsbury and his own home at Upton Flint some miles beyond, he made a sharp right.

Dent's Cross was a small, bald knoll in the middle of the forest at the intersection of two narrow roads. A tottering wooden road sign marked the spot where, according to local folklore, gallows had once stood. Two of the four arms pointed to Coledean and a third had rotted off. A tractor lumbered slowly across and disappeared round a corner into the woodland. Leonard slipped the car back into gear.

As he was about to drive off, his eye caught a glint in the bracken a few yards up a forest track. Moving forwards, he saw it was a bicycle. He recognized it at once. Oh God, he thought: she *has* gone there.

He pulled over and got out. All round the bicycle lay the clear imprint of track-shoes in the soft sand, leading into the forest along a track that curled gently around the wooded slopes. He began to follow, though he hardly needed the trail.

At first, the silence of the forest engulfed him, then gradually as he went, here and there, he began to pick out woodland sounds: a sparrow chittering, a pheasant squawking, a squirrel rustling in the fallen foliage. The sun was already weakening and a reluctant bluish mist had begun to rise, quenching the febrile colours of bracken, briar and brake, while in the upper branches, all but naked now, stillness had descended, casting a hand over the mouth of the forest. After a while, the track grew steeper and the going rougher. More than once he tripped over a concealed tree-root. He came to a fork, and for a moment, he lost his way. But there they were, steadily paced footprints following their determined path, vanishing and reappearing by turns. A chill bit into the air, yet he felt hot from the exertion and loosened his tie. Brambles snagged his suit and his lightweight shoes were mud-clodded and full of grit.

The track levelled off and broadened until, around a gentle bend, it broke into the wide grassy clearing. At once he spotted Grace, standing in the centre. He was about to call out when he held himself back. Falling to a half-crouch, he inched his way towards the cover of a tree.

Grace stood in half view to him. She was swaying gently backwards and forwards and holding one arm up to her face as if to shield her eyes. Suddenly, as he watched, she slipped to her knees and thrust out the other arm in a desperate fending-off gesture. Then, very gradually, she sank back onto her heels and lowered her arms and, raising her head, stared out fixedly at some point ahead and slightly above her. He followed her line of sight across the clearing to the small entrance into the disused mine, now heavily overgrown and, from where he stood, apparently properly barred and sealed, and, rising steeply behind it, the shallow embankment covered with bracken and surmounted with a line of silver birch trees. But that was all. No man nor bird nor creature of any kind appeared to move in the slope ahead of her. What was she staring at?

Then, as clearly as if he'd been within inches of her, he saw her drawn white features relax and, without blinking or breaking her gaze for a second, her whole face slowly spread into a sublime, beatific smile.

Four

Slowly the soft white sheet of light begins to draw in towards the centre, condensing into a single oval orb of shimmering, pulsing radiance. Beams of light spark and jet out at the rim like rays from the sun. The centre is growing denser now, the very light itself coalescing into substance.

Gradually, within the womb of light, an outline begins to form. Line by line, it crystallizes into human shape, a woman's shape, robed in pale blue and white. One hand gestures towards her heart; the other, outstretched, is beckoning. Shafts of sunlight radiate out from behind her figure like spokes of white fire. Above her head hovers a luminous gold halo. She smiles, her head gently inclined. The eyes offer comfort, the halo glints reassurance, the arms promise safe haven.

Come to me, they are saying.

*

From afar off, Grace became aware of a tugging at her arm. She felt herself being lifted to her feet. *No, no, leave me alone*, she wanted to cry. Where was she? What was happening? She was now being shaken bodily. A voice was calling to her, shouting at her. *Let me stay, don't pull me back*. The light was fading, the image dissolving, and from the sides of her vision the familiar drab greys and browns of the woodland were eating in towards the centre. The voice grew louder, more insistent, calling her name over and over again. Gradually a face appeared, Leo's face, his eyes wide with alarm, and slowly around it re-formed a world she knew, all very dull and down to earth.

*

Leonard glanced across at the girl in the car beside him. She was sitting bolt upright and staring fixedly ahead, neither moving nor speaking. In the failing light, he could see her face still bore a distant, expressionless cast. Back in the forest, gripped by horror and fascination, wanting to intervene yet not wanting to break the spell, he'd remained watching as she fell under the grip of an extraordinary, overpowering trance. When she finally slumped to the ground in a faint, he'd rushed forward and seized her in his arms. He'd taken her pulse, checked her retinas, made a guess at her blood pressure, he'd even examined her tongue and her arms for evidence of pills or needles, but everything looked normal. She was in no pain – far from it, she seemed lost in some private, transcendent delirium. He'd questioned her, he'd called her by name, he'd even shaken her quite roughly, but she'd seemed hardly aware of anything going on about her. At first she'd barely been able to stand, but eventually, supporting her like an invalid, he'd managed to steer her slowly back down the treacherous, twisting pathways to the car. All that time she hadn't uttered a single word. She simply wasn't *there*. And now she was sitting beside him, her face drained of expression, while he felt somehow guilty for bringing her back, like a man returning an escaped prisoner to jail. This was the strangest fit he'd ever seen.

He tried a different tack.

'I bought you a book,' he said. 'Duchess?'

'You shouldn't have,' she murmured distantly.

'It's not a first edition or anything. Consider it an early Christmas present.'

He carried on for a while but he could tell she wasn't

really listening. Finally, he gave up and continued the drive in silence.

Before long they reached the village and he turned off down the drive to the mill house. By now the sun had disappeared behind the line of poplars bordering the river, and the irregular stone mill with its low-crouching outbuildings and its shrubbery frayed by the first winds of winter stood bathed in a leaden yellow afterlight. The Volvo was still not back. Pulling up by the front door, he climbed out and went round to the boot to fetch her bicycle. He was wheeling it towards the small iron gate that led into the back garden when she stopped him. In the flat, wan light, her oval face was pale.

'Thanks, Leo,' she said, taking the bicycle.

'I'll fix you a hot drink,' he began, moving forwards. 'I'm sure Laura won't be long.'

She stood in the gateway, blocking his path. 'I'll tell her you came,' she said.

'Oh, I'll come in and wait.'

'She could be ages.'

'Grace, I think I ought to take a proper look at you.'

'I'm okay. I'd rather be alone. Please, Leo.'

'But something's wrong, I can *see* it . . .'

'Please.'

He touched her arm, and met neither warmth nor resistance. 'Well, go inside and look after yourself. I'll call later.'

He returned slowly to the car but paused, then retraced his steps after her. At the small gate, he stopped. She was already half way down the path, pushing her bicycle with a slow, dreamlike gait. He stood in the gateway, following her slender figure with his gaze as she went first to the shed, then without a backward glance disappeared into the house.

*

With the twilight a fine mist had descended, absorbing the woods on either side and gently diffusing the pale beam from her bicycle headlamp. An occasional car passed, momentarily lighting up the road ahead, only to be quickly lost around a bend in a dull red trail. Coming to a small rise, Grace pedalled harder. She was letting Mary Nolan down, but she couldn't help it. She had to know – she had to *ask*. And there was only one place to do that.

Eventually, the gaunt outline of the slate works told her she had reached Abbotsbury. She cycled on past the disused corrugated-iron sheds and mounds of shaly waste, now long overgrown, and on into the town, where sodium streetlamps at irregular intervals marked out the main street and cast a sulphurous pall over the meagre whitewashed cottages along either side. Lights burned behind double-curtained windows, some red, some orange; others flickered in the bluish light of televisions. All were familiar, explicable. Not like that strange, dazzling, shimmering luminescence she had witnessed.

She rode past a group of men waiting outside for the pub to open. One, a gardener at the convent, touched his hat to her. Further down the street, the woman who ran the mini-market opposite the convent waved. She carried on until she came to the wrought-iron gates with the large white board that read, CONVENT OF ST DOMINIC. On her left as she cycled into the convent grounds, she passed the small brick and stone lodge-house where Father Gregory lived. Lights were on downstairs, and at the side his white Mini stood parked. She slowed for a moment but didn't stop. She couldn't tell him. He wouldn't believe her for a moment. He'd call it sinful vanity and upbraid her for her wicked blasphemy.

She cycled on up the tree-lined drive between the cloistered garden on one side and the school games field on the other. Ahead lay the convent, its steep gables dimly silhouetted against the darkening sky and its tall, gothic windows glowing eerily through the mist. Behind, in an irregular complex converted from old pantries, outbuildings and the former stable block, stood the school, while further down the drive as it swept to the right, linked to the convent by a glazed walkway, was the chapel. Convent, school and chapel were all quiet, for it was the supper hour.

She rode up to the chapel and, parking her bicycle out of sight at the side, hurried round the front. Constructed after the war out of austerity materials, its crude stained glass and rain-streaked concrete façade adorned with an angular bronze Crucifixion bore the stamp of a dated modernity. She'd never felt that, seen from the outside, this could be a place of God. But now, once inside, she began to feel the familiar stirring in her heart, the strange and precious sense of the *presence* about her to which she had been a stranger for so long. The pews, in comfortless bleached pine, were empty. From the ceiling hung clusters of lights in small futuristic constellations, dimmed almost to extinction, while on the altar, itself merely a simple trestle in matching pine and spread with lace cloth and silver plate, electric candles flickered each side of a central triptych. Above, flanked by narrow stained-glass windows, rose a gilt and tempera statue of the Madonna and Child in the Renaissance style.

She genuflected and hesitantly made her way to the front. There, grateful to be alone, she sat down and, raising her eyes to the statue before her, slipped to her knees in prayer.

*

Leonard swore. The sink was full of unwashed pans and plates, and a pile of sheets and shirts lay mouldering in the washing-machine. The fridge was bare but for a rind of cheese and a bottle of rancid milk. He took a whisky into his study; it'd have to be a liquid supper tonight. He really ought to move to the city, where you could get a meal at any time of day. This house was far too big, anyway. He'd kept it on after Angie left, now four years ago. At first, Vanessa and Mark used to come to stay for weekends, but now that they were growing up and making friends in London, Gloucester had become too far away and too little fun.

He stood over the phone, wondering what he should do

about Grace. Call Dr Stimpson and get him to refer her to the hospital, where he could run some tests? Or simply tell Laura? As he thought back to her cool dismissal, his anxiety turned to hurt. Did all the trust he'd built up over the past years, all his efforts to bring her out from the darkness of her beliefs into the light of reason, all the love and care he'd shown her, did all of that count for nothing – now, especially, when she was tormented by this terrifying, overwhelming physiological trauma, now when she needed him most?

Pull yourself together, he told himself angrily. He took a large slug of whisky and, having lit the gas log fire, switched on the answering-machine and settled down to listen to the messages left while he'd been away.

Click.

Hi, Lenny, this is Marianna. Who the hell was Marianna? Ah yes, he remembered: the young doctor from St Thomas' he'd met a while back at a drinks party in London. Blonde and busty and breathlessly fascinated in his work on tumours. *I'm coming down your way on Thursday. Let's meet up for a drink. Call me if you're free.* Too bad it was Friday today. He might just keep her number in case, though.

Click.

Dad, you sound so pompous on that machine! It's me. Vanessa. *Mum wants to know about Christmas. Hang on, she's saying something. I'll hand you over. Did I tell you, I'm trying for film school? All right, Mum . . .* Angie came on and began her usual confused tirade. He went to the kitchen to refill his glass, leaving her haranguing an empty room. Where *had* their marriage gone wrong? He'd given too much to his career, worked crazy hours, neglected her. All the familiar reasons. All his fault. There was never any suggestion *she'd* been at fault – too demanding, too insecure, requiring too much attention. She was still talking when he returned, going on about some problem with dates. Let her do what she wanted. He hated Christmas anyway; the season of goodwill divided as many as it united.

Finally she came to an end, and a few clicks followed

where people had called but left no message. Then came a voice that sent a violent jolt through him.

Hello, Leonard? This is Tom Welland. The voice bore a hard, tense edge. *Leonard, I wonder if you'd give me a call. It's fairly important.*

He stopped the machine and replayed the message, trying to read what lay behind the scientist's words. His mouth had gone dry and he'd broken into a light sweat. He jotted down the number Welland had left and reached for the phone, but stopped. Suddenly he crumpled up the paper and tossed it away and, erasing the message from the machine, stood staring into the fire. As far as he was concerned, all that was over and done with. Whatever he'd agreed to then was no longer relevant now. Things had changed, the world had moved on. Sorry, Tom. No calls. No contact. Nothing.

What mattered was *Grace*. He reached for the phone book and looked up Dr Stimpson's number, then he pushed it away and turned back to the fire. This whole thing needed more thought.

*

'Grace?'

Grace awoke from the depths of her meditation to find the soft, round face of Sister Bertram regarding her intently.

'I'm sorry,' she began, momentarily disorientated.

She struggled to her feet, but the nun motioned for her to stay seated.

'What brings *you* here, Grace?' she asked wryly. 'Aren't you supposed to be off sick?'

'It's nothing, Sister Bertram. I just wanted to think.'

'Will you share your thoughts with me?'

Gathering her habit round her, the nun slid into the pew beside her. Her wimple and collar accentuated the roundness of her moonlike face, and not even her frown of sympathetic concern furrowed the creamy smoothness of her complexion. Her hair, though rarely seen, was the colour of ripened corn and she bore herself with a stately, ageless serenity. She taught English Literature, and after Matthew's death, feeling sorry for Grace, she had become a special friend to her, someone in whom she could trust and confide her grief.

'It sounds too ridiculous.' Grace gave a short nervous laugh.

'Whatever's on your mind, tell me. You don't have to be afraid.'

Grace looked into the kindly hazel eyes. How she yearned to confide her worries, but she was afraid that Sister Bertram, for all her goodwill, might not believe her. Would anybody? They'd say she was making it up or, worse, she was mad.

'Sister Bertram . . .' she began tentatively.

'Go on, Grace.'

She looked down at her hands. This wasn't going to be easy.

'Suppose,' she began, 'someone came to you and said they'd . . . seen something. What would you say?'

'Grace, I think you should start at the beginning.'

*

Sister Bertram sat without speaking for some while. Far away a bell was tolling, but the chapel was quite silent. Grace bit at a fingernail. This was terrible. She'd told her everything – about the flashes of light she'd been seeing, about the strange glimpse of Matthew, and now about this astonishing apparition. She should have kept quiet and said nothing.

'Am I to take it,' said the nun at last, 'you're saying Our Lady herself has appeared to you in a vision?'

'I knew you wouldn't believe me,' replied Grace, shifting uncomfortably in the pew.

Sister Bertram held her in a stern gaze.

'Think very carefully what you're saying, Grace,' she warned.

'I'm telling you what I *saw*, Sister.'

'And you saw the figure of Our Blessed Lady standing in the middle of the woods.'

'I did!' Grace shook her head in despair. 'I know you'll think I'm mental. Or I had a hallucination. Or it's hormones. Or hysteria.'

'No, Grace. It sounds to me more like heresy.'

'But it's true! It *happened*!'

Sister Bertram considered her carefully. 'It's one thing to say you truly had an astonishing experience,' she said with quiet precision. 'But quite another to say the experience *itself* is true and you'd seen a holy apparition.'

'I . . . I don't know. It just seemed so real.'

'Seemed,' repeated the nun doubtfully.

'Yes, as real as Our Lady there.' She pointed to the statue above the altar.

Sister Bertram took her hand and slipped to her knees.

'Don't say any more,' she said. 'To lie about a matter like this is a terrible sin. Don't make it worse. Come, we'll pray together.'

Grace fell to her knees beside the nun. She *hadn't* imagined it: it *had* to be real. But was it from some divine source, or was it a trick of the Devil? How could she ever tell? As she raised her gaze to the statue of the Holy Virgin, she fancied she saw the merest hint of a smile soften her features.

Five

In the early hours, unable to sleep, Grace slipped downstairs. A low, moaning wind encircled the house, rising in waves to drown the perpetual rush of the mill stream. Wrapping her dressing-gown more tightly about her, she stared out into the moonlit garden. Was She out there? Might She visit her again right now, there, in the middle of the cloth-of-silver lawn? Or was the apparition in her head, sprung from her own mind?

With a shiver, Grace turned away and curled up on the sofa. She would spend the night there; she didn't feel easy cooped up in her small room upstairs. As she was settling down, a book fell onto the floor. She picked it up and tilted the spine towards the moonlight. The title read, *The Oxford Companion to the Mind*. She switched on the table lamp and opened it at the bookmark. The main entry was headed, *Hallucination*. At once she understood. Leo must have phoned Mum while she'd been at the chapel. She felt sick, betrayed.

But she couldn't close the book. Held in the grip of a terrible fascination, she began reading the entry.

'Children often suppose that what they imagine is external and perceptible to others,' she read. 'Adults sometimes fail to make the distinction, especially at a time of high expectation or arousal. A widow mourning her husband may see him or hear his voice or footsteps repeatedly after his death . . . Hallucination is common in patients who have suffered damage to the brain . . . Schizophrenics . . .'

She snapped the book shut. Had she really just imagined it all? For a while she sat motionless, her eyes closed. She would say a prayer. Father Gregory was right: comfort was always to be found in prayer. Better not to ask questions, but simply to trust. Over the space of two thousand years, the best brains in Christendom had addressed themselves to every imaginable question, and they'd found reassurance. She remained sitting quite still, forcing her mind to grow quiet and calm. But almost at once the first, insidious doubt crept back in. She silenced it firmly, but just as quickly another took its place. For a moment she pictured hordes of small flies crawling out of the dark onto a pure white surface, and she had to swat them one by one, but as fast as she killed them more came on. *Why you, Grace Holmwood? What singles you out for God's special grace? Vanity. And fear. Fear that if it's not a miracle, then it's madness. If you're not blessed, you're just plain barmy. Which is it? What are you?*

She jumped to her feet and pressed her hands over her ears. Her eye fell upon the photo album lying on the coffee-table. Picking it up, she sat down on the carpet and began flicking through the pages. A lump rose in her throat as she looked back over the seaside holidays, the birthday parties, the boating trips and outings and expeditions. She stared into the eyes of the girl she recognized she'd once been, but the face returned her stare impenetrably, refusing to yield its secrets, and far from any vital insight all she found were memories. A tear fell onto a photo, raising a bubble in the emulsion. No, the past was a different world. The Grace in that album had nothing to tell the Grace in this room now. They were strangers. She was on her own.

A sudden wave of drowsiness washed over her, and she closed her eyes and sank back against the sofa. She was barely aware of the album sliding out of her hands onto the floor before sleep engulfed her. She slept fitfully, her mind crowded with confusing dreams. Some time later, in the early hours, she stirred, finding her limbs stiff and cold. She switched out the lamp and stumbled her way sleepily across the room and up the stairs to bed.

*

She woke in the morning with a renewed attack of anxiety. A strange dread burned in her stomach. She dressed, and as she came downstairs she heard her mother speaking on the phone. Just as she entered the kitchen, Laura put down the receiver and shot her a worried glance.

'That was Sister Bertram,' she said.

'What did she want?'

'She's very concerned about you. Grace, is there something . . . ?'

'No, Mother. And I wish everyone would stop interfering and just leave me alone.'

She turned away and busied herself making the coffee. Sister Bertram had driven her back home the previous night, but hadn't stayed. What had she been telling Mum? Goodness knew what Leo had told her, too. It was all crowding in on her. This was her own problem, and she had to sort it out by herself. She should never have confessed to Sister Bertram as freely as she had. Leo called confession a clever Catholic trick to get people to police their own consciences. Far from giving her peace of mind, it had only created more trouble.

During breakfast, her mother kept up a cheerful monologue, but the atmosphere was tense and uneasy. Not waiting to finish her toast, Grace hurried back up to her room and sat on her bed, her knees tucked under her chin, thinking. A pencil-thin shaft of sunlight reflecting off the glass vase on her desk sprayed brilliant coloured darts up the far wall. She stared for a while at the pattern it made, interrupted now and then as a frond of ivy brushed the window-pane and broke the beam, and she strove to conjure up some meaningful form out of the dancing specks. Was there something special about that clearing in the forest, some strange refraction due to the topography of the place or the weather at the time, or some trick of the light to do with the time of day? Come to think of it, both times it had been late in the day, with the light failing. Twilight notoriously played tricks. Was it all merely an optical illusion?

She glanced at the alarm-clock. It was Saturday, and she ought to be getting over to the stables. Or should she go back to Dent's Cross and try and work it out on the scene? She shivered. No, she dared not risk *another*. Her mother's voice from downstairs interrupted her thoughts.

'Grace?' she was calling. 'Are you ready?'

Grace went onto the gallery landing. Her mother was dressed for Mass; she frowned as she looked up.

'But you're not changed,' she exclaimed. 'I left clean jodhpurs out . . .'

With a brief hesitation, Grace went to the top of the stairs.

'I'm coming with you, Mum,' she said.

*

As they walked briskly down the frosty paving, her mother cast her a warm, satisfied glance. Grace turned away, knowing what she was thinking. The air was crisp, and above the last lingering skeins of mist the sky rose in a perfect, uninterrupted gradient from the palest pink to an infinite blue. She went round the car scraping the frost off the windows, then climbed in. For a moment they sat in silence, swathed all around in white billows of exhaust, waiting for the heater to demist the windscreen.

'Father Gregory *will* be pleased,' said her mother at last.

Grace said nothing. Laura let out the clutch and pulled slowly away down the drive.

'He's got a difficult job,' she went on conversationally. 'I don't think the Bishop quite realizes how *entrenched* the people are round here. The Church is having to struggle. Every one of us counts.'

'Nonsense,' muttered Grace.

'It's very serious.'

Hard people, with the hard morals and austere Protestantism of any mining community, the folk in this secluded backwater of the country were by nature suspicious of any who did not belong. As a small minority, the Catholics among them were considered outsiders, and this created

64

divisions that not even the tireless pastoral efforts of Father Gregory could bridge.

'For goodness' sake, Mother,' Grace blurted out suddenly, 'the way Father Gregory talks you'd think it was the Crusades. Methodist, Baptist, Catholic, what does it matter? Or does he win credits in heaven for the souls he recruits?'

'Grace! This is no state of mind to be coming to church in.'

'I've changed my mind. I'm not going.'

'It's too late to take you back to the stables now.'

'I'll wait in the school library, then.'

'Don't be so silly!'

'I mean it,' she said with vehemence.

They drove the rest of the way in silence, through the main square of Abbotsbury town, where the Saturday market was in full swing, and on until the iron railings of the convent grounds came into view. Turning in through the gates, they proceeded slowly up the drive and drew up in the parking area behind the main building. Father Gregory was standing at the chapel entrance. Before Grace could peel off to the library, he'd seen her. He came forward, a curious gleam lighting up his face. She was trapped. He reached out and took her hand in greeting and asked solicitously how *everything was*. She gave a dull, noncommittal reply and lamely followed her mother inside. The service dragged on interminably. The prayers sounded empty, the voices dead. She rested her gaze on the face of Our Lady and sought some reassurance in the mysterious half-smile there, but nothing came back. She'd lost contact. And all the time, whenever he turned to face the small congregation, Father Gregory's eye seemed to single her out and fix itself upon her. So, he knew, too: Sister Bertram had told him everything.

Afterwards, on the doorstep, the priest bid her goodbye with a lingering handshake and a hushed remark that they would be having a word together soon. In the driveway outside, she fancied that everyone was staring at her. Two of her school friends seemed to be whispering behind her back. She spotted Sister Bertram coming down the glazed arcade. The Sister stopped, but being separated by the sheet window she could only raise her hand in a gesture of benediction. Grace returned to the car in silence, and all the way home she uttered not a single word. Already she dreaded going back to school on the Monday and facing the same looks and stares. She'd stay away, sick. She'd pretend she had a migraine. Pretend? She really didn't know anything any more.

*

Laura glanced in through the oven window; the Sunday roast would be ready any minute now. From the table she transferred the third place-setting onto a tray: Grace wasn't coming down to lunch. A grunt behind her made her turn. Leonard stood over by the dresser, examining the bottle of tablets Dr Stimpson had prescribed.

'Methysergide,' he remarked, returning the bottle to the shelf. 'Won't do a blind bit of good.'

She looked at him intently.

'Leonard,' she began after a pause, 'do you think this business is physical or . . . mental?'

'Mental *is* physical,' he replied with an easy laugh. 'That's to say, the mind is an electro-chemical process going on inside the brain.'

'You know what I mean.'

'Is she mentally disturbed? Nonsense! She's *seventeen*, Laura. Remember what you went through at that age.'

'I didn't see funny flashes. I didn't have terrible fits and nearly drown.'

'Laura, she's growing up, that's all.' He smiled reassuringly, but his eyes remained distant, thoughtful.

'What do we *do*?'

'Nothing. Wait, and it'll all blow over.' He reached into a drawer for the carving knife. 'I'll take hers up. If she can eat, then there's nothing wrong with her. Anyway, she's well enough to be having Emily over for tea.'

She kissed him lightly on the cheek.

'Thanks, Leonard.'

'What for?'

'For being such a comfort.' She took the roast out of the oven. 'Come on, let's serve up. Then I want to hear about Brighton and how it all went.'

*

The light was beginning to fade as Grace climbed over the stile after Emily and followed her on the homeward stretch down the muddy tow-path that led alongside the river towards the mill. She lagged behind her friend, lost in her own thoughts. After a while, Emily turned with a swirl of her long dark hair and threw her a suggestive grin.

'Dreaming of the beautiful Benedict?'

'It's not like that,' replied Grace shortly.

'Oh no? Everyone knows what you get up to in the stables.'

'Don't be stupid. I'm fond of him, but that's all.'

'He's got the hots for you, Grace. And he's a good Catholic boy.' She began humming the wedding anthem.

'Oh, shut up, Emily. Anyway, Mum says I shouldn't encourage him.'

'Socially inferior, is he?'

Emily laughed and skipped ahead. Grace followed, sauntering. Downstream, the river branched in two; part was channelled off in a narrow gully that ran alongside the house into the mill race, where it fell a good twenty feet before rejoining the main flow below the weir fifty yards beyond. But here, the river was flat and sluggish, stretching like a ribbon of mercury in the failing sunlight and bordered on either side by banks of reeds and sedges already lost in the twilight. She paused to look at a broken willow bough lying in the water and at the intricate eddies it cast in the surface. A mallard suddenly exploded out from the bank and took wing, rising steeply into the air with an angry squawk. She followed its flight as it circled wide and high in the

67

wintry pink sky. She blinked, then blinked once again. The sky seemed to be growing brighter. A flush of alarm prickled her skin. She dropped her gaze. Somewhere in the back of her consciousness, she became aware of that ominous purple taste. *Oh God, no!* she wanted to cry aloud. *Not here, not now!*

She looked ahead. Emily was now some way in front; she turned a bend and was momentarily lost to her view. To the left, between the willow trunks, the water flowed on silently, steadily. To her right lay an open field, stretching to a distant wooded hillside. But even as she cast about her, the entire scene grew another degree brighter, as if she were witnessing the dawn speeded up. The light grew thicker, denser. Gradually, it invaded her whole field of vision in a vast sheet that pulsed relentlessly in and out, in and out. As it swelled it grew more diffuse, masking everything up to the perimeter of her sight, but as it shrank it grew more opaque, coalescing at each pulse into a denser, more vivid ball that followed her gaze wherever she looked – one moment dancing upon the water, the next floating just off the ground in the middle of the field, until as she finally settled her gaze on the path ahead, the shimmering light came gradually to rest, too.

She grabbed at a tree-trunk for support. Her whole stomach seemed to rise to her throat, as if some force were trying to turn her inside-out like a glove. Clutching the rough bark, trying to shield her eyes from the searing light as it grew ever denser and more solid, driven beyond wonder and terror and robbed of any will to resist, gradually and irresistibly she sank slowly to her knees.

*

The light shimmers in a soft white sheet. It furls at the edges, draws in towards the centre. Rays spurt out like spokes. The eye of the light-storm is growing still denser, still thicker. Clotting, solidifying into sub-stance. Line by line, it crystallizes into human shape. *Her* shape.

She stands in a simple hooded robe of pale blue and white. It is hemmed with golden ribbing and it falls to the ground in ample folds. Around her head the cape forms soft, crenellated pleats, as if riding on the waves of her dark hair. Her skin is pale, the texture of fine wax. One hand gestures towards her heart; the other, out-stretched, is beckoning. Her halo radiates gentle sparks of fire. She is smiling, her head indulgently inclined.

Her lips do not move, but somewhere a low voice is audible, speaking softly.

'Eternal peace and life everlasting.'

*

Suddenly, with no warning or word of farewell, the appa-rition began to fade. Within a moment it was quite extin-guished, leaving only a ragged, carbon-grey hole in her vision. Blinking hard, she looked up to see Emily standing over her, her eyes wide with alarm. She struggled giddily to her feet. Her wellingtons squelched water and her jeans were soaked, but she was hardly aware of anything.

Emily reached to support her.

'You okay?' she cried. 'You look as if you've seen a ghost!'

Grace grasped her arm.

'You saw her too?' she demanded hoarsely.

'Saw who?'

'Our Lady!' She tugged her closer. 'Did you see Our Lady? There, just there, where you're standing.'

Emily pulled away. She gave an odd laugh.

'Sure, I saw her. And the Apostles too.'

'For heaven's sake,' Grace pleaded desperately, 'didn't you see that amazing light? And then *her*? Didn't you hear the voice? Didn't you see anything?'

'Hey, what is this?'

'You didn't see *anything at all*?'

Her friend slowly shook her head. 'Only you grovelling around on your knees.'

Grace let out a small cry and covered her face with her hands.

'Oh, God,' she sobbed.

'Grace?' Emily was shaking her now. 'You sure you're okay?'

Grace nodded. She was defeated.

'It's nothing,' she mumbled. 'Don't take any notice.'

Emily took a step back. She shook her head.

'You're really loopy, girl. Seriously nuts. You should be on the funny farm.' She shivered. 'I'm getting back. It's really spooky out here.'

*

Eternal peace and life everlasting. Lying in bed, Grace stared out of the window at the stark, clear night. As she repeated the words, she felt a strange warm glow gradually spreading throughout her. It was all beginning to make sense at last.

It was, after all, a vision. There could be no doubt now. A vision with a message. About Matthew. Our Lady had heard her prayers and come to tell her that Matthew was in heaven and everything was fine. That first time, Leo had interrupted before the message could get through properly. But next time, at the pool, Our Lady had actually let her glimpse him as he now was, in heaven, bathed in light and surrounded by pure whiteness. He had shed all the pain and suffering and found eternal peace and life everlasting. Tears of joy welled up in her eyes. How could she have been so blind to the obvious? And what message could be more wonderful?

Six

Grace rose early and, putting on her tracksuit, went for a jog in the damp dawn fields. As she passed the spot by the river where she'd had the apparition, she stopped; slipping off the small elephant-hair bracelet Matthew had given her, she tied it to a branch of the willow tree. She stood quietly for a moment, her head bowed, before setting off down the track at a steady run.

Back home, she dressed quickly and went round opening up the house. She brought her mother tea in bed and ran a bath for her; she laid the breakfast table, she squeezed fresh orange-juice, she percolated the coffee and put croissants in the oven to warm.

'Five-star service today,' smiled her mother when she came down. 'And you're looking so much better, darling.'

'Sorry about yesterday,' said Grace, sitting down. 'I was very off with Leo, too.'

'I wouldn't worry. He understood.'

'He didn't.' She paused. 'I didn't either. Not then.'

'Oh?'

She met her mother's eye.

'I've worked it all out. It's really quite simple. You see, he's only trying to tell us that he's fine. That he's happy where he is and everything's wonderful.'

'Leonard?'

'No, Mother. Matthew.'

Her mother gave an uneasy smile.

'Oh, come on, darling! This isn't like you. You're so — what did Father Gregory call it? — intellectually stringent. I'm sure Matthew is fine wherever he is, but to say he's trying to get through to us, well . . . Grace, you're not dabbling in spiritualism, are you?'

'No, no, you don't understand.' She looked into the worried eyes and turned away, unable to explain. 'It sounds too stupid.'

'I think you should tell me, all the same.'

'Well,' she began hesitantly, 'you know we've often talked about life after death, and, well, I'd never really believed in heaven, at least not the kind of heaven with angels sitting on clouds and playing harps. I always saw it more as a state of mind.'

'It is, it is,' agreed her mother quickly. 'Going to heaven won't be like walking into a Tiepolo fresco. That's just metaphorical.'

'But what I'm trying to say is, it's *real*.'

'Yes, but on a level we can't comprehend.'

'I mean *really* real. And very beautiful. Light and bright, and everything white. That's where Matthew is. He's completely happy, perfectly at peace. We don't need to be sad at all.'

'So we must believe.'

'But I *know*, that's my point. I've *seen* him.'

Her mother let out a small, sympathetic sigh.

'I used to dream about him quite a lot after he died, too. It was the same after your father died. I even once dreamt I saw him in heaven. Well, I dreamt he was happy and safe, and it did give me a lot of comfort.'

'It was no dream, Mother,' said Grace quietly.

'Well, a daydream, I suppose you'd call it. I'd generally be dozing off in my chair . . .'

Grace checked herself. She couldn't expect people to understand, let alone believe her. Until yesterday, she'd have laughed at such a claim herself. But now everything was different; she felt she'd passed through a door and left everyone else on the other side. She glanced across at her mother, sitting tight-lipped in her own private world. She got up and wrapped her arms gently round her shoulders.

'He's happy, that's all,' she said simply. 'He just wants us to be happy, too, and to remember him.'

'Yes, darling, I know.'

Grace could feel her shoulders tautening with the effort of fighting off the pain. But there was no need for pain or grief, that was the whole *point* of the message. It offered reassurance for the present and hope for the future. And that called for burying the grief for the past.

'You know, Mum,' she said after a while, 'I think it's time we did some rearranging. Let's go through Matthew's room and clear out his things properly.'

*

During school break, Grace slipped away to the convent chapel. The place had a quite different feel to it. The pews of bleached pine no longer felt austere and comfortless but aglow with an all-embracing warmth, while the light that streamed in through the stained glass, dappling the statue of Our Lady, now appeared cheerful and pure in its simple, primary colours, rather than crude and harsh. She sat down in a pew just inside the door and knelt to pray. A feeling of irrepressible exhilaration gradually swelled up within her. She wanted to laugh and weep all at once. Any moment, she felt, she might burst open with the sheer hugeness and wonder and happiness and relief of it all. She was flying, soaring, higher and higher, without wings, without weight, into a pure, clear realm where nothing hurt, nothing cloyed, and all was light and ease.

Dimly some earthbound part of her heard the door squeak on its hinges and she sensed a light draught brush her face. A moment later, she felt a hand on her shoulder. The touch struck her like lightning down a conductor, grounding her instantly. Disorientated, she looked up to see Father Gregory leaning over her, his eyes narrowed and his florid face set in a hard cast.

'I'm glad to see you here, Grace,' he said. 'In a spirit of penance, I trust.'

She looked up at him quizzically.

'I don't follow, Father.'

'I think you know what I mean.' He glanced around the chapel; at the far end, by the altar, one of the Sisters was at work polishing. 'I'd like to talk this over with you, Grace. Not here, though. Let's go into the vestry.'

Reluctantly, feeling her peace of mind threatened, she followed the priest down the side aisle and into the vestry. There he prised a bucket-seated chair off a stack and motioned to her to be seated. Leaning back against a table with his arms folded and his legs crossed at the ankles, he pinned her with a penetrating eye. Confused, she looked away. Briefly her gaze roamed over the row of vestments hanging on the wall and, above, a framed photograph of the chapel consecration ceremony. In the small, hot, airless room the fumes of pine-wax and plastic mingled with the musty aroma of incense made her head swim. She met his eye again. His smile was falsely reassuring.

'Now, Grace, what's all this I've been hearing?'

'All what, Father?'

'What Sister Bertram has been telling me.' She detected a hint of mockery in his tone. 'Our Blessed Lady has been appearing to Grace Holmwood in a vision.'

'What do you want me to say, Father?'

'Tell me what you mean by it.' His tone softened. 'It's not like you to go round inventing wild stories.'

'It's no story, Father,' she said quietly. 'It's true. I did see Our Lady.'

'May God forgive you!' he exclaimed, then checked himself. For a moment he appeared to struggle to find the right approach. 'We're a small, closely knit family here,' he began reasonably. 'False rumours can cause immeasurable harm and undermine the trust and faith we're building. You're a popular girl, Grace, and a lot of the younger ones look up to you. You know how impressionable they can be, and you have a responsibility to see they're kept on the right tracks. Now, you're a sensible girl . . .'

She stood up; she was shaking. She didn't have to listen to this.

'Father, would you excuse me? I'll be late for Art.'

Hastily he pressed her back into her seat and drew up a chair for himself opposite.

'Don't worry, I'll speak to Sister Ambrose. Let's take this calmly, step by step.' He smoothed a hand across his beard. 'Now, why don't you just tell me exactly what happened.'

'I'd rather not, Father. You wouldn't believe me. It doesn't matter any more, anyway: I've worked it out, and it's okay.'

'Oh but it *does* matter,' he retorted. 'I have the spiritual well-being of a hundred and twenty girls to think of. That's my first concern.'

'That, and not the truth?'

A light flush appeared high on his cheeks.

'What is Truth? That's not an easy question, Grace. We can often be mistaken. Sometimes temptation appears to us in the form of truth. The Devil is very clever. Now, in small matters, that's not so important, perhaps. But *this* is quite different. It's a very serious matter indeed. Claiming divine visions is a direct challenge to the authority of the Church—'

'Father . . .'

'—and a blasphemy against the holy sacraments.'

'You don't understand!'

'Oh, I think I do, Grace.'

'I know what I saw!' she blurted out, feeling hot tears of distress welling up. 'I know you think I'm imagining it. Or deliberately inventing it. But I'm not. It's true. Our Lady *did* come to me, she appeared just like that, without any warning, and not just once, either, but twice. There was this huge dazzling bright light, out of nowhere, and she just sort of materialized out of it. Our Blessed Lady herself. I can't say how, I don't *care* how. But I saw her, Father. Right there, in front of me. As real as you are now.'

Father Gregory regarded her in shocked silence for a long moment, then he leaned forward in his chair and appealed to her more urgently.

'Grace, will you start from the beginning and tell me what happened? *Please?*'

*

After Grace had gone, Father Gregory stood staring out of the high vestry window. Think calmly, he told himself.

There seemed to be a whole spectrum of possibilities. On the one hand, Grace could be just a mischievous girl, deliberately fabricating a subversive lie. On the other hand, she seemed to believe in her experiences with total conviction. Perhaps, then, she was deceiving *herself.* During the hormonal holocaust of adolescence, girls often imagined seeing things that weren't there. But again, what if she were neither lying nor hallucinating, and the things actually *were* there? What if Grace, of all the girls in the convent, of all the people across the country, laity and priests, novices and nuns, had genuinely been granted a visitation from Our Lady?

His pulse quickened. As a boy, taking his first Communion, he'd had a brief but indelible experience of God, a sudden momentary insight into the wonder and mystery of the Holy Ghost. Those few transcendent seconds had decided him upon his life's vocation; he was in love with God and he could imagine nothing finer than spending his days in closeness with the Divine presence. But that experience had never happened again, and as the years passed in empty hope, he grew to feel detached from his God, an onlooker at Christ's table, not a participant. He'd carried on with his pledge and taken his vows, but he'd never felt that presence again. He'd seen it in others, and at times he made himself do penance for envy, but as time went by he gradually accepted that in some way he had been passed over. Removed from the higher mysteries, he'd devoted his ministry to the mundane daily concerns and troubles of the people of his parish. If now, therefore, one of his flock had received no less a blessing than a visitation from Our Lady, this was an unimaginable blessing upon him, too. How could he not, in his deepest heart, *want* to believe Grace? Yet that, by itself, ought to make him mistrust his judgement. This was indeed a critical test of his own faith. If it was a sign, he must embrace it wholeheartedly and rejoice. If, however, it was a deceit of the Devil to inflame erroneous passions, he must stamp it out to the last ember.

Gripping the window-sill to steady himself, he turned his gaze upon the small wooden crucifix on the wall. How should he act? Should he speak to the Reverend Mother? Or directly to the Bishop? Or first to Laura? He returned to his chair, drew it up before the crucifix and knelt down. With his elbows resting on the seat, he closed his eyes and prayed for guidance.

*

Laura sat at the drawing-board, staring sightlessly at a jam-jar of fading anemones in a cluster of pots of paintbrushes. Her lunch – orange juice, cheese, bran biscuits, a stick of celery – lay untouched on the tray beside her. Father Gregory had just left. *Visions?* She'd laughed at first: it was nonsense, a practical joke. But no, the priest had been serious. Very serious. He'd even mooted the possibility that they might actually be true.

Of course, that was absurd. As a priest, he should be more responsible than to entertain the idea. It would be wrong to lead Grace along: she'd only end up disappointed and hurt. But where had the story come from? It was inconceivable that the girl had deliberately fabricated it. She told innocent fibs like anyone else, adult or child, but never lies, and certainly none so wicked. What possible motive could she have? To gain attention? She had no lack of that. To ridicule her religion? She'd gone to Mass on Saturday *and* Sunday. And Father Gregory himself said he'd found her that morning in the chapel, praying.

She must be imagining it all. Father Gregory had dismissed the idea it might be psychological, to do with adolescent sexual repression, but perhaps that was it, after all. This wasn't a matter for a priest but a doctor. Leonard was the man to talk to.

Laura called the hospital and had Leonard paged. They spoke for a full twenty minutes. He was calm, easy and reassuring. He said he'd cancel his afternoon case conference and collect Grace from school himself. Laura agreed to be out when they came back, to give him time and space alone with her. Maybe, as a close and trusted friend, he could get her to open up in a way that she, as her mother, couldn't.

As she put the phone down, she felt sudden misgivings. Deep down, she mistrusted all doctors. What had they ever done for her family? For Alec? Or, worse still, for Matthew? For three terrible, sleepless weeks she'd stood helplessly by, watching the poor boy visibly ebbing, while they took tests and more tests and tried first this treatment, then that . . . All along she'd never been able to shake off the feeling that they'd never really known what it was, let alone how to cure it. 'Gastro-intestinal failure, aggravated by pneumonia' was the cause shown on the death certificate, but no-one, not even Leonard, had ever explained to her satisfaction what had caused *that*, or why a tough, healthy little boy of twelve who'd survived his share of knocks and scrapes and never lost a day's school through illness, should suddenly, for no apparent reason at all, develop a mysterious and devastating illness, suffering all those vicious stomach cramps and that bloody diarrhoea, that terrible external ulceration and the unstaunchable internal bleeding. Or why, despite constant blood transfusions and even a severely painful bone marrow transplant, he should fail to pull out of the relentless downward spiral. And why, above all, with all the skills and equipment at their disposal, Leonard and the others had simply been defeated. How could she ever really put her trust in them? Was it because they looked so convincingly the part, wearing their white coats and speaking of *immuno-deficiency* and *thrombocytopenia*, or was it perhaps simply because everyone around them – above all the patients themselves, out of sheer desperation – had such conviction

78

in the omnipotence of modern medicine that no-one ever dared question their authority? What gave them the right? Leonard was a priest of his own calling in just the same way as Father Gregory was of his; the hospital was Leonard's chapel, the Hippocratic oath his creed, and the salvation he offered, though of the body rather than the soul, nonetheless demanded the very same thing: *faith*. Faith in man and in his works.

Well, she'd lost that faith.

She swivelled her chair round and stared out across the back lawn. She'd rely on herself to work it out. She thought back to Grace's strange remarks that morning. If the poor troubled girl was seeing imaginary presences, it must be because they were serving some psychological function, satisfying some deep, repressed need. The more she pondered what the priest had told her, the more the answer seemed inescapably obvious.

The key was Matthew.

As children, Matthew and Grace had been inseparable and virtually indivisible. They shared the same aches and pains. If one fell off a bicycle a mile away, the other would scream. A secret shared with one was a secret imparted to both. Games like chess held no fun for them, since each could foresee the other's moves. Their conversation together was rapid and elided, half spoken and half thought and very hard for others to follow. There could hardly have been a crueller trauma for Grace than her brother's death. At the time, she'd appeared so calm and strong – unknowingly, she'd even given Laura herself the strength to cope, too – but somehow she'd never fully *resolved* it. At the time, Laura wondered if Grace's problem was that she had never really allowed her grief to express itself or even fundamentally accepted that he was dead. She kept his room exactly as it had been, she cleaned and tidied it herself and, but for Leonard's well-intentioned efforts at redecoration, you could put your head round the door and you'd think for all the world that the boy had just popped out and would come tearing back up the stairs at any moment, laughing and chattering in his usual excitable way. Maybe only now, five years later, was Grace beginning to reconcile herself with reality. Inventing a happy picture of him in heaven, an absurd fiction though it might seem, was perhaps her subconscious way of laying him to rest. For five years he had lain unburied in her mind. Now she was clearing it all up – clearing out the room, too – and, with it, according him due burial.

Laura rose and, leaving the studio, walked thoughtfully across to the house. She went up the stairs and followed the gallery to Matthew's bedroom. Just inside the door, she halted. The sense of his presence was overwhelming. His very smell seemed to linger in the air, just as if the room had been inhabited five minutes before, not five years.

It all had to go. Grace was right. You had to free yourself from the past, not try and cling onto it. Wasn't she herself just as guilty? She had a trunk of Alec's memorabilia lying in the cupboard in her own bedroom. With sudden decisiveness, she turned and, closing the door behind her, went briskly down the landing. She'd go through the trunk right now and clear it all out – Alec's old suits and shoes, his tennis racquet and cricket bat, the old love letters and the honeymoon photographs, the party invitations and the playbills, even the white roses he'd brought to the hospital after the twins were born and which she'd pressed in a book . . . Yes, the past was dead, and it was time it was buried for ever.

*

Sitting in his Jaguar, Leonard watched Grace's class come out and disperse, some to bicycles in the sheds, others to waiting cars. One by one the lights went out and within a few minutes the school was deserted. Could he have missed her? He was on the point of going inside to check when the slender, fair-haired figure emerged. She took a few steps forward, half in a dream, then looked about her. The moment she saw him she hesitated, evidently wondering if it was too late to turn back.

Throwing open the passenger door, he called out to her. Uncertainly, she stepped forward.

'Hop in,' he said cheerily. 'Your mother's had to go to a meeting, so I'm here.' He leaned across to take her school bag as she climbed in. 'How did it go today? It's Art on Mondays, isn't it?'

'I missed it,' she replied in a flat tone.

'But you love Art. Something the matter?'

'I'm not stupid, Leo. I know perfectly well why you're here. Father Gregory got on to Mum, and Mum got on to you.'

His laugh struck a false note.

'Very astute, Duchess.'

She withered him with a glance and turned away. She sat toying with an end of her hair, staring straight ahead. They drove in silence down the convent drive and headed westwards through the town and into the yellow and crimson streaks of the setting sun. He looked across at her and struggled to find a tone that would draw her out. They'd always found it so easy to talk, before.

'It seems you've really been giving them the run-around,' he began with a chuckle. 'Father Gregory's got his cassock in a right old twist. Still, no doubt a few Hail Marys will straighten him out. Or, knowing him, a few *Bloody* Marys.'

'Stop the car please, Leo.'

'Hey, it's only a joke.'

'Stop the car! I'm getting out.'

He pulled up. She reached for the door. Her eyes blazed with fury. Shaken, he tried a conciliatory smile.

'Don't get upset, angel,' he said. 'I just thought, well, seeing a ghost is one thing, but the Virgin Mary herself is really pushing it. If you're not careful they'll sanctify you. Saint Grace Holmwood. They'll have the last laugh.'

'That's no way to talk! These things are very precious.'

A chill ran through his blood. Could she actually be *serious*? What had happened to the Grace he knew?

'Come on, Duchess, you're talking to Leo! You don't

need to kid *me*. We've talked about these things together dozens of times. About the Church as a political institution, dedicated to its own survival. Very successful it has been, too, I don't deny that.' Keep talking, he told himself; get a dialogue going, play for time, don't let her slip away. 'The dogma, the creed, the sacraments – that's all just ideology, nothing to do with any truth. Far from it,' he hurried on, aware he was beginning to sound like a textbook. 'It has everything to do with *opposing* the truth. Suspending one's disbelief. Denying one's reason. Ignoring objectivity. I appreciate that man has an inbuilt, primitive need for mystery. Robbed of one mystery, he'll invent another. Every inch science rolls back the carpet of ignorance, the primitive element in us all is forced to look for something further still beyond the reach of reason – something, literally, unbelievable. Religion fulfils a *need*. It's comforting, yes; it's socially useful; it's even therapeutic in some cases. But it's as far from being the *truth* as I am from being a Chinaman.' He paused. 'We agree on all that. Don't we?'

All the time he was speaking, she had been holding his eye with a blinkless gaze. For a moment he wondered if she'd actually heard him, if she was really there. Eventually a frown deepened over her brow and, lowering her eyes, she shook her head slowly, sadly.

'I'm sorry, Leo.'

'Sorry? Why?'

'I'm just sorry you'll never accept it. You, of all people, can't.'

He felt a spurt of alarm. He had to re-establish common ground.

'Look,' he began, 'we can't talk properly here. Let's go back home and you can tell me everything.'

She shrugged sorrowfully.

'What's there left to say?'

'*Explain* it to me. Logically. I promise I'll keep an open mind.'

'But it's *not* logical!' she blurted out. 'Don't you see, Leo, this is something beyond reason and logic. I don't expect to convince you. I don't even care any more if no-one believes me. I only know what I saw. What I felt, and heard. I know what you'll say. You'll say I was imagining it, hallucinating, my subconscious was playing tricks, a neurotic delusion . . . I'm not going to argue with you. You choose whatever makes you comfortable, Leo. I'll stick with what I know.'

'What you think you know,' he corrected.

'What I *know* I know,' she retorted fiercely. 'I was there, Leo. It happened to *me*, not to you or to anyone else. It was real, authentic, actual.' Her voice was trembling now. 'I wish everyone would just leave me alone! I don't see why I should have to have these conversations.'

A silence lengthened between them. His mouth was dry and his pulse pounded in his temples like a drumbeat. He looked across at the girl, biting her lip and holding back tears, and pressed his hand gently on her arm.

'Come on,' he said at last. 'I'll get you home and we'll talk about something entirely different.'

*

Late in the evening, with darkness already fallen, Leonard left the mill house without waiting for Laura to return and, climbing into his car, retraced the route he'd taken a few days before, at the start of the trouble. He'd finally got Grace to tell him the whole story, and he was profoundly shaken. A terrible, sneaking, impossible suspicion had driven him to this place.

He slowed down as his headlights picked out the small knoll of Dent's Cross, surmounted by the lop-sided road sign, then continued slowly for a hundred yards until he found a field where he could park the car out of view. He switched off the lights and sat for a moment, letting his eyes adjust to the dark and asking himself what on earth he was really expecting to find. Finally, he reached into the glove-box for a torch and stepped out into the chilly air, where he stood still for a moment, allowing his senses to adjust to the night. A pale moon leered at him over the tree-tops; a field away, carried alarmingly close by the wind, a fox coughed. With a shiver he turned up his coat collar and headed back towards the crossroads, where he made off down the track that led into the deep forest.

The moon, lying full ahead, cast a green pallor over the sandy ribbon of the path and threw into jagged relief the outline of the spruce trees banked on either side. A sudden commotion brought the undergrowth alive – a shrill squawk, a sharp snarl, a brief flapping tussle, then silence. He hastened his step. The soft sand absorbed his footfalls. At the crack of a twig behind him he glanced uneasily over his shoulder to see his own footsteps stretching in a winding trail behind him, betraying him as clearly as a set of fingerprints. Don't worry, he told himself sharply; no-one can ever *know*.

As the track grew steeper and the going rougher, he had to slow his pace. In the light of the torch the route was confusing and treacherous, and at times the path disappeared completely. At one point he took a wrong turn and found himself caught in a moonless trough, trapped in brambles and deep bracken. Eventually, with his breathing labouring and his pulse rising, he stumbled out into the grassy clearing.

He stepped slowly forward. In the centre, at the spot where he'd seen Grace kneeling, he stopped and bent to examine the grass. For what? Scorch marks? He flashed the torch around. Grass, bracken, trees, shrubbery: nothing unusual, nothing significant. The silver birches on the embankment ahead returned a dim gleam. He lowered the beam to the rusty iron door that barred the entrance to the disused mine and moved carefully forward, step by step, until he reached the metal grille.

The padlock was firm and the chain, though rusted, was sound. The lock and hinges bore no sign of tampering. Drawing back the creeper and roots, he quickly satisfied himself that the concrete frame was immovably bedded into the red-brown rock face. A PRIVATE sign hung at a slight angle; from the rust and rain marks running in vertical streaks he could tell that it hadn't been disturbed in years. He shone his torch inside. A solid wall stood a few feet within, firmly sealing off the passage. He quickly scanned the surface, now flecked with moss and lichen. Everything looked fine. He was about to turn away when he froze in his tracks. Far down in the bottom corner, just at the point where the mortar joined the rock, ran a fine hairline crack. A pearly white sediment had built up on each side of the crack, forming two ridges like the bloodless lips of a corpse, while down the centre oozed a thin, glistening thread of moisture that ran along the rough concrete sill and leached away into the earth, leaving a large, irregular stain fringed with silvery crystals.

He stepped back sharply. The patch had seeped out under the grille, discolouring the grass in a long spur. Christ, had he trodden in it? His mind reeled sickeningly. Backing away, he broke into a stumbling run across the clearing and, pausing only to cast a final, fearful glance behind him, headed back down the track the way he had come. *Red* oozing from the earth – red oxide, red haematite, red ore – okay. But not that evil, suppurating white. That could mean only one thing.

*

Back home, Leonard hurried into his study. He went straight to the wastepaper basket and rapidly sifted through the contents until he came to the scrap of paper on which he'd written down Tom Welland's number. He grabbed the phone and dialled. It rang without reply. Of course, he thought with a muttered curse, that'll be the number at the labs. He replaced the receiver and went to the kitchen for a drink to calm his nerves. He'd have to wait till the morning.

Seven

The car-park at the rear of the Department building was empty except for a pale blue car in the bay marked 'T. J. W.' Above, the rain-streaked concrete façade rose sheer and windowless, relieved only by ventilation grilles. The front and other two flanks of the building were ribbed by small metal-framed windows; struggling pot-plants on the sills singled out the offices from the labs, which were mostly shuttered behind venetian blinds. At the main entrance, beneath the discreet 'Department of Medical Research' sign-plate, a bright orange diamond-shaped sticker was affixed, with 'HAZCHEM' in bold black lettering across it. Inside, the fire-doors, spaced at intervals down the corridors, bore the standard yellow squares with their circular black trefoil logo, warning of radiation danger.

In the reception area, the night security guard was coming off duty, and before long the first secretaries and lab technicians would start arriving for work. Upstairs, in a large room on the third floor, beyond a reinforced door that had automatically locked itself behind him, with a plastic beaker of machine-made coffee in one hand and a cigarette in the other, Tom Welland was going over the computer print-out once again to make absolutely certain that in his elation and relief he wasn't misreading the results.

The suspense was nerve-racking. He'd been here before many times, but never with tissue quite like this. The vital question was always the same, however: Had the process of freezing and thawing destroyed the tissue's ability to synthesize protein? Was it inert, or could it be made to regain *life*? You could never quite tell. For all the sophisticated computers and the special cytological assaying equipment in that room, regenerating tissue was really more of an art than a science. He'd done his doctoral thesis, fifteen years before, on radiation damage to neural tissue in the common laboratory mouse. Genetically, mouse and man were curiously close, and the one made a useful template for the other. But even so, a technique that worked a hundred times on murine material didn't necessarily work on human material, especially on the tissue of such a complex organ as the human brain. Life itself was just too elusive, the spark too fickle. But then, that was the challenge.

He came to the end of the sheaf of print-out and rubbed his eyes behind his glasses.

'Jesus!' he breathed.

He went over to a unit mounted on a trolley beside the isolation chamber. Fine plastic tubes hooked up to the cerebral blood vessels inside the chamber led out to this small unit, carrying a constant circulation of enriched plasma. A further tube, finer than the rest, branched off and fed samples to the differentiometer, an instrument which tested for changes in the concentration of oxygen and glucose in the plasma. If what came out was the same as what went in, the organ clearly remained inert. But any change, especially any significant oxygen uptake, indicated that some neurochemical event was taking place there, some vital metabolic activity, some cluster of cells firing somewhere in among the ten thousand million, and however tiny the stirring, however dim the glimmer, nevertheless the spark of life was present. And, as the print-out clearly showed, there was indeed metabolism here.

Still cautious, though, he quickly checked for any obvious malfunctions – the tube connections, the electrical leads, the temperature and flow-rate monitors. He glanced at the switch marked Pulse Control that controlled what he called the 'spark plugs' – the electrodes through which, every few days, for a brief period towards the end of the day, he would squirt a few millivolts of electricity in controlled bursts in an

87

attempt to kick-start the cells back to life. He peered in through the two-inch glass panel. There lay the brain, pinkish-grey and wrinkled and looking strangely withered and shrunken in its small perspex cask. He ran his eye over all the joints and wires, the tubes feeding in and out, paying special attention to the pair of electrodes themselves, bedded deep into the pre-frontal lobes like two micro-fine tooth-picks.

Standing back, he wiped a sleeve over his brow and drew a long, deep breath. Yes, all was fine. The process had begun.

Suddenly, behind him, the phone rang. He started violently. Bracing himself with a pull on his cigarette, he reached for the receiver.

'Tom Welland speaking,' he said.

'Ah, Tom. It's Leonard Grigson. I got your message. Before we get onto anything else,' the voice hastened, 'there's something I'd like you to take a look at.'

*

'And you saw nothing at all, Emily?'

The tall, dark-haired girl shifted uneasily. From his position by the mantelpiece, Father Gregory threw a glance towards Sister Bertram; seated at the desk near the Reverend Mother, her hands folded in her lap, she'd kept a severe silence all through the interview. The clock beside him continued its measured tick, resonating flatly in the sparsely furnished study. Through the high-set windows filtered the distant clamour from the playground.

'Emily?' repeated the Reverend Mother.

'I'm not sure,' the girl replied at last. 'I could have.'

'Did you or didn't you?'

'Well, not *as such*.'

'Emily, you've been spreading tales which, by your own admission, aren't true. That's a very serious thing to do, and it must stop at once. If you hear any of the other girls talking this idle nonsense, it's your duty to correct them. Do you understand?'

'Yes, Reverend Mother.'

'Thank you, Emily. You may go now.'

As the door closed behind the girl, Sister Bertram broke her silence.

'I foresee trouble,' she said quietly. 'Remember what happened with Bernadette Gilmore and how the rumour spread? Half the school reported seeing Our Blessed Lady, and when it was investigated the girl admitted making the whole thing up.'

Father Gregory couldn't contain himself any longer.

'Now wait,' he protested. 'Perhaps Grace is *not* making this up. I mean, we can't be *sure*.'

'With all due respect, Father,' replied Sister Bertram, 'you've only got to look at the family history. I know Grace very well.'

'As I do, Sister, and she is simply not that kind of girl. She's perfectly normal, well balanced and down-to-earth. Bernadette Gilmore had a history of mental instability.'

The Reverend Mother raised a hand. Her complexion folded itself into a mass of tiny wrinkles, like cracked glaze on a china vase.

'Let's not be too quick to judge,' she said. 'Grace may be one of the many, as St Augustine put it, who "have tried visions and found only illusions". On the other hand, she may not. It's not for us to determine which. Our task is simply to see if there is a case at all to investigate, and after that it's a matter for the Bishop – and ultimately, I suppose, the Holy Father and his offices. For our part, though, let us keep an open mind and approach the question with humility. I shall talk to Grace myself. Meanwhile, I'd like you, Father, to keep a record of everything you and Sister Bertram have heard, including what Emily O'Dwyer has just told us.' A wry smile briefly softened her features. 'Grace may not be the most devout of our girls, but we mustn't jump to conclusions. At the same time, we must have regard to the effect on the rest of the school. I'll speak to the staff at this evening's meeting and ask them to exercise restraint and common sense. In the meantime, I suggest we all pray for Grace and for our own guidance.'

*

Leonard sat in his car in the gateway to a field, listening to a tape of Mahler songs and trying not to think of all the alarming possible implications. Mary Nolan hadn't claimed visions, but then she didn't have the imagination of a girl like Grace. If what he suspected this meant was true, then God help the poor girl. And God help him.

The dashboard clock read three-forty. Welland was late. Irritably, he snapped off the music and waited. After a while, the note of an engine in low gear caught his attention. A pale blue car came slowly into sight and drew up beside the tottering signpost that marked Dent's Cross. The driver changed his glasses to consult a map, then switched them back again to check the sign. Leonard smothered an oath. The fool was wearing a white lab coat.

He went up and tapped on the window.

'Hello, Tom,' he said coldly. 'You made it.'

'Your grid reference was spot on.'

'Brought the box of tricks?' He nodded with relief as Welland pointed to a small black case on the seat beside him. 'Good. Put the car over there, behind mine. And for God's sake take that bloody coat off. You don't want to be a walking advertisement.'

Welland parked his car and, clutching the black case, hurried over to where Leonard was waiting, a few yards up the track. The past five years showed in him: he'd grown somehow flatter, more compressed, his wire-framed glasses were thicker and his bald patch had spread to resemble a large white yarmulka. Leonard headed off briskly up the path, keeping a step ahead to discourage conversation. The scientist struggled to catch up.

'I'm glad we're in touch again, Leonard,' he called out, growing short of breath as the going grew steeper. 'I need some information.'

'I can't help.'

'Just background stuff. Family medical history. That kind of thing.'

'Sorry, Tom. Can't oblige.'

Eventually, cutting a corner, Welland managed to get ahead. He stopped in the track, blocking the way. He held the black case pointedly between them.

'One good turn . . . you know what they say.' He paused and tried a blunter tack. 'I'm talking about a *quid pro quo*, Leonard.'

'I'm sure you are.'

'Well, then?'

'Come along,' replied Leonard, mollifying his tone. 'Let's get this over with, and then maybe we'll see.'

'What's with you, Leonard? You've changed.'

'The world's changed, Tom.' He pushed past and took the lead again. 'Follow me. It's not far now.'

They continued in silence. A cold, steely sun cast harsh shadows across the sandy path. A pheasant burst out suddenly from a thicket barely an arm's length away and broke into frantic, clumsy flight. High above the trees, a flock of pigeons spotted their approach and wheeled quickly away to another part of the woods. At last they reached the clearing. Beckoning the scientist to follow, Leonard led the way across the expanse of wiry grass. Twenty yards from the embankment into which the entrance to the mine-shaft was hewn, he stopped. He gestured towards the iron gate.

Welland set the case down and flipped open the catches. Carefully he withdrew a cylindrical metal instrument shaped like a heavy-duty flashlamp; in the upper face, beside a handle, was set a calibrated dial and a row of knobs. He waved it around a few feet off the ground, then made an adjustment to the setting. He took a few steps forward, sweeping the ground ahead of him with the instrument held out in front. Once again, he stopped to adjust the scale. A short, crisp *toc* resounded around the clearing, then another, and another. Stretching out his arm, he ran the unit a few inches over his watch-face. The clicking rose to a wild chatter. He stepped gingerly forward.

Ten yards from the iron gate, Leonard fell back. The clicks were coming sporadically, at about one a second. Welland bent and carefully grazed the machine over the patch in the grass where the ominous white fluid had leached into the earth. The slow rhythm of the *tocs* barely changed. More boldly now, he ran it over the base of the grille and over the concrete plinth the base of which, even from where he stood, Leonard could see was moist. He swept the posts, the chain, the bars themselves, the signboard, then more widely around, covering the stones caught in the ivy roots, the grass on the embankment slopes, even the shrubbery on either side. Not once did the tell-tale clicks approach anything like the chatter over the luminous watch dial.

Finally he straightened and turned to face Leonard.

'Clean as a whistle,' he said.

'But that white stuff . . .'

'I'm no geologist. Rock salts, at a guess.'

Leonard swallowed. His throat was desperately dry.

'Thank Christ for that,' he rasped.

*

Leonard hummed gaily to himself as the car cassette burst into the triumphal march from *Aida*. He turned up the volume and took the bends a little faster. He felt light-headed with relief. Then abruptly he grew quiet. Damn fool he'd been: if he hadn't been so paranoid, he wouldn't have had to involve Welland and risk opening up that whole can of worms again. Still, too bad. He would simply block any further discussion. The chapter was closed and must stay closed. He had no real reason to feel so relaxed, either. All right, *that* wasn't the immediate cause, but the problem still remained. It didn't necessarily take an external event to trigger it off.

Grimly, with the music off, he turned up the drive to the

mill house. He wanted to look in on Laura and have another word about Grace; he had to find some way of examining the girl. As he pulled up on the gravel beside her studio outhouse, he saw through the window Laura's slim figure bent over a layout board. He climbed out and tapped on the pane. She looked up and beckoned him, beaming with delight.

'This *is* a welcome surprise,' she said. 'I phoned the hospital, but they said you were on a call-out. Can you stay for a cup of tea?'

'Sure.' He glanced admiringly at the design. 'You're really brilliant, you know.'

'So are you, Leonard. Come on, let's go across.'

As they crossed the gravel drive, she turned to him.

'So, how did you get on yesterday? Grace wouldn't tell me a thing.'

'Made no headway at all. She told me about these experiences of hers, but I'm afraid our interpretations differ.'

Laura led the way into the house.

'I have my theories,' she said quietly.

'Yes. Some are pretty obvious. For instance, she's at the age when girls get interested in boys.'

'Come off it, Leonard. Not Grace.' As they reached the kitchen, she caught his eye and laughed shortly. 'Surely you're not seriously suggesting . . . ?'

'Freud saw all hysterical conditions as based on repressed sexual drives.'

'So you think it's hysteria, at root?'

'I don't know. I'm just voicing possibilities.'

Her hand rested on the kettle as she reflected.

'Certainly,' she admitted, 'there's no doubt it's all in her mind. I've been considering taking her to see a psychiatrist after all.'

'I'm not sure that's necessarily the best thing,' he said quickly.

'But you said . . .'

'I'm not sure one wants to involve too many people,' he

responded, watching her carefully. 'Better to keep it in the family, so to speak.'

She cast him an uncertain glance, but he could see she had taken the bait.

'Pity psychiatry isn't your field,' she said.

'Laura, who's to say this thing *is* purely in the mind? What if it has some simple physiological cause? We could have her in . . .'

'To hospital?'

'And run some simple tests. If it's a form of epilepsy, for instance, it'll show up on the EEGs and the scans.'

'*Brain* scans? Leonard, what are you saying?'

'Relax! Leave it to me.'

She turned to him, her face full of anxiety.

'Well, I suppose you could have another talk to her. At least, you could try. When do you have to get back? You could always stay for a while after I've collected her.'

*

Hugging the edge of the ploughed field beside a thick copse, Leonard struggled through the heavy, cloying mud. Ahead, Grace stopped in her tracks. She looked out over the fields to the village lying below, a distant cluster of roofs and spires beneath a quiff of pinkish cloud. For a brief moment, as he caught her in half-profile with the light against her flowing fair hair, he felt a sudden jolt. He'd seen her in so many modes over so many years, but he'd never seen her quite like this, with the poise and beauty of the young woman she was unselfconsciously becoming.

Turning, she caught his eye.

'Leo, you give me the creeps, staring like that.'

'I was just thinking.'

'I can *hear* it from here.' She gave a short, impatient sigh. 'I hope you didn't drag me out here to talk about *that*.'

'Course not,' he replied quickly. 'Though you must admit, it *is* fascinating.'

'For you, I expect it is.'

She set off across the field and over a stile into a meadow of grazing sheep. After a while, he drew alongside and searched her expression for the right approach, knowing that whatever he tried would be wrong.

'I've been reading up some interesting clinical cases,' he began. 'The thing that characterizes all delusional states is how *real* they feel. Absolutely real and lifelike. Of course, they must, if they're to serve their psychological function.'

She considered him coolly for a moment, as if deciding how to respond. When she spoke, her tone seemed a deliberate mockery of the kind of debate they used to enjoy together.

'Aren't you perhaps prejudging the issue?' she asked. 'There's another class of things that appear absolutely real and lifelike which you seem to be ignoring. Those things that actually *are* real.'

'Ah, but where does their reality *lie*? Does the tree in the quad still exist when there's no-one around to observe it? Of course it does. Our perceptions don't create reality, they reflect it.' He paused. 'Now, one simple test of objective reality is whether other people perceive the same thing too. Emily was there, you say, but she certainly didn't see it, did she?' Grace had gone white, but remained tight-lipped. He went on, compelled to press his point home. 'I'll give you an even simpler test. Next time it happens, just close your eyes for a moment. If the apparition disappears, then it really does exist out there. If you can still see it, then it's a product of your mind. Is that fair?'

Suddenly she rounded on him, her eyes filling with tears.

'Leave me alone! I don't want to play your stupid games. I don't *need* to.' Her voice was cracking. 'I *want* to believe. It's all I've got. It's my *hope*. And you're trying to destroy it with your clever reasoning, your cynical logic. You're so *limited*, Leo. I don't care if science got men on the moon. It doesn't give you something to live for, it doesn't give you hope and happiness.' She backed away. 'I won't listen to any more – I've had enough! I want everybody to leave me alone!'

With a pained cry, she turned about and stumbled away across the meadow. Leonard stood frozen to the spot with shock and dismay as Grace reached the gate at the end and, climbing over, headed off into the woods, quickly disappearing from sight.

*

She didn't go to school the next day, or the day following. She kept to her room, where she lay on her bed for hours on end, staring up at the ceiling. Everything that had been so beautiful and special had been reduced to public property, defiled and tarnished by the common touch. She spent the time in a mixture of fear and anticipation of the next visitation, and towards the end of each afternoon, at the right hour, she would hide away in the loft, locking the door behind her, and sit quietly among the fusty old carpets and packing cases, preparing herself. The first day passed without incident. On the second, the vision repeated itself but it was over in a matter of seconds, leaving her feeling alone and cheated – puzzled, too, for it took exactly the same form as the time before. She'd wanted to ask Our Lady for guidance and instructions but the vision had ended too abruptly. She felt somehow there was more to come, and yet it all was fixed and predetermined, like a film sequence unfolding, rather than live and allowing variation and interaction. But, most of all, it was the mystery of the apparition itself that defeated explanation, and scarcely an hour passed without some sceptical remark of Leo's creeping insidiously into her mind, confounding her afresh. Her moods swung alternately from joy to despair, from hope to fear, reducing her to misery and confusion.

On the third morning, Dr Stimpson called. He declared she was 'run down' and prescribed a glucose and iron drink. Her mother clearly hadn't told him everything. Was she afraid he'd refer her for psychiatric treatment and there'd be the stigma of mental illness in the family? She was certainly very solicitous, though, trying to keep up their spirits and always taking great care to avoid any mention of 'that business'. But that merely showed she had made up her mind what it was. And if proof were needed, going downstairs after lunch that day, Grace found the bookmark had been moved a few pages forward. It now marked the entry on Hysteria.

Later that afternoon, she was walking down the gallery landing on her way up to the attic, when she heard the front door open. A moment later, Father Gregory entered the living-room below. Her heart sank. She took a step back to move out of his line of sight, but trod on a loose floorboard. He looked up at once and saw her.

'Ah, Grace, there you are!' he said. 'I've just been with your mother across the way. How are you feeling? I should like to have a word with you. Will you come down, or shall I go up?'

*

'Grace?' Seated on the living-room sofa, Father Gregory leaned forward in alarm. 'Are you all right?'

Grace had stopped in mid-sentence and a distant look had entered her eyes. Even as he spoke, slowly, as if in a trance, she turned towards the tall window that overlooked the garden, then suddenly she gave a low, choking moan and began to tremble violently.

'Grace!' he cried, now starting out of his seat.

The look of fearful dread that spread over her face stopped him short. Her eyes widened and began to roll wildly about. Holy Mother, he thought, she's *possessed*. Her breathing was growing faster, more agitated, and she was muttering something indistinct. She seemed unable to tear her gaze off the window, and suddenly she rose to her feet and stumbled forwards. He leapt up after her.

'Grace, what is it?'

But she hardly seemed to hear him. She was staring fixedly at a point apparently in mid-air about ten feet off the ground, between the window and where she stood. He followed her line of sight. Nothing, only the glass panes reflecting the gallery lights against the darkening sky outside. Then gradually, as he watched, her expression began to soften and her breathing grew calmer. He took a step closer.

'Tell me what you can see!' he whispered urgently.

'Brighter . . .' she mumbled. 'It's growing brighter. See, see it!'

'What? Where?'

'There. The light. It's soft . . . white . . . like the sun, but different . . . more *natural*. She's coming, She's coming.'

'Go on!'

'I can't . . . It's too . . . I . . .'

He strained to catch her words, but her speech broke up into short, inarticulate fragments, some no more than exclamations and sighs of wonder. She stood inclined slightly forward, her hands held out before her, her eyes wide and glistening and a look of sublime rapture spread across her face.

'Holy Mary,' he muttered, making the sign of the Cross.

He wiped a hand behind his collar. Gradually, hardly realizing it at first, he felt a strange trembling in his limbs. A strange lightness began to fill his whole body, as if the weight of mortal life had been lifted from him. Beside him, through the corner of his eye, he could see Grace had fallen to her knees, clasping her hands in an attitude of prayer. The joy swelled irrepressibly in him, lifting him aloft. He could hear music, singing, laughter. He breathed the air of love. He wanted to weep with simple wonder. And gradually he was transported to that small church where, as a boy, he'd knelt in supplication before the altar and felt the touch of God. Overcome, his legs weakening beneath him, he, too, sank slowly to his knees and, folding his hands, raised his tear-filled eyes to heaven.

*

That night, alone in his small study in the convent lodge-house, Father Gregory struggled to come to terms with his experience. He felt different – renewed, reborn, revitalized. Time and again, he closed his eyes and gave thanks, in gratitude for the Divine grace, in relief for all his years of despair and in repentance for all his doubt and disbelief. Surely, he thought, this is a sign. Grace has indeed been blessed with Divine favour, and I have shared in it.

Towards midnight, driven by curiosity, he turned to his books and took down St Teresa of Avila's record of her remarkable visionary experiences. Possibly because this sixteenth-century Spanish Carmelite nun had received her first visions when in her mature years, her accounts were some of the most complete and informative ever recorded, describing in great detail what the experience was actually like.

He read through the pages slowly and carefully, but as he came to one particular description, he caught his breath.

'It is not a dazzling splendour,' he read, 'but a soft whiteness and infused radiance, which brings great delight to the eyes and never tires them with the sight . . . It is a light so different from what we know here below that the sun's brightness seems dim by comparison with that brightness and light which is revealed to our gaze and makes us quite loath ever to open our eyes again. It is like looking upon very clear water running over a bed of crystal and reflecting the sun, compared with a very muddy stream running over the earth beneath a cloudy sky. It seems rather to be natural light, whereas the other is artificial.'

He reread the passage, his hand trembling.

'The rapture is irresistible,' he read on. 'Before you can be warned by a thought or do anything to help yourself, it sweeps upon you so swift and strong that you see and feel yourself being caught up in this cloud and borne aloft as on the wings of a mighty eagle.'

He closed the book. He reached into his cassock for his small ebony crucifix and kissed it. Squeezing his eyes shut, he bowed his head once again in prayer.

Eight

The phone woke Tom Welland from a dream. He was addressing a Ministry inner committee, but his voice was paralysed and he couldn't get the words out. Somewhere a bell was ringing. Behind him, a screen showed a Golgi stain of a cluster of short-axon neurons. As he pointed to it, it began writhing, twitching, seething like a can of fisherman's bait. 'Life out of death, gentlemen,' he was trying to say. 'You are witnessing *resurrection.*' The ringing grew more insistent. It broke through finally and he awoke sweating, disorientated. He fumbled for the light. Beside him, with her back turned, his wife was lightly snoring. He reached for his glasses before lifting the receiver. He couldn't think if he couldn't see.

'Tom Welland here,' he grunted.

The voice echoed hollowly down the line.

'Night security here, Dr Welland. Sorry to disturb you, sir, but there's an alarm gone off in your lab.'

'My lab?'

'The indicator panel says Room 313, sir.'

'I'll be right over.'

The night was still and clear. Beneath a bright moon, frost sparkled on the empty pavements and coated the cars lining the kerbs in a uniform white crust. The city centre was deserted. Slipping through red lights and ignoring speed limits, Welland headed past the railway station, noting its clock showed ten to four, around the Georgian crescents and up to Bath General Hospital, where he turned off towards a complex of buildings at the rear of which stood the plain, undistinguished structure that housed the Department of Medical Research. Parking at the front, he hurried up the steps and rang the night bell. The security guard was at the door in an instant. Brushing quickly past, Welland made straight for the stairs, not trusting the elevators at night.

At the first set of locked doors, he dropped his electronic pass-card in his haste; the guard stepped forward from behind and opened it with his own. He strode down the dim-lit corridor and through the further doors. As he reached Room 313 he could hear the intermittent bleat of the electronic alarm. He unlocked the door and, snapping on the light, tore across to the control console. There he quickly keyed in an instruction.

'QUERY STATUS?' he typed.

Immediately the reply flashed back:

'PLASMA DEFICIENCY.'

He quickly examined the unit on the trolley; the drip bottle was empty but there was no sign of any leak. He turned to the isolation chamber, dimly lit by a single blue safety bulb, and flicked on the inspection light. Peering in through the thick glass window, he saw the problem at once. A joint in the plastic tubing had failed, spilling the enriched plasma uselessly into the trough below. Inside its perspex cask, the brain lay dull and limp, sagging lop-sidedly under its own weight like a jelly-fish washed up on a beach.

'Trouble, sir?' asked the guard, shifting from foot to foot.

'Would you mind, please . . . ?'

Catching his glare, the man retreated to the door and left the room, muttering under his breath. Numb, Welland turned back to the chamber. He stood very still, staring in at the ruins of his work, while his mind frantically scrambled all the possible courses of action. This was, quite simply, the worst catastrophe he could imagine. He could patch the leak and get plasma circulating again, but was there enough left to salvage? It had been purified from the actual blood collected at the time of death and the group it belonged to was rare, very rare. He could run a full analysis, but what were the chances of sourcing replacement material to match? Very slim indeed. And what about the brain itself? At room temperature, the normal organic processes of decay, which freezing had arrested, would already be under way.

As he stood there, the sheer scale of the disaster began to dawn on him. Years of work lay in shreds, all for the failure of a miserable piece of plastic. Certainly, there was post-Chernobyl tissue on the market, at a price – in the same way as if you were a geologist, there were particles of moon dust to be bought. But never a whole rock, landing intact on your doorstep. Equally, as a neurophysiologist, he knew he'd never again find a whole organ quite like this.

*

Father Gregory stayed up all that night, keeping vigil. He prayed that his judgement might not be distorted by his own human frailties and desires, he prayed for protection from the lures of vanity and the temptations of pride, and he prayed for strength and courage in the difficult time he could foresee ahead. Between prayer, he read and studied. Around dawn, stiff and cold, he went to the typewriter and began a preliminary report to the Bishop. There was unquestionably a case to be investigated.

At seven he took a hot bath and dressed. By eight he had left a note for the Sister who came down to clean for him, raked out the ashes from the boiler and filled the bird tray in the garden and was already huddled deep in his overcoat, his breath smoking on the frosty air, crunching his way down the gravel drive with an eager step towards the convent chapel. At eight-thirty, after contemplating a while alone, he led a small congregation of nuns, pupils and parishioners in a celebration of Mass. *Hic est enim calix sanguinis mei novi et aeterni testamentum, mysterium fidei, qui pro vobis et pro multis effundetur in remissionem peccatorum.* The age-old incantation rose within his head like incense, filling him with a trembling sense of excitement and awe. *Mysterium fidei*: dulled by a thousand repetitions, the words suddenly came alive, and he felt that, for the first time in his life, he really understood.

At ten o'clock, having discussed the matter with the Reverend Mother and agreed this next course of action, he retraced his steps to the lodge-house presbytery, climbed into his small white car, shutting the door on the skirt of his soutane as usual, and headed off towards Gloucester, to deliver his letter to the Bishop's palace in person.

*

Two miles across the city from the Bishop's palace, in a private room on the cancer ward at the Royal Hospital, Leonard was struggling with sorrow and rage. A girl no older than Grace lay dying of leukaemia. By her bedside, her parents sat trying to comfort her as she slipped away. The family believed in faith-healing and had refused drug treatment. As he stood looking on helplessly at the pale, emaciated shell of this once-pretty girl, he felt a generalized anger at the blindness and superstition he saw all around him. There was Grace, in the face of all common sense, believing in some absurd Divine vision; here was a family sending their child to her death, believing in some equally absurd power of the human mind to override human matter. He had a pharmacopoeia of drugs he could offer them – all tried, tested and, apart from some unpleasant side-effects, generally successful. The side-effect of *their* treatment, however, would ultimately be death.

And he thought of Grace. What would he do if it got to that stage with her? Force her to take treatment? Would he risk administering cytosuppressin, that new drug he'd learned about at the conference? It was absolutely essential that he got her in for tests. He had to try again.

Shortly after four, with no appointments until a hospital Ethics Committee meeting at seven, he left the hospital and drove into the declining sun in the direction of the Forest of Dean.

*

Father Gregory followed the winding drive up to the mill house but drew up abruptly thirty yards short. He'd recognized the silver Jaguar parked outside the front door. For a moment he hesitated; then, reaching for his document case, he clambered resolutely out of his car. He was the bringer of great glad tidings; this was not time for trivial animosities. The Bishop had been tied up in meetings, but he'd seen one of his aides, Monsignor Jerome Rolfe, a young and thirsty priest, who had shown considerable interest in the case, commended him for his prompt and proper action and promised to bring the matter to His Lordship's attention at once.

With an eager step, Father Gregory walked up to the studio and looked in through the window. Laura was there alone, working at the drawing-board. He tapped on the door and put his head round.

'Father!' she smiled, looking up. She laid down her ink-pen. 'Do come in. Or shall we go across? Grace is in. And Leonard.'

The priest stepped inside.

'I'm happy here.'

'Well,' she said, drawing up two wicker chairs beside a low cane table, 'let's be comfortable. Coffee? It's only instant, I'm afraid.'

Refusing with a gesture, he sat down and leaned forward, unable to contain his eagerness.

'I'm glad of the chance to talk on our own, Laura,' he began, laying his briefcase on the table. 'We're going to have to work closely together.'

'Father?'

'Ultimately, of course, it'll be up to Rome and the powers that be, but I have a feeling.' He tapped his nose. 'Still, I must warn you against raising your hopes. The Church moves in mysterious ways.'

'Hopes, Father?'

'About Grace, Laura, *Grace*.' He smiled. 'I rather feel the name is well chosen.'

Laura's eyes widened in disbelief.

'You can't be suggesting . . . ?' she began.

'Laura, a healthy scepticism is one thing, but don't let's be found Doubting Thomases. It'd be terrible to deny Our Lady because we didn't have the courage to believe.' He held up a hand to silence her protest. 'Yesterday, when I was here, right there in your living-room, I witnessed with my own eyes what I believe was Grace receiving a visitation. And,' he dropped his gaze, 'I, too, felt the touch of the Divine presence. I didn't say anything to you at the time, I know: I was very confused and perplexed. I had to think it through carefully. When one wants to believe something, it's easy to delude oneself. I've been up all night, thinking and praying.' He returned his gaze to her with the full strength of his conviction. 'Without wishing to pre-empt the proper investigations, Laura,' he said firmly, 'it is my honest belief that we have received a great and wonderful blessing here, in that Our Lady has favoured your daughter Grace and appeared to her in Her Holy person.'

*

'Do your fingers go numb? Do you feel nauseous? Does your head hurt when you move it? Are you aware of being hypersensitive to sound? Do you get an unbearable feeling beforehand that something is wrong?'

Leonard followed at Grace's elbow as she moved about the kitchen, from sideboard to sink to table. Picking up a slice of bread and jam in one hand and a glass of milk in the other, she pushed through the door into the living-room. He kept just a step behind.

'Do you get phosphenes?' he persisted. 'You know – shooting-stars, boiling and fizzing away in the corner of your vision? Does the light form a kind of horseshoe shape with zig-zags at the edges? And then does it turn into a hole? Do faces disappear or seem as if they're missing? Do you get a sense of *déjà-vu*?'

'Leo, *please*,' she protested, sitting down and reaching for the newspaper.

'Duchess, it's important.' He sat down beside her. She turned the paper noisily. 'Look, I know how you feel. It's frightening to lose control of one's perceptions. We *are* what we perceive. When that goes wrong, we feel our whole identity is threatened, our whole sanity. But having migraines is not the same as being mad.'

'It's not migraines.'

'That's the thing about hallucinations, you see: you take them for real. Like dreams, while you're dreaming them.' He leaned closer. 'Now, what I'd like to know is, What brought them on? Was the sun flickering through the trees or on the water in some particular way? At eight to twelve cycles per second, you know, flashing light can cause epileptic fits, and migraines are, after all, simply slow-motion seizures across the brain . . .'

Throwing down the paper, she sprang to her feet.

'*They're not migraines!*' she cried. 'They are what I said they are.'

She stormed into the study, slamming the door behind her. Biting his lip, he held himself back for a moment, then went after her. She sat curled up in the chair at the desk, buried in a magazine. He browsed briefly among the shelves and, finding the book he was after – one that he'd given Laura – took it out and sat down quietly in an armchair.

'I'm sorry to have to say this, Duchess,' he began again after a while. 'But you aren't the first girl to believe she's seen a saint or had a religious vision. Have you heard of an eleventh-century nun called Hildegard of Bingen? Well, Hildegard had visions, and she actually drew pictures of them. She saw showers of falling stars, for example. Now, anyone who has dealt with migraine sufferers will recognize at once that these are precisely the phosphenes you get with a bad migraine attack. She had visions of the Heavenly City, with the walls zig-zagged and castellated; there again, these are clearly just what we call "fortification spectra", perfectly common in migraines. Here, look for yourself.' He held out the book – Oliver Sacks' classic study on *Migraine* – but she merely hunched her shoulders and let out a bitter, exasperated sigh. 'Hildegard, too, believed in her visions sincerely,' he said more gently. 'But the simple, hard truth is that she was just a chronic migraine sufferer with a rather vivid imagination.'

Grace looked up. Her eyes were red-rimmed. 'Can't you see? I don't want to know.'

A wave of pity swept over him. Reality was often painful, but how else could he bring her to see it? How else, indeed, would he persuade her to agree to tests?

'I'm sorry,' he repeated firmly. 'But it has to be said.'

'It *doesn't*! Nobody asked you to!'

'You've got to face facts . . .'

'Facts!' she snorted. 'I have my facts, you have yours.'

'Oh come on, don't be childish,' he snapped. Ignoring the glare she shot him, he went on, 'Take your precious saints, for instance. Let me tell you about some of your Church's "facts" about them.'

'I'm not listening.'

But he couldn't stop. Pain, frustration and, above all, anger – anger at Grace for her blindness and at himself for being unable to get her to see through it – drove him to recklessness. He rose to his feet and took a step forward.

'Did you know St Patrick was a Welshman?'

'I don't care if he was a Chinaman . . .'

'St Sebastian did not in fact die from arrow wounds. St Cecilia knew nothing at all about music. St Catherine didn't die on the wheel. St Francis of Assisi's real name was something else – Giovanni, I think. And as for St Christopher, he was a real phoney, one minute up there on High Table, the next demoted . . .' He was sweating heavily, his fist clenched tight around the book. 'How can you possibly believe in all that mythological claptrap? How can you possibly want to be part of it?'

Grace was now on her feet, too. White in the face, crouching as though his words were blows to be warded off, she skirted round the edge of the room to the door. As she tore it open, she looked back at him.

'You call yourself my friend,' she choked, the tears streaming down her face. 'If you really were, you'd *go away and leave me alone!*'

At that, she turned and fled from the room. He heard her hesitate momentarily in the hallway outside, then she raced into the living-room and away up the stairs. As he reached the hall after her, he saw what had arrested her. Just inside the front door, with a look of horror on their faces, stood Laura and Father Gregory.

The priest opened his mouth, then seemed to think better of it. A flush spread over his already florid jowls and his hand went to his crucifix. For a moment the two men held each other's eye, then with a muttered scowl, Father Gregory brushed brusquely past him and hurried after the girl.

Desperate, Leonard turned to Laura.

'She's really hooked on this thing,' he said. 'She won't see sense – she won't even talk about it. This isn't *Grace*. What's got into her? Who's got at her?' He looked through the open door to the far end of the living-room, where the priest was already hurrying up the stairs.

'Don't blame Father Gregory,' replied Laura shortly. 'He hasn't put anything into her mind. In fact, until last night he was every bit as sceptical as you.'

Something behind her words stopped him short.

'And you, Laura? Laura?'

She held out a conciliatory hand towards him.

'Look, Leonard . . .' she began uncertainly.

He took a step back. 'Laura, I don't believe it! Am I hearing right? Have we gone back to the Dark Ages? Laura, come on, don't be so *gullible*. Don't let that priest trick you. He'll be proclaiming a miracle here next.'

Laura stood her ground and met his eye unflinchingly.

'That's rather how he has come to see it,' she said solemnly.

'You mean . . . ? Oh my God. How pathetic.' Unnerved by the trancelike lustre in her eyes, he looked away. 'I think I'd better be going,' he said thickly.

She laid a hand on his arm. Her expression was soft, full of compassion.

'Leonard . . .'

'Don't, Laura.'

He headed for the door. There he turned and cast her a final, incredulous glance. Shaking his head in despair, he marched out of the house and headed over to his car. He gunned it angrily into life and let out the clutch, spinning the tyres savagely on the gravel. In the rear-view mirror he could see the slim, dark-haired figure standing in the doorway, looking pale and perplexed. As he pulled away down the drive, he saw her give a forlorn wave.

He drove badly for the first few miles, overtaking on blind bends and revving the engine to a scream. Gradually, however, his anger abated and he slowed down until, some ten miles down the road, he pulled up at a deserted picnic area and switched the engine off. He had to think.

This was a calamity, and he'd only made it worse by his behaviour. He'd alienated Laura and shown up their irreconcilable differences. As for Grace, though, he'd undone the trust he'd built up so patiently and lovingly. Now she had rejected the whole foundation on which their relationship was built, the very spirit of enlightenment which had pulled her through her long depression after Matthew's death. The Jesuits were right: a child given to them for the first seven years was theirs for life. Grace had had twelve years of conditioning when he met her. Now, at a stroke, faced with an overwhelming and inexplicable experience, she had thrown over all the principles of enquiry and positive scepticism he'd painstakingly helped her develop since then and she'd regressed to her childhood world of religious superstition. The same stroke, too, had robbed him of her trust and respect – of her love, even. He sat in the car, staring at the small tide of litter eddying round the empty log tables. His stomach was knotted tight. He loved this girl so dearly, but for all the reasons that had suddenly re-arisen to haunt him, he needed her so badly to love him. Oh God, what a bloody disaster.

*

'I'm not disturbing you, Grace?' said Father Gregory respectfully, putting his head round her bedroom door.

Grace lay curled up on the bed, her fair hair clinging damply to her cheeks. She struggled to sit up.

'I'm sorry, Father,' she sniffed, wiping her eyes.

'I'm sorry,' he countered. 'Sorry you've had to face the slings and arrows so soon. Leonard is only the first, I'm afraid.'

'Leo thinks he understands everything. He's ruled by his head: he doesn't listen to his heart. I sometimes wonder if he's got one.'

'Don't be uncharitable, Grace. Though it's hardly for me to reprove *you*,' he added with a wry smile. Seeing the puzzlement on her face, he went on more forcefully, 'Since yesterday, I've done a good deal of thinking. I want you to know that, whatever I may have said before, I sincerely believe you. I'm with you. All the way.'

'Father . . .'

'Better than that, I've already set things in motion.' He pulled up a chair and unzipped his document case. 'Now, of course it's up to the Bishop whether he puts the case forward, but I had an interesting chat with a Monsignor Rolfe this morning, and I feel sure they'll refer it to Rome.'

'Rome?'

'I expect you've heard of the Sacred Congregation of Rites, Grace. First of all, they'll probably appoint a Medical Tribunal to check that everything is okay with you – medically and psychologically speaking, I mean.' He saw her frown deepen and hurried on. 'You see, our critics will obviously challenge your state of mind, Grace. They'll say

IIO

you're just an emotional teenage girl who has lost her father and her brother and who has a history of some difficulties in adjusting . . .'

Her face had been growing longer as he spoke. Now she shrank back and fixed him with fearful eyes.

'I'm not sure about all this, Father,' she whispered plaintively.

'Let me explain again, then.'

'I mean, it's private and I'd rather keep it to myself.'

'That's not possible.' He leaned forward. 'Grace, I don't think you quite realize what we're dealing with here. If it is as it seems, then Our Lady has chosen you to receive a message, a message of peace and everlasting life. That can't be just for you alone but for the whole world, too. It's the same message Our Lady imparted to the visionaries at Fatima, the same as at Knock, the same as at Medjugorje. The news belongs to the world. You *have* to share it. You have no choice.'

A look close to terror flashed across her face, then she dropped her gaze.

'I'm sorry, Father,' she mumbled. 'It's just all rather sudden.'

'That's more like it.' He smiled. 'Why not come and see me before Mass tomorrow? I should like to pray with you.'

'Father?'

'If I may,' he added.

'Well, yes, of course.'

'I'll leave you now,' he said, rising. At the door, he smiled again. 'You're a special girl, Grace: I always said so. If we are not being deceived, this is a rare and precious blessing you have received, and I am blessed to be part of it. God be with you.'

'Thank you, Father. And with you.'

*

A cold, diffuse light filtered in through the skylight, robbing the stacked packing cases and rolls of old carpet of colour

III

and shadow. Grace sat on the dusty boards, resting her chin on her knees, waiting. Idly she looked around. In the centre of the attic lay Dad's old tin trunk, its lid open to reveal neatly packed shirts and shoes, tennis racquets and cricket pads. So this was as far as Mum had got, throwing his things out. She hugged her knees tighter. It wasn't cold, but she was shivering.

Everything was slipping from her control. She didn't belong to herself any more. Everyone wanted a part of her. They had already begun fighting over her – Leo pulling her one way, Father Gregory the other, with Mum hovering nervously in the middle. She was being torn in two.

She glanced at her watch: five-thirty. Still no hint of that strange, tell-tale purplish taste in her mouth. She stared out of the skylight at the low, darkening clouds and wished she was somebody else. Everything was changing. Even in ordinary small ways, people were treating her differently. Mum was watchful and untrusting; she smiled at her in the way you smiled at a child who was mentally disturbed. Father Gregory was all humble and respectful, Leonard was all hurt and resentful. Poor Leo: she imagined him as a father in a folk tale, left on the shore, shaking his fist at the ship that was abducting his daughter, a sad, angry figure growing smaller and smaller and his cries further out of earshot. The only person who'd really seemed to understand was Benedict. She'd told him at the stables last time, and he'd accepted it all without incredulity or doubt or any attempt to meddle. Benedict was rather simple, but that was the beauty of him.

Ten to six. Was it not to be today? Perhaps yesterday had been the last time. Pray that it was. Then it would soon all be past and forgotten. She didn't want to be *special* if it meant being the rest of the world's property.

By six-fifteen, still nothing had happened. She felt disappointed for all her sense of relief. Still, she could get back to normal life at last. She thought of all the things she'd forgotten or neglected in those past days. She hadn't been to read to Mary Nolan for ages. It was Friday today, she suddenly remembered, and Mary would be expecting her: what was she thinking of?

With sudden resolve, she jumped to her feet and ran downstairs. From the kitchen came quarrelsome voices from a radio play, mingled with the comforting aroma of baking. She hesitated outside the door. Mum was all for her visiting Mary but she disapproved of Benedict – he was rough and common – and was worried she was encouraging him. He probably would still be at the stables, anyway. Turning away, she slipped quickly across the living-room into the hall, grabbed her anorak and headed out into the blustery twilight. She could be there and back in time for supper.

*

She walked briskly to the end of the drive, then cut across the road and took a small, poorly lit track that ran along the backs of the houses in the main street. She waved to the woman from the village store, out filling a coal scuttle; in a garden further down, pulling potatoes, the butcher's son who'd once shown her how to snare rabbits called out a greeting. She hurried on, over a small cart-bridge and across a paddock full of broken jumps and rusty oil drums, until she came to a piece of wasteland on which stood a pair of stone farm-workers' cottages. One was derelict, its windows boarded up. In the other, a solitary light burned downstairs in the front room while from the chimney, barely discernible against the darkening sky, rose a thin strand of smoke.

She knocked. There was no reply. She knocked again. Still silence. She waited a moment, then looked in through the window. The front room was empty. She frowned: Mary was never out at this time of day. Returning to the door, she crouched and peered in through the letterbox.

She let out a gasp of horror.

Mary Nolan lay sprawled at the foot of the stairs, twisted and contorted, her face grey and bloodless and her blanked-out glasses thrown askew.

Grace frantically tried the door, but it was locked. She rushed round the back. The door there was open. She raced inside and threw herself on her knees beside the inert body. Desperately trying to remember her First Aid, she grabbed her wrist and felt her pulse. At first she couldn't find it and a flush of panic welled up inside her, but then, hardly perceptibly, she began to feel the slow, faint throb of life. She looked about her: of course, there was no phone in this house! Careful not to disturb the unconscious woman, she let herself out of the house and ran for all she was worth across the wasteland, through the paddock, over the small bridge and up to the first house where she could get help.

Nine

After the Ethics Committee meeting was over, Leonard rode down in the elevator with the Administrator and two other senior consultants in a taut, brittle silence. He stood with his fist clenched about his briefcase handle and his eye fixed impatiently on the indicator. They'd spent most of the meeting discussing a surrogate motherhood case, and the decision had gone against him: the hospital was going to refuse to perform a controversial embryo implant. He knew he'd become too emotional over the issue. He was outraged by his colleagues' pious, reactionary attitude, but what lay behind his anger was really the hurt and distress he felt at Grace's rebuff. From the moment he'd walked out of the mill house, he'd had moments of fevered foreboding. In that parting glare on the priest's face he could see the thirst of a Church in need of miracles to feed its flock, and he couldn't help worrying obsessively about what would happen if they really took these hallucinations seriously and teams of clerics started grubbing around, raking up the past, asking about things better left dead and buried . . . If he had any sense, he'd be taking precautions now.

The lift opened at the ground floor and the three men headed for the main exit. In the foyer, Leonard turned back, saying he'd left some papers behind upstairs. Instead of returning to the lift, however, he waited until the other two were out of sight, then followed at a distance until he reached the front desk. Beside the middle-aged admissions nurse sat the night porter, a cheery young Jamaican with a mouthful of capped teeth like a boxing guard. Leonard approached with a disarming smile.

'I need to get into Radiology, Charlie,' he said. 'They forgot to send up some X-rays.' He broadened his smile. 'Understaffed – but who isn't?'

'No sweat, sir,' said the porter. He rose to his feet and reached for a bunch of pass-keys from his drawer.

'Don't you trouble. Give me the keys and I'll see to it myself.'

Leonard took the keys out of the porter's hand and, assuring him he'd be right back, returned to the elevator hall. There, instead of taking a lift up to Radiology on the fifth floor, he slipped through a side door, down a flight of concrete steps and through another door marked 'BASEMENT LEVEL I'. Here the corridors were narrower, for no beds or trolleys came down this far, and dark and empty, too, since this was an administrative area and the staff had gone home long ago. Hurrying along the dim-lit corridor, he finally reached a door with a sign in regulation hospital lettering that read, 'RECORD OFFICE'.

He tried six keys from the bunch, but none worked. From around the corner came the sound of a vacuum cleaner, growing ever closer. He was sweating. The tenth key finally opened the door. In a flash he was inside and locked the door behind him. As the fluorescent light flickered on, switching on the ventilation fans with it, he scanned the small, windowless room. Along each wall stretched uniform green metal filing cabinets. In the centre stood the records officer's desk on which sat a microfiche reader and, beside it, a bank of card indexes plastered with garish post-cards of seaside resorts and pictures of wildlife and wide open spaces torn out from magazines, betraying the sorry dream of one who worked far away from natural light and air.

A glance at the filing cabinets showed him they were arranged chronologically, in order of the patient's admission date. In a moment he'd found the drawer for February 1981. It was locked. There was bound to be a key somewhere: the librarian wouldn't take those home. He riffled through the desk drawers. In a small tin of throat pastilles, among hair-grips and luncheon vouchers, he found a small ring of keys. In a second, he had the drawer open and was thumbing through the files. Groves, Gulliver, Hanrahan, Henderson, Hicks, Hilary, Hodges, *Holmwood*.

'HOLMWOOD, Grace. Age: 12. Admitted . . .'

No, that wasn't the one. He flicked to the next file.

'HOLMWOOD, Matthew Francis. Age: 12. Admitted 15 February 1981. Referring doctor: Dr P. Stimpson, Abbotsbury General Practice. Consultant: Dr Leonard Grigson. Initial diagnosis . . . Drugs Prescribed . . . Path Lab Results . . . Consent to Surgery . . . Case conference . . . Intensive Care Report . . . Cause of Death . . .'

A wave of sickness swept over him as the memory of that harrowing time flashed through his mind. In a single, swift motion he took the file out of its pocket and thrust it into his briefcase. Realizing he'd left a noticeable gap, he reshuffled the pockets so that the sequence appeared unbroken. Then he turned to the card index and tore out the entry for Matthew Holmwood. As he did so, he noticed that the card bore cross-references to Consents and to Postmortem. Retrieving the relevant cards from these trays too, he threw them into his briefcase and hurried to the door. Then, with a final glance to make sure he had not left any obvious traces, he switched off the light and, checking all was clear, slipped out into the corridor and retraced his steps to the ground floor.

*

The first sheet caught quickly and burned greedily. Leonard dropped it in the grate as the flame reached his fingers and lit the next sheet from it. Adding one after another, he'd soon built a blaze that sent burning fragments up the chimney in cascades of sparks. Phosphenes, he thought to himself, *migraine* phosphenes . . . With a sudden flash of irritability, he seized the poker and swiftly pulverized the charred residue into a small heap of black ashes. Then he stood back. All record of Matthew Holmwood's treatment at Gloucester Royal Hospital had been erased.

As he reached towards the mantelpiece for his whisky, his eye fell on a photo of his daughter Vanessa receiving a cup at a school sports day. She couldn't have been any more than twelve, the age Grace had been when he'd first met her. He turned away, feeling a stab of pain. God, he'd made a real mess of his life. He'd even lost Laura and Grace now, too, and, with them, the hope of a new family and the chance in some way to make good the past.

He sat down in the armchair and stared into the cold grate. From the bottom of the garden came the plaintive hoot of a barn owl; something, perhaps a frond of ivy, clawed persistently at the window-pane. He gritted his teeth. It was a mistake to look to people to complete your life: they only let you down. You came into the world alone and you left it alone and, whatever anyone said, you lived the time between alone, too. Birth, copulation and death: the three loneliest acts in life.

He swallowed back his whisky in a single, punishing gulp, recognizing in it the source of his melancholy, and went into the kitchen to refill the glass. Behind his mood, he knew, lay a terrible truth: the crisis was finally breaking. Something which had started with the best intentions and the most honourable motives and which had lain comfortably at rest long enough for a new truth, a new reality, to take its place, was now slowly rising, like a corpse from a tomb, propelled by a force of its own that was quite beyond the power of reason to refute. And he could do nothing but watch helplessly from the sidelines at the relentless onward march of the madness.

This would not do! He *had* to find a way back in. He had to win back Grace's trust. But how? Not by further argument or appeal to reason. He returned to his study and, sitting in his armchair with his eyes closed, he gradually began to see the way through.

The issue was one of faith, not facts. Of trust, not truth.

In order to win back her trust in him, he had to break her trust in one man. Father Gregory: he was the key. The task was to undermine her faith in this priest, to discredit him in her eyes.

But what of the Church's faith in her? If they shared Father Gregory's conviction, they were bound to mount an internal inquiry into the validity of the visions. The first thing they'd look at was her psychological state, and that would involve investigating her whole medical background. Nothing would escape the inquisition once it began. He'd taken steps to destroy the more obvious records of her brother's death, but there were still other people – not many, true, but one alone was enough – who had been involved at the time and who *knew*. Questions would be asked of him, too. Could he refuse to answer? Should he?

And then, there was Laura. He felt almost in a state of shock at the chasm that seemed so suddenly to have opened between them. He wished he could turn the clock back to a time before . . . But there never had been a time before: he'd lived with this for as long as he'd known her. And yet he'd been able to love her and, he felt sure, in her own funny way, she'd grown to love him, too. He couldn't let her go like this. A dialogue had to be kept going. For every reason. Maybe he should not see her for a few days, but that didn't mean he couldn't communicate in other ways.

With sudden resolve, he went to his desk and took out a sheet of paper. He'd write to her. He'd be very understanding. She was going through a terribly difficult time. He felt for her. But she mustn't let her feelings, her hopes, run away with her good judgement. How tempting it was to seek reassurance in signs and wonders! Caution was the safest course. The danger was that everyone would want to be in on the bandwagon. He could foresee all kinds of difficult and intrusive questions being asked about Grace and her psychological health. There'd be medical tribunals, investigating committees, psychiatrists, paediatricians, doctors of every kind . . . Did she want to go through all that? And what might it do to Grace's already fragile mental state? He'd end the letter enclosing an article from *Nature* on insect pheromones for Grace and, for herself, tickets for a performance of *Così fan tutte* in Bath in a fortnight's time. Some light relief was called for, he'd say. Doctor's orders.

He rewrote the letter twice before he was satisfied the tone was right and that he'd hit the right note, arousing her fear with one hand and allaying it with the other. Some time after midnight, he retired to bed. He'd done the best he could.

*

Grace poured a cup of weak tea, adding a sweetener tablet just as Mary Nolan liked it, and replacing the kettle on the small range made for the kitchen door. Benedict, pale even with his ruddy cheeks, followed her with a forlorn, hangdog expression, but he hung back shyly at the foot of the stairs, letting her go up alone. At the stables that morning, he'd implored her to come back; somehow the story had reached his mother's ears and she had been calling for her. With a sad heart, Grace tapped on the bedroom door and went in. They mustn't put their faith in *her*.

Mary lay on her back on a high old-fashioned bed, her head propped up by pillows. Her cheeks were sunk and her skin as white and lifeless as marble. One hand lay above the bedclothes, tightened around a rosary. As Grace came in, she inclined her ear forward. The room smelled of lavender and polish and damp plasterwork, and despite her blindness the curtains were drawn shut against the midday light.

'Bless you,' she mumbled as Grace put the teacup down beside her and steered her hand towards the handle.

'Drink it slowly,' said Grace. 'It's hot.'

Between sips, Mary tried to talk, but her speech was so slurred as to be almost incomprehensible. Benedict had said Dr Stimpson had come by again that morning and was worried it was getting worse; he'd wanted to send her into hospital right away, but she'd refused. Her abiding terror was that she'd be sent off to a home, and hospital was the first step along the way.

Finally, Grace relieved her of the cup and stood up.

'I have to be going now,' she said. 'I'll look in again later and bring you some tea-cakes.'

As she was turning to go, Mary reached out a bony hand and clasped her wrist.

'Grace,' she struggled, 'will you pray to Our Lady for me?'

'We'll say a prayer for you at Mass tomorrow.'

'No. You pray for me, Grace. She listens to you.'

'Of course I will, Mary.'

Shutting the bedroom door quietly, she made her way slowly down the steep narrow stairs. Benedict still stood sentinel at the bottom. His eyes were rimmed with red. Without a word, he took the cup and laid it aside, then opened the front door to see her out. On the doorstep, she reached out and squeezed his hand. His eyes filled with helpless despair. With a small cry, he drew her towards him and clasped her to his strong chest in a tight embrace. Overcome by pity and sadness, she in turn wrapped her arms around him, and for a full minute they both stood there, out in the open, hugging each other in silence and drawing from one another the comfort each so desperately needed.

∗

Father Gregory had grasped the wooden post in one hand and was about to mount the stile when he looked up. He stopped abruptly. Across the stretch of wasteland, standing in front of the door of the cottage he was coming to visit, stood two figures locked in a close embrace. He recognized them at once. For a moment, he stared in disbelief. Then with sudden resolve he turned and swept back across the paddock the way he had come, stopping only when he'd reached the spot where he'd parked his car. He climbed in but sat without driving off. He'd wait until Grace appeared and let it seem he'd just arrived. This was something he wished he hadn't seen.

*

On a table in the centre of the classroom, laid out on a lace altar-cloth, lay the jug and bowl of fruit that made up that Monday's Still Life composition. Grace was hatching in the shadow tones to her drawing when she saw Sister Bertram enter the room and exchange a word with Sister Ambrose on the rostrum. The Art teacher glanced up in Grace's direction and gave a nod, at which Sister Bertram made her way through the circle of easels and drawing-boards towards her.

'Father Gregory would like to see you, Grace,' she said in a lowered voice.

'You mean, now?'

'Yes, now. Come with me.'

Grace put down her pencil and board and, casting Emily beside her a helpless shrug, followed Sister Bertram to the door. Outside, instead of turning towards the main body of the school, the Sister headed down the corridor, through a set of tall double doors and into the convent itself. The corridors there were painted chocolate-brown gloss to shoulder height and, above, plain white emulsion up to the high ceilings. They went past the refectory, where the tables were being laid for lunch, and a small chapel, in the dim light of which she could just make out white-robed figures at prayer. Sisters in work habits passed them with a demure greeting. Finally, Sister Bertram led the way across an imposing panelled hall, her heels snicking softly on the highly polished flagstones as she went. In a niche set in one wall stood a small statue of Our Lord dressed in white robes and wearing a red thorn-circle heart on his breast; the golden halo reflected each flicker of the little glass lamp that burned on the pedestal at his feet. Sister Bertram eventually stopped outside an ornately carved oak door on the far side. She tapped. A voice that was not Father Gregory's bade them enter. With a considered smile towards Grace, she ushered her in, then withdrew.

The room was narrow and tall and painted a uniform pale cream. The windows were set too high for anything but a slip of sky to be visible. Behind a large, ornate desk sat a man Grace had never seen before. His face was that of a young man but his hair was silver, and though his lean features softened into a half-smile as he saw her, his dark eyes held hers in a calculating, blinkless stare that seemed to penetrate her very thoughts. At his elbow stood Father Gregory, beaming encouragement like a circus-master. Unlike Father Gregory whose clothes were ill-fitting and crumpled, this man was immaculately tailored and almost self-consciously neat. Around his waist he wore a crimson sash, and on a narrow table beneath the window, on top of some leather-bound books, lay a small purple-trimmed biretta. In the centre of the desk before him lay a large-scale Ordnance Survey map, while on the blotter at his elbow was a slim pink folder. Upside-down though it was, Grace could easily make out the embossed crest resembling a cardinal's hat and, underneath, written in bold italic script, the title:

Grace Holmwood Inquiry:
STRICTLY CONFIDENTIAL.

Father Gregory stepped forward.

'Ah, Grace,' he said warmly. 'Let me introduce you. This is Monsignor Rolfe. He has been appointed by His Lordship the Bishop to conduct the investigation —'

'Thank you, Father,' said Monsignor Rolfe quietly, without taking his eyes off Grace.

'I wanted to explain,' returned Father Gregory, evidently thrown off balance, 'that you have the full authority of His Lordship and the office of the Congregation of Rites in Rome —'

The Monsignor held up his hand.

'We shall have plenty of time for the credentials. Won't

we, Grace?' He finally broke his stare and turned to the priest. 'Perhaps you would leave us now, Father. I'll ring through if I need anything.'

'If you're sure . . .'

'Thank you, Father.'

'Well, I'll leave you both, then,' said Father Gregory and, with a small, crestfallen frown, he left the room.

Monsignor Rolfe turned back to Grace. Now he gave her a full smile, showing a perfect set of teeth, but his eyes remained hard and watchful.

'Bring up a chair, Grace,' he said. 'I want us to get to know one another a little.'

His eyes bored into her, paralysing her, robbing her of movement. She felt strangely detached, too, as if she were watching herself from a great distance.

'Grace?' he repeated.

'I'm sorry,' she heard herself reply meekly.

Forcing her limbs into action, she drew up a chair opposite and sat down. She lowered her gaze to the hands in her lap. After an eternity's silence, she gradually raised her eyes and met his. He was still watching her.

'That's better,' he whispered. 'Now, let's begin.'

While he spoke, she focused her eyes on an imaginary point midway between them, so that his face dissolved into an indistinct blur, then slowly she pushed the point forwards until she was looking *through* him to the wall behind. It was an old trick she'd used when hauled before the Reverend Mother to answer for some misdemeanour. She tuned her hearing out, too, so that while she gathered the gist of what he was saying she didn't actually *listen* to it. Her own mind was teeming. What was this all about? She wanted no part of any investigation. They might want to authenticate her story, but she didn't. Why should she be forced to parade her private experiences before strangers?

'Grace?' The note in the voice hardened. She realized the priest had been asking her a question. 'You're not making this easy for me. You won't help yourself if you keep silent.

I was asking for some basic background details. Now, shall we start again? Your date of birth?'

'26th May 1968, Monsignor,' she answered dully.

'Call me Father. Where?'

'The Middlesex Hospital, London.'

He had the pink folder open and was referring to a page of notes. It was just a device to get her to talk. And she found herself gradually drawn into going along with it. First he asked simple personal details: dates of schools, places they'd lived in, Mum and Dad's dates and places of birth . . . By degrees, the questions grew harder: her views on moral issues, the strength of her religious conviction, her position on tricky problems of right conduct. And then her feelings, her secret thoughts, right down to the deepest concerns of her soul. Little by little, drop by drop, with infinite patience, he was drawing the very heart out of her, like a spider sucking its prey dry of all its vital juices, leaving her an evacuated husk, drained of all that was personal and particular, of all that made her *her*. Question, answer, question, answer: the minutes lengthened into hours. She dug her nails into her palms until she almost cried aloud, telling herself that she could always hurt herself more than they did, that whatever they did to her, however they probed and tormented her, they could never rob her of the final act of selfhood, that even if they threatened to bleed her to death she would bleed herself first, by her own choice, and by remaining that step ahead she would always remain herself.

*

Leonard picked his way across the wasteland. At the stile into the paddock, he turned and glanced back at the small farmhand's cottage. Poor Mary Nolan, he thought bitterly: another victim of fear dressed up as faith.

Dr Stimpson had called him and asked him, as the specialist who'd first treated her, to look in on her and try and persuade her to go into hospital for tests. But she'd adamantly refused. She was terrified of being taken in and never let out again; if she should die – as she certainly would if she didn't have immediate treatment – she would die at home, and such would be the will of God. For a fleeting instant he pictured the dying girl whose parents had been too intransigent to allow her medical treatment, and he recalled his anger at himself for not intervening. Could he stand by again and watch a deliberate act of suicide? Was it right to force someone to take a treatment they didn't want? How could he do so anyway, short of sending in the men with the stretchers and straitjackets? But he had to – not only for the woman's sake but also for Grace's. If he'd read the ominous signs correctly, *her* life was in the balance here, too.

He was about to return to the cottage and try one last appeal when a sudden idea struck him, sending a thrill of hope shooting through him. Without tests and scans he could guess that Mary Nolan's brain tumour, triggered off by her fall, had broken through the surrounding infarcted areas that had hitherto contained it and was spreading afresh. Short of major surgery, her only hope was some drug to arrest its spread by shrinking the tumour itself. And he knew of the very one.

Climbing over the stile, he strode purposefully across the paddock to his waiting car.

*

For the next few days, Leonard lived in a state of nervous excitement alternating with long periods of soul-searching and doubt. Was he really thinking of administering a drug not yet clinically approved? *And* without the patient's knowledge? But Mary Nolan would die anyway, and if the drug worked it would resolve any anxieties over Grace for ever. He stayed late at work, he caught up on months of unread periodicals and paid longer visits to the other hospitals in his area than were really necessary, but nothing he did could take his mind off the issue. It obsessed his every waking thought.

His son Mark's birthday fell on the Saturday, and he'd promised to go up to London and take him out to lunch. He'd find himself only a few miles from London University, where the research into cytosuppressin was going on.

Towards the end of the Friday morning, with his ward rounds finished, Leonard returned to his small office on the top floor and stood for a moment at the window, staring thoughtfully out at the city spread below. The cathedral rose clear and confident from amid the sprawl of multi-storey car-parks, shopping centres and congested traffic systems, a fearless Gothic statement of faith in a sea of modern material-ism. He thought of the hospital building in which he was standing and of its tawdry functionalism, and wondered briefly whether spiritual belief was a prerequisite of beauty and whether scepticism created only uglinesss. But what other course was there, once you had known doubt? Which was more valuable: some unknowable, unpredictable life hereafter, or life now? One was at best a promise, and a highly contingent promise at that, while the other was real and actual and tangible. If he had a God at all, it was the God of life, the life-force of all animate things. How could he stand by and see it deliberately denied?

Suddenly the answer became very clear. Reaching for the phone, he asked to be connected to the central switchboard at London University. There he asked for Dr Williamson. He was put through almost at once. The conversation lasted a few brief minutes, and by the time he hung up he had an appointment to meet the research scientist at eleven the following morning.

He rose early and drove up to London, reaching the Medical Research department building in good time. The meeting went more smoothly than he could have imagined. Dr Williamson told him that he'd just obtained approval for a limited programme of clinical trials, and he was keen to involve senior hospital consultants to participate in the tests. By twelve-thirty, without having committed himself firmly, Leonard was on his way to meet his son at a trattoria in

Fulham, carrying a small sample bottle of tiny white tablets in his pocket. The first hurdle was over.

The atmosphere at lunch was relaxed but empty. Over two bottles of Chianti, Leonard tried to rediscover his son, but he left feeling only sad and disappointed. He felt shocked that the boy only seemed interested in a life of hedonism and glamour. For Mark, the problem of right or wrong was a problem of the right or wrong set to be in, the right or wrong place to be seen at. As Leonard drove home, he pondered why it was that other people seemed to have so much less trouble with their moral decisions, while he himself faced his dilemmas with such tormented perplexity. It wasn't just that he was ageing. He had a past, a past comprised of actions, some good, some bad but all irreversible, whereas a boy of Mark's age simply did not.

But on this issue he had made up his mind, and he'd satisfied his conscience. All that remained was to work out how to do it. He puzzled over it during the long drive back west. He had stopped at a motorway service station for a cup of coffee and happened to glance at a woman at the next table slipping sweeteners in her tea. The answer came to him in a flash. He reached into his pocket and took out the small bottle of tablets Dr Williamson had given him. He shook a few into the palm of his hand. They *exactly* resembled saccharin sweeteners! His mind raced back to his recent visit to Mary Nolan's house. Hadn't he seen Benedict stirring one into a hot drink for her? He rose at once and headed for the service station shop, where he bought a small tin of sweeteners of the brand he'd seen in their house. Returning to the car, he carefully emptied out the contents and replaced them with the cytosuppressin tablets.

When later he reached Upton Flint and home, he drove on without stopping and made his way through Abbotsbury and on to Coledean. There he paid Mary Nolan another visit and tried one final time to get her to change her mind about going into hospital, but she was as adamant as ever. On the way out, he slipped into the kitchen for a glass of water and, without Benedict seeing, he switched tins. As he was leaving the room, he stopped. What about the dosage? He called Benedict and told him that an excess of sweeteners was aggravating his mother's condition and made him promise to see she restricted her intake to six a day. Then he headed for home, where he hurried inside and poured himself a very large drink. His hands shook and he felt a guilty dread gnawing at his stomach. He had done the right thing, hadn't he, in the circumstances? Only time would tell if this would be the salvation of Mary Nolan. And of Grace.

II

Ten

The boy ran wildly through the freezing February dawn, his heels flying and his breath steaming as he tore across the frost-locked wasteland. Vaulting the stile, he headed diagonally across the paddock. The frozen earth was pocked and rutted by hooves, and twice he tripped and fell sprawling on the iron-hard ground. But he picked himself up and struggled on past tumbledown horse jumps and rusty oil drums and down to the five-bar gate at the far end. Clambering swiftly over, he raced off down the lane. On the cart-bridge he came upon a farmhand from the manor estate trudging off to work.

'It's Mum!' he cried as he flew past.

On he ran without waiting for a reply. His chest ached and his windpipe scorched in the frosty air. The brook alongside the track was frozen. He glanced up; pink streaks were gradually prising apart the steely grey bars of the sky. The track widened as it met the road. He dashed across without looking and followed the road for a hundred yards until he reached a drive marked with a signboard all but whitened out by the rime: COLEDEAN MILL.

∗

Grace glanced at the bedside clock. Still only six-thirty. The nights seemed so unending when you couldn't sleep. Beyond the open curtains, the sky was pitch black – all the blacker, too, because she'd taken to sleeping with the bedside light on. She lay back and stared at the ceiling; she knew every line and crack intimately.

A sudden wave of nausea swept over her and for a moment

133

she thought she was going to be physically sick. The previous morning, she actually had been. Otherwise, however, things hadn't been too bad during those past three months. The apparitions had stopped: she hadn't had one since that time in the living-room with Father Gregory.

A general sense of routine had settled over her life. Monsignor Rolfe's investigation was continuing very slowly, very painstakingly. Once a week, on Fridays like today, he'd arrive at the convent and set up his discreet little court of inquiry. She'd lost count of the interviews she'd been called for, sitting in the same chair and giving the same evidence over and over again, while he picked her up on tiny inconsistencies with earlier accounts until she couldn't be certain any longer what *had* actually happened or even if anything had happened at all. In all the telling and retelling, her memory had been rubbed so smooth that the events themselves now slipped from her grasp. To protect herself from being trapped into contradicting herself, she had written down everything she could remember in a blue school exercise-book, but even then, when she came to refer back to the record, the experiences seemed far removed and beyond her power to re-create, as if they had happened to someone else, and she was thrown into a panic, wondering if she was a deliberate fraud after all, as she was sure the Monsignor secretly believed, or whether she had actually conjured up the whole thing through some aberration of her imagination. It made her feel all the more guilty over her mother and Father Gregory, both of whom seemed determined to believe these were Divine visions, for she knew that, sooner or later, she was going to let them down.

She glanced around her room. It all looked much the same. She'd taken Matthew's little statuette of Our Lady and placed it on her bedside table – just as he had always kept it, whether at home or in the hospital – and on her dressing-table she'd pinned to the mirror a photo of Troy, Ralph Cottrell's chestnut stallion and her favourite in the stables. But in most ways she had deliberately tried to keep her life the same. She went to Mass no more often than before, for instance, though she knew it surprised Father Gregory and disappointed her mother. Why should she change?

Despite Monsignor Rolfe's efforts to keep the case strictly *sub judice*, the story had begun to leak out, and though she could never be certain who actually knew – she'd been forbidden, on pain of the direst consequences, to discuss it with anyone or even to admit that there was an investigation taking place at all – she felt constantly watched, pried into, observed and her behaviour the subject of comment behind closed doors. Some people, such as Sister Bertram, seemed to expect her to show greater piety and lead a reformed, model life; others, such as the Monsignor, seemed to expect the opposite, as being more consistent with the image of a girl who told wicked lies. Even with Father Gregory, for all his evident conviction, she couldn't help sensing some ambivalence, as though, deep down, he resented the fact that Our Lady had appeared to her and not to him. In the end she simply felt tired. Tired of being pulled in different directions, her freedom of mind taken over, her will coopted, tired of being an unwitting subject of everyone's selfish needs and motives.

She badly wished she could talk to Leo in the way that they used to. She felt upset they'd somehow become strangers. He still came over to supper or to take Mum out to plays and concerts as often as before, and though he always acted in a friendly and cheery way towards her, she sensed a coolness, an awkwardness, behind it all.

Faced with such confusion and muddle, she decided the best plan was to keep her thoughts to herself and merely live from day to day. To tread warily, assume nothing, take no-one's loyalty for granted. And above all, not to let that smart, conceited, sarcastic Monsignor get to her.

She had closed her eyes and was sinking at last into a welcome doze when she heard the distant sound of footsteps pounding up the gravel drive, growing rapidly louder as they approached. A gate clanged, and the steps fell to a muffled padding sound. She was instantly alert. Someone was in the garden, running across the lawn! She jumped out of bed and flew to the window just in time to see a figure disappearing from view onto the path beneath her. A second later came an impatient hammering on the back door. Grabbing her dressing-gown, she hurried downstairs to the kitchen.

There, framed in the back door, stood Benedict, his cheeks flushed apple-red, his dark hair all awry and his piercing blue eyes burning wildly. As she unbolted the door and threw it open, he fell inside, grabbing at her to save himself from falling.

'It's Mum!' he cried breathlessly. 'Come quickly!'

*

Grace followed a few steps behind him, stumbling over the rough, frozen ground as he urged her to hurry faster. The sky was growing rapidly brighter, and a hard, wary sun was already tingeing the crusty frost a pale pink. They ran down the lane, along the track, across the paddock and finally over the stile into view of the pair of tied cottages. As they crossed the wasteland, he slowed down and let her catch up. Just ten yards away, he took her by the arm and pointed.

'Gracie, look!' he puffed exultantly.

At the window of the front room, staring out across the strip of rough ground between them, stood Mary Nolan. Her dressing-gown wrapped about her, she gazed out at the scene, open-mouthed.

Benedict squeezed her arm.

'Watch!' he said.

He raised his arm and began to wave.

Gradually the expression on his mother's lined and sunken face changed. Her whole complexion lifted and spread in a wonderful smile. And slowly she began to wave back.

*

Leonard checked the dashboard clock. Five to nine: he was going to be late. How many Hail Marys were you given for keeping the Inquisition waiting? Back in early January he'd received an invitation to appear before Monsignor Rolfe's tribunal; he'd already put it off twice, in the slender hope that the Church might give up and wrap up its case without his evidence. But from what he gleaned from Laura – he avoided discussing it directly – it seemed that they knew a good marketing proposition when they saw one and they were sparing no effort in checking it stood up. He bit his lip. That was no attitude in which to approach the meeting.

By now he had reached the outskirts of Abbotsbury and slowed down. As he drove through the small town, he was struck momentarily by the way the sun played on the frosty slate roofs, reversing the usual state of things so that the parts in shadow were white, while those in sunlight, where the frost had cleared, were dark grey. If he were to ask the priest what tone a shadow was, wouldn't he reply, 'Dark'? Only a scientist would say, 'it depends upon the conditions.' White could actually be black, but not to Monsignor Rolfe: *his* truths were absolute. They belonged, quite rightly and properly, in books of prayer.

He frowned; what common ground was there for any dialogue? Still, he'd make an effort. He'd stick to the physics and avoid the metaphysics. He'd have to tread carefully, though. The other day, Grace had let slip the name of the doctor appointed to the tribunal. He'd checked up on the man: a developmental psychologist from the Maudsley, and reputedly very good. All the more worrying.

As he drew closer to the convent, his thoughts turned to Grace herself. The atmosphere between them was still deeply strained. He tried to talk to her as before, but he could feel it jarring. This whole ludicrous business of the apparitions stood between them like a chasm growing gradually wider all the time until they could barely hear each other's voices across it. But he had to wait for her to come round, to come *back*. He'd pursued her with reasoned argument already too far, and to do any more would only push her further away than ever. Still, he'd managed to maintain his rapport with Laura, and that allowed him to keep a close eye on things. But, most encouragingly, there'd been no sign of any recurrence of the hallucinations. Could he hope that it might be getting better all by itself?

He'd reached the convent and was about to pull in through the gates when a small white Mini burst out of the drive and shot right across his path. He jammed on his brakes and came to a halt with a screech of tyres, missing the Mini by inches. The other driver didn't stop – he didn't even seem to notice – and without looking to left or to right, he tore off down the road. But not before Leonard had recognized the square head and tousled hair of Father Gregory.

Shaken, he drove on slowly up the tree-lined drive and around the back of the convent to a car-park. For a moment he stood on the gravel, sizing up his surroundings. The building rose before him tall and stately and self-assured, while behind stretched lawns and flower-beds that bore the stamp of years of confident care. Clenching his jaw, he strode forward and headed resolutely for the main entrance.

*

A thin beam of sunlight filtered in from a high window and fell with absolute precision upon the young Monsignor's silver hair. He sat at the side of the table, as if to give a less formal feel to the meeting. From his tall-backed chair opposite, Leonard observed with cautious amusement the well-practised dance he was being led, from the opening pleasantries, through a little light skirmishing to the engagement of the business in hand.

'Frankly, Dr Grigson, I envy you,' the priest was saying with a disingenuous smile. 'In my far more modest way, I'm trying to do something you do every day in your work. I find myself confronted with a puzzling case. I must diagnose the condition. I test one hypothesis against another. I'm looking not for where they fit the apparent evidence but where they don't. I'm looking, if you like, for reasons against. Psychological, medical, physiological . . . That's why I asked you to come here today. To lend me the benefit of your experience.'

Leonard leaned forward. Was this some trap?

'You want me to give you medical grounds for dismissing the case?'

'Let's just say I'm asking you to play Devil's advocate. So to speak.'

'So that you can then demolish the scientific arguments?'

'Perhaps,' responded the priest carefully, 'you will demolish *mine*.'

Leonard held the man's eye, trying to read the subtext. Was it possible the Church authorities wanted Grace's visions *dis*proven?

'One tends to think of miracles happening in Ireland, Portugal, France,' he said easily, while watching the Monsignor's reaction closely. 'Or in places like Yugoslavia, where Church and State are in conflict. I imagine a miracle in England, right here in the Forest of Dean, could be rather . . . unpolitic.'

Monsignor Rolfe gave a smooth, insincere smile. It seemed to say everything. 'I'm after the truth, Doctor. And the truth is not a matter of politics.'

'Indeed, one would hope not,' responded Leonard quietly, then continued, 'I'm not sure how far I can help you. In my opinion, both as her physician and as her friend, there is, and never has been, anything wrong with Grace.'

'Never?' Monsignor Rolfe consulted a pink file at his side. 'Could we go back to the time of her brother Matthew's illness? According to Dr Stimpson's testimony . . .'

'Yes, Grace was under the weather for a few days.'

'And you treated her?'

'Dr Stimpson referred her to me – he'd already referred Matthew. It wasn't anything serious. A mild stomach upset, that's all.'

'A sympathetic illness?'

'No, not if you mean hysterical.'

'And you treated her at the hospital?'

'Hardly.'

'You treated her at home, then?'

'I mean, she was no sooner admitted than discharged.'

'So you did treat her at home?'

'I didn't say that. Yes, I did visit her at home once or twice. In a professional capacity.'

'Wasn't that rather unusual for a hospital consultant?'

'I was a friend of the family.'

'You knew the Holmwoods before?'

'I *became* a friend of the family,' Leonard snapped. 'Look, if there'd been anything seriously wrong with her, I'd have kept her in. She had a temperature, stomach cramps, diarrhoea – perfectly normal for a child whose twin brother was ill. Critically ill.'

'And, as it turned out, incurably.'

Leonard glared at the priest.

'You might like to know that Grace spent night after night on her knees, praying to God for him. I'm not sure his death can be laid at medicine's door alone.'

Monsignor Rolfe met his glare with a faint, ironic smile, then turned aside and began jotting down notes in the file. For a moment they sat with only the sound of the priest's fountain pen scratching on the paper to fill the silence. Then suddenly, abruptly, the phone rang. With an irritable frown, the Monsignor picked it up. He listened to a garrulous outpouring from the other end, interjecting only the odd word.

'Yes. No. I see. What was the woman's name? It's a bad line: could you spell it, please? N-o-l-a-n.' His frown had deepened and he wrote down the name in heavy, angry capitals. 'Right. If you think so, Father. Yes. Thank you, Father.'

He replaced the phone and turned to Leonard, looking strangely discomfited.

'It appears that some blind woman in Grace's own village

is now claiming a miraculous cure.' He shook his head. 'These things are like rashes – they have a habit of spreading. Still, we shall see.' He regained his composure. 'Now, Doctor, where were we?'

*

Father Gregory put the phone down with a triumphant flourish. he turned to find the door of the small village store back room slightly ajar and the woman who kept the store standing within easy earshot, busy pretending to be restocking a shelf. What matter? News of this wonder would be over the whole county in minutes anyway. Monsignor Rolfe would have no hope of claiming an embargo on it this time. The sceptics might try and dispute a young girl's visions to which there had been no other witnesses, but they couldn't dispute *this*. Everyone knew that Mary Nolan had been blind as a bat for years – she'd even suffered a damaging fall not so long ago, too – and now, suddenly, with no treatment or medical intervention, Our Lady had answered her prayers – no, Grace's prayers for her – and had given her back her sight. Here was living, breathing, *seeing* proof. Let the doubters sit up and take note! Grace had truly been blessed with Our Lady's favour.

He hurried out of the shop and round the side to the path along the back of the row of houses. As he came to the paddock he noticed Dr Stimpson's car parked by the gate. Loosening his scarf, for the sun was already bright and warm, he hastened back across the rough ground to the cottage. Inside, he found Dr Stimpson in the front room with Mary Nolan, packing away his ophthalmoscope after finishing his examination. The doctor's face bore a look of profound perplexity. Father Gregory waited until he had bidden his patient goodbye and followed him back out of the house.

On the doorstep, Dr Stimpson stopped and shook his head in disbelief.

'Beats me,' he muttered.

Father Gregory smiled confidently.

'I don't suppose you've ever been to Lourdes, Doctor? The physicians there accept miracles as a part of daily life.'

Dr Stimpson caught his eye.

'God help us if that happens here. I'm busy enough without being inundated with cases of mass hysteria. For that's all your faith-healing is.' His tone grew more reasonable. 'Of course, these things do happen. I know of a case where a man was blind for years, got knocked on the head by a mugger and regained his sight.'

'No-one's mugged Mary Nolan.'

'My point is, we'll find a perfectly valid explanation for this, in terms of normal medical cause and effect.'

Father Gregory maintained his unruffled smile.

'We *have* a perfectly valid explanation,' he said quietly. 'In terms of Divine cause and effect.'

The doctor stared at him with incredulity.

'Father,' he said, 'you aren't *really* serious . . . ?'

'Never more so in my life.'

'Then God truly help us all.'

'He will, if you ask Him.'

Dr Stimpson was about to reply but stopped himself. With an impatient click of the tongue, he turned and walked briskly off across the waste ground. Half way, he paused for a moment, but apparently thought better of it. Carrying on over the stile into the paddock, he was quickly lost from sight.

Father Gregory went back inside. He felt overwhelmed with joy and wonder. He would sit with Mary for a while and hear the whole story all over again, starting with her asking Grace to pray for her all those weeks ago.

Eleven

Grace sat on the edge of the bath, gripping the cold enamel tightly as she fought off another swell of nausea. Her dressing-gown hung loosely around her and, with her head bowed, her long fair hair fell lank and clammy about her face. A dull pain throbbed in her temples, and even the diffuse, foggy early morning light from the window hurt her eyes. After some while, the sickness gradually passed and she struggled to the mirror. A death-mask faced her. People expected her to look radiant with joy, but she felt only dread and foreboding. She hadn't *really* been instrumental in Mary's cure, she knew that. True, she'd mentioned her in her bedtime prayers to Our Lady, and she'd asked Matthew to pray for her, too, but no more than millions of people did every night. If anything, it showed her up for what she was – a fraud, a fake, accepting the credit for something she hadn't done. It was Mary's own faith that had healed her.

She took a shower and, still shaky, made her way back to her bedroom. Downstairs, she could already hear her mother preparing breakfast. Mum meant well, of course, but if only she'd stop treating her so *preciously*. She herself hadn't changed; she was still untidy, she still fiddled with her hair when she was embarrassed, she still wore sloppy jumpers and threadbare jeans, she still played her records too loudly and skipped homework. Throwing open her wardrobe, she ransacked the drawers until she found her tightest jeans and her most colourful sweatshirt. She dressed quickly and went downstairs without putting shoes on, knowing how Mum disapproved of stocking feet.

Her mother began filling the teapot as she entered – Grace could tell she'd been waiting, to keep the brew fresh – and a light frown crossed her face.

'You're not coming to Mass like that, are you, darling?'

'I thought I'd go up to the stables,' replied Grace. 'I haven't been for ages.'

'But it's far too foggy to go riding. Besides, your jodhpurs are in the wash.'

'These jeans will do. Mum, do sit down and let me do the toast.'

'No, no, it's done.'

She spooned the marmalade into a cut-glass dish and poured tea into two china cups.

Grace caught her eye.

'Are we expecting a visitor? Or perhaps a visitation?'

'That's not funny, darling.'

'Come on, Mum. Everything's become so precious round here. I liked it before when things were rough and ready.'

'I thought we could be a bit more civilized. At least, at weekends when we don't have to rush.'

'I'm sorry.'

'Things *have* changed, darling,' sighed her mother, sitting down. 'They're bound to have.'

'But not here, with us. We're still the A-team, right?'

'Of course we are,' she laughed. After a pause, she went on, 'Mary's coming over this afternoon. *Walking* over, by herself. She wants to come and clean for us again, but I said it's quite out of the question. She should take things quietly. Readjusting isn't going to be so easy. She admitted it was all quite frightening. The world was so much bigger and brighter than she'd remembered.'

Grace nodded as she spread her toast.

'The worst is people who are blind from birth suddenly getting sight,' she said. 'Some can't take it and end up killing themselves. I'm not sure if a miracle is always such a blessing really.'

'Not everything is as it first seems,' her mother said mildly.

144

Grace looked up, puzzled by her tone.

'What do you mean?'

'It's strange. People who believe are always praying for a sign, for proof. When it comes, it's not so helpful. The whole point of faith is that there should be no proof. For me, it's as if what has happened to Mary has actually taken away room for faith.' She cast her a sympathetic smile. 'If it's hard for me, it must be doubly hard for you, darling. Don't think I don't see that.'

'It's okay, Mum.'

'Is it, really?'

Grace hesitated.

'Well, it isn't *that* okay.' She looked down at her plate, wondering how much she should open up. 'It's just that everyone looks at me as though I'm some kind of freak,' she said ruefully. 'I feel they're watching me all the time. I can't bear to think what it'll be like now.'

'But the fact is, you're special.'

'I'm *not* special and I don't *want* to be!' she blurted out. 'I want to be like everyone else. I want to be *me*!' She gathered herself. Of course Mum didn't understand; why should she? 'I'm sorry,' she said lamely.

Her mother reached out and squeezed her hand, but Grace couldn't bring herself to look up and meet her eye. Silence fell, broken only by the sound of rushing water from the mill stream. She turned and stared out into the garden. The fog swept across the lawn in thick swathes, sponging out the grand chestnut tree at the foot and reducing even the nearest apple trees to nothing more than a faint suggestion of form. Was it really too thick to ride in? Perhaps it would be clear on the higher ground.

As she turned back she caught the puzzled, pained look on her mother's face. 'I'll come along if you want,' she said quietly.

'No, you do what you were planning. We'll go together tomorrow. I'm not sure about riding, though. Best if you just stick to the stables.'

'Don't worry about me, Mum,' she replied, squeezing the hand back. 'I'll be all right. Promise.'

'I love you very much, Grace.'

'I love you too, Mum.'

*

The chestnut stallion bucked and frothed at the bit as he fought against the reins holding him tightly in. Suddenly out of the mist loomed an orange plastic fertilizer bag, swept against the hedge, and with a terrified whinny the horse shied, his hooves skidding wildly on the metal road surface. Grace leaned forward in the seat and patted his neck, calling softly, *Easy, Troy, easy, boy.* She hadn't ridden him out for several weeks and he needed a good gallop, but that was out of the question in this visibility. A car approached, its headlamps boring two funnels into the mist, and she steered the horse's head in towards the hedge. Again he bucked and whinnied.

For a moment she wondered whether to turn back, but she carried on, and before long the tottering signpost that marked the knoll of Dent's Cross rose up before her. Turning off the road, she headed up the sandy path that led into the forest. As she went she felt in the pocket of her riding jacket for the white camellia she'd picked from the bush in the garden; she would lay it on the spot where she received the first visitation. For whatever part she did or didn't play in them, she felt the need to acknowledge them – not in church with everybody else, but by herself, in her own way.

Boughs brought down in the heavy January snows threw obstacles across the path, compelling the horse to keep to a stumbling walking pace. From time to time he slipped on the mulch, for with the fog had come a thaw, and at one point she had to dismount and lead him on foot for a short way. The track grew steeper but the mist scarcely thinner. As it finally levelled off and widened into the broader ride, she remounted and allowed the horse to break into a trot.

No sooner had they reached the gentle bend than he switched stride to a canter. She fought to keep him in, afraid of the fallen logs and low branches that suddenly swept up upon them without warning. The ground was heavily rutted, too, as though a logger's tractor had ploughed its way up there – and quite recently, to judge from the bare scars. The horse was now straining to break into a gallop as they rounded the bend and . . .

Suddenly, a fence!

A chain-link fence. Higher than a man. Topped with barbed wire stretched tight between angled concrete posts. And a signboard racing towards her, its bold red and black lettering searing into her mind: KEEP OUT – BY ORDER. Closing now, closing too fast! Tug back the reins! Too close, too close to stop! The horse is collecting his stride for a jump, galvanizing the powerhouse of his legs, gathering speed, and more speed. He's going to go for it . . . No, don't! It's impossible! We'll never clear it! But he digs in his heels and with a violent thrust he explodes upwards, catapults bodily into the air, forelegs outstretched, neck straining forward, flecks of froth whipping past my face, the stirrups loose, but we're flying, flying like a Pegasus, hang on, grip the mane, tighten the knees to a vice, go higher, Troy, higher! We're not going to clear it, *we're not going to* . . . Suddenly we're caught, tugged back, belly-hooked. A wild shriek, a terrible bloodcurdling animal scream, and the whole horse's body twists and contorts, the ground suddenly rushes up, the reins go slack, the saddle slips askew, his front legs hit the earth and buckle, his vast weight-mass follows, forelegs crumpling, head slewing, body grounding, no way of staying on, find a soft patch, bale out, ditch, slide off, that's it, slither off, tuck your head in, roll over and over, grass and sky, grass and sky . . . Grace crawled to her knees and, wiping the mud out of her eyes, looked out across the clearing. The stallion had bolted. She could just make out his form, bucking violently every few yards as if trying to shake off some creature clamped to his chest, before he disappeared into the mist, leaving the sound of his frantic neighing to echo around the empty arena.

She climbed slowly to her feet, shaking in every limb, and checked herself over. She seemed all right; nothing broken, nothing even sprained, only a deep gash along the side of her hand and up her arm. But her horse? Thick spots of blood spattered the grass and led off in a broken trail into the mist.

She set out after him at a run. At the far side of the clearing she plunged back into forest. She tripped on a tangle of brambles and fell forward onto a tussock of dead grass. As she clambered, winded, to her feet, she saw to her horror that her hands and chest were red with blood. The straw-pale grass below was stained like the floor of a butcher's shop. She stood still, listening. Somewhere beyond the steady drip, drip, drip from the mossy oak above her, came the sound of a large creature blundering through the undergrowth. She stumbled on, torn and battered, until she was brought to an abrupt stop by another fence. She paused. It was made of the same heavy chain link, bolted to concrete posts that were angled inwards at the top and laced with a treble strand of barbed wire. Looking closer, she could see the mesh was flecked with strange yellow froth, and the grass below was treacled with blood. Thick and sticky, the trail wound back into the undergrowth.

Fifty yards away, at the edge of a clump of birches, she found the horse.

He lay on his side, vainly pawing the empty air. His head was twisted and thrown back, the whites of his large brown eyes rolled in grotesque circles and from his nostrils foamed a hideous yellow froth. From his chest down towards his groin ran three savage gashes like the claw-marks of a lion, each one biting deeper as it went, ripping open his soft grey belly.

With a cry, she rushed forward and fell to her knees, cradling his head in her arms. But that was no use: she must get help! Tearing off her riding jacket, she laid it over his shivering chest and, with an anguished promise to be as quick as she could, her eyes misting with tears, she blundered back along the track the way she had come.

It was only when she had crossed the clearing and reached the fence they had jumped that she realized she was trapped inside a circular enclosure. With a frantic howl she threw herself at the mesh, but it absorbed every blow without yielding. Forcing herself to keep control, she followed along the fence until she came to a double metal gate. It was padlocked and chained. Underneath, dug into the sandy soil, ran two deep tyre ruts, snaking round to join the track she'd taken into the clearing. Seizing a stone, she began scraping out one of the ruts deeper and wider until finally, crawling on her hands and knees, she managed to worm her way under the gate through to the other side, where she scrambled to her feet and headed off down the main track at a flying run.

*

A nervous mood of unease had settled over the stables. In their stalls, the horses circled restlessly, and the din of neighing and hooves beating on wood filled the late morning air. The vet's car stood parked in the yard and beyond, no longer veiled by the mist, rose the tall brick and stone manor house. Wrapped in a horse blanket, Grace stood in the courtyard, looking over the half-door into the stable where the great chestnut stallion lay on the straw. Beside him knelt the vet, with an array of surgical instruments spread on a towel at his side, busy sewing up the wound. Spent hypodermics and capsules lay in a metal dish on the straw amid piles of bloodied daubs and rags.

In the corner stood Ralph Cottrell, a stocky, swarthy figure in a red waistcoat and loud check jacket. He caught Grace's eye and scowled. She looked down at her boots. She felt terrible. It was all her fault. Troy was his prize hunter, but the real source of his anger seemed to be that she'd gone up to the mine. She thought back to how she'd stumbled exhausted into the stables, how Benedict had run off to fetch his boss and how, purple with rage, the man had grabbed his Range Rover and trailer and raced off up to Dent's Cross. The three of them had lurched and bumped their way up the rough sandy track and along the rutted path to the gates in the tall fence. Ralph had jumped out, taken a bunch of keys from his pocket and unlocked the gates. She'd been puzzled: how come he had the right keys? When they'd found the horse, he'd insisted on winching the poor animal onto the trailer and carting him back home.

At the sound of footsteps she turned. Benedict was hurrying across the courtyard carrying a pail of boiling water. As she opened the stable door for him, he cast her a sympathetic look.

'He'll be fine,' he said bravely, though she knew better: she'd seen the vet shaking his head. Then he added, 'There's a feller at the gate asking for you, Grace.'

Ralph looked up sharply, bristling.

'Who?' he barked.

'From the *Western Post*, Mr Cottrell.'

'A reporter? Jesus *Christ*!' He pushed past to the door. 'I'll sort him out. Now listen here, Grace, if anyone asks anything, anything at all, you don't know a thing. That goes for you, too, Benedict. Get me?'

Abruptly, he stormed off across the courtyard. Benedict put the pail down beside the vet, then returned to where Grace was standing, nursing her bandaged arm. For a while they stood in silence, watching the vet finishing his work. Then she turned to the boy beside her. She couldn't rid her mind of the question.

'Ben,' she asked, 'is that Mr Cottrell's land up there?'

'It's all his land.'

'So he put up that fence? Why?'

The boy shrugged. 'No idea.'

'But nobody ever goes up there. It's only a disused old mine, all bricked up.' She paused. 'Do you suppose he bricked it up, too?'

'Search me.' He touched her arm tenderly. 'You're shivering fit to die, Gracie. Come on, I'll walk you home. There's nothing you can do here. Don't worry, it's not your fault. It's *his* fault, for putting up that stupid fence. You can't enclose Forest land, anyway. There's some old law against it. Serve him right.'

*

Grace sat curled up in the armchair in front of the fire, picking at a box of chocolates. She felt feverish, shivering one moment and sweltering the next. Her mother reclined on the sofa in a new red woollen dress, gazing towards Leo who stood by the dresser peeling the foil off a bottle of champagne. At the pop of the cork, he made a droll remark and she laughed almost skittishly. Grace clenched her teeth. Some people could be poles apart on the fundamentals and yet have fun together as though none of it mattered. They were just too afraid of being alone. Well, *she'd* never compromise with anyone.

'Try this, Duchess.' Leo was standing over her with a glass in his hand. 'It'll cheer you up.'

'I don't feel like celebrating,' she replied dully.

'Let's drink to Mary, then,' he proposed, forcing the glass into her hand and raising his own. 'To Mary.' He chinked glasses. 'Come on,' he persisted. 'Candy is dandy but liquor is quicker.'

She looked away. She could only think of the poor horse.

'The vet said he's worse,' she mumbled. 'I just *assumed* the track was clear. You don't expect fences in the middle of the forest. What gave Ralph the right?'

'Ralph Cottrell can do anything,' remarked Leo with a hint of bitterness.

'Just because he owns some crummy old iron mines that haven't been used in donkey's years?'

'He happens to own half the land round here and most of the local businesses, too,' he replied soberly. 'He's on the county council, he's even on the Board of Governors at the hospital – not that he ever turns up. He's a man with fingers

151

in a lot of pies. If he says, *Keep out*, then I'd do just that. Keep out. Anyway,' he added, 'the mines are dangerous. The whole place is derelict; bits could fall in at any moment. I doubt if it's ever been properly mapped since Roman times.'

She held his eye, feeling her anger rising.

'People only put up fences when they've got something to hide,' she said.

Her mother leaned forward.

'Getting cross won't make the horse any better, darling.'

'I'm serious, Leo,' said Grace.

Leo gave a pained shrug. 'You don't get where Ralph Cottrell is without the odd skeleton in the cupboard,' he responded, then added quietly, 'Which of us hasn't got something to hide? Something one has done or something one hasn't.'

Her mother looked askance. 'I'm not sure I know what you mean, Leonard,' she said.

'He's having a dig about Mary, Mother,' replied Grace shortly. 'He's saying I'm taking the credit for something I didn't do.'

'I didn't say that, Duchess,' responded Leo.

'But that's what you mean, isn't it?' she cried. 'Maybe you're right. What of it?'

'Easy now, angel,' he smiled. 'I wouldn't presume to judge. Mary Nolan has at last agreed to come in for a scan, yes. But that'll only tell us what we know already, that she's regained her sight, not how and why.' He held up his hand defensively. 'Don't give me that burn-the-heretic look of yours. I'm prepared to be persuaded. Give a poor heathen a chance.'

'I'm sorry, Leo,' she said more mildly, returning his smile in spite of herself. 'I don't want to spoil things this evening.' She raised her glass. 'All right. Let's drink to . . . whatever you like.'

'That's more like it,' her mother chimed in. 'To life and love.'

'*A nos amours*,' said Leo. He drank his glass in one, then turned back to Grace, his expression hardening again. 'I'm serious about that place. Best not hang around up there.'

'Ralph Cottrell can't stop me,' she retorted defiantly.

'He told me he's thinking of putting dogs in there.'

'He told you?'

'Well, we spoke at the Board meeting the other day.'

'I thought you said he never turned up.'

'Come on, don't take everything so literally! It was an exaggeration, a hyperbole, a figure of speech.'

She finished her glass and held it out to be refilled.

'In that case, I shouldn't take the rest of what you say literally. Should I?'

'Grace!' her mother broke in.

'Sorry, Mum.'

But she could see she had hit a tender nerve. Why should he be so concerned about her going for her walks and rides up there in the woods? And what was that business about everyone having things to hide? Did *he* have something to hide? How could they ever talk properly and openly again if he didn't come clean?

*

Leonard groaned at his reflection in the cloakroom mirror and sluiced more cold water over his face. He always drank too much when things were on his mind. He should have kept off the booze, if he was going to drive. And he *was* going to drive: no broaching that subject with Laura again. Drying his face, he took a deep breath and returned to the living-room. Grace had gone to bed and it was time to go. The sound of a coffee-grinder told him Laura was in the kitchen, but as he reached the foot of the stairs, he paused. All evening Grace had been giving him strange, suspicious glances. He couldn't leave without establishing a more comfortable note.

He slipped up the stairs and crept along the gallery. As

he reached her bedroom, he heard her voice speaking. Who on earth to? He stepped quietly forward and stood outside the door, listening.

'Please, Matthew, *please* . . .' she was muttering softly.

Matthew. A sudden chill shuddered through him. His hand hovered over the doorknob. No, he'd better not. Turning, he retraced his steps down the stairs just as Laura came through the kitchen door carrying two cups of coffee on a tray. She looked up interrogatively.

'She's asleep,' he said, 'and dreaming.'

*

As another violent sneeze racked her body, Grace leant forward and groped around for the box of tissues lying among the cold-cure packets and the Sunday papers strewn across the duvet. Sinking back into the pillows, she looked about her with pain-blurred eyes. Beside Matthew's small statuette on her bedside table stood an array of glasses, some glistening stickily from honey and lemon drinks, others white with the residue of aspirin powders. The midday sun streamed into the room, giving a false hint of spring. Downstairs, she heard the front door bell ring and her mother hurry across the living-room floor. There was a brief exchange, the door slammed and the footsteps stomped back across the living-room.

She stared up at the ceiling. Troy was dead. The horse had simply lost too much blood in the forest. She closed her smarting eyes. She knew the grief of loss all too well, but this was all the worse for being her fault. If only she'd listened to Mum when she'd warned her it was too foggy to ride. If only she'd chosen a more sensible route. If only she hadn't allowed the horse his head on that last stretch. Accidents, Leo said, were just particular conjunctions of time and place. If only time and place hadn't conjoined particularly then and particularly there.

Someone was now rapping on the back door. She heard a window being thrown up and her mother calling out in an irritable voice, *I've told you no! She is not to be disturbed. Now please leave or I'll have to call the police.* The window slammed down and footsteps receded down the flagstone path.

She winced. The world was closing in. Word had got out about Mary, and everyone was thinking it was *her* doing. People were coming to see this girl who had visions and worked miracles. But it was all nonsense. Why hadn't she managed to cure Troy, then? Why hadn't Our Lady heard her prayers this time? She'd prayed more fervently than ever. Had the line gone dead? Or had there never been a line in the first place?

For a while she dozed fitfully. Gruesome, savage images floated through her consciousness in an incoherent muddle. At one point she woke with a jolt, choking back a scream as she pictured herself at a bullfight seeing a horse with its belly ripped open being stuffed with straw . . . Turning over to face the light, she gradually lapsed into a deeper, less troubled sleep.

Some while later, as she rose more gently to the surface of consciousness, she became distantly aware that the light had grown strangely brighter and was flickering gently.

She half-opened her eyes as she felt the familiar flush of panic. Was it happening again? Or was it just the sun? It had moved round behind the small statuette of Our Lady so that its rays spilled round the figure and shone directly in her face. She swallowed, tasting for any hint of that purple flavour, and lay very still, not moving a muscle. She'd work this thing out once and for all. She'd catch it unawares this time, she'd surprise it, smoke it out . . . The sunlight seemed to be pulsing now, or was that the throbbing behind her eyes? As she watched, it seemed to wink, working its way around the outline of the holy figure, reducing the background to a dull dark blank and growing more vivid every moment, as one spot, more brilliant than the rest, sparkled off the golden halo and held her in an unshakable, mesmeric grip. And as she lay there, through her mind slowly passed the words of one of the descriptions she had recorded in her notebook.

The light shimmers in a soft white sheet. It furls at the edges, draws in towards the centre. Rays spurt out like spokes. The eye of the light-storm is growing still denser, still thicker . . . Line by line, it crystallizes into human shape. Her shape.

She stands in a simple hooded robe of pale blue and white. It is hemmed with golden ribbing and it falls to the ground in ample folds. Around her head the cape forms soft, crenellated pleats . . . Her skin is pale, the texture of fine wax. One hand gestures towards her heart; the other, outstretched, is beckoning. Her halo radiates gentle sparks of fire. She is smiling, her head indulgently inclined . . .

With a sharp cry of horror, she drew back violently against the bedstead. Her hand flew to her mouth. Gradually and tentatively, as if in terror of it coming alive at any moment, she reached out and touched the statue. Her fingertips met cold, stony plaster. She recoiled with a shudder. Steeling her nerve, she eased her body inch by inch back to its earlier position. Then, extremely slowly, she stared back up at the figure.

It *was* Our Lady . . . *Exactly as she had seen her!* Standing in a hooded robe. Gesturing towards her heart with one hand. Beckoning with the other. And smiling that beatific smile.

With an anguished moan, she buried her face in the pillows. She wanted to suffocate, to die. She was a fraud, an impostor, a mental case. She had imagined it all in the sickness of a very sick mind, and here was the absolute incontestable proof.

Twelve

Only the steady whirr and click of the scanner as it progressed slice by slice through Mary Nolan's brain, tracking in a line from the crown of her head to the base of her skull, punctuated the tense silence in the Radiology room. Leonard stood at the console across the room, his fists clenched in the pockets of his white coat, looking over the radiologist's shoulder at the twin display screens set up side by side. The screen on the right showed the results of the CAT-scan she had been given four years before; the tumour had already stabilized but he'd decided it was too risky to operate, and he'd had to break the news to her that her blindness was irreversible and she must not expect ever to see again. On the left screen, synchronized to show the comparison, were displayed the X-rays being taken at the moment. Whirr, click, whirr, click . . . step by step the scan probed deeper towards the crucial region of the midbrain.

He glanced up. She lay on the narrow padded couch in her thick hose stockings and a Sunday-best serge suit, with her head entirely enclosed in the circular hood of the scanner. On a side table lay her dark glasses and white stick which she'd brought along *in case*. Unknown to herself or the rest of the world, this woman was about to make medical history.

The radiologist was tapping the right screen. Leonard bent forward quickly. Yes, here was the original tumour coming up again. It appeared like a hole at the base of the two oblongs of the lateral geniculate, while around it glowed the familiar bright ring where the blood vessels surrounding the growth had become engorged.

'Hold it there,' he ordered.

Then he turned to the left screen, showing the present condition of the same region of the patient's brain. He drew in his breath sharply.

There was no dark hole, no ring enhancement or any sign of abnormal microvasculature. Only the faintest shadow where the tumour had been and, in the centre, a small dense area the size of a pea where the necrosed tissue had shrunk and collapsed.

He caught the radiologist's eye.

'Ever seen anything like that?' he breathed.

'Never in all my time.'

'Take it back a bit, would you? I want to check for coning.'

He tensed himself for a problem. Some drugs given to shrink malignant growths inside the brain tended to make the brain press downwards in a cone through the tentorium cerebelli, inhibiting respiration and other vital functions and eventually, if unchecked, leading to death. Slowly the radiologist tracked back and, increasing the resolution, focused on the critical region around the brain stem.

Leonard leaned closer. Slowly he let out his breath. There was no hint of any misshaping.

He stood back. The drug had worked beyond his wildest dreams. And the proof was patent in every frame.

*

He saw Mrs Nolan downstairs. In the lift he made her press the buttons herself and in the corridors he let her navigate her own way round the trolleys and other obstacles. She followed the EXIT signs without prompting and by the time they'd reached the reception area, she was walking confidently in the centre of the corridor, rather than hugging the side. As they passed the main reception desk, he took her thin white stick and snapped it in two. She let out a peal of girlish laughter.

Through the glass door at the entrance, he could see Benedict waiting beside a car in the driveway. The boy was engrossed in conversation with a man who carried a camera slung over his shoulder and was making notes on a pad. Leonard halted abruptly and held out his hand.

'I'll leave you here, Mary. Ben's just out there . . .'

'I've seen.' She took his hand unerringly. 'You're a good man, Doctor,' she said. 'May God bless your other patients as He has blessed me.'

As she stepped out into the bright sunshine her son came forward. The reporter unshouldered his camera and began taking photos. Two nurses leaving the building stopped to watch, then a family arriving for visiting time, and soon a small, inquisitive crowd had gathered.

Leonard retraced his steps back to the lifts, feeling a crooked grin spreading over his face. Well, in its way, it *was* comic. Gradually, however, the smile hardened. It would be more comic if it weren't so damn pitiful. How feeble was mankind, clutching at the straws that fell from their straw gods. Nietzsche got it slightly wrong: God was not dead – He'd never been alive in the first place. Man was the creator of God, not the reverse. Who else could man look to for help but to himself? In the beginning was the *logos* – reason, logic, order. *That* was the true God; the other gods were just fabrications of the human psyche. Childish man playing in the doll's house of his mind. He sighed. Still, let the people have their opium. His job was to restore sight to blind bodies, not blind souls. Not for him to bring enlightenment to the great unlit corners of darkness lurking in the human mind. Not even in this case, where he had incontrovertible proof of the real truth of the matter. For, whether he relished the irony or not, this truth had to remain his truth alone.

*

But that couldn't stop him *caring*. That night, over supper heated up in the microwave, he thought of Grace.

He'd phoned Laura to see if she was better. She still had a bad cold, Laura told him, but she was very depressed because the stallion had died. 'It was a fine creature and it meant the world to her,' she'd said, perplexed, 'but it was only a horse, after all. She seems to have forgotten the wonderful things that have been happening. She keeps asking *questions*. Sometimes I really don't understand her.'

He pushed away the food half-eaten and poured himself a whisky, then went into his study. Picking up the photo frame from the mess of books and papers on his desk, he stood for a while scrutinizing the face of the girl standing with her arm round her mother's shoulder, looking so composed, so knowing, so *intelligent*. He stared deeper into her eyes. Could *he* understand her? Think his way into that mind? Probe it so carefully he could hear it actually tick?

She was a girl of seventeen, turning eighteen. People thought she was special, that she had a gift, a hot-line to God. But all she probably wanted was to be ordinary, normal. Just plain Grace Holmwood. Schoolgirl, not saint.

She was convinced her visions were real, but did she never wonder if they were *authentic*? A blind woman had just regained her sight: did she really ascribe that to her own intervention? The other night he'd heard her praying to Matthew – to save the horse? – but the animal had died. Now, a true believer would have called that God's will. But from what Laura had been saying, it appeared that Grace didn't. She had, in fact, begun to ask questions. What did that signify? Surely that, deep down, she didn't really believe all that garbage at all! Try as she might, she couldn't bring herself to believe unconditionally as she was supposed to. She was still the girl he'd steered through adolescence, whose mind he'd helped shape. Still a child of reason, not superstition. Still his child.

A surge of hope shot through him. Grace, Grace, he wanted to cry out, I'm still here, still your Leo. Let me help you. Can't you see the danger in blaming yourself for that horse's death? Once you start on that, you'll never be free. You could intercede for all the ills of the world and your prayers would go unheard. There is a peril in all idealism: for any ideal there is an equally valid counter, for any principle a valid exception. Can't you see you're human like the rest of us all, can't you recognize your humanity and within that find all the richness and reward you seek in life?

Slowly he leaned forward and reached for a sheet of writing-paper. Maybe the device would work a second time where it was really needed.

'Dear Duchess,' he began carefully . . .

*

Father Gregory closed the carved oak door and stood for a moment in the hall of the old Victorian convent while Mary, shaking and white-faced, took out a handkerchief and dabbed her eyes.

'I'm sorry, Father,' she mumbled. 'It's just I didn't expect it would be like that.' She collected herself and cast him a wan smile. 'It's his job, I suppose. He's got to be sure.'

'I suppose it is, Mary, I suppose it is.' He took her by the elbow. 'Come along, I'll take you home.'

He led her across the hall, down the brown and white corridors and through the kitchens to the back door. Was it really necessary to leave by the rear entrance? Had it really been necessary, too, to subject the poor woman to such an interrogation? She was only a simple soul and the Monsignor had easily tied her up in knots, cunningly casting serious doubt on her mental faculties. He'd almost had her admitting that she'd been taking some kind of medication but that her memory was so unreliable that she must simply have forgotten.

Half way across the car-park outside, he noticed she was walking with her eyes closed. A gentle smile had softened her wrinkled features. He squeezed her arm.

'What's the good of the Good Lord working a miracle, Mary,' he reproved her with a chuckle, 'if you go around with your eyes shut?'

'I was looking at the birds in that tree.' She opened her eyes and fixed him with a direct gaze. 'You know, Father, I can see better with them shut.' She stopped and grew suddenly serious. '*You* believe, don't you, Father?'

'I do,' he answered quietly, ushering her into the small

161

white Mini. 'And so will the others, eventually.' He paused; how far would he have to take it if they didn't? All the way. 'Have you ever been to Rome, Mary?'

'Never set foot beyond Gloucester, Father.'

'*That*'ll open your eyes,' he smiled.

But in the car she kept her eyes shut all the way back to Coledean. Perhaps the sight of the world in all its brightness, colour and movement frightened her. Or maybe the shock was still too great.

Reaching the village, he took the narrow road that led in a meandering sweep over cattle-grids and through barred gates to the back of her house. As he drew up, he noticed a car already parked at the side. It was empty, but on top of the dashboard lay a card bearing the word, PRESS. He saw Mary to the front door but excused himself from coming in. If the Monsignor asked, he hadn't seen that car. Why shouldn't the good news be broadcast? Climbing back into his car, he made off quickly before any gentlemen from the press came after *him*.

*

Leonard unclipped the X-rays from the light-panel and slipped them back into the file, which he tossed into his out-tray. The case was of a middle-aged man with cancer of the lymph glands. The platelet and leukocyte analysis showed he had cancer no more. One hundred per cent remission. Another small triumph for his team.

It was gone one o'clock and a Saturday, too, and he wasn't on duty anyway. He decided he'd go downstairs for a bite of lunch, then head into the city to catch up on the week's household shopping. Slipping his bleeper into his jacket pocket, he left his small office and took the lift down to the staff canteen. As he entered the large, airless room with its steamed-up windows and smell of boiled cabbage, he heard his name called. The radiologist was waving at him from a table in the corner. As he came up, the man handed him a newspaper with a silent smile. It was that week's *Western Post*.

'BLIND WOMAN'S MIRACLE CURE –
BY DIVINE GRACE'

ran the front-page headline.

Leonard sat down slowly, his pulse quickening with unease. He scanned the article quickly. Full in the centre of the page was a photo of Mary, taken outside the Royal Hospital. *It's a miracle from God,' says Mrs Nolan*, read the caption. Lower in the page, beneath a sub-headline that ran, CURE DEFIES MEDICAL SCIENCE, was a grainy, blown-up photo of Grace in school uniform, squinting into the light. Underneath, the caption read, *Schoolgirl Grace Claims Divine Visions*.

He skimmed the copy.

Four years ago, Mrs Mary Nolan, 55, was certified blind. The doctors said she would never see again. Today she can read this newspaper . . . When Mary recounts her incredible story of hope and faith, the tears fill her newly sighted eyes. 'It's a miracle,' she told our reporter. 'Grace is a saint. Our Lady appears to her in visions. I asked her to pray for me . . . Then, just the other day, I was getting the breakfast when I began seeing funny flashing lights.'

Grace, 17, is a pupil at the Convent of St Dominic in nearby Abbotsbury. Yesterday, however, she was at home in bed – with a cold . . . Attractive, fair-haired Grace has had her share of bad luck. At the age of eight, she lost her father. At the age of twelve, five years ago to the day, her twin brother Matthew died suddenly. Grace now lives with her mother, Laura Holmwood, 42, a children's book illustrator, at their home in the old mill house, Coledean.

Mary is a devout Catholic, and the miracle claim is being investigated seriously by the Church. For several months now, an inquiry has been going on behind closed doors into schoolgirl Grace's amazing visions.

The Bishop's man on the case, Monsignor Jerome Rolfe, was unavailable for comment.

Leonard slowly put the paper down. He poured himself a glass of water. He hadn't faced up to the implications of publicity. Would the story die as such stories did, or would the nationals and the media at large take it up? And if so, would the men of the ink dig deeper than the men of the cloth? At least, thank God, he'd done his work in the Records office.

The radiologist was shaking his head.

'We're still in the Middle Ages,' he said. 'Why don't they write about all the bloody miracles that walk out of *here* every day?'

'Our miracles,' responded Leonard drily, 'aren't news.'

'I don't see why not.'

'Because we can explain them. I can turn that glass of water into air, but you wouldn't call that a miracle. You do it each time you boil a kettle. But if I could turn it into wine . . .'

'Then you'd be a darn useful person to know, Leonard.'

He laughed tersely.

'Yes, it's as remote a chance as that.'

*

Father Gregory replaced the receiver gingerly. His ears rang and his head spun with the wrath of Jehovah.

His eye returned to the headline: 'BLIND WOMAN'S MIRACLE CURE.' Well, so it was. But why had the Monsignor reacted like that? The Church had to scrutinize every claim of a miraculous intervention, and rightly so. But need the inquiry be so systematically *negative*? Frankly, if all the stories of the lives and works of the saints were scrutinized so closely, even those of the Gospels themselves, not a single one would really stand up. Yet they were hallowed articles of faith, beyond any permissible questioning. Why should doubt be heretical in that case and yet one's bounden duty in this?

Pushing the newspaper aside, he stood up and went to the window. He opened it an inch or two and stared out into his small back garden. God's will be done, he muttered softly to himself. Humility might be hard towards one's fellow man, whether pope or priest, cardinal or canon, but humility towards God, one's Creator, was all that mattered, and it was as natural as breathing the pure, fresh air coming in through this open window, bearing the faintest hint of spring on its sweet breath.

*

Grace leant her bicycle against the rusty railings and scanned the ill-kept churchyard beyond. A tree-root had swollen at the base of the iron gate, jamming it shut, and she had to climb over the railings to get in. Clutching her two small bunches of snowdrops, she made her way through the straggling dead grass to the two graves lying side by side in the far corner. Behind her rose the small derelict church, its windows boarded up and its stonework crumbling. Abandoned four years previously in favour of the newer and larger chapel at the convent, it stood as a sad reminder to her of happier times.

Clearing the graves of the leaves and debris that had collected, she laid a bunch of snowdrops first on Dad's and then on Matthew's. She felt the tears rising as she stood back. Not for Matthew – she knew he was happy where he was – but for herself, for the deep and unassuageable loneliness she felt.

'I so wish you were here,' she whispered to the headstone. 'I miss you so. I *need* you so.'

A light wind ruffled the grass, and from the eaves of the church a pigeon cooed, but otherwise all was silence. Thrusting her hands in her pockets, she turned and retraced her steps. She was alone. It was fruitless to pretend or to hope otherwise.

*

Tom Welland sat at the desk in his box-room study and turned up the Mozart on the tape-cassette so as to drown the tantrums going on downstairs. His wife had been reading some Skinnerist rubbish in a magazine at the hairdresser's and was trying unsuccessfully some behavioural control on the kids. With a sigh, he began his Saturday afternoon task of going through the week's unread papers. Turning the pile face down, he started on the previous Sunday's heavies first. It was towards four o'clock when he turned face-up the final newspaper, that morning's *Western Post*.

At first he gave the front-page story no more than a smirk of mockery at the gullibility of the mass of humankind, but as he was turning the page, a phrase at random caught his eye. He stopped. *At the age of twelve, five years ago to the day, her twin brother Matthew died suddenly . . .*

Five years ago. A boy called Matthew.

Matthew? Could that possibly be the donor's name? The age was right: he'd known that from the size of the organ. The sex was right: he'd told at a glance from the first chromosome spread. But in all other respects he'd only known him as a number.

Where was Coledean, where this girl lived? He rummaged in a drawer and pulled out a map. A flush of sweat prickled his arms. Coledean was just four miles from Dent's Cross.

Five years ago. That made it early March 1981. he stood up and reached for his 1981 diary. He muttered an oath. Of course, his work diaries were back at the lab. But, come to think of it, it *had* been in early March or thereabouts . . . there'd been a sudden, unseasonal freeze, the car wouldn't start, he'd nearly arrived too late, Leonard Grigson had been nervous as hell . . .

He reread the article more carefully, and as he came to the blown-up photo of the girl, something tingled in his veins. He found he couldn't tear his eyes off that face, the face of this girl who had lost a brother exactly five years ago.

A twin brother.

Thirteen

In-two-three-four, out-two-three-four, keep the breathing steady. Shoulders up, chin down, body erect. Pump the knees higher, pick up the feet, push until it hurts and then push harder. Leonard muttered an oath. He hated jogging. Nonsense to say it was good for you. It compressed the spine, it punished the in-step, it jarred the brain around in its sac of fluid and somewhere he'd read it ruined the sex life. (What sex life?) No, he did it because physically he lived too soft. He drove in a comfortable car to an overheated hospital and spent his evenings sitting in plush chairs at restaurants or theatres or at home by the study fire and drinking far too much.

Or maybe because the countryside was just so beautiful, first thing in the morning. He stretched his gaze down the winding lane to the white patchwork quilt of fields rolling far into the distance. The frosty air burned his nostrils and his ankles ached numbly. Perhaps he'd take the short-cut home and sink into a hot bath.

Hearing a car behind him, he automatically took to the narrow grass verge. The car slowed as it grew closer, but instead of overtaking, it changed to a lower gear and slowly drew up on his left side. As he turned, he felt a sudden tightening in his stomach. He knew that pale blue car. And he knew that flattened, balding head and those thick wire-framed glasses.

Tom Welland wound down the window and leant out. His breath smoked on the frozen air.

'Been trying to track you down for days,' he called cheerily. 'You're damn hard to get hold of.'

Leonard carried on without replying or breaking his step.

'Go jogging often?' Welland continued. 'It'll ruin your health. Killed the bloke who invented it.'

'What do you want?' demanded Leonard finally.

'Matthew Holmwood: does that name ring bells?' The scientist followed the bend, keeping alongside. 'You know what I'm asking, Leonard.'

'I can't discuss it.'

'But I need to know. I've got a problem.'

'That's none of my concern,' he retorted, speeding up as the short-cut came into sight.

'My problems are *your* problems, Leonard.'

Leonard shot him a hard glare.

'As far as I'm concerned, there's nothing to talk about.' He grasped the post of the stile and swung himself over. 'Goodbye, Tom.'

He broke into an angry run along the frost-hardened edge of the broad ploughed field, not slackening his pace until he had left the road far behind. God *damn* the man. He joined a bridleway at the far side and followed it through the small wood that stood on a rise above his own house. As he emerged into the open, he caught his foot in a hidden rut and pitched forwards, twisting his ankle, and he had to hobble painfully and slowly all the rest of the way home. With his temper by now at boiling-point, he stumbled in through the ramshackle wooden gate at the foot of the garden and made his way up the side path between the rhododendron bushes and the shuttered summerhouse and round past the old greenhouses to the back door that led into the utility room. Kicking off his track-shoes on the doorstep, he flung the door open and collapsed gratefully against the warm boiler.

A faint aroma of coffee attracted his attention. His heart gave a momentary leap. Laura? Coming in by the back way, he wouldn't have seen her car at the front. He'd taken her out to supper the previous night, and they'd had a lovely time – fun and uncomplicated. Had she dropped in for breakfast? He glanced at his watch. Surely she'd be taking Grace to school. Or was Grace staying away, after that piece in the newspaper? She'd been up in her room when he'd collected Laura. He didn't even know how she'd reacted to his letter yet.

He limped over to the door that led into the kitchen and threw it open, ready with a bright, welcoming smile. His face fell. Over by the range, still wearing his raincoat, stood Tom Welland. Beside him, on the stove, the coffee percolator bubbled away.

'For Christ's sake, Tom!' cried Leonard. 'This is a sodding liberty.'

Welland gave a flattish grin.

'Coffee?'

'Bugger off.'

Unabashed, the man poured two mugs and set them down on the table, then lit a cigarette. He drew up a chair and sat down.

'I was telling you about my problem,' he began chattily. 'There it was, all going along sweetly, no signs of cryogenic distress to the tissue, the first evidence of glucose uptake, when guess what happens.' He sipped his coffee, but behind his thick glasses his eyes didn't move from Leonard's. 'A junction fails and we lose the blood. I retrieve as much as I can, but it has de-oxygenated. It's useless. *Kaput.*'

'I don't want to know —'

'I whip the works straight back in the cryostat, of course, but I'm not about to risk revitalizing it without a guaranteed blood match. Now, as you well know, Leonard, the blood is a rare group. A very rare group.' He lowered his coffee with the same hard smile. 'So you see, when I heard there might be a *twin* involved . . .'

Leonard took a step forward, his fists knotted.

'Get out of my house,' he hissed quietly.

Welland stood up and began backing away towards the door.

'Thanks, Leonard. You've confirmed my hunch.'

'I've confirmed no damn thing. Just get out!'

169

'I'm not asking much, ten or twenty fluid ounces will do, that's all, you can find a way, you know the girl and her family . . .' His voice rose as he grew desperate. By now he was in the hallway and retreating steadily. 'Leonard, I *need* this! The whole project's screwed if I don't get it! You can't back out of it now!'

'*Out!*'

Leonard grabbed him by his raincoat collar and thrust him out through the door, where he fell sprawling onto the gravel. Scrambling around to recover his glasses, the scientist darted to his car like a scalded cat and clambered quickly in. He started it up and revved it wildly.

'Think about it, Leonard,' he yelled out of the window. 'Think about it good and hard.'

Leonard stood in the middle of the drive, his hands hanging by his side in unspent rage, as the car disappeared down the road until gradually the sound of its engine died away out of earshot.

*

'Gloucester Royal Hospital? Records, please.'

Tom Welland drummed his fingers on the phone as he waited to be put through. He glanced around the lab. Above the glass inspection panel the amber radiation warning light was black, and inside the chamber all was dark. He turned round in his swivel chair so that he wouldn't have to be reminded. For the nth time he read through the blood analysis on the print-out in front of him. An extraordinarily rare group. Virtually unmatchable. Damn bad luck.

A woman came on the line, asking if she could help him. He cleared his throat self-importantly.

'Dr Welland here,' he began. 'I'm working with Dr Grigson on a blood-group survey . . . yes, Leonard Grigson . . . and I need to check a small point about a patient you had in here back in March eighty-one.'

'You must know patient files are confidential, Doctor,' came the response. 'We need authorization in writing.'

'I have a photocopy of his blood analysis from the files, but it's come out too dark to read. I wondered if you'd just check the original. I need to confirm the group. Would you please?'

There was a perceptible pause.

'What was the name?' came the hesitant reply.

'Holmwood, spelled H-o-l-m. First name Matthew. Aged twelve. I don't know the date of admission, but the date of decease was 6th March 1981.'

'One moment, please.'

He waited. Down the line he could hear much ruffling of papers. He frowned; it seemed to be taking an unusually long time. Eventually, the woman came back. Her tone sounded puzzled.

'You did say Holmwood, initial M? We have nothing under that name, Doctor.'

'But that's not possible! I know for a fact . . . I mean, I have the copy right here.'

'No Matthew Holmwood listed.'

'There's got to be some mistake.'

'We do have a *G* Holmwood, female, a minor, admitted as an out-patient about that date, but I've got no note of any death.'

He could feel the perspiration breaking out. *Grace!* Could there be a record of *her* blood-group?

'Ah . . . the wretched photocopy . . . I must have misread.' He forced a casual note into his voice. 'Give me what you have, and I'm sure it'll be what I'm after.'

'Hold on.'

She came back after a moment and began reading out the full breakdown of Grace Holmwood's blood composition. He grabbed a sheet of paper and started jotting it down. The further she went, the higher his excitement soared. At the end he thanked her as calmly as he could and replaced the receiver. Numb with astonishment, he sat for a while looking backwards and forwards from his jotted notes on Grace Holmwood to the print-out of the donor's blood profile.

They were identical!

Rising slowly, he went over to the isolation chamber and switched on the lights. Behind the insulating wall stood the cryostat in which the organ now lay, frozen and inert. Reaching his arms into the pair of heavy gloves sealed into the wall that allowed him to work inside the chamber from the outside, he carefully unscrewed the cap of the small stainless-steel cylinder. Liquid nitrogen vapour curled out. Suspended from the centre on a short steel rod hung a small polythene netting sack. He withdrew it a few inches. It resembled a large, dirty snowball, swathed in coils of vapour. After subjecting it to a careful visual scrutiny, he finally slipped it gently back. Then checking the liquid level, he screwed the steel cap back on.

Everything seemed fine. There was a fair chance he'd get it to revitalize, given a perfect blood match. And now he knew where to go for that.

He dialled the Royal Hospital again and asked to be put through to Dr Grigson, but before he was connected he put the phone down. Leonard would only give him the brush-off again. The affair was delicate and confidential, certainly, and it had troubled Leonard's conscience badly enough at the time, but now he seemed, frankly, *nervous*. Had 'the world changed', as he'd said when they'd re-met recently? Or did he have something else to hide, some other secret shame? Or again, had he simply gone soft and moralistic? Welland frowned. Knowledge was power, and in that quarter he was very weak. He'd have to know a lot more before he could confront Grigson again and be sure of screwing out of him what he so desperately needed.

He slipped off his white coat and, reaching for his car keys, headed purposefully for the door.

*

Tom Welland's first call was to the cuttings library at the *Western Post* offices in Gloucester. The room was hot and airless, and the odour of perspiration mingled sourly with the starchy chemical smell of old newsprint. Loosening his tie, he went up to the reception desk where a rabbit-faced man sat pasting cuttings onto filing sheets.

'Excuse me,' he began. 'You had a piece in last week's *Post* on a girl called Grace Holmwood . . .'

'File's out on the tables,' replied the man, returning to his pasting. 'You're the third today.'

The file contained very little. A picture of the father, Alec Holmwood, speaking to a local architectural preservation society. A photo of Grace, aged ten or eleven, pictured with a horse, receiving a rosette for winning some gymkhana event. Next a small item in a long list, recording the funeral of Matthew Holmwood. Then Grace again, this time leading a charity fun-run . . .

A *funeral*?

The significance took a moment to sink in. He whipped back to the previous cutting.

'The funeral of Matthew Francis Holmwood took place on Saturday afternoon at the Church of Our Lady, Coledean . . .'

Had they *buried* the boy? Jesus Christ.

He closed the file very slowly. His mouth was dry and he felt a drumming in his temples. Something was badly amiss here. Either he was tracking the wrong boy, or somebody had made a very serious slip-up indeed.

*

Welland hated churches and especially graveyards. He understood death, and resurrection, better than most, but all this morbid obsession with preserving the dead body, with the name and relatives and expressions of grief recorded on stone, was primitive and barbaric. Life was nothing more than protein synthesis. What made the living body a *person* was merely a particular neuronal firing-pattern. Extinguish that and you extinguished the person. He frowned briefly as he thought of what lay in the cryostat back in the labs, for the corollary must also hold: revitalize the firing-pattern and you resurrected the person.

The small iron gate seemed to be jammed and he followed the rusty railings, looking for an entrance. Eventually he was forced to climb over, taking care not to knock the small black instrument case he was carrying. A sharp wind had risen, rippling restlessly through the straggly grass and whistling in the crumbling stonework of the derelict church. Out of sight behind the building, he opened the case and took out the small aluminium unit. Adjusting the calibrated dial, he briefly passed the base over the face of his watch. *Toc . . . toc . . . toc*, came the rapid chatter. Fine. Stepping out into the churchyard, he began his search for the grave.

He found it in the far corner. A wilting bunch of snow-drops lay at the base of the marble headstone. *In memoriam*, it read, *Matthew Francis Holmwood, aged 12, Departed this life 6th March 1981, Dearly beloved son of Laura and brother of Grace . . . 'Suffer Little Children To Come Unto Me'*

Holding the instrument at arm's length, he carefully swept the ground surrounding the grave, then he ran it over the grave itself, as close as he could.

Nothing. Not a single click.

He stood back. Thank God for that: someone had had the sense to take precautions. Or did it still mean he was following the wrong trail? Deep in thought, he retraced his steps to the spot where he'd left the case and packed it carefully up. Huddling deeper into his overcoat against the biting wind, he climbed back over the railings and hurried off to his car, glancing about him as he went to make sure he had come and gone unobserved.

*

An invisible choir sang celestial music in the background, and against the wall, framed by purple curtains and lit as if from some supernatural source, stood a vase with a large display of plastic orchids. Behind the desk sat the funeral director, a robust man with a complexion reddened by drink, working his way through the dusty pages of an old ledger-book. Welland sat opposite, a shorthand notebook poised in the manner of the newspaper reporter he was purporting to be.

Eventually the undertaker stubbed a finger at an entry.

'Ah, here we are,' he said. A frown furrowed his heavy brow. 'Funny, I don't seem to have a record of charging for a coffin.' Then his face lit up. 'I remember now. It came all ready sealed. Only a young kid, but did it weigh a ton! Must have been solid teak. For a child's interment it's usually just me and my partner do the necessary. I had to get a couple of the lads to lend a hand.'

Welland made a pretence of writing a note in his pad, but his mind was racing.

'Ready sealed?' he echoed. 'So you didn't get a look inside? I mean, the body wasn't put on show?'

The man winced.

'We respect the wishes of the family,' he replied piously, then added in a more confidential tone, 'Mind you, the state of some of the post-mortem cases, it's just as well.'

Welland slipped the pad in his pocket.

'Just one more thing,' he said rising. 'You don't happen to have a note who did supply the coffin?'

The undertaker shook his head.

'It came in a white van. I remember thinking, "That's not showing much respect". Anyway, they were come and gone before you could say "spade".' He chuckled, a hoarse, wheezing sound. 'Anything else I can do for you?'

'No thanks,' said Welland. 'You've been most helpful.'

In the street outside the small prefabricated funeral parlour he paused for a moment in thought. Four men to carry the coffin of a child of twelve? A *sealed* coffin? Suddenly he understood. Thumping his fist into his palm, he turned and headed off smartly towards his car.

He had the answer. His hunch *had* been right.

*

175

He had to finish off some routine lab work he'd been neglecting, and it was several days before he had time to take a proper close look at his target.

At the edge of Coledean village stood the remains of a railway bridge. Though the arch had been dismantled, the sturdy brick piers still stretched back up the embankment on either side, providing perfect cover. From where he was parked, tucked in tight behind a pier, he could see the driveway entrance to the mill house. Shortly before eight o'clock on a bright, sharp morning, he took up his position. From an attaché-case he took out a camera and, screwing in a 200mm telephoto lens, rested it on the dashboard. Sighting through the viewfinder, he focused on the signboard COLEDEAN MILL, then sat back to wait.

Cars passed at irregular intervals: a school bus, gravel lorries, telephone engineers' vans. Eventually he saw movement down the winding drive and a green Volvo estate car appeared at the entrance, stopped, then pulled away down the road. As it passed he swivelled the camera round and continued shooting. Through the image-finder he caught a brief glimpse of a slim woman with short greying dark hair at the wheel and, beside her, a pretty, smiling girl with a long blonde pony-tail before the car vanished around a bend.

He looked at the dashboard clock. Having timed the journey to the convent in Abbotsbury and back, he reckoned he had a good forty minutes clear. Steeling his nerve he started up the car, drew out into the road and, fifty yards further on, pulled over into the mill drive.

*

He parked facing the exit and left the keys in the ignition. The garage was empty and there was no sign of anyone in the studio outbuildings. His collar turned up against the wind, he hurried up to the front door and rang the bell. No-one answered. With a glance around to make sure he was alone, he went to the window and, cupping his hand against the glass, peered in. It was a small, book-lined study, quite empty. He moved on round, following a tall yew hedge to a small iron gate that led into the garden.

Through a tall window at the side of the house he looked in on a large living-room, with rough stone walls, polished oak furniture, faded rugs and soft leather chairs. Above ran a gallery evidently made from old church fittings. He carried on round until he came to the back door. He rang the bell, but still no response. His pulse pounding furiously, he tried the door handle. It was locked. Was there a key hidden somewhere? He looked in the small shed nearby; he ran his finger along the lintel, upended flower-pots and searched beneath seed-trays and pieces of sacking, but without success. He was about to give up when he noticed, just beside the back door itself, a sheet of slate covering a drain. Underneath lay a key.

Cautiously, he let himself in. For a moment he stood listening, but apart from the constant rush of the mill stream still audible indoors, all was silent. His hand was shaking; he wasn't in the lab now – this was someone's home and he didn't belong here. What was he after? He didn't quite know. He slipped through into the main living-room. Magazines and books lay scattered on a low table in front of the sofa, dusted with the pollen from a vase of overblown anemones. He crossed to the sideboard. Decanters, coasters, a wine cooler, a phone whose number he mentally recorded, an engraved silver tray . . . nothing useful there. He opened a drawer. Among the place-mats and napkin-rings, an object folded neatly in tissue-paper caught his eye. It was a silver cigarette-case, inscribed, *To Laura, with all my love, Leonard.* He glanced quickly around the room; there were no ashtrays to be seen. Presumably she'd given up smoking . . .

And then the implications hit him. *With all my love . . .* Leonard was in love with the girl's mother! *That* was how his world had changed, and that was what he was so desperate to protect.

On a shelf beneath he spotted a photo album. Pulling it out, he rapidly skimmed through the pages. Holidays by the sea, birthday parties, boating trips. And then he found confirmation: a snap of the three of them – Leonard, Laura and Grace – laughing and drinking at a restaurant, evidently on holiday abroad. This was Leonard's *family*!

Suddenly the phone at his elbow rang. He jumped so violently that he nearly dropped the album. A swelter of terror gripped him. With a quick movement, he ripped out the photo and jammed the album back on the shelf, then hurried back across the living-room, through the kitchen and out of the house. There he slipped the key back under the slate, glanced to check the shed door was shut and made off round the side of the house, through the iron gate and across the gravel drive to his car. He tore away down the drive and out through the village, not looking to right or left until he was a good five miles clear. Only then did he slow down and pull off the road. He stumbled out of the car and, doubling up, retched emptily into the hedgerow. After a while he slowly straightened and drew in deep gulps of the pure, crisp air. Still shaking in every nerve, he took out the photo and examined it more carefully.

At last he had the key to Leonard.

Fourteen

'*Benedictus benedicatur, per Jesum Christum, Dominum nostrum.*'

'*Amen.*'

Lunch was over, and the large, whitewashed refectory suddenly exploded with the noise of scraping chairs and the chatter of a hundred excitable voices.

Emily turned to Grace and pulled a face.

'Let's get something decent to eat.'

'We don't have time.'

'Course we do. Come on.'

Grace followed her friend out into the bright, cold sunshine and headed off at a jog down the tree-lined drive. They were due on the hockey pitch in twenty minutes. She broke into a run as they approached the convent gates and, darting across the road, raced Emily to the small mini-market a few hundred yards away.

Inside, she flew around the shelves, grabbing packets of potato crisps and bars of chocolate. She was opening the fridge cabinet for a can of Coke when she caught a glimpse of a figure reflected in the glass door. As she turned, she shrank back with an involuntary gasp. Close behind her, watching her intently, stood a man. He wore a stained cable-knit jersey beneath a torn donkey-jacket, and greasy dark hair, parted in the centre, fell in hanks down to his shoulders. But it was his face that gave her a jolt of horror. Every inch of his skin was knobbled with wens and boils. Grabbing the drink, she hurried to join Emily at the checkout. She paid quickly and ran out into the street.

The woman on the till had recognized her, and Emily

skipped alongside, laughing and teasing her that she was a star. They hadn't gone far when she became aware of foot-steps behind them. She turned. It was the man from the shop, following them. A few yards away, he stretched out a leprous hand. His eyes pierced hers with a terrible pleading.

'Stop!' he gasped. 'Wait!'

Smothering a shudder, she slowed down. Emily had seen, too, but she tugged at her arm, dragging her on.

'You're *her*, aren't you?' rasped the man. 'The girl who heals people.' He was almost touching her now. His out-stretched hand looked like a boiled toad. 'Help me.'

Emily tugged her sharply out of his reach.

'Go away!' she hissed violently.

But the man continued coming on. People were turning to stare.

'You can cure me,' he was saying. 'I know you can. Stop a minute!'

Grace shot Emily a helpless glance.

'The poor man, surely we can . . . ?'

'Come *on!*'

Dragged away, she struggled to free herself, but the man was already giving up, and by the time they'd reached the convent gates he'd come to a halt. Raising both hands he let out a terrible howl.

'Bitch!' he screamed. 'Prig! Running away like all the rest! You can't stand to look at me! You could pray for me, you could heal me, but you won't! You're all shit, all of you!'

Weeping and hysterical, Grace stumbled inside the con-vent gates. She turned to catch one final, indelible image of the man as he staggered back against the railings, his blotched face contorted with despair and a long, agonized cry wrench-ing from his throat. A sudden wave of giddiness swept over her and she clutched frantically at Emily's arm. The world was spinning about her. She was screaming inside and no-one could hear. She was panting for air but she was suffocating. A vicious stabbing pain slashed her low in the stomach. The sky was growing dark. Everything was dissolving. Her legs were buckling under her. Stars appeared everywhere, spinning round and round, faster and faster, and then suddenly . . . blackness.

*

Father Gregory put the phone down and turned to Grace.

'Your mother's on her way.' He paused. 'How are you feeling now?'

'Better, thank you, Father.'

'Keep that rug tucked round you. You may look like a geriatric in a bathchair, but you've got to keep warm.' He brought the teapot over and refilled her mug; tea dribbled down the spout onto the carpet, but he didn't seem to notice. 'Make sure you get Dr Stimpson to look at you. It might be appendicitis.'

'It's all right, it's gone now. Just a pain like . . . well, you know.'

She'd fainted just outside the lodge-house and Emily had rushed in to fetch Father Gregory. The crisis had passed, but she still felt weak and queasy. She glanced around the room with its single fireside chair, its single place-setting laid for a single supper by one of the Sisters. She shivered as the sound of that man's abuse rang in her ears, and she felt the weight of his curse upon her shoulders. At least the Sisters were secure within their cloister, safe from men like that.

He drew up a chair and reached forward for her hand. His eyes were tender with sympathy.

'I understand, my dear,' he said quietly. 'It's all terribly distressing for you. But God knows best. If He'd wanted you to help that man, He would have shown you the way.'

'I suppose so, Father.' She frowned. 'But I wish everyone didn't expect me to *do* things. To be something I'm not.'

'Blessings don't come without their responsibilities,' he replied gently. 'You do have a certain duty to people now, Grace, and you must learn to cope with it. It won't go away.'

'I didn't ask for it.'

181

'Maybe not. But now you have it, think of all the hope you can bring to people.'

'I destroyed that man's hope.'

'Grace, listen,' he said firmly. 'Don't go on questioning. If we had the answers, there'd be no mystery. And it *has* to be a mystery.'

She nodded but remained silent. She was so tired of the debate. Father Gregory thought he understood, but he didn't really. He was like the rest, stuck in his particular rut. For him, the key to everything was mystery; for Leo, it was reason. But the whole thing was not about this principle or that: it was about *people*. People like that poor disfigured man. People like Mary, once cast aside as a useless blind old woman but now sought after as a miracle. People, too, like herself, treated as a symbol rather than the person she really was.

Father Gregory was holding her gaze.

'Well?' he enquired.

'I suppose you're right, Father,' she conceded, exhausted.

*

Her stomach pains returned at home and she spent the evening curled up double on the sofa, nursing a hot water bottle. She went to bed early, and first thing in the morning Dr Stimpson came by to visit. The pain had subsided during the night, but the doctor still insisted on examining her. He stood beside the bed, probing her bare stomach with his cold fingers. After a while, he stood back with a puzzled frown.

'Been putting on weight recently?' he asked.

'I don't know. Well, yes, maybe. I've got a bit of a crush on chocolates.'

'When was your last period, Grace?'

'Can't remember. I'm not exactly regular. Is something wrong?'

Instead of replying, he took out a small plastic phial from his bag and handed it to her.

'Slip along to the bathroom and give me a sample, will you? Mid-flow, please. If you get me.'

'I can imagine,' she replied with a small shudder.

In the bathroom, she stepped quickly onto the scales. Yes, she was a few pounds over. Had she got some awful internal growth? Her mind flashed back to the man who had accosted her the day before. She saw it in everything – in the mottled lino on the bathroom floor, in the woodchip paper on the ceiling, in the bubbles that formed on the inside of her toothmug. Had the man stricken her with his curse? She splashed water over her face and, reaching for a towel, buried her face in its soft nap. She felt sick. She was going mad.

Finally she made her way back to her bedroom, feeling more composed. Mum had now arrived and was talking in a hushed, urgent tone with the doctor. Their conversation stopped abruptly as she walked in.

'Something *is* wrong, isn't it?' she persisted.

'Nonsense,' replied her mother. 'Dr Stimpson says you can go to school, only you shouldn't play games or exert yourself.'

The doctor gave her a false, morale-boosting smile.

'That's right. Just take things gently.'

He broke off, and a brief, uneasy silence fell. Grace felt a stab of anger: did they have to treat her like a child not to be entrusted with the truth? But a moment later he began gathering up his bag and Mum started talking away, and everything went back to normal. He repeated his strictures against playing sports and climbed into his overcoat, while Mum thanked him, telling him not to forget his gloves, then saw him downstairs and finally ushered him out of the house.

With a sigh, Grace went to the chest of drawers and chose a clean blouse. She could hear the radio on in the kitchen below; she'd better go down and help with the breakfast, while doing her bit to pretend that nothing was the matter.

*

Laura was airbrushing in a sky when the phone rang. She let it ring for the machine to pick up and continued the delicate work of spraying on the paint so that it made a seamless gradient from the lightest cobalt on the horizon to the deepest indigo at the top. The moment she heard the doctor's voice over the machine, she stiffened.

'Laura, this is John Stimpson. I have the test results on Grace. I think you should call me right away. You can reach me for the next hour on —'

Laura had already put down the airbrush and hurried across to the phone.

'I'm here, John,' she said. 'What's wrong?'

She stood stupefied as the doctor gave her his diagnosis.

'But that's not possible!' she gasped. 'Not *Grace*. She's too young. She has never . . . well, she never *would* . . . I mean, who could it be?'

'I'm sorry, Laura,' came the reply, 'but the results are here in black and white.'

'There's been a mix-up! You've been given someone else's.'

'That's simply not possible.'

'Then there's something wrong with the test.'

'A false negative is possible, but never a false positive. No, the result is absolutely clear, I'm afraid. Now, what concerns me is *Grace*. I think I should come over and discuss it with you. Hello? Laura? Are you there?'

It was a long time before she could trust her voice to reply.

'Whenever you like, John,' she said in a half whisper.

Replacing the receiver, she went back to her board and stood staring dumbly at her day's work. The paint was drying in irregular patches, ringed with hard edges that would be impossible to remove. Distantly she knew she'd have to scrap it, but she couldn't focus on anything except the appalling, inconceivable news the doctor had given her. She shut her eyes tight and winced with pain. She could never have foreseen this. Never, in her wildest imaginings. Not *this*.

What should she do? Returning to the phone, she picked it up and dialled Father Gregory.

*

Grace opened her bedroom door quietly and stood for a moment listening to check all was clear. The central heating was coming on and the ancient wooden boards creaked and cracked, making sounds like human footfalls. She glanced down into the living-room below, lit by a glimmer of cold dawn light; on the low table stood the empty mugs of Ovaltine over which she and Mum had sat for hours, going over the same ground time and again. She looked away, feeling again the stab of despair: however hard she'd protested her innocence, her own mother would not believe her.

Careful to avoid the boards she knew were loose, she tiptoed down the landing to the bathroom. Locking herself in, she bent down to the cupboard under the basin and retrieved from the depths the small square carton marked 'Predictor' she'd hidden. She undid the packet and read the instruction pamphlet carefully.

For half an hour, she sat on the edge of the bath, waiting for the result. She gave it another five minutes, then a further five. Finally, sick with dread, she went over to the small clear plastic cube sitting on the washstand.

There it was: a dark brown circle the size of the pupil of an eye, ringed with thinner bands of pale brown, standing out clear and distinct against the pale yellow background.

She let out a choking cry. Frantically she looked from the image in the mirror to the instructions pamphlet and back again, but there was absolutely no doubt. She clutched the side of the basin. It wasn't possible, it couldn't be! She hadn't been with anyone. Never!

But somehow it was true. She was pregnant.

Fifteen

'Grace?' repeated Laura. 'Answer me, darling. I was asking you a question.'

Grace pushed away her bowl of cereal uneaten and hung her head in silence, hiding her tearful face behind a curtain of hair.

My poor darling girl, thought Laura. They'd just begun to cope with life as it was, and now *this* had to happen. Grace was only making it worse for herself by blocking it out. She was shutting her eyes to reality, just as she had done after Matthew died. The simple fact was that she was carrying a child, and no amount of saying it was impossible would make it go away. Every day it would become more obvious, and sooner or later she'd have to face up to it. They had a new life to think of now, a life that should be wanted and cherished, not shunned and disowned. Laura sighed. What could she do? Just carry on as normal and hope that eventually, with love and understanding, the girl would trust herself enough to admit the truth.

She poured a glass of milk and passed it across the table.

'At least drink this,' she said. 'You need your strength. It takes a lot out of you.' Unable to bear seeing her in such pain, she reached out and squeezed her hand. 'We'll make the best of it, darling, I promise. I've been thinking. You'll have to take the summer term off, but you can sit your A levels again next year. If you got into Bristol I could drive you in every day from here, or maybe you'll have your licence by then, either way we'll get a nanny to look after the child during the day – I don't see why she shouldn't live in, in fact she could have the spare room, there's a bathroom just next door, and the baby could be in Matthew's old room . . .'

Grace withdrew her hand.

'Don't go on, Mum.'

'But we need to get organized. Then I was thinking about Mary. She'd love to come and help.' She hesitated for a moment. Could Mary be the child's *grandmother*? 'Anyway,' she continued quickly, 'a place this size needs a proper family. Children make a place a home.'

She stopped and poured herself another cup of coffee. The implications were, frankly, terrible. Grace was only *seventeen*! What future, what career, what *life* could she have, handicapped at such an early age by the responsibility of a child?

She looked down into her cup, stung with guilt. It was *her* fault. She'd brought Grace up too innocently. Years before, she'd taken her on one side and talked about the facts of life and taking precautions; Grace had known it all already and seemed uninterested anyway. Maybe it had been wrong to bring up a girl in the company only of her mother. For *her* sake, she should have remarried. Why had she always kept Leonard at arm's length? She'd always told herself it was because no man could ever live up to Alec and she could never hope to match what they'd had together, and, in Leonard's case, there was a fundamental difference in religious outlook, but wasn't it really because she was afraid of making a commitment again? She'd lost her husband and her son, and she was clinging onto her daughter in this suffocating, isolated, hot-house atmosphere for fear of losing her as well. *She* should face up to reality, too. At root, *she* was responsible for the girl's predicament.

Grace had got up. Laura reached out a hand, but she brushed past.

'I'll phone and say you're sick,' she offered.

'Doesn't matter,' came the dull reply.

'And we'll go for a drive somewhere and sort it out

properly, like adults. I'll take you out to lunch, what do you say?'

'It's *okay*, Mum,' mumbled Grace and left the room.

She stared at the door after her. Everything was careering out of control and she couldn't handle it any more. She needed help from someone who really knew, someone she could really trust. As soon as she got back from the school, she'd call Leonard.

*

Father Gregory sat on the edge of the hard school bench, waiting for Grace's reply. He glanced briefly around the empty classroom, at the desks stained with ink and carved with initials, at the walls exhibiting a nature study project and the blackboard conjugating French irregular verbs. He looked back at the abject, silent girl and repeated his question.

'So tell me how *you* explain it, then.'

'I don't *know*, Father,' replied Grace, scuffing her shoe on the floor.

'Grace, you are putting me in a very difficult position,' he began again. 'I've supported you all along, I've backed your word, I've given you my trust. You owe me a straight answer.'

She looked up, her eyes red-rimmed and her lip quivering.

'I've told you the truth, Father. I can't *make* you believe me.'

He leaned closer. In the distance he could hear the bell ringing for the end of break; any minute the others would come back in and he'd have to take her off to see Monsignor Rolfe without any notion of what he was going to say by way of explanation.

'I know you're telling the truth as far as you see it,' he responded with growing urgency. 'But I don't think you realize how easily these things *develop*. What starts off as perfectly innocent fun and games can go much further before you know it. Things can happen without *realizing*.'

She cast him an impatient, scornful look.

'Do credit me with some wit, Father,' she cried. 'I'd know if I'd got myself into that kind of situation, and I haven't. I haven't been anywhere near anyone. I haven't even kissed a boy.'

Father Gregory felt the force of the lie as though it struck him a physical blow.

'That's not true, Grace,' he said quietly. 'I saw you with Benedict on the doorstep of his house.'

'When?'

'A while ago, when Mary was poorly.'

'Oh, then! He was very upset, that's all. Anyway, I often hug Ben. He's my friend.'

He leaned closer. The first footsteps were approaching far down the corridor.

'Grace, are you asking me to believe you have never been with . . . had intercourse with . . . anyone, ever?' He pulled out a small Bible from his jacket pocket and pressed it into her hand. 'Swear to me! Swear on the Book!'

She turned aside, her whole body screwed up with pain. He leaned closer still so that his face was almost touching hers.

'Lie,' he hissed, 'and you'll be in a state of mortal sin.'

For a split second they sat facing one another, frozen in a silence like the silence between lightning and the thunderclap. Then she grabbed the book and rounded on him, ablaze with fury and conviction.

'I swear!' she blurted out. 'I swear on Our Lady and all that's most holy! *I swear I haven't been with anyone!*'

A cold shiver ran through his veins. He recoiled, trembling.

'God have mercy upon us,' he muttered quickly and made the sign of the Cross.

She thrust the Bible back at him and stood up with a scornful glare. Then, with dignity, she turned and moved towards the door just as the first of her classmates came running in.

'Don't let's keep the Monsignor waiting,' she said tartly and led the way out of the room.

*

Laura reached for the bottle of Frascati and refilled Leonard's glass. For a moment he did not reply but sat with a closed, set expression, steadily pulverizing a breadstick on his plate. The trattoria reverberated with lunchtime clamour – waiters calling out orders, cutlery clattering on crockery, sudden bursts of laughter rising from this table or that – but she barely heard any of it. His silence puzzled her. Surely he didn't have to *think* about it.

'Well?' she prompted. 'It's not physically possible, is it?'

He lifted his eyes and smiled briefly.

'Snails can. So can greenfly. And some lizards. Even turkeys, I believe. To a limited extent.'

'*Leonard,*' she reproved.

'All right, Parthenogenesis – virgin birth – is impossible for humans. It takes two to tango. Although, theoretically,' he mused into his wine glass, 'I suppose it's conceivable, in that the human ovum contains exactly half the genetic material required to make a complete person. You could imagine an egg that failed to divide during meiosis. Or two that somehow got fused together in the ovaries.' He looked up. 'But then, we're in the real world. If it could happen, it would have. There are three thousand million people on this planet, and there's never been one single authenticated case of virgin birth. Well,' he corrected himself with another brief smile, 'there was just one. Two thousand years ago.'

'Our Lord?'

'Although, by rights, he should have been a woman.'

'What do you mean?'

'The offspring from a virgin birth can only ever be female. In the egg, both the sex chromosomes are Xs – female – and you need an XY to make a male. The fact that Christ was male rather suggests that Joseph had something to do with

190

it.' He held up his hand and added sardonically, 'But then that's what makes it a miracle, isn't it?'

She shifted uncomfortably in her seat. The restaurant was hot and the noise level seemed to be rising. She was finding it difficult to separate the different strands of the problem in her mind.

'But why won't she admit it?' she said eventually. 'Who is she trying to protect? It's not like Grace to tell serious lies. I really don't know what to do, Leonard. I'm at my wits' end.'

'Perhaps she genuinely can't remember,' he suggested calmly. 'The experience was so traumatic that she has suppressed it. It happens in rape cases: the victim sometimes denies it actually took place, despite all the evidence, because psychologically she can't *afford* to admit its reality.'

She nodded slowly. This lined up with her own theory.

'They'll use this as ammunition,' she said, more to herself.

'Delusional identification with the Virgin Mary,' he agreed, understanding she was referring to the Church. 'An hysteric doesn't make a good candidate for a holy visionary. Still, she'd be better off if they threw the case out, whatever the grounds. Look at what the poor girl's going through, day after day.'

'Leonard, you'll never understand what it *means* to a Catholic.'

For a moment she felt the gulf between them was unbridgeable. Was this why she'd never really contemplated sharing her life with him? They stood on opposite sides of the street, seeing different faces of the same things passing by between them.

The waiter brought coffee and the bill on a saucer. She reached out and put down a credit card.

'Mine,' she smiled. 'For the consultation.'

But he was toying with his glass, a thoughtful frown on his face.

'I don't think we've talked about the real problem, Laura,' he said after a while. 'Grace is far too young to have a baby.'

'Yes, but it's no use trying to wish it away.' Suddenly she caught the meaning behind his expression. She drew in her breath sharply. 'Absolutely *not*, Leonard!'

'Look,' he said more urgently, leaning forward, 'if she goes ahead with it, think how it'll blight her life! It'll ruin her career. She'll never make it to university. She'll just be yet another single-parent tragedy. Even suppose the father comes out of the woodwork, then what? My guess is that'd only make it worse. Laura, be *sensible*. Think what she's letting herself in for.'

'How can you say that – you, a doctor! Dr Stimpson thinks she's four months gone. We're talking of a fully formed human being. A human *life*.'

'For God's sake, Laura, what about *her* life? She's got another twenty-five childbearing years – plenty more chances for having kids, but only one chance for her education. Surely you aren't really going to let her go through with it?'

'Life starts at conception. Even you admit it's a human being after fourteen days. Abortion is murder.'

'At least let's get her an amniocentesis.'

'What for?'

'In case . . . well, suppose there's something wrong with the foetus.' He was noticeably flustered now. 'Suppose it's deformed, or has some congenital defect . . .'

'What, and murder it *then*?'

'Spare it the misery. You'd do so with an animal.'

'We are *not* animals, Leonard! Animals don't have *souls*. Children with disabilities may not live so long, but they can be given happy, loving lives. It's their right, and you or I can't deprive them of that right just because we'd rather do without the inconvenience or the unsightliness.'

'But think of Grace. Spare *her*.'

An uneasy feeling was creeping into her mind. Why was he assuming something would be wrong?

'Disabled children give their parents a lot of happiness in return. A chance to show selfless love.' She glared at him. 'You think that society shouldn't waste its limited resources

192

on these cases. Well, look at what good they can do for society. I know of a man born with congenital syphilis. You'd probably have given the mother an amnio and had the thing terminated. That man's name was Beethoven.' She paused to collect herself. 'Anyway, I don't know why we're talking like this. Grace's child is going to be fine. Why shouldn't it be?'

'I'm sure it will be,' he persisted, 'but there's just a chance. An amnio would tell, that's all.'

A tense, deadlocked silence fell. They'd come full circle. There was nothing more to say. You either believed the unborn child was a gift from God, that its life was God's to give and to take away, or you saw the world as one vast farmyard where people were merely superior animals whose lives were commodities to be traded, to be given or taken according to other people's convenience and self-interest. She felt sorry for Leonard. Believing in nothing beyond material expediency must be very bleak and comfortless. Was such a man, who'd never known Divine love, really capable of human love?

He'd reached out for her hand.

'Sorry,' he said simply. 'I'm desperately worried for her, that's all.'

She squeezed his hand back with a flush of tenderness. Of course he was capable of love.

'I know. Thank you, Leonard. We may disagree, but I always know you care.'

*

Leonard stood at the hospital entrance watching the Volvo disappear down the sweeping drive-up. He was back to square one. All the anxiety that had lifted with Mary's recovery and the reassurance that the drug actually worked had returned with a vengeance.

Grace was *pregnant. Christ!* How the hell had she got herself in that mess? Goodness knew what the hormonal changes of pregnancy might do to the *other thing*, now apparently dormant for these past months. If it provoked a relapse, if it triggered off a fresh onset of the hallucinations, what on earth would he do? Cytosuppressin was a tumour-shrinking drug and, as such, far too dangerous to administer to a pregnant girl. His safety-net was quite useless. Behind his anxiety, too, he recognized a strange twinge of hurt. Somehow she'd always been a child in his mind, pure and virginal . . . He turned abruptly and strode off down the corridor. Such thoughts were absurd. He was feeling the pain of a rejected father. No, of a rejected *lover*.

Laura said she'd vehemently denied having been with a boy. Naturally she would. But to suggest for a second that she had conceived without intercourse was lunacy. Laura was in danger of becoming affected by the collective madness. They'd seen one miracle and were thirsty for another. She'd told him that the Monsignor had arranged an appointment for Grace with a gynaecologist for an internal examination. The poor girl, what would she make of that? What would *they*, for that matter? To be medically intact didn't necessarily mean the conception was parthenogenetic: there were plenty of cases on record of fertilization taking place with a maidenhead intact. Equally, with an athletic girl such as Grace, who especially loved horse-riding, a broken hymen didn't necessarily mean intercourse *had* taken place. Typical papist quackery, he thought. They'd subject the girl to a humiliating physical examination, all for a result that would tell them nothing anyway. They might as well go back to the ducking-stool.

But the really terrifying question was not so much about Grace as about the *child*. There it lay inside her even now, clusters of billions of cells relentlessly dividing and replicating, growing irreversibly towards term, and only he with his particular knowledge of all that had happened in the past could ask with any serious basis for doubt, *Would it be normal?*

He carried on down the corridor towards the hospital library. With a deepening sense of dread he entered the small, cramped room and stood for a moment, puzzling out how to tackle the problem. The whole point was there had never been any research on second-generation effects. Where the hell should he begin? With the Hiroshima cases?

*

Grace stumbled to the top of the ploughed field and collapsed, breathless, on the grass verge by the barbed-wire fence. Below her the ground fell away in a broad sweep down to the river. She let her gaze follow the silver ribbon of water, lost here and found again there, cutting its way through lower-lying fields, criss-crossed with short, bristly hedgerows that separated the grass from the winter corn. The river disappeared briefly behind the mill house, reappearing further down in a fast, frothing weir, below which it eased into a wide, sinuous meander. From the mill chimney a thin coil of smoke rose almost invisibly into the sharp, bright sky. Already the afternoons were perceptibly lengthening, and on the still air, echoed in the chatter of birds from the copse behind her, floated the scent of spring with all its hopes and promises. She traced the line of the drive to the point where it met the road and wondered if the black car with the photographers was still there. She'd been walking down the drive when one of them jumped out of a hedge and began taking photographs. She'd turned and walked away with as much dignity as she could muster, but the moment she was out of sight she'd broken into a run and fled all the way up here without stopping.

Gradually, as she regained her breath, she began to feel calmer. Here, away from everybody, she could be herself. She wished she could stay here all her life and never have to face anyone again. If she had to go back, she'd die.

She put her head in her hands and let out a long, racking sob. She *hadn't* been with anyone. No-one would believe her. They called for an explanation, but she couldn't give one. She really had no idea how it had happened, no idea at all. Was it some Divine favour, and had the visitations

195

been some kind of Annunciation? Or was it more likely a trick, and she was carrying the Devil's child, the progeny of some terrible incubus that had possessed her in her sleep? She shuddered violently. She'd get rid of it. She'd stab it out with knitting-needles, she'd drown it with gin and hot baths, and then she'd kill herself.

As she sat staring out at the fields below, she felt lonelier than ever before in her life. There was no-one she could trust and no-one who would trust her. She couldn't even trust herself. Pulling the hood of her anorak over her head, she curled into a foetal crouch and prayed that she would dwindle to nothing and the rich, dark earth would swallow her up.

*

Benedict hesitated at the edge of the field and stood indecisively for a moment, looking at the figure of the girl curled up on the ground a short distance ahead. Was she ill or in pain? He took a step forward, then halted. She hadn't turned up at the stables that morning. Mrs Holmwood had told him curtly that she'd gone out and wanted to be left alone, but he'd tracked her up here. As he stood watching, she stirred with a low groan. She looked more sad than in pain. What was wrong? He wanted more than anything to take her in his arms and comfort her, as she had done to him when he'd been in such sorrow. Perhaps she really did want to be left alone, though. Better not to intrude.

Without a sound, he turned and, slipping over the stile, made his way back across the deep-furrowed fields towards the village.

Sixteen

'His Lordship will see you now, Father.'

Father Gregory rose and, tucking his document folder under his arm, followed the old manservant across the library, across a withdrawing room, through a small ante-chamber and into an elegant, book-lined study. The Bishop was at his desk. He looked up, his quick, handsome features flashing a smile of welcome. Laying down his pen, he rose from his tall-backed chair and stepped forward. Father Gregory was bending to kiss his ring when he noticed Monsignor Rolfe standing silently over by the window, half hidden against a dark brocade curtain. The Monsignor gave him a slow, expressionless nod.

'Come and sit down, Father,' the Bishop was saying, ushering him to a chintz suite beside the fire. 'This is an informal chat, not *ex cathedra* as it were.' He smiled again, showing a perfect set of teeth. 'Will you care for a glass of sherry? Jerome, do the honours, would you?'

Father Gregory sat down and tried to respond in like vein to the Bishop's light-hearted badinage. He felt awkward, conscious that his trousers were too short and his shoes were probably muddying the Persian hearthrug. When the sherry arrived, the pleasantries came to an end.

'I must commend you for your diligence, Father,' said the Bishop. 'I have been reading your reports with great interest. You write with such passion. This girl and her case are very close to your heart, are they not?'

'I've known Grace all her life,' he replied. 'She's an honest, responsible girl, and brought up as a good Catholic.'

'Passion can blur one's judgement, however. And judgement, above all, is what we need here. Judgement and objectivity.'

'Of course, my Lord, it's not for me to judge how the Church will acknowledge her . . .'

The Bishop's smile had vanished.

'You misunderstand me, Father,' he said evenly. 'There can be *no* question of any formal acknowledgement.'

'But surely the doctor's report *proved —*'

Monsignor Rolfe interrupted quietly from across the room.

'Grace Holmwood may be *virgo intacta*,' he said. 'That does not imply a *conceptio virginis*.'

'But taken with all the other facts of the case,' protested Father Gregory. 'The visions of Our Lady . . .'

'Delusions of a disturbed adolescent,' responded the Monsignor.

'. . . the miracle of Mary Nolan . . .'

'Our doctors are still investigating that, but even if a miracle is confirmed, who is to say it was wrought through this girl rather than through the woman's own faith?'

Father Gregory looked from one man to the other. In their closed faces he could read closed minds. This latest and most startling revelation about Grace might well destroy her credibility at a stroke; on the other hand, it might be further evidence of Divine intervention. He felt less sure than before of the answer, and he was prepared to face disappointment, but at least he was trying to keep an open mind. Of Grace herself, however, he *was* sure.

'But Grace is not lying!' he persisted. 'She wouldn't, she *couldn't*. She swore to me, on the Bible.'

The Bishop spread his hands with a sad helplessness.

'I'm sure she's not lying *deliberately*, Father. She is simply the victim of self-delusion. This latest absurd business clearly proves it. Not content with merely seeing Our Lady, she now has to become *like* Our Lady. Apart from the grotesque blasphemy, such a claim is quite ridiculous. Why *her*, why *now*, why *here*? Are we to suppose that this Grace Holmwood has been chosen to bear – what? – Our Lord Christ in His Second Coming? Quite unthinkable! It would make an utter mockery of the Church. And it shows up the rest of her claims for what they are.' He shook his head. 'The mystery of the Virgin Birth is the coping-stone of our faith. One coping-stone is quite enough. But destroy it and the whole edifice collapses.'

'But, my Lord . . .'

'Your job now, Father, is to contain the situation. We will have to be seen to be continuing the investigation, naturally, but in due course a formal ruling will be issued. In the meantime, we must do everything possible to limit public interest in the affair. This is where your contribution is vital, Father. You know the local scene. Speak to the girl's mother and her friends, have a quiet word with this Mary Nolan and a few of the key tongue-waggers in the village. Jerome will take care of the convent; he has already spoken to Reverend Mother. As for the press, the chairman of the *Western Post* has been seeking my help in arranging an audience with His Holiness the Pope in Rome . . .'

Father Gregory sat on the edge of his chair, unable to believe what he was hearing.

'Wait a minute!' he broke in. 'This is not giving her a fair hearing! You've made up your minds. You *want* to throw her claim out!'

The Bishop shot the Monsignor a swift, almost puzzled glance, as if he, in turn, was unable to believe what he was hearing. Then his former smile returned. He signalled for more sherry and sat back.

'My dear Father Gregory,' he said expansively. 'A man of the cloth must also be a man of the world.'

'I would hope a man of the truth, too.'

The Bishop turned to the Monsignor.

'Jerome,' he said wearily, 'explain to our innocent friend.'

Monsignor Rolfe took up his position in front of the fire. A strange brilliance entered his eyes.

'The Church is at war, Father,' he began. 'At war with

hostile ideologies – materialism, Marxism, humanism, not to mention other faiths. The truth may be ours, but truth doesn't triumph just by itself. It needs encouragement.'

'But here we have living, tangible proof!' cried Father Gregory, tapping his document folder. 'What more could we want?'

'Encouragement where it's functional, *dis*couragement where it's not.' The priest paused to let his point sink in. 'In terms of global strategic importance, England frankly rates low. Since the Reformation, we've settled into a comfortable *status quo*. We know we're not going to make converts of the whole population, but neither are we under threat from the State or Anglicanism.'

'Ecumenism, maybe,' muttered the Bishop.

'So you see, Father,' the Monsignor concluded, 'miracles in this country are simply not politically functional. On the contrary, given a literate, educated population with a generally nonconformist background, you could say they were positively *dys*functional. Miracles don't sit well in the minds of thinking people. They suit – let us be honest – the more primitive members of the global flock.' He turned to the Bishop. 'Have I expressed the position fairly?'

'Admirably,' smiled the Bishop, then he turned to Father Gregory. 'We are all just small cogs in a greater machine, servants of a greater truth. Remember your vows, Father. From where we stand, no one of us can see the whole picture. We need faith and trust. Do I make myself clear, Father? Father?'

From far off in a whispered voice he barely recognized, Father Gregory heard himself reply.

'Perfectly clear, my Lord.'

'That's better.' The Bishop permitted himself a sigh of satisfaction. 'Now, Father, I was very interested to read in your reports about Grace's . . . social life. I gather she's involved with the son of this Mary Nolan – Benedict, I think his name was. And this boy, you say, is a good Catholic?'

Father Gregory felt a jolt of alarm.

'Grace has denied having had any . . . close physical contact,' he fumbled.

'What Grace says and what she does may well be two different things, Father. I thought we'd established that.'

'I mean, taken in the light of the doctor's report —'

'The doctor is careful to point out that an intact hymen is no proof that intercourse has not taken place.'

'But the odds are infinitesimal!'

'One might say the same of the reverse,' responded the Bishop wryly, then he sat forward and his manner grew more brusque. 'Let's be practical, Father. Monsignor Rolfe and I have talked through this whole tricky problem at great length, and I think we may have found a way out. It all depends on you giving your full co-operation. I trust we can count on that.' He held Father Gregory's eye for a long moment, then continued, 'Now, tell me more about this boy Benedict . . .'

*

The following morning after Mass, Father Gregory walked slowly back down to the lodge-house and climbed into his car. His heart was heavy. He'd been up most of the night, reading, praying and thinking. His mood lurched between defiance and despair. One moment he was full of righteous indignation: he'd challenge the Bishop head-on, he'd take it all the way to Rome, to the Pope himself if necessary. But then he realized he wouldn't get past the most junior cardinal, for the Monsignor had done his work thoroughly and made sure that all the paperwork supported his line – the Party line, as he realized bitterly it had become. *Miracles in this country . . . were positively dysfunctional.* How could he live within a faith where expediency took precedence over truth?

But what really *was* the truth? He believed in Grace's visions and in the miracle of Mary's cure, but did he actually believe, in his heart of hearts, that Grace had had a virgin conception? *Why her, why now, why here?* he could hear the Bishop reiterating. Yes indeed, why Grace Holmwood, rather than any of a hundred girls at the convent, let alone any in the thousands of convents across the world? Why in this age, rather than in an earlier century when a new Saviour might have counted for more, or in years to come – say, to coincide with the new millennium? And why here in England, a country of no ideological significance on the world religious stage, rather than in Cuba or Chile, Poland or the Philippines? Was Coledean to become the new Bethlehem, the mill house a modern manger, the stable-boy Benedict a second Joseph?

Benedict.

Abruptly his thoughts grew more sober. At the Bishop's insistence, he was off to see the boy. But what was he *after*? The real truth, or the convenient truth? He drove slowly out through the town and, with the bright morning sun behind him, headed across the wooded countryside towards Coledean.

*

He found Benedict in the stable-yard, grooming a dappled grey horse. To his relief, no-one else seemed to be about; he'd made a point of parking across the road, and walking up the side drive. At the sound of his footsteps on the cobblestones, the boy looked up.

'Hello, Father,' he said, straightening.

'Hello, Ben.' Giving the horse a wide berth, he came up to the tall dark-haired boy. 'He's a fine-looking creature,' he said, patting its neck.

'She's a beauty. Are you looking for someone, Father?'

'You, Ben. Can we have a word, in private?'

'Sure.'

The boy tied the horse's halter to a post and led the way round the back, out of sight of the main house, where amid weeds and manure a pile of timber and building materials lay stacked against a tall brick wall. Across the track, fenced around by white railings, stretched a paddock in which stood several majestic chestnut trees already swelling into bud, while on the breeze came the scent of flowering currant and the year's first mowings of grass.

He looked Benedict firmly in the eye and took a deep breath.

'I have to talk to you about Grace,' he began.

'She's in trouble?' asked the boy at once.

'In serious trouble, Ben. I think you know what I'm talking about.'

'Sorry, Father?'

It hadn't occurred to him that she might not have told the boy – if indeed he was the father. Or if there *was* a father. Heavens, he thought, what a wretched muddle. Scrutinizing his reaction, he told him that Grace was expecting a baby.

'I have a feeling you are involved, Ben.' He held up his hand to stem the immediate protest. 'Now, before you say anything, I want you to take a moment to think. Grace is in trouble. She needs the help of those who love her. She needs *your* help, Ben. I want whoever's responsible to come forward.'

'Yes, Father, but . . .'

'Think of the child, growing up with no father to acknowledge it, never having its proper name. Think of Grace, abandoned, struggling to cope on her own. *Think*, Ben.'

The boy cast about him in perplexity.

'What do you want of me, Father?' he pleaded.

'The truth, Ben.'

'But I've never been near her, Father. I'm keen on her all right,' he dropped his gaze shyly, 'but she's not interested in me. Not like that, anyway.'

Father Gregory gripped the boy's arm and forced him to meet his eye.

'Is this the truth, Ben?' he asked in a half whisper. 'It's a terrible sin to lie. And you'll only get her into worse trouble. Now, I'm going to go on till I find out who is behind it. Certain people are taking a very special interest in this, Ben. Well?'

Benedict flushed and pulled away.

'I told you, Father,' he insisted desperately.

'Very well,' responded Father Gregory. 'But God help you, and God help Grace, if you're fibbing. Goodbye, Ben.'

'Goodbye, Father.'

Turning on his heel, Father Gregory made his way back down the flinty back drive to his car, more puzzled than ever. Did he believe the boy? He frankly didn't know. But one thing was certain: he wasn't going to suborn him into a false confession, however welcome that might be at the Bishop's palace.

*

Benedict stopped in the middle of brushing the grey mare's mane and bit his lip. He thought back to Grace lying on the hillside. So *that* was what was wrong with her! Poor, poor Grace. What were they doing to her? He remembered the time Mum came home almost in tears after she'd been to see the Monsignor. She'd said they were putting Grace through the same cruel questioning all the time. No wonder the poor girl looked so sorry for herself. It must be terrible. She was pregnant, and all they could do was send the priest round on a witch-hunt after the father. If she hadn't told them, it was because she didn't want to. Why should she? But if no-one owned up, they'd persecute her until she confessed.

*

Some time before eight the following morning, as he was leaving the vestry to prepare the altar for Mass, Father Gregory stopped dead in his tracks. In the far row of the empty chapel sat Benedict Nolan, bent in an attitude of prayer. After kneeling at the altar rails for a moment, he rose and proceeded down the nave to where the boy sat. Benedict looked up as he approached; his face was ashen and his lips set tight.

'This is a surprise, Ben,' he said.

'Father,' said Benedict, 'will you hear my confession?'

204

He hesitated: people would be arriving for Mass shortly. But he'd never seen such a look of dire need before.

'Of course, Ben. Come with me.'

He led him to the small side chapel where the confessional stood. Gathering up his cassock, he stepped inside the small, dark space and glanced through the grille. Benedict appeared to be wrestling with his thoughts.

'Bless me, Father, for I have sinned,' he began at last.

There was a pause. Father Gregory cleared his throat.

'The Lord be in your heart and on your lips,' he responded, 'that you may truly and humbly confess your sins, in the Name of the Father, and of the Son and of the Holy Spirit. Amen.'

The silence lengthened.

'Don't be afraid,' he coaxed.

Feet shuffled. In a low, struggling voice, Benedict finally spoke.

'Since my last confession . . .' he began, then abruptly broke off.

'Go on, Ben.'

'Father,' he blurted out, 'it *was* me. I did it.'

As he listened to the garbled account of an incident at the stables one afternoon some months back, Father Gregory could not shut his mind to the obvious inconsistencies and the inescapable sense that the boy was making it up as he went along. Was he covering up for Grace? Or was he telling the truth? Either he was making a false confession or Grace had grossly perjured herself. Which was it? But did it actually *matter* which? True or false, the Bishop was getting the confession he wanted. And that would set the seal on the case.

*

Grace saw the white Mini parked in the driveway as she returned for lunch from her walk. She hesitated. She didn't want another heavy session with Father Gregory. As she came round the side of the house, through the tall window she could see Mum ushering the priest to a seat on the sofa. She'd keep out of the way; she'd just grab something to eat and take it back out until he'd gone.

As silently as she could, she opened the back door and, kicking off her shoes, tiptoed over to the fridge. The door to the living-room was open an inch, and through it she could hear their conversation. She paid no attention until she heard her name mentioned. Creeping forward, she stood by the crack in the door.

'I can't tell you,' Father Gregory was replying, evidently under pressure. 'As a priest, what I hear in confession is in confidence.'

'But you know who's responsible, don't you, Father?' Mum's voice returned insistently.

'Laura, please,' protested the priest feebly.

'Someone has confessed to being the father!'

There was a pause before Father Gregory replied.

'I can't comment, Laura,' he said, but the lack of sincerity in his tone said enough.

Grace caught her breath and took a step back. She grabbed the edge of the sideboard for support. She heard her mother's sharp exclamation.

'Who is it?' followed the bewildered cry.

'You know I can't divulge that.'

'But I have to know, Father! Tell me in confidence.'

'Laura, *please*.'

'Is it Benedict?' she demanded. 'Is he the one?'

'I cannot confirm anything,' came the careful reply.

'Deny it, then.'

There was a long moment's silence.

'I knew it!' she cried. 'That wretched boy! I knew something was going on at the stables.'

'I didn't say anything, Laura.'

'No, of course you didn't, Father. Don't worry, I shan't tell her how I know.' Her voice faltered. 'What's to be done? She can't possibly marry him. Father, this is perfectly dreadful.'

'Be calm, Laura. My advice is to send her away for a while. A change of atmosphere, a breath of fresh air. I'm sure Dr Stimpson will agree. Don't worry, I'll settle things at school. Meanwhile, we'd better keep the whole thing as quiet as possible. You know how people talk.'

In the kitchen, Grace choked back a cry. Her head spun giddily. *Benedict?* Were they mad? Was *he* mad? Why should he confess to something he hadn't done? Had they forced him? Or had he done it for her sake, thinking he could help her? How could Father Gregory believe him when she'd actually sworn? Deep down, he didn't *want* to believe her. None of them ever had. They were just using her, playing games with her as if what she felt and what she had actually done didn't matter a bit.

Swaying backwards, she accidentally knocked the tea tin off the shelf. It fell to the floor with a loud clatter. Abruptly the conversation in the next room stopped.

'Grace?' called her mother. 'Is that you?'

Footsteps crossed the room. Grace rushed over to the back door and wrenched it open. She fled into the garden and, without a backward glance, tore down the garden, along the path that followed the river, through the hedgerows and on into the open fields beyond, running desperately, wildly, with tears stinging her eyes and branches lashing her cheeks, until finally, far out of earshot of her mother's calls, she fell sobbing to the ground and buried her face in the damp grass.

*

She came back home well after dark had fallen and went up to her room, refusing supper. Her mother tried every approach to draw her out but all she wanted to do was sit on the edge of her bed rocking back and forwards and staring at the floor in silence. That night she made up her mind that it had to be done. She knew where to go; Emily had given her a name and address.

In the morning, off sick from school, she waited in bed

until Mum called up to say she was going across to the studio. As the front door closed, she hurried downstairs and hunted in the sewing-basket for a large pair of pinking scissors. Returning upstairs to the bathroom, she went over to the mirror and gathered a large clump of fair hair in her hand. With one snip it fell into the basin. Gradually a wild frenzy seized her. Grabbing handfuls at a time, she chopped and cropped with growing fury until the basin was choked and her head was shorn wild and ragged.

Hauling on her jeans and a floppy old sweatshirt, she went to the secret drawer in her wardrobe and took out her building society passbook with her four hundred pounds' life savings – Emily had said that would do it – then she scribbled a note to tell Mum she'd gone out and not to worry and slipped out of the house by the back door. To avoid being spotted from the studio, she headed off down the river path on the further side of the house that took her past the weir, skirting the boundary in a wide arc. Once on the road, she began to walk. A bus slowed as it passed, but she turned and hid her face, not wanting to be recognized. A mile on, she hitched a ride from a delivery van that took her to a village beyond Abbotsbury, where a commercial traveller picked her up and drove her the rest of the way to Gloucester. There she found a branch of the building society and took out all her money in cash, then traced her way to the address Emily had given her.

The house she sought was situated in a well-to-do residential area, set back from the road by a shallow semi-circular driveway in which a black limousine stood parked, its windows darkened. A small brass plate on the gate-post read, DR R. BILDERSTEIN MD, CONSULTANT GYNAECOLOGIST. For a moment she held back, tortured with uncertainty now that the reality faced her. As she stood there, the door opened and a woman came out looking white and frail as a corpse, supported on either side by two nurses who helped her down the steps and into the car. The ache that had been grinding in her stomach all morning rose to a stabbing, knifing pain.

The world took a sudden lurch and she clutched at the gate-post, feeling the tears springing to her eyes. No! She couldn't go through with it. She couldn't cope with facing the suspicious questions, with inventing a false name and address, lying about her age, explaining why she had no form of identification, no consent from a parent or guardian, no referral note from a doctor . . . And then the examination, like the examination Monsignor Rolfe sent her to: laid out on a couch, legs splayed apart, then the cold steel tongs and the interfering hands . . . *No, no!* She'd have it, it was hers after all, it was *her*, her own flesh, her own blood. No, she couldn't do away with it, she loved it, she wanted it, she had to have it, it was *meant*, she'd been chosen, given this child from God, God's own child, whatever that meant, however it had happened . . .

Staggering and choking, she stumbled away. The black car glided past like a hearse. On she ran, towards the city centre, to the anonymous shops and the faceless coffee-bars where she could be among the press and crush of people, people who didn't know her, who were just ordinary souls living ordinary lives, who hadn't been chosen for some Divine purpose, people who had friends and family they could trust and who in turn trusted and believed them . . . Who did she have to turn to? Mum? Father Gregory? Sister Bertram? Monsignor Rolfe? Emily? Benedict? Which one of them had not somehow betrayed her?

As the shopping centre came into sight, she slowed down to a walking pace. At least one person had been consistent and stuck by his principles He had always loved her like a father and cared for her like a friend. Just as he'd said in his letter.

Leo.

*

Leonard tidied his desk quickly. If he hurried, he'd catch the shops: he had his eye on a new pair of climbing boots which he wanted to break in before the season started. With a brisk movement he swept a pile of drug companies' brochures into the wastepaper basket and crumpled into his pocket the yellow telephone memos that had been appearing on his desk all week: *Dr Welland called* and, *Dr Welland called again: urgent.* He slipped some papers in his briefcase to work on that evening, exchanged his white coat for his camel-hair overcoat and hurried out of his office.

The afternoon was blustery and wet, but the air was fresh, in contrast to the hospital stuffiness, and as he crossed the car-park, side-stepping the puddles, he paused for a moment to fill his lungs. Hospitals were such unhealthy places; most of the patients would do far better in the brisk Welsh mountain air. The thought of the crags and rocks spurred him on and he strode over to his Jaguar with an eager step. He had opened the door and was about to climb in when he noticed a figure detach itself from the shadows of the building and make its way towards him. At first he didn't recognize this infant madwoman with her hair cropped short and ragged, her clothes drenched and bedraggled and her large blue-grey eyes staring wildly from a chalk-white face, weaving her way erratically through the cars, tripping and stumbling as she went.

With a cry of horrified recognition, he rushed forward.

'My God! Grace!'

She fell into his arms.

'Leo,' she gasped. 'Take me away.'

*

Leonard took her home to his own house at Upton Flint, mid-way between Gloucester and the Forest of Dean. There he ran her a hot bath and gave her a shirt and towelling robe of his own to wear while her own clothes dried. He called Laura to say she was with him and there was nothing to worry about. Then he turned up the central heating, lit a log fire in the sitting-room and put on a compact disc of the *Emperor* piano concerto at full volume. While she was taking her bath, he pulled a chicken out of the freezer and quick-thawed it recklessly in a sink of hot water, chopped vegetables for the side of the roast and threw potatoes into the oven to bake. By the time she came down, bathed and refreshed and looking so absurd in his oversized dressing-gown and Norwegian knitted slippers that they both burst out laughing, the house was filled with the aroma of cooking and wood-smoke and had begun to regain the feel of a proper home.

In the sitting-room, over a glass of wine, they talked. Later, he brought in their supper on a tray, and she opened her heart to him in a way she never had before. She spoke with numb disbelief of being pregnant, and what she'd been on the brink of doing that afternoon. She wept a little when she described how nobody would believe she'd never slept with anyone, even when the examination the Monsignor forced on her had exonerated her. Her mother had all along suspected Benedict, and Father Gregory had somehow got him to make a false confession. Everyone thought she was either lying or mad and she had no-one she could trust any more.

'Except you, Leo,' she said with a weak smile. 'You were there when I needed you.'

Though her clothes were soon dry, she wouldn't let him take her back home. She couldn't bear to return to the mill house, the village, the convent, to the people hounding her for a story or accosting her for a cure. Couldn't she stay there with him for a bit? He withdrew to his study and called Laura. He told her Grace needed a break, a complete change of scene. Term had only another week to run and she'd be better off well away from there. He'd look after her for a time until she was calmer. He spoke for a long while, trying to allay Laura's anxiety and – what was it? – the tinge of resentment he detected in her tone. But this was an astonishing piece of good fortune, and he wasn't going to let it slip out of his hands.

When finally he returned to the living-room, Grace had fallen asleep in the chair. Her breathing rose and fell slowly, softly, and her fine, long features, so pinched and taut before, were now softened and relaxed. He stood for a moment, awed by her beauty, then he lifted her gently up into his arms and, step by step, steered her up the stairs, along the corridor and into Vanessa's old bedroom, where he eased her carefully into bed and, brushing her forehead with a kiss, turned out the light and left her to sleep.

*

The man in the pale blue saloon watched from across the road with close attention as, one by one, the lights went out downstairs. For a moment the house was in darkness, then a light came on in an upstairs bedroom at the far end. A different bedroom.

He stubbed out his cigarette and a slow smile of satisfaction spread across his face. The girl was staying. Good. He reached for the handbrake and eased it off. The car began to roll forwards. Switching on the ignition and steering just by the sidelights, he let the car coast down the hill until he was out of earshot, then as it gathered momentum he gradually let out the clutch, fired the engine and drove away into the night.

III

VII

Seventeen

Leonard hit the Gloucester bypass at sixty miles an hour and accelerated into the late afternoon sun. In his rear-view mirror, the cathedral spire gradually dwindled to a pinpoint. On the seat beside him lay a large bunch of flowers and an envelope with two tickets to a play in London for the following week. The only day his old friend from University College could see him was Grace's eighteenth birthday. The timing couldn't have been more perfect: he would simply tell her he had to go up to town for a conference and ask if she'd come along as a birthday treat.

She'd been staying with him for a week now, a week both wonderful and terrible. Wonderful because he was rebuilding her trust; terrible because she was suffering so pitifully. On the surface, she appeared to be coping, but at night he'd hear her weeping, and in the morning she'd come down, red-eyed and exhausted. At times he'd catch her staring out of the window with a heart-wrenchingly forlorn expression; he'd say something gently teasing and she'd respond, putting on a brave face, and for a moment there would be the spark of her old, argumentative, vivacious self again. Then, just as quickly, the spark would be extinguished and her face would collapse once more. She'd make light-hearted remarks about the clothes that were becoming too tight or her yearnings for chocolate and Coke, and he'd return the quip in like vein, but behind all that passed between them lay the constantly nagging question: *How had it happened?* For him, it begged a more fundamental question: Was she fibbing, or was she fooling herself? She seemed just too balanced to be harbouring a repressed trauma and just too straightforward to be deliberately lying. Delusion or deception: those were the only alternatives he could see. But for her, neither was the case. Inevitably perhaps, a cloak of unease and forced jollity settled over the household in that first week.

He turned off the main road down the narrow lanes that led through hillier countryside to the village of Upton Flint. Reaching his large brick and stone house, he pulled up in the driveway and hurried up the front steps. As he opened the door he was met by the smell of baking. The chequered tile floor was newly polished, the brass door-plates gleamed brightly and on the oak hallway table stood an arrangement of forsythia, winter jasmine and willow catkins from the garden. From the kitchen came the sound of a radio quiz, interrupted by the din of a food processor.

He pushed the door open. Grace stood bare-footed at the work-table, scooping out whipped cream into a bowl. She wore an apron over a tee-shirt and jeans. Her fair hair, trimmed but still boyishly short, accentuated her large, expressive eyes and the line of her cheek and chin.

'You're back early,' she said, looking up. 'Business falling off?'

'You're supposed to ask if I had a good day at the office and get me a drink.' He handed her the flowers. 'And then I give you these in return.'

'You've seen too many bad Fifties movies, Leo.' She undid the flowers and reached to peck him on the cheek. 'But thanks anyway.'

He went to the drinks cupboard for a whisky, but she came up behind and took the bottle out of his hand.

'It's not even six,' she said severely. 'Tea and scones first.'

'Nursery food?' he groaned.

'Better for your liver.'

'Worse for my arteries.'

She sat him down at the table with a plate of scones, a bowl of whipped cream and a cup of tea. Behind her, the sink was stacked with blackened baking trays and in the room lingered a faint smell of burning. He bit into a scone.

'Improves with practice,' he commented.

She cast him a fragile smile.

'Domestic science isn't my strong subject. You should know that by now.'

'Come on,' he replied more gently. 'Everything you do turns out perfectly, in the end.'

A fleeting frown crossed her face, then she brightened.

'I thought I'd do a roast tonight. When did Mum say she was coming?'

'Drinks time.' He smiled. 'That means any moment now.'

'You can hold off till she comes, Leo.'

Turning to the sink, she began chopping the vegetables. As he sat sipping his tea, a long-forgotten warm, homely feeling began to creep over him. Briefly he wished Laura was not coming over. Already that week he'd cancelled a late committee meeting at the hospital, refused two supper invitations and was forgoing an illustrated talk on an Everest expedition, so that he could spend the evenings at home with Grace. He felt so comfortable having her there. He watched her bent over the board, hard at her work, and he found his eye running down the length of her long, slim body. Abruptly, he looked away. He mustn't ever think of her like that. She was his *daughter* – well, more or less. And, besides, there was Laura. His glance fell upon the tickets on the table. Did he ever do anything without some ulterior motive? Would he be more honest with her if she *was* his daughter? She turned, and he saw the grave weariness in her face again.

'Duchess,' he began, 'what would you say to a trip up to town next week?'

*

'Come in.' Leonard drew Laura in out of the wind and, closing the door, reached for the suitcase she was carrying. 'Did you remember her tracksuit?'

'It's all there,' she replied, taking off her coat to reveal a neat grey suit. 'Books, clothes, shoes – anyone would think the girl was staying for months. Still, if it's what she wants.' She looked around the tidy, polished hall and smiled. 'Don't tell me you've got her spring-cleaning!'

'She's reforming nicely,' he said.

'Don't you believe it! She'll soon have the place a complete tip again.' She handed him her coat. 'Still, I like the Leonard Grigson Finishing School. I'm looking forward to having her back.'

He chuckled and went to the foot of the stairs. The radio was playing loudly from Grace's room upstairs.

'I'll call her down,' he said.

Laura laid a hand on his.

'Before you do, Leonard, a quick word. About her birth-day next week. Well, I thought I'd give her a surprise party. You will be able to make it, won't you?'

'On the actual day?'

'Of course. You bring her over at tea-time and I'll have some of her friends waiting. In fact, I was thinking she could move back in then. She'll have had a fortnight's break. You could bring her stuff over with you, so long as she doesn't see.'

The radio had stopped and footsteps were crossing the floor above.

'Listen, Laura,' he began hastily, 'I'm not sure she's ready to go home yet. I don't think we should hurry things. She's making such progress here. Let's give it time.'

She was about to protest when Grace appeared at the top of the stairs. She skipped down and gave her mother a kiss.

'You're looking great, Mum,' she said. 'Come into the kitchen. I've got to put the roast in.' As she led the way through the swing door, she went on, 'Guess what Leo's doing for my birthday! He's taking me up to London. We're going to a show.'

Laura flashed him a glance of betrayal. He cleared his throat uncomfortably.

'There's an oncology conference I want to look in on,' he

said. 'I thought she'd like to come for the ride. It's just an idea.'

'It's a *promise*, Leo!' interjected Grace. 'You can't slide out of it.' She glanced from one to the other, evidently sensing the atmosphere. 'Why don't you come too, Mum! We can go shopping while Leo has his boring meeting. I'll treat you from my savings.'

'Don't be silly, Duchess.' He forced enthusiasm into his tone. 'Of course you must come, Laura. I'm sure I can get another ticket. It'll be such fun.'

A tense silence fell. Laura braved a smile.

'No, no, you two go. I can't think of any better way for you to spend your birthday. Anyway, you want to do all you can *while* you can.'

Grace's face suddenly clouded over and she turned away. Leonard took a bottle of wine out of the fridge. They all needed a drink.

'Well, there'll be plenty more times,' he said lamely.

No-one spoke as he opened the bottle and poured out the wine. Laura stood by the window, concealing her crestfallen expression. Grace remained far away, lost in thoughts of her own. Leonard handed out the glasses and turned to Grace.

'Put some music on, will you? Something lively, eh?'

*

Grace stood on the balcony of the hotel room and watched the red London buses and black cabs swirling down Piccadilly below her. In the swelling pavements and thickening traffic, she sensed the city quickening its pace as the lunch hour approached.

She turned back to the room and went over to the mirror. The skimpy jacket Leo had bought her made her look so smart, so streetwise. She stroked a hand over the soft leather, inhaling its sensual aroma. Her hand descended to her stomach. She could feel the swelling quite clearly now, a small, hard ball, surprisingly high up. Was it noticeable? Not if she wore her loose-fitting jeans. Nice of Leo, she thought, not to give her something capacious for a pregnant woman.

Abruptly she turned aside. She didn't want to think about this . . . this lump in her belly. It had come from nowhere and would disappear to nowhere. It wasn't real – it *couldn't* be. But as she talked herself through this loop, as she did innumerable times every day, she felt the familiar panic choking and suffocating her, for she knew it *was* real, terribly and cruelly and awfully real. By shockingly rapid degrees the panic tightened its grip, so that she had to walk around the room, then sit down on the bed, then stand up again so as to be on the move and go to the window and take a gulp of air. But there wasn't enough air in the whole of London. She was on fire, her skin burning, and she ran to the bathroom and splashed her face, then drank a glass of water, then turned on the television, but she couldn't stay still and so she switched it off, but she needed sound, noise, any noise, so she whistled a snatch of a tune. But that still didn't work, so she tried reading out loud the notice on the back of the door, then saying the first thing that came into her head, a word, any word, but most of all she had to *think of something else*, anything else, anything at all to blot out those thoughts. The walls were crowding in, her thoughts were ricocheting faster and faster off them, louder and louder, she couldn't contain it any longer.

With a cry, she grabbed her room-key and tore open the door. She ran down the plush-carpeted corridor, past mirrors and tapestries and bronze statues, and flew down the wide sweeping staircase, floor after floor, across the cool palmy foyer and past the eyes of porters and doormen and finally out into the street. There she was brought up short by the sudden rush and turmoil. All at once, she felt very small and very afraid. She stepped out off the kerb and a taxi swerved past, narrowly missing her. Like a blind person she hugged the buildings, crossing only in the safety of a group, until finally she came to a line of iron railings behind which stood the Church of St James. Still shaking, she hurried gratefully into the cool quiet haven.

She made her way to a pew at the side and slipped to her knees. But as the panic gradually eased she grew to realize that she could never escape. She carried the problem around with her, literally *inside* her. Sooner or later, she had to face up to it.

*

At two, she met Leo for a bowl of pasta in Soho. He had been to his conference and met the people he'd had to, and having acquired typescripts of the other lectures, he was free for the rest of the day. Despite his efforts to be lively, he seemed under some strain, and several times over the meal she caught him fixing her with a long, intent stare, only to drop his gaze when she looked up. Perhaps she was imagining it. She really couldn't trust her perceptions any more.

After lunch, however, her spirits began to revive. They walked back down Piccadilly and looked in at an exhibition at the Royal Academy. Afterwards, she suggested a walk in St James's Park. As they made their way along the street, she cast him a sideways glance. She was lucky to have him. He was so strong and secure, so solid and dependable. He'd see her through.

In the park, they strolled across the grass beneath the chestnut trees, already breaking into sticky leaf, and sauntered down to the small central lake. The nervous buzz of traffic receded to a background hum. A brass band was practising from a distant stand, and all about them couples meandered slowly, pausing to feed the ducks or to embrace one another or merely to gaze at the trees and the sky and the beauty of the unfolding season. They came to a halt on a small ornamental bridge and watched as a pair of swans glided imperiously past. At the lake's edge, a heavily pregnant woman was lowering herself awkwardly onto a bench. The hedges bristled with blossom, the shrubbery was bursting into leaf and everywhere swelled the irrepressible rhythm of resurgent life.

She looked up to find him watching her.

221

'Sure you feel all right?' he asked.

She shrugged.

'You know how it is.'

'Nothing actually *hurts*, does it?'

'Leo, everything hurts.'

'Where, specifically?'

She tapped her head.

'In here.'

'Where exactly?' he snapped.

She drew back, puzzled.

'I don't mean literally.' She paused. 'It's just that I wish I *knew*.'

He gripped her by the elbow.

'Grace,' he said with a strange urgency, 'if you do ever get any funny pains, *real* pains, I mean, you will tell me, won't you? As a doctor.'

'I'm fine *physically*,' she retorted.

His manner slowly eased, and he slipped his arm in hers.

'Shall we move on?' he said. As they left the bridge, he gave her a comforting smile. 'You were saying you wish you *knew*.'

'Yes: how it could have happened just like that.'

'Perhaps it didn't happen *just like that*. I mean,' he hastened, 'it does rather fly in the face of the facts.'

'*Here* are the facts!' She pointed to her stomach.

'The *scientific* facts. After all, parthenogenesis is biologically impossible.'

She glared at him.

'It's *got* to be possible.'

'There's never been a properly authenticated case of virgin birth.'

'Well, there is now!'

'I'm prepared to believe you,' he said.

'You don't for a moment! You're just humouring me.'

They walked a short way in silence.

'Actually,' he mused after a while, 'there have have been cases of virgin *conception*. In animals. Mice and, I think, chickens. But never in humans – outside religion and myth, that is. Anyway, you wouldn't *want* it that way. You see, the male sperm carries genes to make the placenta. In the case of those mice, not a single one was actually born. The placenta failed to develop properly.'

'You mean . . . ?'

'I'm merely saying the foetus from a virgin conception would probably miscarry. But then,' he added softly, 'miscarriages are basically Nature's way of getting rid of mistakes.'

'Mistakes?'

'About one in six of all human conceptions are lost by spontaneous abortion,' he continued clinically, 'and half of those are due to chromosomal abnormalities. A foetus conceived without the male input would undoubtedly be abnormal. Probably more like a dermoid cyst.' He caught the alarm on her face and went on, in a matter-of-fact voice, 'They're ovarian tumours made up of the mother's chromosomes only. Sometimes they look like a proper foetus, with teeth and quite long hair . . .'

'Why are you telling me this?' she whispered, ashen-faced.

'I'm sorry. We were talking about facing the facts.'

'Do *you* think it's one of those things?'

'Oh no,' he replied, playing the other tune. 'It's not a cyst. Dr Stimpson has heard a heartbeat.'

'It could still be abnormal.'

'Yes.' He frowned thoughtfully. 'Of course, an amnio would throw up any obvious problems. But there's always a risk of provoking a miscarriage.'

'You said it would miscarry anyway.'

'I didn't quite say that.' His frown deepened. 'Look, if you're really worried, I could always fix you an ultrasound scan. At least that would give us a rough and ready visual check.'

'Okay,' she said quickly.

He appeared to consider this for a moment, but she had the uncomfortable feeling that he had been deliberately leading her up to this point all along.

'Tell you what,' he said finally. 'I know a gynaecological diagnostics specialist at University College here. I'll give him a call, if you like.'

'See if he can see me today.'

He gave her a long, careful glance.

'All right. I'll try.'

*

Leonard let out a quiet sigh of relief as Grace lay down on the couch and the white-coated specialist smeared conductive gel on her bare stomach. So far so good. She'd followed him like a lamb. She hadn't asked him why he was taking her to a medical research laboratory in a university rather than to a normal hospital or clinic. Not even the ubiquitous radiation hazard signs or the glimpses of rats in cages through half-open doors seemed to have puzzled her. She didn't for a moment seem to suspect that he was, in fact, a research scientist and an old friend of Leonard's from college days, or that the equipment was a special high-resolution scanner used for his experimental genetic work. No-one in the country was better qualified to tell from an ultrasound scan the answer to the one terrible question that had been haunting Leonard from the moment he'd learned she was pregnant. Certainly, it didn't even appear to cross her mind that his meeting that morning had been with this very man and that there was, in fact, no oncology conference going on in London at all.

To the side of the couch in the small room stood a trolley of instruments, on top of which sat a monitor screen. It was swivelled away from the couch.

'Just lie back and relax,' said the scientist. 'You won't feel a thing.'

'Can't I see?' she asked.

Leonard shot his friend a quick, warning glance. He would field this one.

'If you're not used to reading these things, it won't mean anything,' he said.

Obediently she lay back and let the scientist run the probe over her stomach. Leonard stood behind him, his throat dry. Gradually, a picture emerged on the screen, flecked and swirling like an untuned television. At the bottom flickered a column of numerals giving measurement parameters and exposure details. The man reached out and adjusted a knob. Suddenly the image jerked into full frame. It was astonishingly clear, almost as if the foetus lay there within the tube. Leonard leaned forward, his pulse thumping. The foetus lay on its back, curled like an astronaut in a space capsule, with its left side facing the probe. Every tiny detail stood out with absolute clarity – the fingernails on the one hand, the eyelashes on one eye, the hair on the ear, the lattice of veins spreading under the thin transparent skin of the skull.

And then it moved. With a small convulsion, it twisted over, exposing its other side. As he saw it, he caught his breath involuntarily. A surge of nausea welled up into his throat. From between the right clavicle and scapula budded a second cranium, a flaccid, soft-boned sac with empty orbital sockets and a lipless mouth . . .

He turned to see Grace staring at him fitfully.

'What's the matter?' she cried.

He clenched his fists and forced himself to remove all expression from his face. Then gradually, using all his will-power, he met her eye and held it.

'Nothing,' he croaked. 'It's fine.'

'Let me see!'

The scientist came to the rescue. Suddenly the screen went zig-zagged, and he affected to play with the controls.

'Lost it,' he muttered with an oath.

'Fine, perfectly fine,' repeated Leonard mechanically, winching his lips into a tight smile. 'That's it, Duchess. You can get up now.'

He turned away, gripping the tubular trolley-frame for support, as Grace leapt to her feet and came round to see the empty screen. For a moment he shut his eyes, hoping to erase the image from his mind. He felt her hand on his arm. He turned. Her face was full of simple trust.

'You okay, Leo?' she said.

'Just a bit hot in here.'

'Let's go, then. We'd better hurry, anyway.'

'Hurry?'

'I'm not going to the show dressed like this. Come on.'

She thanked the scientist warmly and headed cheerfully for the door. Leonard gripped the man's arm in a vice and muttered his own grim thanks, saying he'd get in touch in the morning. Following him downstairs to the reception area, where he signed them out, they shook hands and headed out into the city.

Outside, he hailed a cab and settled down in the seat, wondering how the hell he would get through a night at the theatre and then supper afterwards. But he had to: she needed to stock up on all the happiness she could get. He knew what lay in store for her. The foetus should miscarry – no, it *had* to miscarry – and she would have to find a way of coping with that. By rights, she should have lost it that time she fell off her horse. Why had the wretched thing survived? Far better for everyone if it had miscarried then and there.

But more alarming still was what lay behind it all. Only he knew exactly what this was and how it had arisen. He'd feared it from the start. So, the slumbering demon had awoken. When and where and how it would strike next, he couldn't tell. But it had come out of hiding, and its first offspring was welling and waxing inside her very womb. If it had infiltrated the delicate genetic process of germ cell development, where else might it not also be present, lying dormant and awaiting its moment?

Eighteen

Leonard stared into the kitchen cupboard, momentarily forgetting what he'd come for. Ah yes, the cereals. For breakfast. From his study, through the open door, came the sound of Mahler, playing at full volume. Laura had invited him to a concert that Friday; she'd been very insistent, as though she felt the need to *reclaim* him somehow. As he carried the cereal over to the table, his eye fell on the theatre programme. God, what a strain that evening had been. Still, he was sure Grace had enjoyed herself. He'd certainly done his best to see nothing marred her fun.

He went to the window and, staring out at the lawn bathed in misty morning light, he thought back over the conversation he'd had on the phone with his scientist friend the previous day. The man had been studying the videotape of the scan and had concluded it was a severe case of chromosomal non-disjunction. He'd seen something similar only once before – in experimental rats he'd exposed to ionizing radiation. Radiation could induce malignancy in practically all tissues of the body, including germ-line mutations, but, as he'd gone on to explain, radioactive particles had to be present in the gonads themselves and very close to the nuclei of the germ cells in order to have *genetic* effect. But how could that be so in this case? Could he run more tests? Leonard had thanked him and firmly refused to discuss it further. The less anyone knew, the better. Besides, he was coming to a major decision. Maybe this would not remain a problem for very much longer.

Abruptly the music stopped. Footsteps approached across the hallway. He turned as Grace entered the kitchen, carrying a small sheaf of envelopes.

'Sorry, Leo,' she said cheerily, 'but it's too early for all that heavy Romantic stuff.'

'You'll grow into it.'

'That's what I'm afraid of. Coffee ready?'

'Haven't got round to it yet.'

'You'd make a terrible housewife, Leo,' she said, leafing through the envelopes. 'Just bills and circulars. Except one that looks very official.'

She handed him the letters and went to the sink to fill the percolator. The moment he saw the one marked *Private and Confidential*, his pulse gave a sick lurch: he recognized the type-face and the Bath postmark. Turning his back to her, he tore it quickly open. It contained a photograph, a blow-up of Laura and Grace in a car. The background was too blurred to reveal where it had been taken, but the fact Grace's hair was long gave a clue as to when. He turned it over. On the back was a handwritten message: *Meet me at the Mason's Arms 1 p.m. today. Must talk. Be there. Tom.*

With a flush of annoyance he tore it up and threw the pieces in the wastepaper basket. He had no intention of seeing Welland again, now or ever. He had far too much else on his mind.

He turned to find a slim, gift-wrapped packet lying on the table beside his plate. Grace gestured for him to open it. Carefully he undid the wrapping. Inside was a blue silk tie.

'It's beautiful,' he said, deeply moved.

'What else do you give a fusty old bachelor who's got everything?' She smiled. 'It's just a silly thank-you, Leo, for giving me such a wonderful birthday.'

'They'll think there's a new woman in my life,' he chuckled, putting it on.

'Tell them there is,' she said.

He went to admire the tie in the small mirror that hung above the phone. But all he could see was his own face, the face of Judas.

*

Grace spent the morning sitting at the kitchen table, trying to study. The radio was playing light pop music in the background. Every few minutes she'd get up for a chocolate biscuit or another mug of weak coffee. She hated inorganic chemistry worst of all. Around eleven, Father Gregory phoned to ask how she was. He teasingly called her a 'lady of leisure' and made other remarks that seemed to imply that the school were assuming she wouldn't be sitting her A-levels that summer. Why not? So long as she didn't give birth in the exam-room, she was just as capable as the rest, and having a child was no bar to going to university. The more she thought about it afterwards, the more she concluded they didn't *want* her back. Very well, she'd study at home. She had Leo to help her: she couldn't want a better tutor in her subjects.

After a while, too disturbed to concentrate, she went to the sitting-room and lay down on the sofa, staring at the ceiling, her hands folded over her stomach. Every now and then, she fancied she felt a small kick. If she really *was* to have a baby, she needed to pass her exams more than ever. She wasn't going to give up her hope of a decent career and slip into the slavery of nappies and nannies, losing her identity along with her independence. She'd witnessed how hard it had been for her mother after Dad died, struggling to turn a hobby into a career that would support a family.

Dragging herself up, she went back to the kitchen and her chemistry, but again, after barely quarter of an hour, she gave up and tossed the book aside. Her eye fell upon a pregnancy handbook Leo had looked out for her, and idly she began leafing through it. Her baby, she read, was already about ten inches from head to toe; it had fingernails and eyebrows and the unique thumb-prints that would stay with it all its life. She read about its noisy world, loud with the thump of her heartbeat and the gurgling of her stomach, and how it could hear her own voice and even music, too. She read on with growing fascination until she came to a section on miscarriage. Abruptly she got up and put the book way over on the window-sill. Then she went out into the hall and made for the broom cupboard under the stairs. The only way to stop thinking was to keep her hands busy.

She ran a mop over the kitchen floor and, while it dried, hoovered the study and the sitting-room. She polished and dusted the mantelpiece and shelves and finally went round with a garbage bag emptying the wastepaper baskets. She was tipping out the basket in the kitchen when a torn square of paper fell out onto the floor. She was about to toss it into the bag when she noticed it was a part of a photo. A face . . . *Mum*'s face! Puzzled, she delved into the bag for the other pieces, then took them over to the table where she carefully assembled them into their original picture. Who on earth had taken that picture of Mum and herself in the car? Turning it over piece by piece, she read the message. *Meet me at the Mason's Arms . . . Must talk. Be there. Tom.* This must have been that official-looking letter that morning. She glanced at the wall-clock. One-forty. Was Leo meeting this man at this very moment? Who was he, and why had he sent this photo? What *was* this photo? Did Leo know what it meant? Perhaps he did, and that was why he'd torn it up like that. For a brief moment she pictured his lop-sided, angular face with its large, expressive brown eyes, and she thought to herself, I don't really know this man, there are things going on behind those eyes that I'll never understand. Briskly she swept the pieces back into the refuse bag. He was probably protecting her from some crank who'd read the newspaper reports, one of those people in the car lurking in the driveway at home, or the man in the supermarket who'd followed her, the man with the suppurating skin and the oozing sores . . . Her hand flew to her mouth. Perhaps *he* had found out where she was staying! Perhaps he'd been tracking her, watching her, taking photos of her, trying to get close to her, to talk to her, to touch her . . .

With a shudder, she went out into the utility area and put

on her anorak. She'd do some weeding in the garden. The house felt too claustrophobic.

*

Some while later she was kneeling, tidying up the border of a flower-bed, when she heard a muffled cough behind her. She spun round with a violent start. Silhouetted against the sun stood the figure of a man. She backed to her feet and shielded her eyes so as to see him better. He was short, with the face of a flat-fish and small button eyes that glinted behind thick wire-framed glasses. He wore a green sports jacket, check shirt and brown tie, and bore a strong smell of cigarettes.

'Can I help you?' she asked, recovering.

He contrived a smile. Something struck her as wrong, as if his face wasn't used to smiling.

'Leonard not around? No, I didn't think he would be.' His smile pinched to a frown. 'You feeling all right?'

'You gave me rather a turn, that's all,' she said.

'I did ring the bell, but . . .' He shrugged and looked at the flower-bed. 'Got you hard at it, has he?'

'He won't be back till this evening. Shall I say who called?'

'Just say an old friend.' He picked up a bulb she'd inadvertently dug up, examined it briefly, then lobbed it back onto the bed and cast her a long, intent look. 'You must be Grace. He's told me about you. Pretty name, Grace. I always say there's more in a name than you think.' He paused. 'You had a brother, Matthew, didn't you? I'm sorry. Still, he was in good hands. Leonard's the best in the business when it comes to leukaemia.'

'My brother died of a stomach virus,' she said shortly.

The man's eyebrows rose above his glasses.

'That's not what I heard. Still . . .' His voice trailed off, and for a moment he toyed at the pile of weeds with the toe of his shoe. 'A bone marrow transplant just for a tummy upset?' he mused.

'This is none of your business,' she broke in, feeling the

231

distress welling up. 'I don't know who you are or what you want. Please just go and leave me alone.'

'I'm sorry.' The smile had returned. 'Let me leave my number.'

He took out a pen and searched his pockets for paper. With a sigh of annoyance, she put down her gardening fork and went into the kitchen through the French windows. As she came back with a note-pad, she found him standing just inside the door, his eye fixed on the pregnancy handbook. He flashed a glance at her, then down at her stomach. His smile hardened. She thrust the pad into his hand and waited while he scribbled down a number.

'Don't worry' he said, handing her the note, 'I can see myself out. Sorry for the intrusion.'

He went back through the garden and disappeared round the side of the house. A moment later, she heard a car starting up at the front. She glanced at the note. From the code she recognized it as a Bath number, and it was simply signed 'T'.

*

Leonard was sitting at the kitchen table, catching up on a stack of *New Scientists* when the door opened and Grace came in, fresh from the bath in a towelling dressing-gown. She poured herself a glass of water at the sink and headed back to the door without a word. She'd been withdrawn all evening.

'What's up, angel?' he asked gently. She didn't reply. 'Come on, I know when something's wrong.'

She hesitated at the door. Then, as if remembering something, she went to the sideboard shelf.

'Someone dropped in this afternoon. He left this.'

She handed him a note. At once he recognized the number. A flush of alarm broke out over his skin.

'Did he give his name?' he asked quickly.

'He just said he was an old friend. Is he that person Tom?'

'What person Tom?'

'The man who sent that photo of Mum and me this morning. I found it when I was clearing out the wastepaper basket.'

He stood up and refilled his glass. His mind was racing, but he strove to sound offhand.

'This man Tom works for a local rag,' he said. 'They'll do anything for a story. You're news, I'm afraid. It's up to those who love you to fight them off.' He swallowed, watching her expression carefully. 'But this fellow today – describe him.'

'Thick wire-frame glasses and a kind of squashed face . . .'

'That's, uh, that's Terry. We're old school pals. Don't believe a word Terry says. He's out of his tree.'

'He knew about Matthew.'

'He talked about Matthew?' he snapped.

She didn't respond at once, but cast him a thoughtful look.

'You're a cancer specialist, aren't you, Leo?' she asked quietly. 'I mean, the patients you treat all have cancer.'

'Well, yes, more or less, but . . .'

'He said Matthew died of leukaemia.' Her tone grew pleading. '*Did* he, Leo?'

He took her by the shoulders and drew her close to his chest, so that she wouldn't see through his eyes into his soul.

'You *know* what it was, angel. Matthew had a rare blood disease. He was my patient because at that stage we didn't really know *what* it was. You remember we tried transfusions, transplants, everything. But with all the loss of blood, the infection, the internal haemorrhaging . . . well, as you know, in the end it was his stomach and lungs that packed up.'

He continued elaborating the story, skirting the question of *how* the disease had been contracted and carefully avoiding any mention of cancer, until gradually she relaxed and looked up at him with an apologetic smile. He gave her a kiss.

'Now, go to bed and don't think another thing about it. It's all in the past and done with. You have the future to think of now. Two futures.'

233

She nodded and went to the door.

'Yes, Leo. I'm sorry. And thanks. Well, g'night, then.'

''Night, angel. Sleep tight.'

He waited until he heard her footsteps receding up the stairs, then uncrumpled the note from his fist and took it over to the phone. When he heard the floorboards overhead creaking, he lifted the receiver. He'd sort the bastard out once and for all.

The phone rang interminably, until he realized he was calling the laboratory. He went to his study, pausing to listen at the foot of the stairs on the way, and looked up Tom Welland's home number in his address book. This time the phone answered right away.

'Listen, you cretin,' he hissed into the mouthpiece, 'what the hell do you think you're up to, coming round to the house? Don't you dare *ever* do that again! Leave Grace out of it. This business had nothing to do with her, do you hear?'

But all his fury was futile. Welland insisted on a meeting and made it clear he'd continued the harassment until he got one. And so, full of misgivings, Leonard agreed to meet the following evening at a lay-by on the road home. He was trembling as he put the phone down. How much longer could he go on trying to shore up the crumbling edifice?

*

Leonard was late for the rendezvous. He'd stayed behind until the small dispensary on his floor was empty so that he could work unobserved, grinding up the rest of the cytosuppressin tablets into liquid concentrate. Reaching the lay-by, he pulled up nose to nose with Welland's car and got out. Welland threw open the passenger door, and he climbed in.

Within moments, he knew he'd walked into a very bad deal. Welland produced photographs, documents, records. He had done his research and he knew everything. The meeting lasted no more than four or five minutes. At the end, despite his anxieties, Leonard took the kit in the plain paper bag that Welland gave him and returned to his own car. It was blackmail, but what choice did he have?

He drove home slowly, wrestling with his conscience. The house was in darkness, and for a moment he feared that Grace might have packed up and gone, but he found her in the kitchen, her knees tucked up under her chin, staring out of the back windows into the fading evening light. She stirred briefly when he turned the light on, but said nothing. For a moment he wondered if she somehow *knew*, whether Tom had said more to her than she'd told him, or whether she'd read his mind from his behaviour and simply guessed. He told himself to get a grip: he was merely being paranoid. She was ignorant because she was, and always would be, innocent. Her nature was to trust, not to suspect. He bit his lip; that made what he had to do all the more shameful.

He began to chat with all the cheerfulness he could muster about the day's events on the ward and, finding no response, started preparing the supper. He asked her what she'd done all day, but she merely shrugged and remained silent. He poured her a glass of orange-juice, and she drank that. She might be angry with the world, but at least she wasn't taking it out on herself. That mood of self-punishment, of Catholic mortification, was the one he found hardest to handle.

He unwrapped the meat and washed it under the tap.

'Liver will do you good,' he went on cheerily. 'Put some iron into your system. You look washed out. Really, I'm worried, Duchess. We should get Dr Stimpson to give you a blood test.'

'I can't bear that man.'

'Don't be silly,' he responded quickly, pleased to receive any reaction at all. 'If you're anaemic, it could seriously damage the baby.'

She looked at him as though he were a stranger who understood nothing.

'I didn't ask for it. I didn't do anything to get it. Why should I care about it?'

'Your hormones will change all that.'

'Fat chance.'

He calculated his tone carefully before he responded.

'Well, as I'm *in loco parentis* and a doctor besides,' he said, 'I think I should take it upon myself to check.'

She sighed impatiently.

'Do anything you like, Leo.'

'After supper, then.'

'I'm not hungry.'

Quickly he steered a new course before the wind changed.

'Ah, but wait till you taste this!' he chuckled. 'Mushrooms, onions, broccoli . . .'

An hour later, when she was watching television in the sitting-room after having eaten a good supper in spite of herself, he retrieved the paper bag from his briefcase in the study and emptied out the contents on the desk. He broke the seal on the short hypodermic needle and unwrapped the two small vacuum-filled glass phials. Returning to the sitting-room, he asked her to hold out her arm while he rolled up her sleeve and dabbed anaesthetizing spirit on the vein. As he fed in the sharp needle, she let out a small gasp but didn't take her eyes off the television. He held the hypodermic in place while he plugged in each cartridge in turn, letting the vacuum draw out the rich, dark blood. Then he withdrew the needle and placed a pad of cotton-wool over the spot, telling her to press on it hard, and carefully put the two full phials of blood in his pocket.

He patted her head.

'That wasn't too bad, was it?'

'You're standing in the way,' she said. 'Would you mind?'

He moved aside, but stood steeling his nerve for the real challenge. He'd done Welland's work. Now came his own.

'Fancy another orange-juice, angel?' he asked innocently.

'All right.'

He went to his study. Unlocking the top drawer of his desk, he slipped out the small bottle of cytosuppressin fluid he'd reformulated and took it into the kitchen. Taking the orange-juice out of the fridge, he quickly poured the contents of the bottle into the carton. He gave it a thorough shake to disperse the concentrate, then reached for a glass and poured out a drink. He returned to the sitting-room and handed Grace the glass, then turned away. He couldn't bring himself to watch her drink it.

He returned to the kitchen and poured himself a large whisky. His hands were trembling. He'd thought it through carefully, and he'd reasoned away all the ethical objections, but now it had come to the moment, he was fraught with doubts and the struggle to justify his action.

He'd *seen* the scan: he knew what was growing inside her. Surely it was right to spare any woman the trauma of giving birth to a monster? He wasn't taking away human life: this wasn't a child, it was a *creature*. What kind of a life would it have, anyway, if it actually were born? It would spend months, maybe years, in intensive care; it would have constantly to undergo major surgery; it would be grossly deformed, helplessly retarded, unable to care for itself or feel anything around it or know the warmth of human love. And what of *her* life! Who could wish such a curse on an eighteen-year-old girl? Anyway, with a ninety-per-cent chance it would spontaneously abort, he was merely giving Nature a helping hand, wasn't he? And there again, he couldn't really be sure a drug specifically designed to shrink tumours would provoke a miscarriage. Even if she did miscarry, would he be able to say with any certainty that it had been *his* hand that had brought it on?

Angrily, he swallowed a large gulp of his drink. Too much noise was always made about human moral dilemmas. It sprang from man's overweening arrogance. In truth, we were such puny creatures, and our much-vaunted free will, our loud appeals to grand principles, our high-flown claims for the rights and wrongs of our actions really had very little actual influence on the course of events. Because we could create a ripple, we believed we could stem a tide. Far better to listen to the flow and go with it, and try to make the best decision possible in the given circumstances. Life *was* circumstance: it was random, arbitrary, uncertain, without plan or design. That was universally true, down to the operation of the smallest molecular particles. There was no Grand Unifying Theory after all, try as the physicists might to find God in one. How absurd, therefore, to try and live by absolute principles, to say that life *per se* was sacrosanct, rather than *this* life in *this* place at *this* time, and by the same token *not* that life in that place, *not* the life in that poor girl's belly in this very house at this very moment, for that was a life that should not be.

He poured himself another large drink. He was faltering. Somehow, he couldn't quite convince himself. And behind everything lay the terrible knowledge that from a chain of minor actions, all innocent and done with the best of motives, had flowed an irreversible calamity of which this unnatural pregnancy was but the first showing.

*

Tom Welland sat in his car, chain-smoking. The exhaust billowed out in clouds on the chilly morning air. From the lay-by where he stood parked he had a commanding view of the oncoming stream of traffic. The silver Jaguar was some distance away when he spotted it. Flashing its lights briefly, it pulled in and drew up in front of him. Leonard climbed out and came over. He handed the plain brown envelope through the window.

'Don't drop the bastard,' he muttered. 'And don't bother to call me again, Tom. Okay?'

Not waiting for a response, he got back into his car and roared out into the line of traffic.

Welland opened the bag, his pulse beating fast. There they were, the two phials, filled with black-red blood. The twin's blood.

Turning round, he headed down the road in the direction Leonard had taken, but forked off after a couple of miles and took the signs to Bath. Within half an hour he was hurrying up the steps to the Department of Medical Research, in past the security guards and across the hallway, where he took the elevator to the third floor and, slipping through the security doors with his pass-card, finally reached Room 313. Once inside his own laboratory, he carefully set the two phials in a rack on the bench and set to work. By midday he had made the necessary preparations. Then he went over to the isolation chamber and, taking a deep breath, slid his hands into the rubber arm-gloves and reached for the screw cap on the squat aluminium cryostat cylinder.

Would it work, after all the freezing and thawing and refreezing? In eight or ten hours he'd know.

*

Leonard slowed at the entrance to Coledean village and turned into the mill drive just as the six o'clock time signal sounded on the radio. He'd barely driven ten yards up it when he found a new white five-bar gate barring his way. It was padlocked. Leaving his car, he carried on up the drive on foot. On the verges he noticed fresh tyre marks and as he reached the house he saw the flower-beds beneath the windows were heavily trampled. Around the field beyond a new post-and-rail fence was being erected.

Laura came to the door with an apologetic smile and drew him inside. The house smelled of bath oil and fresh paint and the hall was filled with flowers.

'Sorry!' she said. 'I forgot to leave the gate open for you. You can't imagine what a nightmare it's been in the past few days. People seem to think they have a right to come knocking on the door. The place isn't a shrine!'

'Charge admission,' he smiled. 'That'll thin out the crowds.'

'It's not just us, either,' she went on. 'Mary Nolan's house is like Waterloo station. The *Sunday Tribune* has offered a small fortune for her story. I only hope it'll all die down before Grace comes back.' She glanced at the hall clock. 'Time for a drink before we go.'

She led him into the large open-plan living-room. The furniture had been rearranged so that the focus of the room was now towards the tall window and the view into the garden, rather than closed in towards the hearth. The floor was spread with bright new rugs, gaily coloured cushions lay scattered on the leather sofa and on the far stone wall hung a large tapestry in some bold tribal weave. He gazed in admiration.

'You've done wonders, Laura.'

'You should see the baby's room,' she replied, handing him a whisky. 'I've fixed up Matthew's old room. Want to see?'

'I'll take your word for it, Laura,' he said briskly. As he sipped his drink, his eye fell on a child's alphabet chart lying on the table. His hand froze around the glass. The creature, should it survive, would never be able to pick up a toy, let alone recognize a letter of the alphabet. After a moment he asked, 'It hasn't got out generally about the baby?'

'No,' she replied. 'Father Gregory thinks the fewer who know the better. They're trying to keep it as quiet as possible at school. The people we get coming here only know what they've read in the papers.' She paused. 'At least Benedict is being discreet. I think he's too ashamed to want to tell everyone.'

A moment's silence fell, filled only by the constant, restless rush of the mill stream in the background.

He caught her eye.

'Laura,' he said, 'you don't doubt it *was* Benedict, do you?'

'No, though I could wish it wasn't.'

'Your Father Gregory must be disappointed.'

She managed a faint smile. 'Yes. He did rather like the idea of a miraculous intervention.'

'Maybe it's best that way.' He looked at his watch. 'Shall we make tracks?'

*

The brain lay in its perspex cask, two wrinkled, pinkish-grey lumps cloven down the central sulcus. Into the root of the brain stem fed a set of fine plastic tubes that carried the rich, red, newly formulated blood plasma. These in turn led out through small insulated ports in the wall of the isolation chamber and connected to the circulation control system, while a tube finer than the rest branched off from the return feed to the differentiometer. This tested for changes in the oxygen content in the blood being circulated through the organ. Oxygen take-up would be the first sign of metabolic activity in the neural cells, the first sign of regenerated *life*.

Tom Welland peered in through the inspection window and gave a final visual check to the joints in the flow system. He wasn't going to risk another accident. He glanced at a digital reading on the control console. The micro-thermometer embedded deep in the midbrain was registering a temperature of just over ninety-eight degrees Fahrenheit. Good. The experiment was ready to begin. He hoped to God he'd got the defreezing process right.

Two micro-fine electrodes lay embedded deep in the pre-frontal lobes, their ends sticking out like miniature tooth-picks. A cluster of thin wires led to a small junction-box from which ran a cable ribbon to the main console outside the chamber. There it terminated in a simple ON–OFF switch marked with a Dyno-tape strip, *Pulse Control*. This was the red button.

He glanced at the console clock, a liquid crystal display flickering the time in tenths of a second. It was approaching 22.00 hours. He knocked back the dregs of a beaker of cold coffee and went over to the window. Prising open the venetian blinds, he looked out into the night. The light from the lab reflected off the glass, blacking out the sky. A chequerboard of lights burned in the main hospital block and above, far beyond reach, dimly glowered a yellow moon. He stood for several minutes, thinking through the larger implications of what he was about to do, then with a small shiver of awe he turned back to the small, glistening hemisphere of tissue lying suspended in its perspex frame. At times like this, any man was in danger of pushing the physical that one step beyond, into the metaphysical.

He stood over the console, bracing himself for the moment when he would reach forward and, with the smallest movement of a finger, flip the switch to ON. That moment was close, very close.

*

Grace picked at a plate of cheese for supper, but she wasn't hungry. She'd taken a bath but still felt restless, uncomfortable. She washed up her plate and poured herself the rest of the orange-juice from the fridge. For a moment she leant over the crossword Leo had left unfinished and tried to work out a clue, but she couldn't think clearly. She went back to the sitting-room as Big Ben struck the hour for *News at Ten*, but the television headlines seemed to wash over her without meaning anything. She felt muddled, befuddled, as if the announcer's words had lost their power to invoke meaning. A wave of dizziness swept over her as she finished the glass. Strange how everything seemed to taste odd and *metallic* tonight, she thought.

As she switched off the television, she felt suddenly and strangely disorientated. Where was she? Leo's house. Friday evening. Leo was out with Mum at a concert. Perhaps she was starting flu: it could happen in spring. She'd go off to bed and read a book.

She tried to wash away the strange taste in her mouth with a glass of water, but it seemed to cling to her tongue, bringing back some long-distant echo in her memory. She headed across the hallway. Her limbs felt sluggish and heavy, and it took an enormous effort of will to drive them. Her thoughts were confused and garbled, as if her mind was picking up two radio stations at the same time. As she reached the bottom of the stairs, she felt a flush of panic and reached out to the stair-post. Something was happening. Her baby must be coming. And yet the signs weren't right.

It was happening in her mind, in her *brain* . . . bubbling, fermenting, swelling to burst like a boil, a tumour, a cyst . . .

She had her foot on the bottom stair when the light about her suddenly seemed to grow brighter. She stepped back. The whole hallway began to glow with a brilliant radiance. She struggled to make out the pictures on the wall, the oak chest at the side, the study door half open across the way, but it was as if a luminous sheet, swelling and pulsing, hung between her and the objects. *No!* she cried, *not again, surely that's all over and done with!* She clung to the stair-post, shaking her head in the vain hope of throwing it off, but the brightness followed her everywhere she turned, sticking to her eyeballs, clamped to her brain, growing ever brighter, denser, and gradually coalescing into a shimmering light-ball of terrifying, dazzling brilliance.

*

Sudden black-out. Lights fuse. Blind blackness.

Jerk cut.

A room. Odd viewpoint. I'm on the ceiling. Floating above the room, looking down. Looking down on what's happening.

There's a figure lying on a bed below. White-faced, surrounded by whiteness, garbed in white . . . white sheets, white hospital sheets in a white hospital bed . . .

It's . . . *me!*

A man is bending over the bed, a man in a white coat. He raises his fist and slams it down on my chest once, twice, repeatedly, pounding with all his strength, beating the empty sack of my body . . . Lights are

flashing. Nurses rushing all about. Someone hands the doctor a needle. He holds it
up to the light, squirts out some fluid, I see
his face, angular, lop-sided, I know that
face . . . then he sinks the needle into my
arm and suddenly, up here, I feel shot,
dragged down, hauled back into my useless
husk, back to the fight, back to the agony,
back to the terrible endless clawing
pain . . .

*

She heard her own scream echo through the house. Involuntarily, she doubled up as a thick belt of pain lashed into her,
knocking her off balance. She scrambled desperately for the
stair-post, but it slipped from her grasp as another sickening
wave of pain swept over her. She sank to her knees, clutching
her stomach, and slid back onto the cold, hard tiles. Dazed,
she felt another swirl of pain, but this time a different pain,
clawing at her belly, gripping her womb as in an invisible
vice, tighter and tighter, squeezing out a cry from her throat
as it rose to a peak of agony, then briefly subsiding, leaving
her gasping in its wash, before almost at once it came again
and the next onrush swept crashing over her. Oh God, she
howled aloud, not now, not yet, not here, not *this* . . .

*

Leonard drove home from the Mahler concert, humming
the adagio from the Tenth. The fields on either side of the
empty road glowed luminous beneath a bright full moon,
and with a heady sense of the power beneath the hood he
put his foot down and hurtled through the night. He felt
more relaxed. He'd done all he could, and by carefully
administering further doses of the drug over the coming

days, everything might just, with luck, turn out all right. Laura had been lively and attentive all evening, and when he'd dropped her back home she'd pressed him to come in with unusual warmth, but he'd refused. He was anxious about leaving Grace alone. During the interval he'd phoned home several times but the line had been constantly engaged; he'd assumed she was having one of her interminable chats to Emily or another of her friends. Even so, he'd brought the evening to a close as quickly as he decently could and headed back home.

As he pulled into the driveway, he saw her bedroom light was off. He cut the engine and coasted the last few yards so as not to wake her. As quietly as he could, he let himself in the front door. He'd switched on the hall light and was reaching out to lay his car keys on the pewter plate on the hall chest when he noticed a wet red smear dragged across the tiled floor. He flashed a glance around. At the foot of the stairs, caught in pools by the irregular tiles, spread a thin film of water, stained with threads of pink. The streaks led to his study door. With a cry, he leapt forward. A trail of watery blood ran across the carpet to the desk. Smudged and bloodied, the phone lay with the receiver knocked from its cradle. But no sign of Grace.

He flew back into the hall. Heavy clots of blood spattered the floor by the door to the kitchen. He burst in.

Grace lay sprawled unconscious over an upturned chair. Her nightdress was pulled up high and saturated with blood, and between her gore-streaked legs, half-hidden by her crouching body, he could make out a large red mound of matter and, connected by a glistening bluish cord, the unmistakable wrinkled, curled form of a premature human foetus.

Nineteen

'Almighty and everlasting God . . .'

A soft voice, lowered in prayer, swelled for a brief moment, then faded away. Disjointed words penetrated her blurred senses, small isolated bubbles that surfaced gently and burst into nothing.

'Eternal peace . . . life everlasting . . .'

Then another voice, a woman's voice.

'Thank you, Father.'

Mum? Was that her? Such confusion. Nothing made sense. She felt desperately tired. Her mind drifted in and out of focus. As she rose gradually to the surface, everything grew brighter, louder.

'She's coming round. Grace? Can you hear me?'

Father Gregory's face pressed close. Father Gregory, with his vestry smell. He was smiling. He wants me to smile back, she thought, like a baby in a pram . . . *My baby!* Oh God! What happened? Where am I? I see bottles and tubes and white curtains. I'm in hospital. I remember now. It's all coming back . . .

The terrible nightmare. Matthew lying there, dead. She seemed somehow to be floating outside his body. She saw them trying to resuscitate him, then suddenly she was yanked back into his body. Feeling his pain. The pain, the wrenching, ripping, clawing pain, wave after wave, one hard on the heels of the last, splitting and splicing, tugging and gutting, turning her belly inside out like a glove. For a split second she was a child again, at the seaside, watching old men digging for lug-worms, seeing how they jabbed a thumb on one end and the insides squirted out of the other. She'd felt

246

it squirt and squirm out, warm and slippery against her thighs. She'd heard it fall on the floor with a flopping sound, she'd felt for it with her hand, oh God it wasn't moving, wasn't breathing, wasn't wriggling or kicking, just lying there. *No!* It couldn't be dead! Surely they'd saved it. Surely that was why she was here.

'Grace? Darling?' Mum was speaking again now. 'You're going to be all right. Everything's fine, I promise you.'

'That's enough, Mrs Holmwood,' said another voice. 'Let her rest.'

A nurse. I can make out a blue blur. Nurse! My baby, bring me my baby, nurse, please.

She struggled to speak. The words made sounds in her mind but not in her throat. Suddenly she felt the sharp sting of a needle. The room tipped backwards, the faces melted, the voices receded.

My baby . . . Please . . .

*

Father Gregory led the way into the corridor and laid a hand on Laura's arm. She looked grey and haggard.

'You're worn out, Laura,' he said. 'Go home and get some rest.'

'I think I'll sit here just a bit longer, Father,' she replied with a brave smile. 'I'm so grateful to you for coming.'

He glanced at a clock on the wall.

'I'd better be getting along to Mass. Don't *worry*, Laura. They know what they're doing. She's all right.'

'Thank you, Father. God be with you.'

'And with you, Laura.' He gave her hand a squeeze. 'I'll drop in and see you this evening.'

He turned and walked slowly away to the lifts, barely aware of the bustle about him as the hospital geared itself up for the day. Outside, he paused for a moment under the entrance canopy, gazing out at the fresh young day that had broken while he'd been inside, coming to terms once again with death. Poor Laura; her life seemed beset with tragedy.

Poor Grace, too, having lost father, brother and now child. Blessed with one hand and bereaved with the other, where was the justice in this? What could he say to comfort her, what could he *ever* say at times like this? Sooner or later she would react with common human outrage: why *me*, why *my* child? And all he'd be able to say would be, *It's God's will, have faith*.

As he drove out of the city and headed west towards Abbotsbury, bitter disappointment settled over him. Monsignor Rolfe and the Bishop would try to conceal their real feelings but, frankly, they'd be relieved. Virgin conception or not, at a stroke the miscarriage put paid to any notion of a Divine hand at work, the hand of an Almighty who could override natural biological laws. Who would now believe Grace in *any* of her claims? Could he honestly say that *he* did as wholeheartedly as before? No, with her credibility undermined, the lid would be quietly and firmly put on the investigation into her visions, and into the miracle of Mary Nolan, too . . .

Mary Nolan. Someone would have to break the news to her and to Benedict. In a way, it was his responsibility. Very well, he'd drive over at lunchtime.

*

Leonard drove home against the morning traffic. His shoulders ached with tension and he felt a curious detachment, as if everything was happening a fraction of a second late. He'd spent the night without sleep, true, but that wasn't why he felt so bad. He could persuade himself he'd made the best of the situation, but it was a situation of his own making and a lousy one at that. He drove slowly; he didn't trust his reactions, but also he was not looking forward to the job facing him. He glanced down at the bloodstained blanket rolled up on the floor by the passenger seat and thought back to the horror of the night. He'd wrapped Grace quickly in blankets, bundled her into his car and driven off at furious speed to the casualty department of the Royal

248

Hospital. There, under his supervision, they'd pumped her full of drugs and hooked her up to drips. When her condition was stable, he'd called Laura, who had come over right away, and stayed with her until seven in the morning, taking the opportunity of Father Gregory's arrival to leave.

Reaching home, he made himself a black coffee laced with brandy and set about mopping and swabbing the floors and carpets. As he wiped down the phone in his study, he puzzled over why she hadn't dialled for help. Perhaps she'd tried to call Laura from that phone and found her still out, and then knocked it off the cradle as she staggered away so that later, when she'd tried the kitchen phone, she'd found the line dead. He winced to imagine the terror she must have felt at that moment.

He finished as best he could and wrote a note to his cleaning lady, explaining the accident. Then bracing himself with a shot of neat brandy, he went into the utility room.

Just inside the door stood the large old-fashioned family fridge which he'd thrown out when his children had finally given up coming to stay. In a swift, decisive movement, he opened it. Inside, alone on the empty racks, lay a white plastic bin-liner, knotted at the neck and bulging fatly. He'd turned the fridge up too high, and frost spangled the surface where he hadn't properly wiped off the smears. Through the opaque skin where it swelled he could just make out the dark red organs inside. He reached in and swung the bag out. It brushed sloppily against his leg, and as he dropped it into the old stone sink it fell with a dull, fleshy slap. He went back into the kitchen to fetch a sharp filleting-knife, a small polythene sandwich-box and a roll of paper towelling, then, gritting his teeth, he returned to the utility room, rolled up his sleeves and set to work.

First, he unzipped the bin-liner. A tangle of flesh spilled out, so hideously human with its chubby arms and legs, fingers and toes, its disproportionately large tadpole head, and yet so hideously *un*human with its other semi-formed head, a false, unnatural outcrop budding from one side of its neck . . .

The bile rose to his throat and he had to turn aside for a moment to stop himself retching. Summoning all his resolution, he turned back. Deftly, trying to imagine he was back in the school labs dissecting a rabbit, he cut out a small cube of flesh and placed it in the plastic container. Next, he fished around for a section from which he could fillet out the bone – the femur? the tibia? he shut the question out of his mind – and then, holding up the bag, let a small stream of blood trickle to join the rest in the sample box. Finally, he pressed the lid down tight and turned away, choking on vomit. He would take the remains into the garden and incinerate it, then he'd take a long, hot shower and change into fresh clothes and, after all that, he'd drive the samples out to Bath, where he had a card to call in from a man who was better equipped than any in this field. And then he'd know, definitively, if his worst fears were true.

*

Later that morning, Leonard returned to Grace's bedside and sat for a while holding her hand as she drifted in and out of consciousness. At one point she came round and, seeing him, smiled sleepily. When she spoke her voice betrayed none of the frantic desperation of the early hours of that morning. The dichloralphenazone was doing its work.

'Sorry to be such a fuss, Leo,' she murmured.

'It's my job, Duchess.'

'I thought today was your day off.'

'Save your strength for getting better.'

A frown clouded her face and her breathing grew agitated. He squeezed her hand reassuringly. But her distress seemed to intensify, and she began squirming around until he feared she'd dislodge the drip.

'Calm down, angel,' he soothed. 'You're all right, and that's what counts.'

'Leo, Leo —'

'Take it easy. Don't upset yourself.'

Instinctively he reached to feel her pulse. He'd better call Sister and have her boost the sedative. He was rising to his feet when he stopped. Grace's eyes had rolled backwards and her eyelids were fluttering. Fascinated, he listened as she began to speak. Her voice sounded disembodied, other-worldly.

'He was lying on this bed, quite dead,' she was saying. 'You were there, Leo, and you tried to bring him round, you were thumping and hitting him on the chest, but it wasn't working, he was dead, quite dead. Then you gave him an injection and he came back to life again, back into his body . . .'

A chill shiver rippled over his skin. He knew exactly who she was talking about. After all those years he could recall the scene as if it were yesterday. How the hell could she know?

'You mean, Matthew?' he whispered hoarsely.

'And then he felt the pain again, the terrible pain,' she went on, but then gradually her eyes returned to normal and she turned on him with a desperate, pleading look. 'I *felt* it, Leo. I felt *his* pain. Right here, in the stomach.'

He laughed briefly, uneasily.

'That was your own pain you were feeling, angel.'

'I don't think so.' She paused, frowning. 'Leo, could that . . . that nightmare have brought the trouble on?'

'Come on, Duchess . . .'

'I'm serious. It all started just like one of those apparitions. A brilliant bright light everywhere. Only, it was different. Terrible.' Her frown deepened. 'But I saw him. I *was* him. I felt what he felt. Leo, what's happening to my brain? Am I going mad?'

He shook her hand urgently.

'Grace, listen to me! You were in extreme pain — you, yourself. It's well known that pain can cause hallucinations. You evoked images of Matthew because he's still very much in your mind. It's logically impossible to feel someone else's pain. It might have seemed that way, but it wasn't. Just a confusional state. Quite normal. Don't worry.'

He continued trying to reassure her, but he knew he was partly seeking to reassure himself. Gradually her eyes began to droop and her voice fell to a broken, incoherent whisper. At last, he rose and gently tucked her under the bedclothes.

'I'll look in later,' he said. 'Try to put it all out of your mind. Just rest, and we'll have you home in no time.'

'Leo, you don't think I'm round the twist do you?' she asked drowsily.

'You're as sane as the best of us. You're just coping with a lot of stress, that's all.' He leaned forward and kissed her on the forehead. 'Go to sleep now, Duchess.'

*

Father Gregory paused in the rough paddock and took a deep breath. The air was rich with the scent of fresh grass and sappy new foliage. Behind, on the slope beyond the stile, lay the Nolans' cottage he'd just left. Below stretched the ribbon of slate and stone houses of Coledean village, and beyond, across the main road and hidden behind a copse, stood the mill house where it had all started. A bright sun shone fearlessly in a cloudless sky and the trees were alive with the song of birds. Every blade of grass seemed to affirm the joy of new life. Eternal renewal: that was God's greatest gift. The resurrection of the soil with each cycle of the seasons. One might grieve for a stillborn child, but it was in the nature of God to be *bounteous*, to make His world fruitful and teeming, so that the loss of one small seed, tragic though it might seem in the individual instance, was nevertheless, collectively, a part of the whole thrust of Creation. Mary had shown exactly the right response when he'd told her the sad news: making the sign of the Cross, she'd simply said, 'God's will be done.' Without death, there could be no renewal, no resurrection. Grace's loss was part of the plan. It *had* to be.

And yet it was hard to accept. He kicked at a clump of ragwort with his toe and left it uprooted, to perish: was *that* part of the plan? It was an uncomfortable kind of plan that worked on the general level but never seemed easily to fit the particular case. Abruptly he turned and set off briskly down the hill towards where he'd parked his car. This was no way for a priest to think! He was disappointed, that was all. Disappointed that the sign he'd sought had failed him. But it was his own fault for not having had the courage to walk the tightrope of faith without seeing a safety-net below.

'Father?'

He'd almost reached the gate when a call behind him interrupted his thoughts. He turned. Benedict was bounding across the paddock after him. He stopped and waited. He'd been puzzled in the cottage: the boy had taken the news with more agitation than anguish. Now, as he came to a halt before him, his piercing blue eyes betrayed a deeply troubled conscience.

'Can I talk to you, Father?'

'Of course, Ben. What is it?'

The boy cast around him as if afraid of being overheard.

'Can we go somewhere?'

'My car's over there,' replied Father Gregory. 'Will that do?'

*

Father Gregory looked out across his small patch of garden, but he was scarcely aware of the blossom on the apple tree or the leaves newly opened on the elder bush. The window was slightly ajar, but he hardly heard the distant sound of cheering from the playing-fields behind or caught the scent of freshly mown grass on the mild air. His mind was elsewhere, wrestling with the shock of Benedict's recantation. Could Grace have been telling the truth, after all? If so, did that make any material *difference*? The problem had been going round in his mind so long that it had worn smooth, leaving nothing to form a purchase on. Let other people judge; he could no longer trust his own judgement.

He turned to his desk and rummaged among the books and pamphlets until he found the diocesan phone-list. He glanced at the small silver carriage-clock on the mantelpiece his mother had given him at his ordination and wondered what he might be interrupting in the Bishop's household late on a Saturday afternoon. Still, this was important new evidence. With sudden decisiveness, he picked up the receiver.

It was a while before Monsignor Rolfe could be located. When he finally came on the line, the annoyance was audible behind his smooth tones.

'Father Gregory,' he purred, 'this is an unexpected pleasure.'

'I have two important pieces of news about Grace Holmwood, Monsignor,' he began. 'First, you should know she's . . . she's had a miscarriage.'

There was a split-second pause before the Monsignor replied.

'God rest its soul,' he said quietly. 'And the second thing?'

'Benedict Nolan came and spoke to me after I broke the news to him. He told me he'd lied. His confession was false. He wasn't the father.'

'You believe him?'

'We believed him before.'

'Indeed.' Monsignor Rolfe hesitated, then continued dismissively, 'Thank you for letting me know, Father. I shall make a note on the file.'

'But surely this puts a different complexion on things.'

'How? *This* boy may not be the father, but no doubt we could find another who was, if we cared to look.' A note of impatience entered his voice. 'It seems the whole question is academic now. There can be no miracle in a miscarriage, Father. Whatever ideas still lurk in your mind on that score, forget them. And as for the girl's visions, I would say this settles that question.'

'But surely it reopens the possibility —'

'Father, I really don't have time for this nonsense. Would you please excuse me?'

The line went dead. Father Gregory put the phone down with a growl of frustration. Maybe the Monsignor *was* right, but to use this as an excuse to shut down the whole inquiry was quite unjustifiable. The visions and the miracle should be judged on their own evidence. He remembered the novice priest at his old priory once telling him, *The Church is a human institution, with all that's good and bad about it*: open arms, closed minds. It was a system, and any system was political. The step from the politically inconvenient to the theologically inadmissible was, he could see, a very small one indeed. Was he going to stand by and see that glib transition made here?

Twenty

The early morning sun flickered through the trees, disappearing behind a hill one moment only to reappear around a bend the next. Leonard drove fast, eagerly. Six days had passed, and later that afternoon he was bringing Grace back home – *his* home, in Upton Flint. He'd persuaded Laura it would be best if she stayed for a while where he, as a qualified doctor, could keep an eye on her. Laura had suggested instead that he stayed with them in Coledean, but he'd argued that, with all the local gossip and attention she was attracting, she should be kept safely out of harm's way. That evening Laura was coming over with another suitcase of Grace's things. He was relieved; it was vital to have her where he could monitor her condition in these next few critical weeks. He didn't yet know the full extent of the trouble. But very soon he would, for late the previous night he'd received a call from Tom Welland to say that the results had come through. And right now he was on his way to Bath to collect them.

The city streets were still empty and before he knew it he'd arrived at the Department of Medical Research building. He parked at the back, alongside Welland's blue saloon, the only other car on the lot. It had rained in the night; a light wind scudded across the pools in the tarmac and dark streaks disfigured the windowless concrete façade. He hurried round the front and rang the night bell. A security guard let him in, checked off his name, issued him with a visitor's pass and put a call through to Room 313 upstairs.

A minute later, Welland came out across the foyer. Behind his glasses his eyes were red-rimmed and his white coat exaggerated the pallor of his face. With the barest greeting, he led Leonard to the lifts. They rode up in silence. As they reached the third floor, Welland finally turned to him.

'Who else is in on this?' he asked.

'Just you and me.'

'Good.'

He led the way down the corridor and through the security doors to his laboratory. As Leonard followed him inside, the door closed behind him with a dull clunk. The venetian blinds were shut, and overhead the panels of strip-lighting flickered coldly. Microscopes, racks of test-tubes, trays of gels and other genetic analysis equipment lined the benches. Set into the far wall was a small chamber with an inspection panel, arm-gloves and the familiar yellow and black radiation hazard stickers. The interior of the chamber was dark, but from the soft whirr of a small pump and the flicker of needles on a nearby unit, he knew something was active inside. He peered in. In the half-light, he could make out the unmistakable wrinkled acorn shape of a small human brain. Fine wires led to two toothpick-size probes sticking out of the frontal lobes.

He heard the snap of a cigarette lighter behind him.

'Soon be up and running,' said Welland, coughing. 'Thanks to your kind co-operation.'

'Is it metabolizing?' Leonard asked, unable to resist his curiosity.

'When I zap it, yes.'

Welland pointed to a series of time-chart scrolls pinned up on a board over the desk. Apart from a single short, sharp spike, they showed one continuous straight line. At a quick glance, Leonard read off the timing against the spike: some time the previous Friday night. Fleetingly, it occurred to him that this was about the time Grace had had her accident. It might be six days ago, but it felt like six years.

'I give it a few seconds' kick-start every hundred hours or so,' continued Welland. 'I've got oxy-glucose uptake, so at least some nerve-nets are firing.'

'Why the frontal lobes, though?'

'Concentration of short axon stellate cells.' Welland paused for emphasis. 'Memory cells.'

Leonard gave a short laugh.

'Surely no-one believes memory is located in actual cells any more!'

Welland threw him a wry smile but said nothing. Leaving his cigarette smouldering in a Petri dish full of butts, he went over to a bench where, between a drug cabinet and a large slide rack, stood a coffee percolator. He dusted out two mugs with his handkerchief and filled them with coffee, then pulled a bottle of Scotch out of a filing drawer.

'But that's not what you came here for,' he said, unscrewing the bottle. 'Want a stiffener? I think you'll need it.'

*

'See anything unusual?' asked Welland, sitting back in his swivel chair.

'The whole damn thing is unusual,' responded Leonard.

'Anything *specifically*?'

Leonard leant forward and examined the sheaf of photographs once again. The first set presented a spread of the foetus' chromosomes, neatly aligned in their pairs and resembling striped, banded maggots. There, revealed in black and white, was the astonishing genetic abnormality. He knew that, on average, about six births in a thousand involved some form of chromosomal abnormality. Many of these were caused by the failure of one of the parents' chromosomes to disjoin, as in the case of Down's syndrome, resulting in an extra chromosome being passed on. Here, however, there was a *double* non-disjunction – the foetus possessed *four* chromosome 19s, rather than the normal two, giving it a total of forty-eight as against the normal forty-six. Leonard was shaken to the core; he'd never seen or read anything like it, even in way-out experimental research papers.

How had it occurred? Welland had a theory. He guessed that radioactive beta-particles had penetrated the resting oocyte some while before ovulation, and this had interfered with the second stage of meiosis. He showed him the results of experiments on mice in which irradiation of maturing oocytes clearly led to an extra chromosome in one-cell embryos. But *two* extra? Leonard had kept tight-lipped: he wasn't going to get drawn into speculating on what might have been the cause – he knew all too well. The question burning in his mind concerned Grace herself. If *these* cells carried the damage, expressing it only now, what of the *other* cells in her body, the cells of the thyroid, the liver, the lymph and blood systems that were so prone to carcinoma?

Welland was tapping his cigarette lighter on the table.

'Come on, Leonard, what else?'

'I don't see anything else,' he muttered.

'Look at the *genes*.'

Leonard turned to the next batch of photos. Here, selected gene loci had been isolated and stained. They showed up as pairs of dark blobs, laid out in parallel strips on a pale grey background. Against each fragment was a calibration marking its kilobase size and its position on the arm of its chromosome. He looked from one of the pair to the other and back again. He frowned. He flipped to another photograph, showing a different pair of fragments on a different chromosome. His mouth grew dry.

He looked up sharply.

'The pairs . . . They're *identical*!'

'Exactly.'

'What the hell does it mean?'

'Think about it, Leonard.'

He turned back to the chromosome spread and glanced quickly at the sex chromosomes. The foetus would, of course, have to be XX – female. It was. Even a rough visual inspection showed that the bandings on each member of the pairs was exactly the same.

'My God,' he breathed.

'Look at the HLA test,' said Welland.

Leonard fumbled through the photographs again until he

came to the right one. He knew that the HLA site on chromosome 5 was one of the most commonly switched between parents. But here, he could see at a glance, exactly the same sequences were repeated on each side of the pair. Every gene had its exactly matching opposite number. Its mirror-image.

He sat back, dumbfounded, as the inevitable conclusion forced itself upon him.

There had only been one parent in this conception.

*

Leonard spent the morning in a daze. As soon as he'd completed his morning rounds, he shut himself in his office and, telling his secretary to field all calls, sat down to think.

Virgin birth, he knew, was not uncommon in nature. In fact, about a thousand species, mostly invertebrates, reproduced parthenogenetically. At first sight, it was surprising that more species didn't: requiring two to couple had its evolutionary drawbacks. In theory, a single egg before its final reduction possessed all the genetic material needed to produce a complete offspring. He remembered reading about an institute in Maryland where they'd actually hatched a few parthenogenetically derived chickens and turkeys, and some of these had even survived to adulthood. But it had never worked with mammals. True, mouse egg cells had been induced in the laboratory to self-fertilize, but not a single one of the embryos had ever survived to birth. The fact was, as he'd told Grace in London, that in mammals a gene sequence in the male sperm made a specific contribution to the development of the placenta, without which the foetus itself couldn't properly develop. Virgin conception was possible in mice, yes, but not virgin birth. And neither, categorically neither, was thought to be possible in the most evolved of all the mammals – man.

Until now. Until this very special set of circumstances.

Too disturbed to sit still, he slipped out of the hospital building and wandered out into the open air. The sunshine dazzled him, and for a moment he felt as if it was all an unreal dream, a nightmare of absurdities. He sat down on a bench and went again through the photographs Welland had given him. Was this some kind of trick, a forgery, a fabrication? Surely not: the man could have no possible motive. Anyway, who would ever *think* of such an unimaginable idea? Besides, Welland had been very keen to pursue the case. He'd wanted to get to the mother, to check the foetal blood group could actually be derived from hers; he'd even like to check if a skin graft would be rejected . . . Leonard had told him shortly that the mother had died in labour and refused to be drawn further.

He looked out across the fussily landscaped car-park and the line of warehouses and industrial buildings beyond. What could this mean for his career? His work on tumours, based on his clinical experience, was filling in useful gaps in the general corpus of knowledge, but he'd never make his name in that. Here, however, in his very hands, lay the most phenomenal evidence the scientific world had seen for decades. The first authenticated case of human virgin conception! It was a bombshell. He had to do something with it. But almost at once his enthusiasm evaporated. He might have the key to a major advance in man's understanding of himself and his biological origins, he might even possess the proof to explode possibly the world's greatest religious myth, but it was useless in his hands. He couldn't do anything with it without destroying all that counted in his life – Grace, Laura, their friendship, even his career.

Slowly he rose to his feet and retraced his steps back into the hospital. Right now, all that mattered was Grace and how he could best help her cope with the genetic time-bomb ticking away in the cells of her body.

*

Tom Welland taped up the last of the small sachets and, looping it by its tag alongside the other two, lowered the stainless-steel rod into the narrow vat of liquid nitrogen.

There'd been an awkward moment when Leonard had asked for any unused specimen material back, but he'd told him he'd used it all up in the tests. If Leonard was playing cagey over where it came from, why shouldn't he over where it went? Not that Leonard had fooled him for a moment, though. He knew perfectly well who the mother had been. He had only to think back to the time he'd dropped in on Grace and seen that book on pregnancy to put two and two together. Besides, he'd done the obvious check. He knew all about Grace's blood group from the hospital records office, and the foetus's was identical.

He screwed the lid back on the cryostat and stood back. Peeling off his gloves, he rubbed his eyes. He was exhausted; he'd been up two nights in succession, running the tests, unable to tear himself away. He glanced at the wall-clock. It *was* the most extraordinary, mind-boggling phenomenon, but he had a more immediate worry, one that lay across the room in the isolation chamber. He'd better accelerate the programme and give it its next tweak that evening.

He peered in through the inspection panel. As his eye scanned the fine tubes carrying the plasma, he gave a sudden jolt. That blood was *her* blood. He'd used it on the basis that twin blood was invariably compatible, but he hadn't run a proper analysis. It hadn't been necessary – until now. If some cells in her body had produced the astonishing aberration he'd just witnessed, what about *these* cells? Had they, too, been infiltrated in a way that might cause mutation?

He took a deep breath. He'd damn well better run a proper analysis before going any further.

*

Grace sat with her knees tucked under her chin, staring at the television. A comedian had a studio audience in fits of laughter, but she couldn't make anything of it. The world seemed to lie one step beyond her reach. There was plenty of noise and activity around her – Mum was on her way with a load of her things, the phone had been going constantly and Leo kept coming in to check she was all right – yet she felt all this was happening to someone else and that she herself was somewhere far away. She dug her nails into the palm of her hand, but she hardly felt it. She flicked the television over to a chat show; the faces and voices arrived at her eyes and ears but somehow they went right through. She wasn't a living person any more, just a hollow shell.

She felt empty in her soul. The fault was her own arrogance and vanity, and now she was paying for it. She'd allowed people to think of her 'visions' as divinely inspired, but all along she'd known in her heart she was a fraud. They were just what she'd suspected – the hallucinations of a mad girl. Clever, yes, but then a wicked mind *was* clever. Father Gregory had been taken in by her description of Our Lady, but he'd only have to go into her bedroom and look at Matthew's statuette to know where *that* image had come from. And even the nightmare – the *day*mare – about Matthew dying in hospital: she'd probably just picked up something subconsciously, Leo had said. But God knew. God saw into every heart, listened in to every thought. He'd given her the baby and taken it away, to teach her a lesson. In hospital, she'd cried out at the cruelty of it all, but now she recognized the justice of the punishment, condemning her to madness and casting her out beyond hope of redemption.

Lowering her head, she wept into her arm.

Time grew blurred. Sounds merged. Footsteps crossed the floor above. On the television a muffled burst of applause. All far away, so very far away . . .

Metallic taste. Purplish. No, not this, please not again! The madness lurking inside me, here it comes now, uncoiling, slithering towards me . . .

*

263

Light-flash, searingly bright, bursting from the end of a long tunnel like a fireball. It flickers, then explodes in a million tiny shooting splinters and gradually fades into darkness.

Then suddenly a picture, clear in every detail. A hospital room. A bed, surrounded by machines. Everything is white. A figure approaches, dressed in white from head to toe. White gloves, white overalls, white mask with a window for his eyes. He turns to fix something at the side. On his shoulder is a small badge. A circle, with three black wedges on a yellow background . . .

*

Leonard was chopping the vegetables when he heard the cry. He rushed into the sitting-room to find Grace cowering against the back of the sofa, her arms raised to shield her head and her eyes rolled back to the whites. He clapped his hands loudly once, twice, then quickly checked her pupils and pulse. Taking her in his arms, he held her close and tried his best to calm her. Sweet dear Christ, he prayed, please no, not yet, not till I've had a chance to work something out . . .

Gradually her rigidity eased and her breathing began to return to normal. He took her hands and made her face him.

'You had another . . . turn . . . just then?' he asked carefully.

She nodded. 'Horrible,' she shuddered.

'Tell me about it.'

He listened as she described her hallucination. His mind was reeling. How could she know about that? He'd certainly never let drop any hint. Not even Laura knew that Matthew had been sent to a special isolation unit the moment the real cause was diagnosed. In fact, she'd been allowed to believe he'd died in the early hours of that morning. He could recall how terrible he'd felt, seeing the poor woman blame herself that she'd slipped home for a couple of hours' rest, after days and nights without sleep, and so hadn't been there at his bedside at the final moment. He recalled, too, how painful it had been, discouraging her from seeing the body.

He turned back to Grace. Had Welland let something slip? He shivered. But she was now shaking with long, racking sobs. As he drew her closer, she buried her face in his chest.

'Everything's my fault,' she sobbed. 'I deserve it.'

'That's not true!' he said. 'You've got nothing to blame yourself for.'

'I do. I thought I knew it all,' she went on with rising despair. 'I was so stupid, so *arrogant*. I thought at first they really were visions, visions from God, and I'd been specially chosen. But they were just a test. I knew all along I wasn't special, I was just a fake, but I didn't say anything because I didn't want to let people down. Mum, Father Gregory – they *expected* it of me.'

'Grace, listen to me —'

'And with the baby, I thought maybe, after all . . . I *wanted* to believe it was a blessing from Our Lady. I wanted to be like her, to live up to her, but I couldn't. I failed. God punished me for my vanity. He got rid of my baby.'

'This is terrible, wrong thinking!'

But she wouldn't stop. 'And then the funny things started again, like before but much worse. Nightmares. Horrible, mad nightmares. I'm going mad!'

'No, you're not!' he almost shouted, shaking her. 'You're normal and healthy and blameless.'

'How *can* I be normal?' she wailed.

'Grace, angel, *trust me*.'

He continued talking, repeating that she was wrong to blame herself. But what real comfort could he give her except the truth? How could he ask her to trust him when he was so patently untrustworthy?

Eventually, she fell quiet, still locked in confusion and self-blame. Despairing of reversing her thinking by argument and reassurance, he suggested that she record her experiences as they occurred. She shrugged, saying she'd been writing them down before, but it didn't seem to do any good or make things any clearer. He urged her to try again: once they knew the tap-root of the problem in her psyche, they could look for a way of extirpating it. By now she was exhausted, and he persuaded her to go to bed. When Laura arrived, he sent her up with a light supper, and later he took her up a mild sedative himself. Laura did not stay late – she hadn't slept much over the past nights – and he himself was in bed before midnight. He lay staring out at a restless moonlit sky, unable to sleep, filled with rage at the cruel, anti-human ideology with which Grace had been indoctrinated and which now, at a moment of crisis, came back to her. No-one deserved to suffer so wickedly from such erroneous thinking!

And yet, as much as he raged, a small inner voice told him it was all bluster: his rage was really with himself.

*

Leonard pottered round the greenhouse, tying up canes for the tomatoes and preparing the sweet pea seedlings for potting out. Though it was barely mid-morning, the sun beat down on the whitewashed panes, warming up the dusty old shelves and filling the air with the stuffy aroma of sweating mulch. He pulled off his jersey, all the hotter from annoyance, for Father Gregory had dropped in to visit Grace. He'd left the priest upstairs praying with her. Praying! He'd left them to their superstitious practices and retired to the greenhouse, where the spirits were more earthly and obedient to the laws of nature.

He'd just finished fixing the canes when he heard a footstep on the gravel path. A moment later Father Gregory put his head round the door. An anxious frown creased his brow.

'Have you a moment?' he asked.

'Of course. Come in.'

In the shadowless white light, the priest looked pale and careworn, and his usually florid complexion seemed drained of colour. He came forward.

'I'm worried about Grace,' he began bluntly. 'I think it's time she went back home to her mother, where she belongs.'

Leonard strove to sound civil.

'You don't think she's being looked after properly here?' he asked.

'At a time like this, she needs the support of her family.'

'I thought she wasn't to be exposed to all that foolish gossip.'

Father Gregory ran a finger round his dog-collar.

'I'm only interested in what's best for *her*. She's had a terrible time recently, and naturally she's disturbed and upset. She needs spiritual guidance, and – forgive me if I put it like this – I don't think this is the right household for that.'

Leonard cast the priest a hard glare.

'Father Gregory,' he said quietly, 'I don't think you quite realize that *you* are the cause of a lot of her emotional upset. You people, and your repressive superstitions.'

'This is quite the wrong atmosphere for the girl,' said the priest. 'I'll speak to Laura. Well, if you'll excuse me —'

'Walking away won't help her.'

'Staying here to argue the toss won't help anyone.'

'Look,' Leonard began, taking off his gardening gloves, 'let's get this straight. Grace is in post-partum shock. She has lost her child. She's suffering from a crisis of confidence and self-esteem. She needs to regain a sense of her own worth, her own dignity, her own *self*. She sees the miscarriage as God's punishment for having the vanity to believe she'd been blessed with holy visions. That's what's tormenting her. And yet you can't see how you're to blame.'

'Forgive me, Leonard, I don't think this is serving any useful purpose.'

'Father, I don't mean to teach you your business —'

'Then I suggest you don't try.'

'— but if you care for Grace at all, you'll make the effort to see it through *her* eyes.' He heard his voice take on a tight precision. 'Basically, Grace is a victim of your pernicious myth of original sin. She believes, as you have taught her to believe, that she is *stained* with sin, guilty before she even started, and all she can ever do is struggle to mitigate this curse. It's anti-human and, what's more, it's morally stultifying. It deprives people of the responsibility for their actions. Look at Grace, and you'll see the effects. If you had any charity, you'd stop thinking of her as a soul to save but treat her like a human being in need of proper human love.'

Two pink spots had appeared high on the priest's cheeks. He cast a glance over his shoulder at the door, but turned back, apparently deciding to stand his ground.

'We are all maladjusted beings,' he said tightly.

'And no wonder!'

'I was simply making a theological point. We are all mean, selfish, weak creatures. A Freudian might say it stems from infancy, a Marxist might ascribe it to social conditions later on. My Church puts the fatal flaw a little earlier, at conception. But it's essentially the same.'

'It is *not* the same! Freud and Marx believed in man's ability to better himself, *by* himself. Psychoanalysis offers a means of reversing those early traumas, communism offers a way of restructuring society towards a utopia. They both offer *hope*. In a system where one is condemned before one begins, there can be no hope. Give me hope and joy, not sin and guilt. And for pity's sake, Father, give it to Grace, for by God she needs it!'

Father Gregory inclined his head in a philosophical pose and regarded him with a concerned frown.

'There *is* hope, through God,' he said quietly. 'Hope of redemption, hope of grace. Millions find it.'

'At the price of denying what makes one human.'

'Yes – if you mean by that, focusing on what brings one closer to the Divine.'

'I mean demanding that people take an absurd blind leap of faith.'

'It's not blind if you believe there's something there when you land.'

'If you believe. That begs the question.'

The priest seemed momentarily lost for a reply. He picked up a seed packet and examined it briefly, then put it down.

'Faith is not supposed to be easy,' he admitted.

'Ah, but then you have your miracles, Father. That must be a comfort.'

'Miracles *demand* faith, Leonard. They're not a substitute.'

'And what does your faith tell you about *these* miracles going on under our noses here?'

'I can't comment,' replied the priest shortly. 'Grace's case is under investigation.'

'Come on, you're an old-fashioned miracle-hunter, Father Gregory.' He heard his broken chuckle die with a dry clatter. 'That would be rather endearing if it weren't for what it does to *her*.'

'I don't follow.'

'For God's sake, look at the pain she's suffering! You invent a virgin who gives birth to God, you prop up the story with a whole fabric of miracle and myth, and you brainwash the poor girl from infancy into believing it's true. Then a series of odd events occur, physiological events. She has hallucinations of the Virgin Mary – not surprisingly, as she's been encouraged to idolize her – and the next thing you know, half of her believes these must be visions sent from God and that God has chosen her and endowed her with miraculous powers . . .'

'Now, wait —'

'No, *you* wait, Father! Ask yourself: what happens when it doesn't work? When, for instance, that horse of hers died? Remember that? Do you suppose she didn't pray like hell to your virgin mother to save it? Or worse, when something happens that is simply too incredible for even the most fervent believer to swallow – when, quite without any human contact, she discovers she is a virgin mother, too?' He raised his hand to arrest the protest. 'I'm not judging whether she did or didn't sleep with anyone, I'm just asking you to see it from her viewpoint, and in her own belief she *didn't*. Of course it puts an impossible burden on her. She goes to pieces. Is she a second Virgin Mary or isn't she? *You* can't tell her because you're not sure yourselves and you have to set up an investigation first. She suspects she isn't, but if she's not – if, that is, she's imagining it or it's because she's mentally disturbed – then *she has failed*. Failed God. Failed the Virgin, her ideal.' He couldn't stop now. 'Her first instinct is to respond as she's been programmed to do: she blames herself. *Mea culpa*. She's not good enough, not holy or pure or sinless enough. I tell you, Father,' he went on, stabbing the point home with his finger, 'if you want to help Grace, then take her on one side and say Christ didn't really turn water into wine, that it's just a metaphor, or that even if he did by some amazing piece of alchemy, no-one is expecting her to do the same, just as no-one is expecting her to be another impossible, unattainable ideal of a woman who never existed except as some ideologically repressive feminine archetype.' He was choking on his own conviction and had to pause, but when he'd recovered his footing he found his anger had taken a colder, deadlier turn. 'One thing is for sure, Father. In all that we've seen recently, in the visions, in Mary Nolan regaining her sight, in the question of parthenogenesis, not one single thing has occurred that cannot be completely and satisfactorily explained by natural physical causes.'

Father Gregory had gone pale, and he stood clutching the bench, his knuckles white.

'May God forgive you,' he whispered hoarsely.

'I stand by all I said.'

The priest turned towards the door.

'I will not listen to any more of this blasphemy!'

'It's the truth,' Leonard said hoarsely. 'There is a rational explanation for *everything*.'

The priest had his hand on the doorknob when he turned slowly.

'Everything?' he echoed. 'You may not know, but Benedict Nolan has withdrawn his confession.'

Leonard gave a short laugh.

'I could have told you the boy was making it up, to protect her.'

'You have a rational explanation for the conception, I suppose?'

'As I said.'

'Prove it!'

The two men stood eyeball to eyeball in silence for a long moment, then Leonard clenched his jaw and took a deep, slow breath. He was caught in his own trap.

'Very well, then. Come with me.'

*

Father Gregory hesitated at the end of the short driveway. Should he turn right, towards Coledean, and get Laura to remove her girl from that godless house? Or left, towards Gloucester and the Bishop? He turned left. The news had hit him like a thunderbolt, and as he steered his Mini through the winding lanes to the main Gloucester road, he grappled with the implications.

Leonard had shown him categorical scientific proof that the stillborn child was the offspring of a virgin conception. Of course, he'd told him expecting to refute a miracle and thereby to ridicule the Church. But if one looked at it more carefully, it did nothing of the sort. In fact, for a believer, it served to endorse the omnipotence of God. Leonard's mistake arose from being locked in a false view of science and religion as inherently opposed. That was a Christian fundamentalist hangover and, as Monsignor Rolfe had painstakingly pointed out to him during one of the early inquiry sessions, it relied on an error of categories. God had created

271

the natural world and all the laws that governed it. The most science could do was to reveal what was already established. God had written the dictionary, and man merely groped his way through the pages; when he lit upon a word, it naturally appeared to him as his own discovery, but that was merely an illusion. Now, what God had set up, He could also circumvent. A miracle was precisely that – a direct inter-vention by God, bypassing the secondary action of natural physical forces. In that sense, miracles were *proof* of God's existence.

But, of course, God worked through natural laws as well as apart from them. Daily life was a myriad of tiny miracles. St Augustine had once remarked there was no more of a miracle in the loaves and fishes than in the growing of the wheat that made the bread in the first place. To demonstrate scientifically that Grace had conceived while still a virgin might bar it from the stricter definition of a miracle, but it didn't deny the hand of God in it. It merely showed that God had used the natural route after all, rather than the supernatural one, to mediate His Divine purpose.

He opened the car window. The greenhouse had been uncomfortably hot. For a moment he let his mind drift, and he thought back to Leonard's reaction when he'd asked the obvious question: *how had it happened?* Leonard had been momentarily flustered, then he'd begun on a long-winded scientific explanation all to do with the presence of a twin brother with a similar genetic make-up in their mother's womb . . . He'd lost him in no time. It wasn't important, anyway. The fact was what mattered, and he'd seen the proof in black and white.

But here was clear proof that Grace had not been lying. She'd not been deluding herself or others. Everything she'd said was true. That changed the whole picture. She was demonstrably a truthful, reliable witness after all. Now, that very morning she'd told him she'd been having recurrences of her visions – daymares, she called them – and she'd been writing them down. At the time, in the light of his phone-call to Monsignor Rolfe, he'd not wanted to encourage her to go too far, for fear of her disappointment when she learned that the Church was closing down her case. But now there was all the more reason to pursue it, especially now that the visions had returned and would provide new material.

He was within a few miles of Gloucester when he began to slow down. *Open arms, closed minds.* He could imagine the impatience on the Monsignor's face when he confronted him with this latest development. 'I don't have time for this nonsense.'

Abruptly, Father Gregory drew into the side of the road and made an about-turn. He'd darn well follow this up himself.

*

Leonard stood in the doorway of the garden shed, lost in thought. Turning away, he sat down in the sun on the rockery steps. He couldn't focus on anything except the fiasco that morning. He should never have lost his temper. He plucked at a dead stalk and slowly crushed it between his fingers. God damn it, why hadn't he kept his mouth shut? Of course, the inevitable question had come up: how had it happened? He'd had to think fast. The idea of some genetic interchange between twins in the womb had been clever, but had the priest swallowed it? Anyway, so what? His conscience was answerable to no-one but himself. He'd done all he had deliberately and thoughtfully. He could put his hand on his heart and say he'd done it all for the best, out of human care and concern. Hadn't he?

He rose and headed back into the house. It was time he started Grace's lunch. Today he'd do a tuna salad, her favourite. She was all that mattered, and only he understood what she needed.

Twenty-one

'Laura? A moment, would you?'

Father Gregory hurried across the gravel drive and caught her up just beyond the main convent doorway. Through the window he could see the Sisters and staff were already gathering in the Reverend Mother's study for their usual Sunday morning coffee. He walked with Laura to her car in the park at the rear. Small groups who'd come in from outside to attend the Mass stood by their cars, exchanging gossip. The sun beat down with unreal brilliance, dazzling off the chrome and glass. He could feel its warmth through his cassock, but he still shivered; he was tired from a sleepless night.

He told her he'd been to see Grace the previous day and she's said the strange apparitions had been coming back. He didn't mention the row he'd had with Leonard, from which he was still smarting, nor did he tell her about Leonard's astonishing revelation. That was for Leonard to say; after all, only he could explain the scientific details properly.

As they reached her car, he laid a hand on her arm.

'Laura, it's time Grace came back home. That house isn't the right atmosphere for her.'

'She seems very happy there. And it's a comfort to know Leonard's on hand.' She gave a faint smile. 'But I do miss her.'

'I'm thinking of her spiritual needs. She hasn't been to Mass for weeks now, and I don't know when I last heard her confession.'

'Grace is eighteen, Father,' sympathized Laura, 'and she has a mind of her own.'

'Home is where she *belongs*.' He held her eye. 'Try and persuade her, Laura. I believe it's very important.'

'Well, I've always said . . .' She broke off. 'You're right. Especially if she's having those . . . things again. She'll need you, too, Father. More than ever.'

'I'm here to help all I can.' He opened the car door for her. 'Let me know when it's done.'

He waved her off and stood for a moment in thought, then turned and walked slowly into the convent. Pray God she could wrest the poor child from that man and his corrupting influence. He was crossing the hallway to join the others in the Reverend Mother's study when he met Sister Bertram coming down the stairs. In her hand she held a newspaper. He caught the light frown on her soft, smooth face and stopped. As she reached the bottom, she handed him the paper.

'I think you should see this, Father,' she said gravely.

∗

Grace laid out the knives and forks at the lunch-table and went to the sideboard for glasses. Leo was in the garden, picking mint for the new potatoes. Laura was basting the leg of lamb. The kitchen was filled with the sound of sizzling fat and the aroma of roasting meat.

'I'll never get the hang of this oven.' Her mother slid the tray back. 'Still, we can always put it back if it's too pink.'

'Smells brilliant,' replied Grace. 'How much longer? I'm starving.'

'A few more minutes, darling.' She paused and caught Grace's eye. 'I was thinking. Don't you feel it's time you gave poor Leonard a reprieve? He's had to put up with you for weeks now.'

'He's a sucker for punishment,' she smiled.

But her mother didn't match her smile.

'I spoke to Father Gregory after Mass,' she said. 'He's very worried.'

'For goodness' sake, will everyone please stop worrying!'

At that moment, the French windows opened and Leonard came back in. He beamed at them both.

'Worries, on a day like this?'

'Mum thinks I should stop imposing on your hospitality, Leo,' said Grace.

'I was just saying,' her mother broke in hastily, 'that it's time she came home and let you get on with what you have to do. She's only being a bother, and you've put yourself out enough already.'

'She's no bother!' he laughed. 'I've never been so well looked after. This place is like a five-star hotel. Anyway, I need to keep my beady eye on her.'

'But you're out all day,' protested her mother. 'I'm at home.'

'She's actually coming in with me one day next week . . .'

'But anyway, she's much better. She's got over the worst, haven't you, darling? Thanks to you, of course, Leonard.'

Grace caught the strange, desperate note in her voice and realized this was the tip of a whole iceberg of submerged feelings. She'd never thought of it like that before, but perhaps Mum missed her quite badly. Leonard's expression had hardened. A taut silence stretched between them. Absurd, but it was almost as if they were fighting over who should have her.

'Hey, come on!' she laughed.

Leonard held her with a fixed gaze while he addressed Laura.

'Perhaps Grace should decide for herself,' he said quietly.

'It's not fair,' objected her mother.

'Well, Duchess?'

Grace bit her lip. 'I don't know,' she murmured.

'We both want what's best for you,' he pressed. 'What is it *you* want?'

She looked from one to the other. She felt she was being asked to make a choice that went beyond merely in whose house she should stay. The silence lengthened.

'If Mum wants me back . . .' she said finally. 'You can cope on your own, Leo. You have for ages.'

'But we're having such fun, aren't we?' he protested with a teasing smile under which she could see the hurt.

'But you'll be coming over all the time, just like before – like Mum has here.' She gave a small, self-deprecating smile. 'I'm really best off on my own. I'm just a trouble and a nuisance.'

Her mother reached for her hand.

'Not to your mother,' she said.

Leonard was about to say something, then checked himself. He clapped his hands.

'Right,' he said briskly, 'if it's going to be the Last Supper, we'd better have a really decent bottle of wine.'

Shoulders hunched and hands clenched, he left the room. Grace stared after him as the door swung closed. It had all happened so quickly. She caught her mother's eye.

'I didn't mean to hurt his feelings,' she said.

'Don't worry, darling,' her mother replied quickly. 'He'll get over it. Now come on, let's serve up.'

*

Ralph Cottrell strode out across the cobbled courtyard towards the kennels. As he passed the stables, he screwed up the newspaper and flung it with a muffled oath onto a pile of manure. Rubbishy damn rag! Hadn't they got anything better to print than to rehash the Mary Nolan Miracle story again? How much had they paid the old girl? He'd have doubled it to shut her up. Of course they'd regurgitated all that junk about Grace and her holy apparitions, too. Hadn't they heard what had happened? Saints didn't go round spontaneously aborting. He groaned aloud. A double-page spread in a national Sunday paper! And, worse, to give a map with, 'X marks the spot where Our Lady first appeared to her . . .' Jesus *Christ*!

Unleashing his two German shepherds, he packed them in the back of his Range Rover and headed out towards

Dent's Cross. He was a mile off, driving down a narrow lane, when a camper van forced him up onto the verge; as they drew alongside, the driver called across to ask the way to 'where that girl had those visions'. When he reached Dent's Cross he found the whole area choked with cars and a line of people – families on a Sunday afternoon outing, hikers with rucksacks and maps, a group of middle-aged women in walking boots and sun-hats, even three Hell's Angels on their bikes – winding their way up the sandy track into the forest.

Wheeling about in a fury, he bored his way through the bracken and gorse in a long sweep that took him round the back of the escarpment. He followed round the perimeter of the chain-link fence until he came to the main clearing. There a small group of people was wandering around, trying the fence.

He accelerated towards them.

'Clear out!' he bawled. 'Private property! You're trespassing!'

As they scattered, a movement from inside the fenced-off area caught his eye. In the centre stood a youngish man laying out a makeshift altar. A knotted rope hung down inside from one of the concrete posts.

'Hey!' he yelled. 'Get out of there!'

Racing over to the metal gate, he unlocked the chain and drove in. Ten yards inside, he pulled up and let out the dogs. Snarling and snapping, they streaked across the clearing and leapt upon the man, bringing him instantly to the ground. An angry shout rose from the crowd. Suddenly Cottrell came to his senses. Pulling out a whistle, he called the dogs off, whereupon the man picked himself up and made a terrified dash for the open gate.

Cottrell drove back out after him. He stopped to lock the gates, leaving the dogs inside. As he climbed back into the car, he heard the snarl of motorbikes and looked up to see the three leather-clad figures bearing down on him. One roared by, and as he passed he struck out with a club, shattering the side window, then wheeled around for another pass. Cottrell rammed the car into four-wheel drive. It took a lurch forward but grounded in a deep rut. He revved the engine furiously, shooting the gears from forward into reverse and back again, but he only seemed to bed in deeper. The bike boys were circling now, baiting him. Blows clanged down on the metalwork, glass splintered, the windscreen crazed. And then, suddenly, a wheel bit, and with a violent jerk he was free and driving wildly through the bracken, scraping against tree-trunks, careering frantically this way and that to escape the pursuing furies.

*

Laura drove slowly through the winding country roads with the windows open to the warm late afternoon air, taking the corners as gently as she could. Beside her, Grace sat ashen-faced, complaining of feeling sick. Laura kept up a cheerful one-sided chatter; she'd soon have her home. As she approached Coledean, she became aware the traffic was unusually heavy, and from the old dismantled railway bridge onwards they were reduced to a crawl. Only when she was in sight of their house did she see the bottleneck was caused by a caravan backing out of their own driveway, holding up the traffic in both directions. Behind, another car reversed out of the drive after it.

'I thought it had all died down,' muttered Laura furiously.

'Just ignore them, Mum,' said Grace.

Laura wove through the cars and turned up into the drive, stopping only to unlock the gate that had blocked the interlopers. Hurrying indoors, she sat Grace down in the living-room and went into the kitchen to put on the kettle. As she was reaching for the tea, a flash of sunlight from the garden caught her eye. From the wilderness at the far end of the lawn she could make out the crouching figure of a man evidently with a telephoto-lens camera. She opened the back door and waved her arms until the man backed away into the undergrowth.

Returning to the living-room, she went over to the tall picture window and swept the curtains shut.

'Bright light isn't good if you're not feeling well,' she said.

'It's all right, Mum,' replied Grace quietly. 'I saw him, too.'

'Well, any more and I'll call the police.' She smiled at the lanky, fair-haired girl. 'It's good to have you home, darling.'

'You've done wonders to the place, Mum. I love the African stuff.'

'I thought we needed a change. You sit still while I get us a cup of tea.' The phone rang. 'That'll be Leonard, I expect. I'll get it.'

She took the call in the kitchen.

'Mrs Holmwood?' said a voice. 'This is the *Daily News*. I wonder if you'd care to comment on the article in today's *Sunday Tribune* . . .'

'I don't know what you're talking about and I have nothing to say. Please leave us alone.'

Trembling, she put the phone down. It rang again almost immediately. She picked it up and, listening to check it wasn't Leonard, put her finger on the cradle and left the receiver off the hook.

*

Standing on the back steps nursing a tumbler of whisky, Leonard watched the sun gradually slip down behind the far ridge of trees and suddenly, as if by sleight of hand, disappear entirely from view. He turned indoors. The house felt empty and lifeless, just as it had after Angie and the children left. Did he have to go through all that again? Couldn't heartache work like an inoculation – once suffered, always protected? He recognized the mood. He would put on some Wagner at full volume and catch up on letter-writing, maybe he'd even go for an evening jog: exercise stimulated endorphins, the body's own morphine.

The whisky tasted joyless and he was only forcing it down to spite himself. Pouring it down the sink, he went into the

280

study. As he entered, the phone rang. He recognized the irritable bark at once.

'Leonard? Ralph Cottrell here.'

'Hello, Ralph,' he replied cautiously, at once picturing in his mind's eye the short, rough-cast squire. He'd never liked the man: the son of a humble freeminer, Cottrell had set himself up in the manor, adopting a bogus air of breeding and growing fat off the local people's poverty. Leonard frowned as the routine thoughts passed through his mind. This was not, he knew, the real cause of his dislike.

'You saw the piece in that damn paper?' Cottrell was shouting. 'Don't get me wrong, Leonard, this is trouble. Serious trouble.'

Leonard listened with a sick feeling in his stomach as Ralph Cottrell described the double-page article in that day's *Tribune*. He'd been up to Dent's Cross, he said, and the whole place was overrun with snoopers and God-squad loonies.

'Have they been in touch with you?' he demanded, his tone filled with manic urgency. 'Have they made any *approaches*? They will, man, they will. Whatever you do, don't speak to them! Don't say a word! They'll be hearing from my lawyers. I'll get Securicor guards onto the site. That's the only way to deal with these bastards. I'm counting on you, Leonard.'

'Now look, Ralph,' replied Leonard coolly, 'this is none of my business.'

A nasty edge entered the man's voice.

'Oh yes, it is. You're in this, too. I don't need to remind you . . .'

'That was five years ago. I wish to God I'd never got involved.'

'Don't we all? But you did, Leonard, and you can't back out now.' He paused, then adopted a more reasonable tone. 'Look, we can't talk over the phone. Come over here. Take the back drive. No, better: I'll come to you. Give me half an hour.'

'You're wasting your time. I won't have any part in it.'

'Just stick where you are and don't move.'

Abruptly, the line went dead. Leonard replaced the receiver slowly. He went back into the kitchen and poured a fresh drink. This time it tasted very necessary. He stood at the window again for a moment. All that was left of the day was a pinkish afterglow that merged by imperceptible gradations into the cold indigo of the encroaching night. He swore softly to himself.

*

In the early hours of the morning, Laura was woken by a long, wrenching cry. She flew down the gallery to the bathroom to find Grace doubled up, clutching her stomach. She phoned Dr Stimpson, who came out at once. He examined her and gave her an injection of antibiotics and some painkillers. He suspected she'd caught an infection at the time of the miscarriage; he would come by again in the morning, and if things weren't better he'd have to consider sending her into hospital.

Laura spent the rest of the night sitting in a chair at Grace's bedside. She knew it was no infection. She'd seen that ashen, greenish-grey look on a child's face before. It was a look she'd never forget in her life.

Twenty-two

Father Gregory drove fast through the morning traffic, impatient to arrive in Coledean. Laura had phoned the previous evening to say Grace was back home. On the passenger seat beside him lay a book from the convent library he'd taken out for her. Entitled *The Visionaries of Medjugorje*, it described the recent case of six teenagers in a small Yugoslavian village who had been receiving regular apparitions of the Madonna for the past few years. The more he'd studied it, the closer he found the parallels. There, too, the local Bishop had set up a commission of inquiry; it had stalled for as long as it could, caught between the conflicting pressures of Church and State, then come to a decision which was never published but was rumoured to be negative. The people themselves, however, cared nothing for the politics and made pilgrimage there in their millions, while behind it all, guiding the supplicants and protecting the visionaries, stood a courageous and far-sighted priest. As he drove, Father Gregory felt a warm glow. He'd heed his calling, and to hell with the Monsignor and his politicking.

When he arrived, Laura withdrew discreetly to her studio, leaving him alone with Grace. The girl lay half-reclining on the sofa in the large living-room, with a rug over her legs and a pile of books and magazines on the floor beside her. She looked pale and hollow in the cold, overcast morning light. Drawing up a chair, he sat down and asked her how she felt.

'A bit wobbly,' she replied with a brave smile. 'Dr Stimpson's just been. Doctors always leave you feeling worse than when you started.'

Father Gregory drew his chair closer.

'Grace, I want you fit and strong, because we've got work to do.' He handed her the book. 'Now, you must have wondered why things have gone rather quiet on the inquiry. I'd like you to read this. It may help you to understand. But don't worry, I'm not going to give up. You deserve a proper hearing, Grace.'

She glanced at the title and handed it back.

'I'd only be wasting your time, Father.'

'What's time when we're after the truth? Now, you said the apparitions have begun again . . .'

'Can't we just leave it?' she cried, growing distressed.

'My child, there are millions out there who pray night and day for the merest glimpse of the blessing you've had – you *may* have had. It's your duty to them. And to Our Lady herself. How can she give us her message if the messenger won't deliver it?'

Grace rummaged under the sofa cushions and produced a small blue exercise-book. She thrust it into his hand.

'Read this first, Father.'

Flipping through the book, he recognized the first few accounts of the apparitions from what she'd told him at the time; he noted the three-month gap when nothing had happened, but as he went through the two most recent accounts he felt a twinge of disappointment. She must have read his expression.

'I've read about *real* visions, Father,' she said. 'I know all about Lourdes and Knock and Fatima. I've read this book of yours in the library. I'm not stupid.' She bit her lip. 'Whenever *they* describe their apparitions, it's always "a joy deeper than words" and it feels like "floating on air" and Our Lady is always smiling and kind and sweeter than any friend.'

'Not like these latest . . . occurrences?' he asked hoarsely, already knowing the answer.

She shook her head.

'They're nightmares. Terrible, hideous, frightening nightmares. I don't feel joy, I feel *pain*.'

284

'But the first ones weren't like that,' he protested.

'No. But now they've changed. I don't see *Her* any more. I get the bright light, then suddenly it flips into a nightmare.' She pointed to the exercise-book. '*Real* Divine visions convey a holy message – make peace, love thy neighbour, pray, do penance, make confession. But mine are all about dying and pain and men in terrifying white clothes coming to get me.' She shivered visibly. 'Father, I'm sorry,' she said, staring down at the carpet. 'It's my problem, and I've got to handle it by myself.'

He reached out for her hand. It was stone cold.

'Couldn't there be *some* message there?' he persisted. 'What about the one when you felt yourself dying? Maybe you are being shown what the experience of death will be like.'

'That was Matthew and Matthew's death,' she said quietly.

'It might have looked like Matthew in the bed, but . . .'

'It *was* him. What I saw actually happened at the time. I checked with Leo. He was there: he was the one who saved him.' She cast him a fearful look. 'It's not a message from Our Lady – it can't be. If it's from anyone, it's from Matthew.'

'I don't see how that's possible.'

'It isn't! That's what's so frightening.'

He cupped her hand in both of his, trying to feel for himself some of the reassurance he was putting into the gesture.

'Grace, I know this has all been a desperately disturbing time for you, but you must *not* lose hold of your faith. God will help you if you turn to Him in humility and trust.'

She let out a long sigh of resignation.

'I can't any more,' she said quietly. 'Too much has happened. I feel too lost, too . . . let down. First the apparitions, then finding I was having a baby, then losing it, and now these awful daymares.' Wearily she turned her large grey eyes on him. 'No, Father. Don't ask me that. I can't. I've exhausted my belief. I'm worn out.'

Silence fell between them, measured only by the tick of a clock against the perpetual rush of the mill stream outside.

What could he say in face of such despair? And such erroneous thinking? He'd worried before that she was being tempted to look to the supernatural for an explanation. The Church took a strong stand against suggestions of communication with the afterlife. Either the apparitions were divinely inspired or else they were normal earthly phenomena, but in neither event were they paranormal. He frowned. Perhaps he'd been letting his eagerness to see God's hand at work run away with him. Certainly, the two recent apparitions had a strongly *secular* feel about them. If he checked into the facts surrounding Matthew's death, would he really find her account fitted the events as they'd actually occurred? If so, wouldn't he then have to conclude she was merely an hysteric after all, fantasizing about an episode in her childhood which still exerted an abnormal grip over her?

But the look of utter sorrow and abandonment in her expression brought him up short. All else was of secondary importance compared with such living human torment. Releasing her hands, he folded his own and bowed his head.

'Come, Grace,' he said gently.

And slowly, almost tentatively, he began a prayer.

*

Tom Welland studied the print-out once again while he held on for the hospital switchboard to page Leonard. The news was grim. The results of the blood analysis left no room for doubt. Fortunately for his own experiment, the problem didn't seem to have had any adverse affect. He'd fired the electrodes on two occasions now in this new series of tests, and he knew he would have to rework the readings, but in actual fact the data would be more representative of the real-life situation than he'd planned. After all, even five or ten years after a nuclear holocaust, the general blood stocks in the surviving population, let alone those in any blood banks not already exhausted, would be significantly contaminated. However carefully the human cerebrum had been frozen and later, when the environment had grown less life-threatening, thawed and regenerated, would the doctors and scientists then have any *better* blood than this available to them?

Eventually, Leonard came on the line. Welland braced himself with a deep pull on his cigarette.

'That young friend of yours, Grace Holmwood,' he began. 'Have you run a blood analysis recently? No? There's something I think you'd better know. I took a look myself, from the stuff you kindly procured for me. Why? Why do you bloody think, Leonard? I'm not *that* half-arsed.' He let the point sink in; Leonard couldn't be so dumb as to think he hadn't made the obvious connection with the foetal material. 'I have the results here. Should I mail them to you?'

'No, give me them over the phone, damn it,' Leonard snapped.

'Hope you're sitting comfortably, Leonard.' He read from the print-out. 'Platelets down at $1.1 \times 10^5/\text{mm}^3$. Granulocytes down at $3.5 \times 10^3/\text{mm}^3$. Lymphocytes down at . . .'

'Jesus.'

Welland paused, waiting for an explosion.

'Would you like a copy of the print-out?' he asked finally. 'Leonard?'

It was a long moment before Leonard replied. His voice was tight and controlled.

'Yes, if you wouldn't mind. To my home address. Thanks, Tom. I, uh, I do appreciate this.'

'Doing each other little favours, that's what life's all about, eh?' responded Welland sickeningly.

He let out a sigh as he replaced the receiver. Another man's headache, not his. He'd got quite enough of his own with the experiment. He reached for the list of pre-test checks. The third firing was scheduled for later in the day. He had repositioned the electrodes to a new bank of cells and he would give it a real zap. Maybe he could kick-start a good chunk of the pre-frontal lobes into life this time.

*

287

Leonard stared out of his office window at the overcast sky. A pigeon settled on the window-sill, eyed him uncertainly, then flew off. A light wind had risen, moaning through the ill-fitting metal casement and spattering the window with occasional gusts of rain. Far away on the ground below, tiny figures hurried across the car-park to shelter, and a toy ambulance sped along the reserved lane towards Casualty, its blue light flashing. He turned away. How *dared* life continue as normal after this?

So, it had happened. It had come out of hiding. For five years, he'd held his breath, alternately alarmed and relieved, but the seed planted all those years ago was bearing its ugly fruit.

Dozens of cancer patients had passed though his wards over the period. Many had recovered completely and returned to live normal lives. He'd become one of the top clinical specialists in the field. He'd kept up with the latest research, he'd attended conferences and exchanged information with institutes and clinics around the world, he'd investigated every potential new treatment and tried out many in controlled tests on his own patients. Throughout that period, too, he'd discreetly kept a close eye on Grace. He'd watched her grow from a child into a young woman, but as his love had grown, so too had his dread. Constantly, in the back of his mind, hope had waged battle with fear. The symptoms had been there all along, but he'd chosen not to see them. He'd focused on her morning sickness, for instance, and the pains of afterbirth, refusing to see beyond to the true condition. But now the truth was out. Hope had lost the battle. In his deepest heart, he'd always known that this moment would come, later if not sooner, and he'd prepared himself for it. He was ready.

*

Grace had feared it all afternoon. By five, the ominous metallic taste in her mouth had grown so insistent that she knew the onset could only be minutes away. She felt short of breath and flushed. As the panic welled up she threw open the window and gulped in the cool, damp air, but still she was suffocating. She had to get clear of the house, get on the move, get out in the open.

Bending to put on her wellington boots, she felt a sharp stab of pain in her stomach and she had to cling onto the doorhandle until the wave passed. Could the infection be serious? Perhaps she shouldn't have spat out the antibiotics when her mother's back was turned.

She struggled into the garden. The air was fresh and a light drizzle was falling, and for a moment she felt revived. She had passed the garden shed and was heading up the tow-path along the mill stream when everything around her – trees, path, grass, river, sky – seemed to grow that one familiar, ominous degree brighter. She clutched at a fence-post to steady herself. Gradually, the light intensified, glazing the world about her with a surreal brilliance. Then, feeding in from the edges to the centre of her vision, it began to coalesce into one large shimmering ball.

She dug her fingers into the post. Wait! Hold it off! She had a simple test she wanted to try, something Leo had once suggested. *Shut your eyes and see what happens!* She shut her eyes tight. She could still see it, growing ever brighter and more insistent! It didn't exist for real, it didn't exist out there at all. The vision was a figment of her mind, a freakish aberration spawned by her own diseased brain. This was the *proof*.

With a low howl of despair, she slipped to the ground and submitted to the nightmare.

*

Flashes of light. A haphazard stream of scratchy, grainy pictures, flicker-flashing, dizzy-dazzling, reeling past too fast to catch.

289

Suddenly, a single scene, searingly clear, viewed from above.

A figure lies on an operating table, surrounded by blood-drenched green sheets. A man in white garb, bloodied up to the elbow, works at the head end. As he reaches to the side for a scalpel, he reveals a glimpse of the body.

The head has been unlidded. The dome of the skull, hollow and shaven of hair, has been sawn off in a neat line running just above the eyes and ears. It lies a few inches away from the rest of the body. Out of the stump bulges a wrinkled, glistening, walnut-shaped brain. It's pinky-grey and latticed with tiny blood vessels. Below, exposed where the drapes have parted, the face is visible, its grey-white lips and marble eyes just recognizable . . .

His face . . . *my* face . . .

*

That evening, Leonard visited Laura. His case conference had gone on longer than expected, and it was past eight by the time he arrived. Grace was in bed. Earlier, Laura told him, she'd come in from the studio and, seeing Grace had gone out without taking her anorak or raincoat, had hurried after her. She'd found her huddled beneath a tree, shivering and terrified, apparently having just had another of her apparitions. She'd put her in a hot bath and sent her straight to bed, then called Dr Stimpson. She showed Leonard the prescription the doctor had left. Leonard shook his head: antibiotics wouldn't do any good.

Then he proceeded to tell her why.

They sat at the kitchen table late into the evening. A cottage pie lay cold and untouched between them. Leonard was drinking heavily. Laura, he noticed, had developed a strange tic in her eye and had picked her thumbnail clean of lacquer. She took the news with initial fortitude, but later she broke down. He reassured her in every way he could. Medicine, he told her, had progressed immeasurably in recent years, and great strides had been made in the treatment of cancer. She asked if he thought the apparitions were the result of a growth on the brain itself. He couldn't deny that was very possible. Only a scan would tell. The hospital had one of the few PET-scanners in the country, and he'd already taken the step of booking Grace an appointment late the following day. He would come over himself in the afternoon and collect her. Given her present state of mind, it was kinder to break the news to her then, and he would be there to help answer her questions.

After a while, when Laura had grown calmer, he went upstairs to look in on Grace. She lay asleep, with the duvet kicked off and the bedside light still on. Her forehead was hot and damp. He drew the covers over her and stood for a moment, staring with an aching heart at the strong, brave face, so animated in life and so calm in repose. He thought of how much she'd already been through and yet how she'd need all her strength and bravery to cope with what lay in store. He bent forward and laid a kiss softly upon her forehead. As he straightened, his eye fell upon a small blue exercise-book and pencil wedged between the bed and the table.

He skimmed the pages quickly, then read them again more carefully. Finally, he replaced the book as he'd found it and, turning off the light, left the room. For a long moment he stood outside, staring down from the gallery into the well of the living-room below. Whether some tumorous growth was pressing on her visual cortex creating hallucinations or whether these were the fantasies of a seriously maladjusted teenage girl, the question that burned through his mind like a laser was, Why *these* apparitions, rather than any others? Why this latest and most horrific image? Why all so specific, so particular, so precisely how the actual events had been?

Deeply shaken, he returned to the kitchen. Laura was pacing up and down. She looked up anxiously as he came in.

'She's fine,' he muttered through a dry throat. 'She's sleeping.'

Laura reached out and clung to him. She was trembling.

'She's all I've got left, Leonard,' she said in a high, fragile voice.

'She's going to be all right, Laura.'

'You're just saying that.'

'We've caught it in time. We'll do all the tests and find out exactly what's the matter, then we'll know how to treat it. Laura, this is my *job*. It's the one thing I do know a bit about.'

'Yes, I'm sorry.' She struggled to pull herself together. 'I don't know where we'd be without you, Leonard. I'm sure we seem very ungrateful at times and take everything for granted, but we do appreciate all you do for us, you know we do . . .'

He broke in, unable to bear any more.

'Don't, Laura. Look, why not let's go into the study and put on some music?'

*

He barely slept that night. He'd driven home, recklessly over the limit, and headed for the bottle again. Around one in the morning, he'd put on a coat and wellingtons and gone for a walk. It had stopped raining, but the wind had risen. Storms were forecast. He'd walked for an hour, perhaps two, without purpose or direction, hoping somehow to still the clamour in his mind. But he'd found his thoughts locked in a groove, an old familiar circuit of questions and answers and further questions, balancing those to which he desperately wished he knew the answers against those he desperately wished he didn't.

The day started badly. On the way to work, he braked sharply at a pedestrian crossing, and on the wet roads the car behind skidded into his rear. No sooner had he arrived at the hospital than he fell into an acrimonious dispute with the Administrator over a locum who'd been put on his ward. In the middle of the morning, he learned that an urgent operation to remove a malignant tumour on one of his patients had been cancelled through shortage of theatre staff. When a call came through to his office from Father Gregory shortly before midday, his temper was at breaking-point.

'Yes?' he snapped.

Father Gregory cleared his throat.

'I wanted a word,' he began in a dignified tone. 'It's about Grace. I wondered if I could come and see you.'

'I thought we'd said all there was to say.'

'Leaving aside our differences, Doctor . . . You see, you are the only person who knows what actually happened.'

'I don't follow.'

The priest paused, evidently reluctant to broach the matter over the phone.

'Well, it's about her apparitions. You know, of course, she's begun having them again. It's just that when one looks at them more closely, certain questions spring to mind.'

'Do I hear a Doubting Thomas, Father?'

'Questions concerning what actually happened at the time of her brother Matthew's death.'

Leonard felt his jaw clench.

'I can't help you,' he said shortly.

'But you were the doctor on the case. Laura assures me you were there the whole time.' Urgency entered the priest's voice. 'It's important we eliminate the obvious *secular* explanations. Grace seems haunted by images of her brother's death. Is she simply reliving in her imagination something she has picked up? Something you, perhaps, have told her about?'

'I never discuss the details of cases with anyone.'

'My point is, if we could just cross-check . . .'

'Not with *anyone*, Father,' he repeated.

Father Gregory paused, but he wasn't going to give up.

'Well, then, what is *your* explanation, Doctor?'

'I don't have one.'

'I seem to remember you saying you could give me a rational explanation for *everything* that has been happening.'

'Raking up the past won't help anyone, least of all Grace,' responded Leonard tersely. 'I suggest you stick to your area, Father, and I'll stick to mine. Fair enough?'

Refusing to entertain further discussion, he brought the conversation to a quick close. Damn the meddlesome priest! Things had been altogether better before, when the Virgin Mary was buzzing around making her guest star appearances and the Monsignor was holding his kangaroo court and everyone was locked in theological debate, counting angels on the heads of pins. The Church officialdom seemed finally to have given up, but now there was Father Gregory taking up the cudgels on his own, and his one-man crusade was taking him into areas better left untouched. He already knew far too much. He'd been around towards the end, and of course he'd been the one administering last rites to the boy. He knew his way round the hospital, too: he was forever visiting patients, and quite a few of the staff were among his congregation. If he couldn't get the answers he wanted out of Laura and Grace – and he couldn't, for they simply didn't know – then he'd find other ways. He'd track down the houseman on the ward at the time, or one of the nursing staff . . .

Leonard snapped the pencil he'd been toying with and tossed the broken ends into the wastepaper basket. This had to stop. He went to the window and stared out at the dark, glowering sky. The priest had put his finger *exactly* on the vital conundrum. The real question, however, was how the hell could Grace have possibly *known*?

He thought back to what he'd read in the exercise-book.

One: Matthew is being given emergency resuscitation. He swallowed; he'd actually done it himself, and it had been exactly as she'd described, down to the last detail, but he hadn't told her or her mother about it, not wanting to cause them extra worry. *Two*: a scene in a highly specialized isolation room, with a doctor wearing strange white garb. Grace couldn't possibly have invented that. As far as the family were concerned, the boy was never moved from his room on the hospital ward. And she couldn't have known about the special protective clothing. *Three* – here Leonard shuddered. *That* ghoulish scene could never have been born out of her imagination, not in all its horrific and accurate detail.

Neither she nor Laura had been present at any of the incidents. Who could she have got it from? Not from him: he'd been obsessively careful to avoid ever dropping the slightest hint. From the staff at the hospital? Unlikely: she'd never had occasion to speak to the houseman or the nursing staff, to his knowledge, and, besides, it all happened so long ago they were bound to have forgotten the details of what was a perfectly routine emergency resuscitation. Only two porters could have known the boy was later transferred, too, and they'd been told he was being sent to a hospice.

Then the answer hit him. Only one possible person was in possession of sufficient of the facts. And this person happened to have paid Grace a visit a short while before the new series of nightmare hallucinations began. *He* was the source.

Tom Welland.

Swelling with fury, Leonard threw off his white coat. Grabbing his jacket, he headed for the door. He glanced at his watch. He was due to pick Grace up later for her scan, but if he hurried he'd just have time to sort the bastard out once and for all.

Twenty-three

The sky was closing in from the west, drawing a curtain of dark, scowling clouds over the land. The wind had quickened and the first thick clots of rain were beginning to fall as Leonard parked his car at the back of the tall, drab Medical Research block and hurried round the front, up the steps and into the shelter of the reception hall. He gave his name to the receptionist and asked her to call upstairs to Dr Welland. She relayed the message, then frowned.

'Dr Welland says he's in the middle of an experiment, sir,' she said, holding the receiver to her chest. 'Do you have an appointment?'

'Here, let me speak to him.' Leonard took the phone. 'Tom? Listen, I'm downstairs . . . No, I can't come back later. I need to see you now. Now means *now*, Welland.'

He paced up and down the foyer impatiently. A bike messenger arrived to deliver a package, a visitor surrendered his tag and signed himself out, a young woman in a white lab coat hurried in and cast him a look of unfeigned interest as she passed, but eventually the lift arrived and Tom Welland shuffled out towards him. His white coat was grubby and stained, his glasses magnified his irritable glare and in his hands he carried a pair of surgical gloves he'd evidently taken off on the way down.

'This is bloody inconvenient,' he grumbled. 'Well?'

Leonard glanced around. The receptionist was conspicuously pretending not to listen.

'I can't discuss it here,' he said.

'But I'm just about to run a test,' Welland protested, then

sighed. 'All right, you'd better come up. But you mustn't mind if I carry on while we talk.'

Collecting a visitor's tag, Leonard followed him into the lift. In silence they rode to the third floor and walked through the various security doors to the laboratory. Inside, preparations for the test were clearly well under way. Tiny lights flickered across the banks of instruments lining the wall, while a desktop computer monitor was flashing a check-list of questions. The light was on in the isolation chamber this time, and through the thick glass inspection panel Leonard could make out the glistening, wrinkled cerebrum in its perspex housing, with a pair of fine needles spiking out at the front and a cluster of thin tubes filled with rich red plasma feeding in through the stem at the base. On a nearby trolley stood an oscilloscope and, beside it, a printer traced a line with an ink-pen on a slowly scrolling chart. Both screen and chart showed a continuous unbroken line. The brain was inert, waiting for a jolt through the electrodes to fire it into life again.

Welland was keying in a series of instructions at the console. Looking over his shoulder, Leonard could see a message flash up on the screen confirming that the circuitry was functioning correctly.

'You do pick your times, Leonard,' muttered the scientist, tapping in another command. 'What's the problem?'

Leonard waited until he had to look up.

'Cast your mind back to that time you came barging round and you found Grace at home, Tom,' he began tightly. 'I want to know exactly what you said to her.'

'For God's sake, is that all? Look, in fifteen minutes this thing is due to fire —'

'I need to know, Tom,' he warned, feeling dangerously close to the limit of his patience. Welland gave an exasperated sigh and turned back, but Leonard grabbed him by the shoulder and spun him round. 'What did you tell her? I want to know. Exactly.'

'How the hell should I remember?' Welland caught his

expression and faltered. He gave a feeble shrug and tried to squirm free. 'I don't know. We talked about you. I said how brilliant you were.'

Leonard tightened his grip.

'You told her a lot of things, Tom,' he said in a deadly cold tone. 'Things you shouldn't have told anyone. Things about her brother Matthew.'

Welland winced.

'The boy's name might have cropped up,' he admitted.

'You told her he died of cancer!'

'Not in so many words.'

'What words did you use to tell her the rest?' spat Leonard. 'To tell her that he was transferred to a special unit? That a certain operation was performed on the body, without the family's knowledge, an operation that went some way beyond your average autopsy?' He stabbed a finger at the isolation chamber to emphasize his point. 'You stupid bastard, Tom. Why didn't you keep your trap shut? Do you know what you've started? She's been having nightmares — and uncannily precise they are, too. Nightmares about men in radiation suits. About a certain unauthorized surgical ablation. If this were some ordinary girl, no-one would take any notice. But people *know* about Grace. When *she* has nightmares, daymares, whatever the hell they are, they stop and listen. They ask questions, Tom. They want to know, are they fact or fantasy? And let me tell you, they're going to find out. Jesus Christ, Tom,' he groaned, smacking his forehead, 'why in God's name did you have to tell her?'

Welland had pulled away. He shot him an injured glare.

'I never said any of *that* to her,' he protested.

'Don't lie to me, Tom.'

'I'm telling you: I said nothing whatever about what happened after the boy left the hospital. Why the hell should I? This is my *work*, Leonard. My livelihood.'

'Exactly: why *did* you?'

'I didn't! She told me the boy died of a stomach upset, and I merely remarked that a bone marrow transplant was a somewhat drastic remedy. That's all. Nothing else, I swear to God!' He turned back to the console. 'Now, for Christ's sake, Leonard, let me get on with this.'

Leonard stood back. The man's tone rang true. If it wasn't him, then who *was* it? Perhaps nobody at all. Then *how* was it? Guesswork, intuition, imagination, chance? Telepathy? Was she somehow reading the secrets of his mind? Absurd! For all the Madame Blavatskys throughout history, for all the mediums and clairvoyants that had ever pored over balls of glass or sat around three-legged tables, for all the claims in the pulp press of people who 'knew' when a close relative had suffered an accident, for all the serious experiments, too, never had one *single* case ever stood up to proper scientific scrutiny. If he was reduced to concluding she'd somehow beamed in on it, he was seriously unhinged. In a world governed by natural laws and ordered according to rational principles, there was no place for forms of communication governed by paranormal laws and ordered according to irrational principles.

He drew up short, surprised by the violence of his own reaction. Momentarily chastened, he stood watching Welland at his work. The scientist was moving carefully and systematically about the laboratory, checking the sensitive micro-electronic equipment and inspecting the mechanical pumps and tubes that were feeding blood into that porridge of neural tissue lying in its cask.

'A couple of minutes,' muttered Welland, craning past him at a bank of instruments. 'Would you mind?'

'I'm sorry,' mumbled Leonard, lost in his thoughts.

Stepping out of the way, he turned to the isolation chamber and stared inside. In the thin beam of the spotlight, the two silvery electrodes planted in the forebrain glinted mesmerically against the lead-grey cladding behind. Any minute now, a series of pulses, each just a few millivolts in strength, would be sent down the electrodes into the brain, in the hope of firing the circuitry in that region back into life.

He understood the real purpose underlying the experiment. Civilization was memory. In the wake of a nuclear winter, with wholescale global devastation, where would human civilization and the hope for its renewal reside? Not in the ashes of libraries or in computer data banks wiped clean by electronic storms, not even, probably, in the minds and memories of those who had managed to survive, wandering deranged and desocialized across a lifeless landscape, but in the minds and memories of those who died. Killed by radiation and frozen by the sub-zero temperatures, a crucial few brains of the last of *homo sapiens sapiens* might remain intact with all their functions and memories preserved, waiting only for a spark to restore them to life and, with it, their lost civilization. Welland had been working in this area for many years, funded discreetly by the Ministry of Defence. Hitherto, his work had of necessity been limited to laboratory mice and rats and certain of the lower primates. But the only sure way of studying the effect of fatal doses of radiation on the human brain was to experiment with the actual human organ. There had been accidents at nuclear power stations and in government ordnance research installations, but for their various reasons none of these cases provided suitable material. And then, five years ago, out of the blue, a brain, *this* brain, became available. It had been an absolute godsend.

Leonard frowned; one underlying assumption had always puzzled him. He recalled a well-known experiment in which the American neuroscientist Penfield had stimulated the temporal cortex of an epileptic undergoing brain surgery, and the patient relived an entire evening at a concert. Actually, Penfield later changed his mind and suggested the memory record was not stored in the cortex but distributed in many different places in the brain. Either way, this relied on a mechanistic view of the mind in which memories were physically stored as traces. The trouble was, no-one had ever found a memory trace.

He caught Welland looking at him quizzically.

'Not still on about *that*,' sighed Welland. 'Send the girl to a shrink and forget about it.'

'I was thinking about all of this.' He gestured around the

room. 'You can evoke a neural response, I see that,' he went on, 'but how do you know you're evoking a *memory*?'

'By inference. Electrical activity in this region implies thought, and thought implies memory.'

'But actual *memories*?' he persisted. 'Such-and-such a memory when you hit such-and-such a nerve-net? I thought no-one believed in memory traces any more.'

Welland turned and bent over the console to check off a reading.

'They don't,' he said casually.

'But how, then —?'

'Morphic resonance. It's a process of *tuning in*.' He straightened. 'Everything's set. Are you staying or going?'

Leonard gave a small start. Tuning in . . . beaming in . . . surely no-one *seriously* thought . . . He came to his senses as Welland's question sank in. He glanced at his watch. He should have left already. Still, a few minutes wouldn't matter. He'd give Laura a call as he left and tell her he was on his way.

'I'll stay for the show.'

'Then please clear the stage.'

With a final glance around the room to check all was in order, Welland went over to the panel. He reached forward to a switch marked PULSE CONTROL.

'Here goes,' he muttered, and snapped the switch upwards to the ON position.

At once the line on the oscilloscope screen started jumping up and down, forming erratic, spiky waves. At the same time, the stylus began scratching furiously on the scrolling chart. A needle was flickering on the differentiometer. Life, momentarily, had begun again.

＊

A narrow passage, deep in the earth. It's dark and damp. Torchlight picks out broken wooden pit-props, standing askew beneath the half-fallen roof. The earth is red and sticky. Flecks of minerals glint from the rough-hewn seams.

The torch beam settles briefly on a figure crawling on hands and knees along the low passage. It's a young girl. She has fair hair in a pony-tail and her hands and cheeks are muddied and grazed. She is calling out, 'Wait for me!' Her voice makes a hollow echo.

The light whips forward. The passage leads into a vast cavern. The beam barely reaches the white crystal patches on the roof. The ground is compacted red earth. Ruts show where barrows once ran. The circle of torchlight prowls across the walls, reflecting dull gold flashes here and there. It comes to rest on a small pool, cupped in the rock at the far side. A trickle from the rock slab above feeds the pool. But there's something strange about the liquid. It glitters with an eerie but enticing bluish glow . . .

*

Leonard waited until Welland had finished and flicked the switch off, then reached for the phone. No more time to indulge in the fancies of scientific research; he had his own, practical job to do now. Taking Grace for her scan would only bring one step closer the moment of truth, already perilously imminent.

Laura answered the phone in deep agitation.

'Leonard, thank God it's you!' she cried. 'Where are you?

302

I thought you were coming over. It's Grace. She's had another of her turns. She's okay now, but it was terrible, *terrible.*'

The jolt shot through him like an electric shock.

'When?' he barked.

'When? Well, just now, literally a moment ago. I came in and found her on the floor, gasping for air, her eyes rolled back . . . You can't imagine what I thought.'

His gaze had come to rest on the scroll charts pinned up on the wall above the desk. For a moment, his mind was blank. Then some glimmer of a connection began to form. He glanced across at the printer; the wild jerky wave-forms had returned to a steady, unbroken continuous line. *She's had another of her turns . . . literally a moment ago . . . she's okay now.* He looked back at the past charts pinned on the wall. They showed short bursts of furious electrical activity once every few days, followed by long stretches when nothing was happening at all.

His blood went icy cold.

'Are you there, Leonard?' came Laura's voice.

'Listen, Laura,' he began carefully, 'I want you to do something. It may sound strange, but you must do it. I want you to go upstairs to Grace's room. There's a small blue exercise-book she keeps beside her bed. Bring it to the phone.'

'For heaven's sake, Leonard, not now, not while she's . . .'

'Grace will be all right. Please just do as I say.'

Protesting and puzzled, Laura put down the phone. A minute later she returned.

'Turn to the first page,' he ordered. 'Give me the date and time written at the top.'

Laura read out a date and a time. Gritting his teeth, Leonard ran his eye along the bottom vector of the chart to the exact month, day and time of day she had given. His pulse gave a sickening lurch.

The chart recorded a violent burst of activity in the brain at that precise moment. Before, it showed nothing; afterwards, too, nothing. Underneath the scribble of spikes and waves was the handwritten note: 'Pulse Firing #1'.

'Turn to the second page,' he croaked.

She read out another date and time. Again it matched exactly the timing of Pulse Firing #2. The same with the third, and the fourth . . .

In all, there had been seven occasions when Welland had test-fired the apparatus. In all, Grace had had seven apparitions. And each time at the very same moment!

'Leonard –?'

He barely recognized the strangled rasp in his own voice.

'Just keep her warm,' he managed to reply. 'I'll be over as soon as I can.'

He put the phone down and stood for a long moment staring first at the chart, then at the human brain lying in the chamber, then back again. Years of rage and despair welled up inside him, mingling with the dawning horror to form a violent, explosive mix that now suddenly, without warning, hit flash-point. He turned towards Welland – the scientist was standing with his back to him – and advanced a few steps, then thought better of it. Instead, his hands hanging loosely at his sides, he ground round and took a slow, deliberate step across the room towards the bank of delicate electronic equipment.

This thing had to be stopped. Now.

*

He was a maddened animal. His rage roared in his ears, his fury ran red in his eyes, his whole being howled out to crush and smash and destroy. With brutish ferocity, he reached out both hands and locked his grip onto the handles of the oscilloscope unit, then in a single sweep he swung it off its trolley and sent it crashing to the ground, snapping the cables, shattering the glass screen and bursting open the casing so that small components jumped out and skittered across the floor.

A wild cry burst from behind him.

'What in God's name —?'

But Leonard lumbered forward. He seized the tubular legs of the trolley itself and toppled it over, sending the chart printer sliding to the ground where it suddenly went berserk, frenziedly spewing out endless tangled rolls of gibberish.

Welland rushed forward and tried to drag him off.

'Christ, man, have you gone mad?' he yelled.

'This must end!' growled Leonard thickly and, shaking him off with a brutal blow, went for the next machine.

Welland lunged for the phone and began dialling. Leonard caught the movement out of the corner of his eye. Spinning round, he grabbed the cable and wrenched it out of the wall socket. Welland let out a foul oath and hurled himself upon him.

'You're mad! You're insane!' he yelled.

'Get out of my way!' Leonard shouted back.

The scientist, though shorter and overweight, had the strength of a bear. He gripped Leonard round the neck and dragged him backwards to the ground, but Leonard managed to struggle free and break away. Welland came for him again, fumbling, his glasses lost. Using the man's own weight, Leonard grabbed him by an arm and a shoulder and swung him bodily across the room, where he slithered the length of a bench, sweeping it clean of racks of test-tubes and slides.

While Welland groped blindly about on his hands and knees looking for his glasses, cutting his hands on the broken glass and howling curses of rage and incomprehension, Leonard turned back to his work. He had disposed of the pulse unit in a single blow and was just reaching out for the differentiometer unit when a large heavy object smashed him between the shoulder-blades, throwing him forward so that he struck his forehead sharply on the projecting rim of the inspection panel. He slipped to the ground, momentarily stunned. Through blood-bleared eyes he could make out the white-coated figure of the scientist crawling across the floor, fingering his way along the ledge of the bench towards the wall behind. There, half way up, beneath a large radiation hazard sign, was mounted a yellow and black alarm handle. Already Welland's hand was clawing its way up the wall.

Leonard made a rapid calculation: he'd never make it in time. Instead, he reached up and seized hold of one of the supply tubes feeding blood into the chamber.

'Move and I'll rip this out!' he yelled.

Welland froze. Squinting, he peered back across the room.

'What the hell are you doing?' he hissed. 'The work's critical! You know it is.'

'It's destroying her!'

'The girl? Are you crazy?'

'Each time you zap that brain, she has a hallucination.'

'For Christ's sake!'

Leonard hammered frenziedly on the inspection panel glass.

'It's her brother in there. Her *twin* brother. What did you call it – morphic resonance? Think, Tom, *think*! I'm telling you, man, this stops here and now.'

'Maniac! You're out of your head!'

Welland's hand inched towards the alarm. Leonard tightened his grip on the blood supply.

'I'm warning you!' he yelled.

'Screw you!'

With a sudden, swift movement, Welland lunged for the alarm handle and tugged it down. Instantly, a shrill electronic alarm started up and above the door a red panel flashed DANGER – RADIATION. Somewhere a siren began to wail and all over the building bells started to ring.

Leonard jerked at the thin plastic tube. It sprang from its junction, spraying the wall with a jet of blood. He let it drop to the floor, where it continued pumping the enriched blood in rhythmic spasms, then he ripped out all the other tubes that fed into the chamber. Plunging his hands into the arm-gloves set into the wall, he reached into the chamber itself and snatched the brain from its perspex housing. Tearing the greyish wrinkled organ free of the tubes and wires, he began to pulp it in his fingers, kneading and grinding until all that was left was a lumpy, useless mush dribbling through his fingers onto the chamber floor.

He looked over his shoulder. Welland was staggering towards him, brandishing a chair. Hastily he slid his arms free and rolled out of the way just as the chair crashed down, glancing off his shoulder. He fought to recover his balance. Shouts could be heard outside. Footsteps were already hurrying down the corridor. A loudspeaker somewhere was broadcasting a message to evacuate the building. But Welland was coming after him again, wildly, blindly swinging a broken spar of the chair. Leonard stepped inside the sweep of a blow and, balling his fist, jabbed him a hard uppercut on the point of the chin. The man's head jerked back and, letting out a gasp of pain, he tottered drunkenly backwards, slipped, cracked the back of his head on the bench and slithered, unconscious, to the floor.

Leonard quickly knelt to check his pulse. Satisfied he was merely concussed, he rummaged in the pockets of his white coat for his electronic pass-card. Then, wincing with pain, he stumbled to the door and let himself out. The corridor was clear. He hurried to the first security door and slipped the card-key into the slot; it clicked open and closed automatically behind him. As he reached the second door, he met two men in white protective suits coming down the corridor clutching geiger counters. As he passed, he yelled 'Room 313!' and pointed the way he'd come. Then he forced his body into a hobbling run. Letting himself through the final security door, he half ran, half fell, down the three flights of stairs, slipped out past groups of evacuated staff, past the unmanned reception desk, and dragged himself finally through the squalling rain to the car-park at the back.

Twenty-four

Rain lashed the windscreen in sheets, blotting out all but the tail-lights of the truck in front. Cars swept past perilously close, buffeting him with hails of spray. The wipers kept up a frenzied tempo, and for a moment he found his gaze locking onto them, mesmerized by their rhythmic sweep. Suddenly he realized the truck ahead was braking, and he jammed on his brakes just in time to avoid a collision. Every pulse sent a stab of pain shooting through his shoulder. He was shaking and felt sick, the familiar aftermath of shock. A convulsive shudder ran through him as he thought back to the madness in the laboratory.

Just suppose it *was* true . . . No, it couldn't be! The world *had* to run on ordered, predictable lines. If you let in the merest chink of doubt, then everything changed: the chink became a wedge and the wedge a chasm, and before you knew it the world was random, aleatory, unguided and ungoverned – in a word, *mad*. Perhaps it was. Perhaps he was mad. Once upon a time there were two twins, a brother and a sister, the brother's name was Matthew and the sister's name was Grace, and when they were both twelve Matthew fell ill, and they sent him away to a place where he died and they secretly took out his brain . . . they stored it away for five long years, then they tried to start it up again, but every time they got it going so that it remembered something, his sister Grace, who was living miles away, experienced the memories *herself* . . . Now, Grace was a religious girl, and to some people her experiences began to look rather like religious visions . . .

He let out a harsh burst of laughter. *Memories?* Rubbish! The boy couldn't have known about his own death! That time his heart stopped and they'd given him emergency resuscitation, he was, by definition, unconscious, if not actually clinically dead. But abruptly he choked back his laugh. Reading Grace's account of that incident, he'd been especially struck by the fact that the description was as if it were being *seen from above*, from a viewpoint hovering somewhere up by the ceiling. He recalled once talking to an elderly woman who had, to all intents and purposes, died on the operating table; she'd later recounted to him accurately everything that had happened in the theatre while she'd been dead, things she couldn't possibly have known, describing it all as if she'd been floating above the room, looking down. Later, he'd read some accounts of near-death experiences. They all had two features in common. One was this bird's-eye viewpoint – or, as it was often taken to be – the *soul's* viewpoint. The other was that, having taken leave of their bodies, the patients all underwent very similar experiences of death itself: going down a tunnel towards the light, a glowing orb of light that grew brighter and brighter, shimmering, pulsing . . . He swallowed hard. In his mind's eye he could see one of the entries in the blue exercise-book: *soft white sheet of light . . . a single oval orb of shimmering, pulsing radiance . . .*

Hang on a minute! he said to himself severely. Suppose Matthew *had* somehow 'remembered' his own near-death experience. Suppose, too, he had actually remembered the small isolation unit to which he'd been transferred, where the doctors and nurses had worn special white protective suits. Suppose he had even witnessed, from his vantage-point on the ceiling, the final surgical removal of his own brain. But what about the *other* 'memories', those that appeared as holy visions of the Virgin Mary? How could these possibly be *memories* of his? The boy had never *met* Our Lady in his life. Was it some film he'd once watched, maybe? Or was he seeing her in heaven and beaming back pictures like some space satellite? God damn it, the right theory had to fit all the cases.

With an oath, he hit the brakes and pulled into a driveway at the side. He'd missed the turn-off to Coledean. For a moment he sat without moving, his head pressed tightly in his hands. He was lost, disorientated, an acrobat toppling off the tightrope. He was forcing the facts to fit and coming up with absurd conclusions, while all along he was skirting the real question. *How the hell could one person's memories become another person's experiences?*

Maybe there was something in Welland's 'morphic reson-ance'. He'd often thought about this tantalizing, revolution-ary theory that all natural systems were shaped by fields containing a collective memory and that, far from being stored as traces in the brain, memories resulted from tuning in to the past. This was the nearest science had ever come to a really plausible explanation of telepathy. But it was still a *theory*. Leonard pressed his temples. Was he seriously to believe that, in these recent daymares at least, Grace had been tuning in to her twin brother's memories? On the other hand, what alternative explanation was there?

Hammering his fist on the steering-wheel in exasperation, he addressed himself to the road again. Making an about-turn, he retraced his route until the signpost for Coledean became visible in the driving rain. He'd take it step by step. First thing was to get Grace into hospital. She might have had the last of her apparitions, visions, hallucinations, *memor-ies* or whatever the hell they were, but she was still in a very serious condition indeed and no amount of theorizing about morphic fields would cure *that*. There, at least, he was on home ground.

*

He pulled up in the drive and climbed out to open the gate. The rain fell steadily, and in the distance growled the first broken thunder. He found the gate ajar. Pushing it fully open, he hurried back to the car and drove quickly up the remaining stretch. As he drew up outside the mill house, he saw Laura at the study window, peering out anxiously. He'd barely reached the doorstep when she flung the door open. Her face was wild with alarm.

'Have you seen her?' she cried. 'She's gone!'

'Grace? Gone where?'

'Gone on her bicycle!' She reached for an overcoat. 'I'm going after her. You stay here, Leonard. One of us had better.'

He caught her by the arm.

'Wait. Calm down. Let's think it through. There's no point in rushing out into that. You can't see more than five yards.'

He closed the door and drew her into the centre of the hall. Under the light he saw the worry etched deep into her complexion; her face was taut and in her eyes burned the agony of despair.

'I've phoned around everyone I can think of.' She clutched his sleeve. 'This won't make her worse, will it? *Will it*, Leonard?'

'Relax. Now tell me exactly what happened.'

'She had another of her strange turns, as I said on the phone, and then I took her up to her room, she was so exhausted, the poor lamb. I brought her up a cup of tea, and she seemed all right then, just lying on her bed, writing. I came back down and wrote a few letters myself, then I went back up to see how she was feeling and she was gone. Not a word, nothing.'

A strange, terrible idea crept into his mind.

'Laura,' he said carefully, 'what did you do with that notebook?'

She looked taken aback.

'I put it back. She didn't see me, I'm sure she didn't.'

Pulling himself free, he turned and hurried through the living-room and up the stairs. Laura followed on his heels, protesting in perplexity and distress. He hastened along the gallery landing to Grace's room and went straight over to

311

her bed. In between the bed and the table he found the small blue exercise-book. He snatched it up and turned it to the latest entry. Date: today. Time: barely an hour gone.

A narrow passage, deep in the earth, he read. *It's dark and damp. Torchlight picks out broken pit-props . . .*

Slowly he closed the book. He knew where she was. Or where she was trying to go. He looked up. Laura hovered in the doorway, speechless and lost.

'It's all right,' he said more calmly now. 'Leave it to me.'

As he was reaching to replace the exercise-book, a glint of light caught his eye. It came off the small statuette of the Virgin Mary that Grace kept on her bedside table.

He froze.

Gradually he opened the notebook and turned to the earlier accounts of the divine apparitions.

She stands in a simple hooded robe of pale blue and white. It is hemmed with golden ribbing and falls to the ground in ample folds. He turned to the statuette. The figure wore a simple hooded robe of pale blue and white, hemmed with golden ribbing . . .

He went back to the notebook. *One hand gestures towards her heart; the other, outstretched, is beckoning.* He looked up. One hand gestured towards her heart. The other was outstretched and beckoning.

Behind him, he could sense Laura's impatience, but he ignored her. Very slowly he lowered himself onto the bed. Lying on his back, he turned his head to the side and looked up at the statuette. He moved it a few inches so that the bulb of the light shone exactly from behind its head. And he stared directly into the face, without blinking, for as long as he was able to hold it.

Beams of light jet out like rays from the sun, he found himself mumbling aloud. *Spurt out like spokes . . . shafts of sunlight radiate out like spokes of white fire . . . above her head hovers a luminous gold annulet . . .*

Of course.

Jesus Christ Almighty.

He closed his scorched eyes for a moment. His mouth was dry and his whole body trembling as the absolute inescapability of the truth hit him. Finally, very gradually, he sat up and looked Laura in the eye.

'This statue was Matthew's, wasn't it?' he asked in a hoarse whisper. 'I suppose . . . I suppose he had it in hospital with him when he died?'

'Leonard, please not now . . . Grace . . . it's more important . . .'

'No! I must know! It's *vital*.'

Laura frowned, bemused, and blinked hard.

'Well, yes, he did. He always kept it next to his bed. Why?'

Leonard rose slowly, feeling dizzy and unbalanced. All he could hear was the noise of his own mind, aghast with astonishment.

Matthew's last memories. When a brain was regenerated, would its *last* memories not be the *first* to be revived?

'*Leonard!*' Laura was shaking him. 'We're losing time.'

Dimly, as if from a great distance, he heard his own voice reply.

'It's all right, Laura. I know exactly where she's gone. You just stay here. I'll go.'

*

Matthew. He was calling her. He'd been calling her all along. She hadn't understood at first. But now she did. She was coming. She'd be there.

Grace huddled deep into her anorak and struggled on. As the track grew steeper, the going became rougher. Small rivulets flowed off the hillside, loosening boulders and making a running channel of the path. Every few yards, she'd step on a loose stone or stumble against her own boots and lose her footing. Once when she slipped, her bicycle headlamp fell out of her pocket and skidded away down the track; luckily, it wasn't broken, but in scrambling after it she fell against a jutting spar of rock and gashed her hand badly. The rain got everywhere: it crept in down her neck, it permeated her anorak where the oil had rubbed off and it trickled down onto her jeans, soaking them through. When for a brief moment it let up, she'd glimpse the sky above her glowering black and angry, veiled by low, wind-whipped clouds. Then a sheet of lightning would suddenly throw the skyline into fleeting relief, and seconds later a grumble of thunder would crawl round the ridges, and within moments the rain would begin again more furiously than ever and, with it, the wind, howling, tearing, scorching through the trees. She came upon a silver birch lying across the track, brought down by the storm, and making a detour around it she momentarily lost her way and plunged into a choking tangle of dead brambles. Slipping and sliding, she eventually reached the level ground and followed the track as it widened into the clearing.

A flash of sheet-lightning illuminated the enclosure with its high chain-link fence and concrete pillars topped with barbed wire. She let out a cry of frustration: she'd forgotten. She followed the fence round to the double gates, wondering if she could get in the way she'd crawled out before. But a new concrete base had been laid around the gate, filling in the gaps left by the tyre ruts. She was bending to examine it when a sudden savage yelping made her look up. Two dogs – Ralph Cottrell's alsatians – were streaking across the clearing towards her. Barking wildly as if half starved, they hurled themselves at the fence. She recoiled in terror and scrambled hastily away across the narrow strip of cleared scrub that ran alongside the fence and into the deep under-growth. There she crouched beneath a tree until she'd re-covered her nerve. Then, keeping her distance, yet tracked at every step by the snarling dogs inside, she carried on round the perimeter of the fence, looking for a way in.

*

Dogs? Leonard paused, listening to the distant sound of barking carried in snatches on the wind. No doubt about it. Cottrell must have put some dogs up there, the fool. Pray

God Grace hadn't encountered them. He'd found her bicycle abandoned at the bottom of the track, proving his hunch had been right. And now the dogs . . . He felt in his pocket – tissues, peppermints, chewing-gum, the car-torch – and wished he'd brought a medicine bag. Where the hell did she get the strength from, in her condition?

He hastened his step. He had to intercept her before she did the really dangerous thing.

*

She fought her way up the shallow escarpment, through thorn bushes and ensnaring brambles. Half way down the slope the other side, the fence swung away at a sharp angle to the right and disappeared into the undergrowth. Somewhere, perhaps fifty feet below where she stood, must lie the cavern. But it was hopeless. The dogs, eyes rolling and jaws slavering, continued to paw and claw frantically at the chain mesh. Suddenly she tripped on a tussock and pitched forward, clutching vainly at a branch to save herself. A violent streak of pain ripped through her whole body. With an involuntary cry, she doubled up and for a moment she stood there, retching emptily. As she straightened, a sweltering flush broke over her body and the countryside swirled dizzily about her. She staggered a few steps down the slope, lost her footing completely, grabbed wildly at a thorn bush, then quite suddenly she felt the ground give way beneath her feet and she was slipping, falling, falling into a hole in a chute of stones, falling into the pit of darkness, into the very earth itself.

*

Leonard reached the clearing and paused for a moment to pinpoint the direction of the barking. To the left, beyond the ridge. Hugging his injured shoulder tightly, he set off at a jog down the strip of cleared scrub that ran alongside the fence. The eye of the storm seemed to be passing over his very head, with each streak of lightning followed instantly by a shattering crash of thunder. He blundered on, beating out an unremitting measure, forcing the pace harder still up the slope, until finally, in agony and exhaustion, he reached the crest of the escarpment.

The moment he spotted the two dogs, he pulled up sharply. Caged inside the fence some twenty yards away, tearing at the mesh to get at some target outside, they provided a clear marker of Grace's position. Careful to keep out of their sight, he swung away into the undergrowth and swept around in a wide arc until he was in a direct line from the dogs but a good hundred yards away. Then, more slowly, he proceeded forward towards the fence. She had to be between him and them.

Half way up the slope, still some distance away, he stopped and scanned the ground all around. No sign at all of the girl. Could he have missed her? He took a few steps forward. Suddenly his foot hit a hollow and he fell sideways, twisting his ankle. As he struggled back to his feet, he saw it. His pulse gave a wild leap. Overgrown with grass, buried beneath a clump of thorn bushes, hidden from view from any direction and all but closed over by dead brambles and fallen rubble, lay a low, narrow opening that led directly, almost vertically, into the ground. And at the edge were the unmistakable signs of someone having slipped and fallen in.

*

The shaft wound in a steep downward path. In parts the roof had collapsed, leaving the narrowest gap through which he could only slither with difficulty. Broken wooden pit-props stood twisted askew, crushed under the living weight of the earth. Crouching and crawling, struggling and squirming, gradually he made his way down the shaft. After a short distance he reached a small cavern in which he could just stand up, his head touching the flat lidstone roof. He listened. After the storm raging outside, the silence deep in the earth was all but absolute. From somewhere – he couldn't tell where — came the minute *plink* of dripping water. He felt disorientated, claustrophobic. The cavern was as cold as a grave and deathly still. He flashed his car-torch around. From the creased limestone walls, scoured and pocked into strange, jagged forms, winked small flecks of minerals and crystals. In one corner a seep of water had left a thick deposit of calcite that shone as brilliant as marble, while compacted into the ground were the traces of the rich red haematites, the iron oxides and the ochres that had been mined there from pre-Roman times until just a generation ago.

The quiet was growing oppressive. The walls seemed to creep in still closer. His torch blinked. Hastily he looked behind him. Would he be able to get out? He flashed the light ahead to where a narrow channel led out of the chamber. Was she down there?

'Grace?' he called.

An echo cheekily returned his call. He listened. Did he hear something? A pebble skittering away? A *cough*? Suddenly something flapped past his face, a small flying leather-winged creature, and he recoiled in horror. Whipping the torch round, he caught the dark flash of a bat flicking out and away down the channel. A convulsive shudder ran through his body. With a sudden resurgence of determination he stepped forward and, clenching his teeth, he bent to a crouch and inched his way into the channel.

*

She heard her name called from a far-off distance. It echoed briefly round the large cavern, then was lost. Who was calling her? Matthew? She stopped and swept the beam of the cycle-lamp around. Where was he?

'Matthew?' she whispered.

Silence, then a strange shuffling sound from somewhere she couldn't place.

'Matthew? Are you there?'

How would he show himself? Why here, in this place deep inside the earth? Because he lay buried in the earth?

317

Her torch-beam prowled across the walls, losing itself here in the deep recesses only to be found again there in a glint of gold or silver. Finally the thin circle of light came to rest on a small pool, cupped in the far side. A slow ooze from the seam of rock above fed the pool, depositing a streaky white stain behind it. But this was no ordinary pool. This was *it*. Matthew's magic pool. The potion he'd drunk to make him invisible. Bionic. Travel beyond time. And now to speak from the dead.

It glowed. All by itself, it glowed an eerie, enticing bluish glow . . .

Slowly she moved forwards, her limbs sluggish as a somnambulist's. She bent forward over the glowing pool. She could see her face reflected right through it. She cupped her hand. She reached out gently towards it . . .

*

'*Don't touch that!*'

With a startled cry, she whipped round. Pinning her in the torch-beam, Leonard stumbled forward into the cavern.

'Come away from there!' he shouted, his voice distorted by the echo.

A piercing scream split the air. Shielding her face with one hand, she backed away. Her other hand fumbled desperately along the side of the pool. He flashed the torch briefly on his own face.

'It's me – Leo,' he said. 'Keep away from that water! You mustn't touch it!'

'Leo?' she echoed numbly. 'What . . . ? Why . . . ?'

By now he had reached her. Grabbing her by the hand, he jerked her violently away into the centre of the cavern. There, with a grief-stricken whimper, she flung herself into his arms, weeping hysterically. Her torch clattered to the ground and abruptly went out. His shoulder blazed with agony as she tightened her arms around him. A scree of loose pebbles spattered down the shaft behind him, and for one terrible moment he imagined the channel was collapsing in on itself, sealing off their escape, burying them alive . . .

*

Slowly and carefully he led her back through the channel, across the smaller cavern, up through the steep shaft and finally to the surface. The storm had moved away to darken the sky in the east, leaving a light drizzle skirmishing in the rear. He helped her gently up the escarpment and down through the forest the other side, steering well clear of the enclosure. She was completely exhausted, and for much of the way he carried her like a wounded comrade in arms. She was clearly in terrible pain, and despite his efforts to hush her, she kept struggling to speak, though it came out in a semi-coherent ramble. And so, slipping and stumbling, they limped down through the forest until they reached his car.

He helped her into the passenger seat and wrapped her tightly in a car-rug. He threw her bike in the boot, fetching from a carton there a bottle of whisky, and forced her to swallow a mouthful. With the engine running and the heater on full, the car was warm within moments and the windows soon steaming up.

As he was about to slip into gear, he glanced across at the pale, shivering figure staring at him with large, hollow, haunted eyes.

'Was it . . . dangerous?' she asked in a half-whisper.

'Deadly dangerous.'

'But what is it?'

A strange sense of calm seemed to take hold of him. All those years, he'd been shunning this moment, but now that it had come, he felt almost relieved. What had started as a simple act of kindness to a bereaved family had turned into a deceit, and the deceit into a lie that struck at the heart of the two relationships he held most dear. Truth had to be constantly affirmed; the smallest untruth, if allowed to take root, grew until it overshadowed the whole garden. Now, finally, the time had come for him to reap the harvest of his own untruth.

He looked her full in the eyes.

'That water is radioactive,' he said quietly.

'*What?*'

'It's contaminated with caesium chloride,' he went on. 'A compound of the isotope caesium-134. Highly radioactive.'

She gasped.

'But how?'

He didn't reply at once. How much should he tell her? How little *could* he tell her so as to do the least damage? How would she ever understand, or forgive? The fan heater whirred noisily. The wipers beat intermittently. The windows were quite opaque now, cocooning them in an unreal, timeless womb. Where should he begin?

His voice cracked as he finally spoke.

'Grace, darling, I want you to remember first and foremost that I love you. I love you like a daughter – like a soul-mate, too. You've given me such happy times, being your friend and watching you grow up and sharing things with you. All I've ever done was for your sake, to help you, to protect you . . .'

He broke off. A horrified suspicion was dawning over her face.

'Leo, why are you saying all this?'

'Because it's time you knew.'

He offered her the bottle again but she refused it with an abrupt grimace. He took a swig himself and, thus braced, started to unfold the secret of his heart.

'Cast your mind back to the day before Matthew fell ill,' he began. 'You went exploring in this mine. It was completely derelict; no-one had been down there for years. You followed the mine-shaft deep into the ground. Matthew was leading. Finally you came to that cavern. He spotted that strange, glowing pool. What did he do then? Tell me what he did.'

Bemused, wide-eyed, she muttered a reply.

'He drank it.' Her hand flew to her mouth. 'Oh God!'

'Yes. I'm afraid so.'

'I . . . I don't understand. How could it possibly . . . ?'

'I'll explain.' He paused to collect his thoughts, unsure where to begin. 'I don't know how much you know about nuclear power. No? Well, the fact is, it may well be perfectly safe today – it's all so tightly regulated that mistakes really can't happen – but it hasn't always been like that. In the early days, people did things without foreseeing the effects. And something no-one foresaw was the problem of waste.'

'What has all this got to do with it?'

'Hang on. Now, there are various levels of waste. The really high-level stuff – spent fuel rods and so on – is reprocessed and the waste stored on site in underground tanks. Intermediate wastes get stored above ground, but also on site. But the biggest and bulkiest problem is low-level waste. Some gets buried in land-fill site, but medical and research wastes – and that's what we're dealing with here – tend to be too contaminated. These days, they're shipped to Harwell and packed in special concrete and steel drums and dumped at sea, and it's all very tightly controlled, as I said – NIREX, the AEA, lots of bodies are monitoring it the whole time. But there was a time in the early Fifties, when the nuclear industry was just getting onto its feet. At that time, it seemed reasonable to bury low-level waste in the earth. And you couldn't find a better site than a disused iron mine with good, deep shafts already conveniently dug for you.'

'They dumped some stuff *here*?'

He nodded. 'Ralph Cottrell was then young and hungry. He'd inherited acres of useless, unprofitable land, riddled with dead or dying mines. He was also on the local council. He saw his opportunity. How he slipped it past the committee without anyone taking note, I don't know. Anyway, he got a licence to dump waste on the Dent Cross site. He did a deal with the Ministry of Defence, which had a problem of waste from weapon research. To cut a long story short, they buried a number of canisters down a shaft in that mine and poured in concrete on top to seal it off. And there it lay undisturbed for nearly thirty years.' He paused before adding distantly, 'Which is just about the half-life of caesium-134.'

'And you mean . . . ?'

'The canisters evidently leaked. Maybe there was a land-slip or a mine-shaft collapsed and cracked the casing, or maybe they just corroded, I don't expect anyone knows. Anyway, some material began to leach out. It mingled with water and seeped through the rock into that small pool. Caesium chloride glitters. That's what attracted Matthew. And he did the very worst possible thing: he drank it.'

Her face had drained of all colour and her mouth hung slack in disbelief.

'Why didn't anyone say anything?' she stuttered. 'Why is Ralph Cottrell walking around free, when he's a murderer? Didn't you tell the police? What did *you* do about it, Leo?'

He looked down at his hands, avoiding the accusing glare.

'I didn't know at first,' he replied simply. 'When Matthew was admitted, his condition had me utterly foxed. For a while I even thought it might be meningitis. He was at death's door when I finally diagnosed it.' He looked up. 'Come on, Duchess, put yourself in my shoes. Who'd ever expect to find a twelve-year-old boy with radiation sickness *here*? What you aren't looking for, you don't find. Even if I *had* diagnosed it from the start, there was nothing I could have done to save him anyway. The dose he took, and the way he took it, was bound to be fatal.'

'Why?' she demanded.

'Well, alpha radiation particles aren't especially penetrating – the body's skin will even block them. But ingested they can be very damaging. A medium dose produces severe nausea within hours. Over the first two days, this develops into vomiting, loss of appetite, the skin reddens, the mouth and throat inflame, there's headache and sweating and diar-rhoea and feverishness. Drugs control the symptoms, and invariably the patient seems to get better during the second week – just as Matthew did, remember? But that's a false recovery. In the third week, his condition deteriorates sharply. The blood count falls. Lack of platelets prevents blood clotting and leads to haemorrhage, both internally in the intestines and externally on the lips and gums. You give blood transfusions, and if they fail, you'd consider a bone marrow transplant. The immune system collapses, laying the patient open to infection. The bacteria in the intestines spread, the digestive system breaks down, lung infections add to the complications ... Death generally occurs in three or four weeks. The actual cause could very well be gastro-intestinal failure, aggravated by pneumonia. That's what I put down on Matthew's death certificate.'

She had been listening, horror-struck. He'd held back nothing so far.

'You lied, then,' she whispered, drawing back.

'I did not! He died of the condition I recorded.'

'That wasn't the *real* cause!'

'Grace, suppose someone has AIDS but actually dies of pneumonia, which is the *real* cause? What was the real cause of the last war – Hitler invading Poland, or the whole background of German rearmament and dictatorship? These things aren't so simple.'

'Anyway,' she retorted, 'what I meant was, why didn't you do anything at the time?'

'I did all I could. The moment I realized, I wrote a report to the hospital Board. It so happened they were meeting that day. As you know, Ralph Cottrell is on the Board. The memo never got past him. He came flying into my office to see me. We had a terrible row. Matthew had just had heart failure; I'd managed to resuscitate him, but he was deteriorating so fast he couldn't last much longer. I told Cottrell the whole business was a major scandal and something had to be done to expose it. He argued it wouldn't do anyone any good: Matthew was virtually lost anyway, and it would only cause more grief and distress to your mother as well as spreading general panic and confusion among the local people. He assured me he'd see the mine was properly sealed for good and there'd be no chance of an accident happening again. Later the same day, a man from the MoD came to see me. He said they were sending in a unit right away to seal it off once and for all. So you see, I believed I was doing the right thing at the time.'

He paused. There was no need to add that the man from the MoD had also promised funds for a PET-scanner the hospital badly needed.

'What happened to Matthew, then?' she was asking.

He looked at the alarmed, grief-stricken girl huddled in the car-rug on the seat beside him, and he bit his tongue. Here the story had to end. He couldn't tell her that the man had actually sent an unmarked white van and, under the pretext of taking Matthew to Radiology for tests, they'd wheeled the semi-conscious boy out of his room, down the service elevator and out of the back of the hospital where the van was parked, and that unknown to anyone, to her or her mother or the nursing staff, the dying boy was driven away to a special isolation unit where a team of doctors and nurses, trained to deal with radiation cases, saw him through his last hours and then, when they'd finally certified him clinically dead, they'd removed his brain and quick-frozen it in liquid nitrogen and sent it along to a laboratory at the Department of Medical Research in Bath where it was received into the hands of a Dr Tom Welland. Nor could he tell her that the body, or what was left of it, was returned to the family already in its coffin, a sealed coffin that could not be opened, a strangely heavy coffin, too, on account of the thick lead cladding that had had to be used to line it. Nor, again, could he tell her how he himself had felt at being party to all of this – condoning it at first in the belief that he was genuinely helping further the cause of science, in the still more high-flown belief, too, that Welland's research was of global importance in preserving the civilization of mankind, but with increasing reluctance as, later, he began to see the practical, human toll upon the lives of Grace and her mother. How much individual human suffering was it justified to inflict in the interests of humanity at large? During the months and years that followed, he was to ask himself this question time and again, and in his heart he knew the answer.

'Leo,' Grace repeated, 'what happened to Matthew?'

He turned away again, unable to meet her eye. In his mind he could still picture that look on Laura's face when she returned to the hospital, having just gone home for a brief hour or two, and he told her that Matthew had died while she was gone, and then how he'd persuaded her, for *her* sake, not to ask to see the body . . .

'He passed away, angel,' he mumbled. 'Peacefully.'

A long pause stretched between them. The car was growing suffocatingly hot, and he wound down the window an inch. A cool breath of fresh, scent-laden air wafted in. He glanced back at the girl, sitting rigid and expressionless. He had yet to tell her the worst – about herself and her own condition. Perhaps he'd best leave it until she was home and warm. He reached towards the steering-wheel.

'Was that why you sent us off on holiday?' she asked suddenly. 'So you could check Matthew's things? So you could get rid of his clothes and the bits that were contaminated?'

He caught her eye. God, she was quick. He winced to recall that absurd farce. He hadn't wanted to have any part in it, but he'd already got himself in too deep to pull out. They'd used him as a convenient front. He'd even driven mother and daughter to the airport and collected them again, to make sure the coast would be clear for the men with geiger counters to come in and sweep the house clean. He'd even allowed himself to be consulted on suitable replacements for the sofa and the other furniture they'd insisted on taking and destroying. He shook his head. Each step might seem just an inch, but before you knew it the inches had become a mile. That, he knew bitterly, was the trouble with taking the expedient course, rather than taking the stand.

'Yes,' he replied quietly. 'That was why.'

'You told Mum you were clearing out all the old reminders, when in fact you were covering up your tracks.' Her eyes were full of tears. 'Leo, how *could* you?'

'I . . . I thought it was for the best.'

'Why didn't you just *say*?'

'It would have only made it worse.'

'At least we would have *known*.'

'Think of your mother, Duchess. At least she always had the comfort of her religion. If she'd known, she'd have got all embroiled with Cottrell and the government and the law, and she'd never have had any peace. All for what? Nothing could bring Matthew back.'

'For *justice*, Leo. For what's right. Mum isn't so feeble. She's capable of being responsible for her feelings without needing you to come along and spare them for her. You've no right to take other people's decisions for them.'

'I love you both,' he muttered glumly. 'I meant it for the best.'

'Well, you should *think* first.'

'It's easy to speak with hindsight.' With a bitter sigh, he reached for the gear-stick. 'Come on, let's get you home.'

He was about to move off when he felt her hand on his arm. Her face wore an expression of a new and yet more desperate anxiety.

'Leo,' she haid hoarsely, 'what about *me*? I didn't drink that water, but I was there too, you know. I got splashed . . . I think.'

'I know.'

'All these funny things that have been happening to me recently, are they a result of that? They *must* be, mustn't they?'

'You're cold and wet, angel. Let's get home first.'

'No! Tell me now, Leo. *Don't fib to me any more!*'

He drew out into the road and pulled slowly away.

'I'll tell you all I know as we go along.'

Twenty-five

Grace lay in bed, staring up at the ceiling. From the kitchen downstairs came the muffled rise and fall of voices; Mum and Leo were *discussing* it again. She closed her eyes. There was nothing to discuss any more. The facts were beyond dispute and, for all Leo insisted, the case beyond cure. She knew: she wasn't stupid. Matthew had been there before. For her, it had taken five long years, but in the end it had come out of hiding.

She could feel a broad swathe of pain, dulled by some tablets Leo had given her. She could feel it worst in her head, a swollen, jabbing pain that prodded her deep inside with every pulse of her blood. She was riddled through – that was the phrase they used, wasn't it? *Riddled through with cancer.* She imagined it working its way through her body, attacking where the matter was softest, creeping through her brain, eating its way silently through her bowels, a myriad of deadly cells bubbling away in a hideous ferment. She wondered how it actually *looked*. She thought of snails in the garden she'd seen that had eaten bait, lying upended and deliquescing to a slimy froth. She imagined tumours like blood-blisters, puff-balls filled with yeasty spore, evil yellow mushrooms that spawned in dark, hidden corners of rotting sheds. And she thought back to Matthew in his last days, with his gums bleeding and his skin blistered as if it had been sandpapered, and later, when his very blood had failed him, lying there in the bed, half blotched and half blanched and terminally drained. Yes, she knew what to expect. Except that for her, because she'd merely got splashed with the lethal water and it hadn't entered her body, it had taken these years to show itself. For the same reason, too, her death would be all the slower and more lingering and, for all Leo's desperate talk of the miraculous powers of medical science today, no less certain. *People don't die of cancer these days like they used to*, he'd insisted. Yes they do, Leo, they still do.

Painfully, she sat up and reached down the side of the bed for her blue exercise-book. She flicked through it briefly, then lay back and let it drop to the floor. She'd been wrong all the way along. They hadn't been divinely inspired visions at all. They hadn't been messages from Matthew either. Nor even fantasies born of madness. They'd been just plain hallucinations, plain *cancerous* hallucinations, brought about by a tumour on the brain. All to do with pressure on the secondary visual cortex; she knew her biology. It was so very clear now.

We mustn't jump to conclusions, Leo had kept on saying. *First, we must do tests.* Tests! He was staying the night and taking her into hospital with him in the morning, for tests. What use were tests when the outcome was so obvious? The proof was everywhere you looked. Take her pregnancy, for instance. Leo had himself admitted it had come about as a direct result of her exposure to the contaminated water. Radiation had been shown in mice to interfere with re-duction division during egg formation, he'd begun to ex-plain. Something had probably been wrong with the foetus, anyway, he'd added as if by way of comfort; spontaneous abortion was Nature's way of dealing with mistakes. 'Nature's way' – the phrase people used for making the abnormal sound normal.

Tests. She shuddered, recalling all the tests they'd done on Matthew, and to what good? She felt the panic rising. She understood the system. First thing was to get you into hospital. Once you were there, you never got out. They made a show of asking your permission, but you were too drugged up and too frightened anyway to make balanced decisions. They gave you radiation therapy that made you sick and your hair fall out. They cut you open. Stomach cancer meant operating on your stomach. Brain cancer meant —

No!

She shrank up against the bedstead. She was drowning, suffocating. In the morning they were coming for her, with the hood and the straitjacket. They'd probe and pry, they'd stick in tubes and jab in needles . . .

Clawing her way across the room, she threw open the window and frantically gulped in the cool, damp air. She had to escape.

*

Somewhere in the small hours of the night, in that silent no-man's-land when the burden of the day past is laid aside and that of the morrow not yet assumed, Grace awoke from a beautiful dream. She was walking down a path in a garden, surrounded by flowers – foxgloves, delphiniums, hollyhocks, snapdragons, flowers of an old English country garden. At the end of the path stood a small low white gate, set in a hedge of trailing dog-roses and honeysuckle. Beyond this gate stood Matthew. He was dressed in his old jeans and shirt, but they glowed a bright, creamy white. She knew he wasn't alone, for she could feel there were other people about although she couldn't see them. He seemed unsurprised to see her. He just smiled, with a look that suggested he'd been waiting a long time, and beckoned her over. She stepped up to the gate. Somehow she knew that if she went through she would leave everything behind. He was waving her forward. His smile sparkled. 'Come on, Grace,' he was urging her, 'don't wait, hurry up.' Slowly she reached out to the latch.

For a while she lay in bed, staring at the pattern of moonlight on the ceiling, her spirits crushed with disappointment at having to leave that world of joy and brightness for this world of anguish and gloom. Slowly, pressing hard into her stomach to contain the pain, she rose and hobbled over to the window. The sky had cleared, and a half-moon shone brilliantly across the garden, glinting off the stream and tracing the fields and trees beyond in delicate silverpoint. Heavy, dark nectars made her senses swim. The world out there was beckoning her, the world of the night and its cool, wide embrace. Turning, she slipped a light dressing-gown over her nightdress and fumbled her way to the door.

She tiptoed along the gallery, pausing at the top of the stairs to listen. In the living-room below the clock chimed a single stroke: one o'clock, or the quarter hour? Outside, the mill stream had grown strangely quiet, as it did when swollen by heavy rains. From the spare room opposite came the sound of gentle snoring. She frowned. How *could* he have behaved like that? Not telling the truth was the same as telling lies. Five years, built on a lie. Five years of false smiles and sham fun. All that she'd loved and admired in him, all that she'd confided of her deepest secrets in the friend and father he'd appeared to be, all the ideas and influences she'd gladly adopted from him and the 'enlightenment' he'd prided himself on having brought into her life . . . all of that was now wiped out. She felt betrayed but, strangely, not bitter. She didn't forgive him, but nor did she condemn him. She felt numb, untouched. None of it mattered any more.

Gripping the banisters, she made her way sideways down the stairs, step by step. At the bottom, a nauseous wave of pain broke over her, leaving her choking in its wake. Finally straightening, she glanced around. All was still. Long shafts of moonlight fell slantingly across the floor and up along the leather sofa. Leo's sofa. She turned quickly towards the kitchen. There she poured herself a glass of water and stood clinging onto the edge of the sideboard through another long surge and ebb of pain. Then, quietly unbolting the back door, she stumbled out into the night.

She followed the narrow path past the garden shed and through the shrubbery to the tow-path by the river. Underfoot, the mud was cold and sticky. A sudden rustle in the undergrowth startled her, bringing her momentarily back to her senses. What was she doing out here? But she was too tired, too exhausted with the struggle, for any more thinking. All she wanted was to be out in the wide open where she could breathe freely and stretch the wings of her being. She stood for a while at the river's edge. Upstream, to her left, spread the fields she'd so often explored on her walks; there, only a hundred yards up the path, lay the spot where she'd been walking with Emily that time when she'd had one of her . . . *go on*, she said to herself . . . yes, one of her brain-blips, one of her tumour-turns.

Choking back a sob, she turned to the right. A short way down, the river divided. A smaller stream split off beneath the path along the side of the house, gathering speed as the channel narrowed until suddenly it gushed out in a solid jet down into a deep shaft where, no longer having a mill wheel to turn, it dropped in an unbroken twenty-foot fall to rejoin the main river below the weir. With the water so high, the cascade fell askew onto the side of the house itself, muffling the usual drumming of the waterfall with an eerie quietness.

Like a sleepwalker, she followed the path. On her left, the main river glided swiftly, silently. Trailing willow fronds spread eddies that coruscated strangely in the moonlight. A moorhen, startled by her approach, fled squawking into the darkness. On she forced herself, pausing every few steps to let out a gasp of pain. The weir was very close now and the downrush growing louder all the time. Already she could make out the three tall, stout pillars with the teeth of their rack-and-pinion tracks clearly outlined against the sky. The sluice-gates must be down. The path swung inwards as the river banks closed, concentrating the water flow into the weir. By now she had reached the wooden rail-posts and, stumbling on, hauled herself up the three small steps onto the narrow bridge that spanned the weir itself. She clutched the hand-rail and looked down. In an unbroken stream, the water sluiced over the draw-gate, falling down, down in a gleaming curve of molten glass, where it broke up into a bubbling, boiling, frothing cauldron. She leaned over, pressing her stomach where it hurt against the rail. The roar would drown her pain. The rush would carry it all away. The force . . . the violence . . . cleansing her . . . washing through her . . . She leant further forward, further towards the dancing spray, towards the molten sheen, towards the endless downrush, folding in on itself, pulling, tugging, beckoning, *Come on, Grace, don't wait, hurry up,* urging her through the small white gate, drawing her closer, inviting her to embrace the light, to topple into the shimmering, pulsing light, closer, closer still, just that little bit more . . .

*

Leonard woke at six o'clock to the bleep of his watch alarm. Hurriedly he slipped on his old shirt and mud-stiffened trousers and tiptoed round the gallery, past Grace's half-open door and down the stairs to the kitchen. They'd stop off at his own house on the way in for a shower and a change of clothes and, with luck, he could be in the hospital early to get her on the scanner before the day's bookings began.

He made a pot of tea and took it on a tray back upstairs. He tapped first on Grace's door. When there was no reply, he pushed the door open. She was evidently already up. She must be in the study, he thought. He knocked on Laura's door and woke her, then went back downstairs to the study. The room was empty. Frowning, he checked the other rooms on the ground floor, then went back upstairs. He looked in the bathroom, in Matthew's old room and even in the attic at the top, but there was no sign of Grace. With growing alarm, he went back to her bedroom. The bed was cold. Christ, he thought, she's tried to do it again! He hurried down to the kitchen. He'd check if her bike was still there.

The back door was unbolted. He raced into the shed. No, the bike hadn't gone. Just as he was turning back into the house, an imprint in the muddy path caught his eye. He looked closer. It resembled the mark left by a human heel. He glanced around. A few yards towards the river was the unmistakable print of a foot. A bare foot.

At the river, he turned left and followed the path for a short distance until he realized he'd lost the tracks. Returning, he picked them up again going in the other direction, along past the side of the house. He broke into a jog. As he passed the mill race he stopped and, sick with dread at what he might find, peered over the sheer drop into the chasm. No: no sign of her there. Heaving a deep sigh of relief, he carried on at a brisk pace. He hurried over the weir bridge, glancing with a shudder into the boiling ferment below, and followed the path as it descended to the wider, slower spread of river. He was half way down when he realized the footprints had petered out again.

He looked around. In the pearly light of early morning, all was very still, very calm. He cupped his hands.

'Grace?' he called. 'Grace!'

No reply. No sound at all, save the chittering of birds just audible above the constant bubbling roar from the weir. He retraced his steps to the bridge from where he'd be able to command a view over the land around. Carefully he scanned the rolling fields all about for any sign of movement. Through gaps in the trees he caught the occasional flash as a car passed along the main road, and in a barn two fields away a tractor started up and lumbered away down a track. He was about to turn back and check she hadn't got back home by following the far boundary when a fleck of white far down the river caught his eye. For a moment he stood screwing up his eyes trying to make out what it could be – whether a discarded fertilizer bag or possibly an abandoned fridge or pram . . . But somewhere in the depths of his mind, an ominous drumbeat was sounding. With his pulse thumping, he set out down the path to check.

For much of the way the object was hidden around a bend in the river. He quickened his pace. As he rounded a clump of thorn bushes, he froze in his tracks. There, twenty yards away, against the river's edge, trapped in a mat of sedges, floated a bulky tangle of clothing. An arm, a human arm, bent awkwardly against the bank, projected from one side, while the waves as they lapped against the water's edge gently stirred the form, revealing a body, pale and stiff, beneath the brownish water.

With a terrible howl, he leapt forward and threw himself into the water. In a single movement he swept up the body and carried it to the bank. One glance at her eyes and her blanched skin told him she was dead. No! She couldn't be! Digging her mouth clear of mud, he pressed his lips over hers and breathed hard. She made no response. Weeping, he sat her up and bent her head forward between her legs to try and empty her lungs, but she was as limp as a rag doll. He grasped her to his chest and yelled.

No!

He shook her, he squeezed her, he slapped her, he rubbed her arms, he buried her against his chest, everything and anything to bring back the smallest spark of life, but he knew it was hopeless. Lifting up his head, with the tears streaming down his face, he howled out his rage and pain.

Twenty-six

After the first rage came the disbelief, the numbing sense of impossibility that the two worlds should co-exist simultaneously, one in which school books littered the study and magazines lay scattered on the sofa, where a game of solitaire lay half-finished on the coffee-table, a postcard written to Emily, as yet unstamped, upon the kitchen table and by the back door a muddy pair of yellow wellingtons size six, a world where the cupboard shelves groaned under packs of the favourite cereal and the fridge was filled with the special fruit yoghurt, where everywhere you turned, from the shopping list upon the kitchen scratch-pad to the record catalogue upon the stereo, there was the characteristic handwriting . . . and, side by side, another world in which the person who gave form to all this lay in a bed upstairs, covered with a sheet. And then followed the second rage, the rage that nothing could be *done* about it. Life was so fragile, a switch that took only the merest touch to flip over. Nothing he or she or anyone had ever done, no love given, no prayer uttered, no kindness shown, not even all these things taken cumulatively, had sufficient weight to unflip that switch. Leonard had seen death a thousand times; death on the ward, death in the streets, even death at home when, the one shortly after the other, his parents had died. But nothing had prepared him for *this* death. For here he saw himself responsible.

At first, he turned to the immediate practicalities so as to busy his hands and silence his mind.

Dr Stimpson was called. Having certified the death and attended to Laura, the doctor arranged for an ambulance to come and take the body away. He would write a report, which would go to the Gloucester coroner. There'd be a post-mortem and an inquest . . .

'Please not a post-mortem,' pleaded Laura desperately. 'What's the need? We know what happened.'

Dr Stimpson instinctively looked to Leonard to respond. Inured though he was as a medical practitioner, Leonard, too, felt appalled. Grace had been so pure, so lovely.

'It's routine, Laura,' he replied thickly.

'It was an accident and she drowned,' she went on. 'What do they hope to prove?'

Relatives naturally found the prospect of an autopsy deeply upsetting. But here he recognized an underlying fear, too. For Laura, with her religious beliefs, it *had* to be an accident. His mind flashed back to that dreadful moment when he'd lifted the drowned girl into his arms and carried her lifeless body, so light and insubstantial, back to the house, where he'd laid her on the sofa in the living-room and gone upstairs to tell Laura. 'There's been an accident,' he'd said blandly, in that cruelly innocent phrase used for breaking the very worst news. And an 'accident' it had since tacitly remained. Just once she had turned to him and started, 'You don't think she could have *meant* to . . . ?' but instantly she'd cancelled the thought from her mind. The implications of thinking it could be anything other than accidental, of admitting even the smallest possibility that Grace had taken her own life, were so unbearable that *her* own life would become unlivable.

He turned to Dr Stimpson.

'Death by misadventure,' he said. 'That'll be the verdict, wouldn't you say?'

'Unquestionably,' replied the doctor loyally.

Yet *he* knew the reality, with a dreadful and absolute certainty. He knew what he'd told Grace the previous day in the car. Laura did not. He hadn't told her, and he'd agreed with Grace on the way home that they wouldn't – or not yet, with all the other worries she had on her mind. Knowing what he did, it was glaringly obvious what the poor girl had done. From a purely practical point of view, besides, could anyone really believe that she'd gone for a midnight stroll, bare-footed, with no more than a light dressing-gown over her nightdress, and that she'd chanced to stroll not this way nor that but precisely there, down to the weir, where it was most dangerous? And, once at the weir, that she'd somehow slipped or lost her footing or in the confusion of sleep mistaken the river for land, the scum at the edge for the path . . . ? When he later took Dr Stimpson to the spot, he found the footprints clearly showed that she'd walked onto the bridge and stopped in the centre where the water ran fastest and deepest. The ground there was rough and quite unslippery, and the rail was firm and intact and set at waist-height. Laura might close her mind to the evidence, but could anyone with an open mind call that an accident?

Laura, wrestling to create a story she could live with, had suggested she'd suffered one of her 'turns' at the crucial moment. This, at least, from what he'd done in the laboratory, he knew with absolute certainty to be impossible. Perhaps, nonetheless, she'd had a moment of dementia. With the thunderous noise of the rushing water and with all the deceptive tricks moonlight could play, maybe she had suffered some kind of sensory deprivation and momentarily lost her bearings. Fast-rushing water was well known to exert a mesmerizing power – wasn't 'white noise' precisely that? – and in her mood at the time she'd have been especially susceptible to any hypnotic influences. Under the right conditions, such sensory deprivation could rapidly lead to total physical and mental disorientation. Here, too, to cap it all, was a psyche desperately seeking escape from the reality of the senses . . .

Words, empty sounds, specious gobbledegook. They might comfort Laura, but he couldn't kid himself. He *knew*. Grace had committed suicide, and he was directly to blame. How could he go on living his own life, with that knowledge?

There were other more immediate lives, however, for

whom he was responsible. He called the hospital and cancelled his morning's appointments, leaving instructions for the locum to stand in for him. Laura had phoned Father Gregory, and the priest was on his way over. In the meantime, he'd leave her with Dr Stimpson and slip off home. He'd clean himself up and make one important and very long-overdue phone-call, then return to Coledean and stay with Laura for the rest of the morning.

*

Ralph Cottrell put his foot down on the accelerator with a savage oath. Damn Leonard Grigson! The man had been trouble from the start. He'd just had him on the phone accusing him of criminal incompetence, saying he'd failed to seal the mine adequately, that he *himself* had been up there last night and actually got inside. He was coming over later for a show-down. Cottrell kicked the Range Rover into a lower gear and swung off the road up the track that led into the forest. He'd have to find a way of getting the doctor transferred; he should have had it done ages ago.

Soft drink cans and other picnic debris littered the trail. Here and there he saw evidence of camp fires, and, half way up, he found two campers pitching tent. By the track further up, pointing the way, stood a makeshift cardboard placard, disfigured by rain, with a cross boldly painted on it and, beneath, the words, *Ave Maria*. He swung over to the side as he passed and rode it brutally down. By the time he'd reached the clearing, his temper was at breaking-point. He drove straight up to the gates, switched off the engine and climbed out. He'd see for himself what the hell Leonard Grigson was talking about.

He undid the padlock and chain and let himself into the enclosure, shutting the gates quickly behind him just as the dogs, yelping shrilly, came streaking across the clearing towards him. He stormed forwards, heading for the grilled gate on the other side that blocked the entrance to the mine, calling out to the dogs as he went to come to heel. He'd

338

taken no more than a dozen paces before he slowed in his tracks. The two alsatians had shuddered to a halt a few yards away. Their hackles were bristling, their ears flattened and their teeth bared, and they stood growling in a strange, throaty note he'd not heard before. Keeping a distance, they began slowly to circle him.

'Back off, you two!' he called and reached into his pocket for the whistle.

Wrong jacket.

He called them by name. He put out a hand to one, but it suddenly lunged forward and snapped, gashing him with its sharp teeth. With a stab of alarm, he began to brush his way past. With a snarl, the second dog made a dive for his heel. He spun round and booted it hard on the jaw, knocking it backwards. What had got into the brutes? Anyone would think they were starving.

The dog let out a savage howl and, wheeling round, flew at him. He threw up his arm to defend himself and felt its teeth sink into the flesh. With a yell of pain, he flung it off, and it fell back again, ripping and tearing him as it went. But the first dog now leapt in under his guard and went straight for his throat. He stepped back just as its jaws snapped closed an inch from his face, but the force of the onslaught knocked him off balance. Toppling backwards, he tripped and fell bodily onto the ground.

At once they were upon him. He fought back, kicking and punching however he could. He grabbed one by the throat, determined to strangle the brute with his bare hands, and together they wrestled in the mud. He dug his fingers into its windpipe, fighting off its twisting, snapping, slavering jaws, crushing its body under his own to smother its hind claws lacerating his thighs. But the other dog attacked his exposed face and head, he could feel its teeth grazing his skull, he could see its eyes rolling red just inches away from his own, and with a terrible scream he released his grip and rolled over into a tight foetal huddle, wrapping his arms tight around his head. A searing blinding pain tore through his buttock. He rolled over onto his side, then a blaze of agony ripped through his groin. The howling rose to a crescendo, greedy and feral. He fought his way onto his knees, blood everywhere, his hands shredded, the flesh hanging from his face in strips, and through a haze he looked out towards the fence and the Range Rover beyond. He fell onto all fours, his hand outstretched, and began dragging his broken body forwards towards the fence, inch by inch towards a hope that never grew any nearer, then fell for the last time, brought face down into the earth, into the mud, the blood, the teeth, the eyes, the sky, the earth . . .

*

She'd been here before, she'd been here twice before. First with a husband, then with a son. People said Nature had ways of preventing you remembering pain. Nature was cruel: the memory of how she had coped before might have helped her now. Nothing that had gone before left any legacy to equip her for what she was suffering now.

Laura sat on the sofa looking out of the tall window into the garden. She sat very still, for there was nothing to move for. The phone rang, but she let it ring. She had nothing to say and there was nothing she wished to hear.

Father Gregory, heartbroken, had spoken his words of comfort, and she had found some momentary glimmer of solace in the familiar litany of prayer. The doctor had made the noises of his own profession, about taking rest and medication three times a day and soon she'd be ready to face life and make a new start. A new start: how hollow the words sounded. There could be no life ahead, for there could be no future, only an eternal, empty present. Leonard alone had said nothing. He was bereft, too, and in his grief he felt the sorrow went beyond words.

She glanced at the clock: it was past six. He said he'd be over soon. Sooner, later, it didn't matter when. Time didn't exist any more. Dimly she recalled Mary Nolan once describing what it was like to be blind. It wasn't like being in a dark room, in the presence of darkness, she'd said, but rather it was an absence of dimension. That was how she felt. She could see things – the trees, the window-frame, the chair-arm, her own hands – but they didn't register as having meaning. She was absent, in a one-dimensional world. The real world had stopped twenty hours before, when she'd said goodnight to her daughter. Her mind stood frozen at that moment, locked in a perpetual loop in which she went over and over that final scene, trying to remember for all time exactly what she'd said to her and how Grace had responded and whether there had been any hidden clues, any unspoken cry she should have heeded, while with each replay the mental videotape grew thinner and fainter, until she ended wondering how much was real and how much a construct of her own. If only she'd stayed with Grace all afternoon. If only she'd gone in to see her in the night. If only this, if only that. The lost dimensions of her present world were locked in those worlds that might have been.

Distantly, she heard the front door bell ring and, a moment later, Leonard's footsteps cross the hall into the living-room. He came up to her without a word and, bending to kiss her on the forehead, drew up a chair near her and sat down. He was ashen, drawn, and for a long while he didn't speak.

'I've just come from the manor,' he said finally. 'Ralph Cottrell has been found up by Dent's Cross. Mauled to death by his dogs.'

'My God,' she muttered when the news sank in. 'His poor wife.'

He nodded.

'Fitting, though,' he added quietly.

'How can you say that?'

'Things he did . . .' He looked up. 'There's always a reckoning, Laura. You believe that.'

'But not like that. Not like *this*!' She turned away to hide her tears. 'It's so unfair. What harm had *she* ever done anyone?'

Out of the corner of her eye she saw him rise and sit down

beside her, then she felt his arm close around her shoulder, drawing her towards him. He stayed sitting there as the minutes ticked past, slowly and quietly stroking her hair until at last the welcome numbness returned and she felt calmer.

*

Above the drone of Father Gregory's voice, Leonard could hear a bird singing from the top of a spreading yew tree, a lone, pure melody that rose and fell like the bubbles in a fountain. The day was insolently beautiful. He looked about the small churchyard. In the days that had lapsed since Grace's death, some attempt had been made to tidy it up. The nearby graves had been roughly weeded and the grass rather poorly mown, leaving an ankle-deep mulch of cuttings. Behind the main group of mourners stood the derelict chapel, its stonework crumbling and its windows boarded up. The funeral service had been held in the convent chapel but the interment here at Coledean; Laura had been adamant that Grace should be buried beside her father and her brother.

Laura was standing beside him, very calm and composed. Her courage and strength astonished him. He didn't know what went on out of sight in the privacy of her room during the lonely hours of the night, but he felt she must have a resilience he lacked. Perhaps it was simply her faith. He would go over for supper, or for such of a meal as they could stomach, and he'd stay until a sedative or natural weariness overcame her, then return to his own house and seek solace in the whisky bottle. Solace he never found, but silence he did. Silence from those endless gnawing questions that all ended in a cul-de-sac of self-recrimination. Often she pressed him to stay, and he knew he was walking back into the old familiar issue.

She looked up and, catching his eye, gave a small, brave smile. He dropped his gaze. Christ, he thought with a flush of shame: I can't even look her in the eye.

'Forasmuch as it has pleased Almighty God in His great

342

mercy,' Father Gregory continued intoning, 'to take unto Himself the soul of our dear sister Grace here departed . . . grant, we beseech Thee . . . eternal peace and life everlasting . . .'

Leonard gave a jolt. *Eternal peace and life everlasting.* That phrase rang bells. Hadn't he read it somewhere in Grace's exercise-book? Then he felt a grim smile creep over his face. Of course: the words spoken by the priest over the dying boy at his hospital bedside! The final piece of the jigsaw was in place.

The service dragged on slowly. For a while he scrutinized the faces of the people about him, composed in prayer. The Reverend Mother, wise and wrinkled; Sister Bertram, smooth and moonlike; the Monsignor, suave and subtle; Emily, tough and truculent; Benedict, ruddy and lean; his mother Mary, lined and sunken. And he thought to himself that the one thing all those faces shared was belief. They saw a coffin disappear into a hole in the ground, yet they believed that Death had been vanquished. He looked across at Father Gregory, his cassock slightly crumpled and his cheeks flushed with the warmth of the day and the fervour of his prayer, and he felt a moment's envy that these people had found something that bypassed the mind and spoke directly to the heart. Were they maybe, inadvertently, tapping into some resonance to which he'd made himself blind and deaf? Un-questionably, they found comfort in their ritual, and comfort was what he most badly needed. He might choke on the Creed, but could he not somehow re-interpret it for himself and so tap that wellspring of solace? Did they claim a monopoly on comfort, and was subscribing to their dogma the price to obtain it?

The service ended, and the diggers began shovelling the first clods of earth into the fresh grave. Slowly the mourners started to file down the path to the small gate where Father Gregory had taken up his position to shake hands as they left. Leonard was escorting Laura down the path, and as they approached the gate they drew alongside Sister Bertram.

The nun began to exchange a few sympathetic words with Laura, while Leonard took the chance to fall a few steps behind. He wanted to pass the priest by himself.

As his turn came, he held out his hand. Father Gregory hesitated for an instant, flashing him a look of surprise, then dutifully clasped his hand, mumbled a greeting and turned to the next in line. Steeling himself, Leonard kept hold of his hand and drew him closer.

'I'd like the chance to talk to you, Father,' he said. 'Could I come round and see you? Later today?'

'I'm really not sure . . .' the priest began, drawing back.

'Just for a chat.'

'Well, I have Mass at six-fifteen, but maybe afterwards . . .'

'I'll be there. Thanks.'

He rejoined Laura, who was now with a group of Sisters. He already felt an absurd sense of relief. Somehow he had to unburden his soul to somebody, and it couldn't be to Laura. Father Gregory was a professional confessor. He'd drop in after work, on the way over to the mill house. He was taking her out to supper so that she wouldn't be alone on this of all evenings. But when should he turn up at the priest's? He had no idea how long Mass took.

*

Father Gregory stood at the door of the lodge-house and watched as Leonard's silver Jaguar disappeared through the wrought-iron gates of the convent. He felt too shocked to move. His world had been turned upside down. He'd sought the hand of God here, there and everywhere, but it had all been an illusion. Leonard *had* got a rational explanation for everything, damn him. Our Lady had not shown herself to Grace in visions, Mary Nolan's cure was no miracle and the virgin conception was nothing but a freak of biology caused by exposure to the natural earthly forces of radiation. *Radiation*, he repeated to himself with a small shiver. Invisible, intangible, all-powerful, omnipresent: could there be a closer earthly parallel to God?

He turned indoors and refilled his wine glass. Leonard's glass remained half drunk; his taste was clearly too sophisticated for the home-made stuff. He went to the window and stared out across the garden into the dying sun. He'd treated Leonard harshly – too harshly? Had he once again let his own feelings interfere with his duty as a priest? True, he was angry with himself for having rushed to see evidence of visions and miracles and disappointed, too, that these grand hopes had been finally and convincingly dashed and, perhaps no less bitter a pill to swallow, that the Monsignor and the Church had been right all along in their scepticism. But it had obviously cost Leonard a great deal to come and open his heart as he had. As one human being to another, shouldn't he have done more to ease the man's troubled conscience? But how else *could* he have reacted? The confession was, frankly, the most shocking he'd ever heard.

'I don't quite know what you expected I could do,' he'd responded when Leonard had finally finished.

'I hoped I could find some . . . peace of heart,' Leonard had replied humbly.

'I offer you my sympathy but I can't offer you absolution, if that's what you're after.'

'I assumed that confessing to a priest —'

'I'm not your priest, Leonard, because you're not a believer. Unburdening the heart naturally makes one feel better in oneself, and I respect you for your courage in coming here. But a formal confession to a priest is a different matter. The priest is merely a mediator. You're making your confession to God. If you don't believe in God, what meaning can it have? Unless you're merely seeking to ease your conscience. I'm sorry, but the Church isn't in the business of letting people off the moral hook so they can sleep more easily at night, Leonard.'

'I understand that, Father,' he'd said quietly. 'I suppose I want to make some kind of apology . . .'

'You're a humanist, Leonard. I suggest you apologize to

the *people* you've harmed, not to God. That's more likely to give you the peace of heart you seek.'

That had been the best he'd felt able to offer, and in the circumstances he felt he'd been very restrained.

He opened the French windows and stood on the doorstep, all but oblivious to the scents and sounds of the evening. After all, what about Laura? If Leonard didn't tell her, should *he*? What was his duty now? He surely wasn't bound by obligations of confidentiality, was he? One thing was clear: leaking nuclear waste in the mine posed a very real and present danger to the people of his parish. What if another child found the unmapped entrance? Or, more likely, one of the public who came flocking to the site? The more he thought about it, the more his anger swelled within him. Natural justice demanded a reckoning. If he wanted a crusade, let it not be a clerical crusade, crossing swords with the Monsignor and the Bishop, fighting at a level where dogma interwove with diplomacy and the orthodoxy was as much politics as faith. Rather, let it be *pastoral*, at the level of the people and of religion in practice, the level at which he saw and knew God.

Turning to his desk, he took out a pen and pad of paper and began making a list. First he'd write to the chairman of the local council on which Ralph Cottrell sat. Then to the local Member of Parliament, to the editor of the *Western Post*, to Friends of the Earth, to Greenpeace.

*

Laura unlocked the front door and led the way into the hall. Instinctively, she listened for a voice calling from the living-room, but smothered the thought before it could take root. She turned to Leonard.

'That was a lovely meal, thank you.'

She hesitated. He stole a glance at the clock behind her.

'I've got an early start,' he said.

'Leonard, don't you think . . . I mean, with the way things are . . .'

'Don't worry, I'll be over tomorrow. We could go to a film.'

'Yes, all right.' She touched his cheek. 'You're such a kind man, Leonard. It's just such a comfort to have you here. I'm sorry if I've been distant. Maybe we could find a way . . . one day . . . I mean, there was a time when things were different.' She looked at the carpet. 'I guess I haven't made much of a success of that side of life, either.'

He drew her towards him and gave her a firm hug.

'Don't say that, Laura. There's the whole of the future ahead. Things to see, places to go. The Canaries are wonderful this time of year.'

'Then won't you stay? It doesn't have to be the spare room, Leonard.'

'Laura —'

'I'm sorry,' she said, pulling away. She'd said too much.

'No listen, Laura,' he went on with sudden urgency. 'I want to . . . I don't know how to put it . . . I want to come to the table, *clean*. A clean break, a fresh start. There's too much that's gone on. Too much that needs to be settled. Do you know what I'm saying?'

'I think I understand.' She drew him towards her with a sigh and kissed him lightly on the lips. 'Go along now. Get a decent night's sleep. And don't take chances on the road.' She smiled weakly. 'You're all I have left now.'

She saw him off at the door, then turned back inside and went into the living-room. She stood for a moment, looking around. She'd left everything as it was before the accident. The school books and magazines still lay scattered over the sofa and the game of solitaire remained untouched on the table. Slowly she picked up the books and magazines and stacked them on the sideboard, then sat down and finished the game of solitaire. Yes, there *was* the whole of the future ahead. She'd keep the shrine to Grace's memory in her heart, not in her house. Leonard had been right to clear everything out after Matthew's death. In the morning she'd make a start on Grace's room. She, too, would come to the table, clean.

*

Leonard prowled restlessly around his study, whisky glass in hand, trying to avoid Grace's eye and her brave, innocent smile shining out from photo frames everywhere he turned. He loosened his tie – *her* tie – and went over to the window, but against the pitch-black night outside all that met him was his own reflection in the glass.

At the time, what he'd done had seemed reasonable, even right. Nothing would have been gained, no practical purpose served, by shouting 'Scandal!' from the rooftops. Cottrell had been right, factually speaking: the boy was all but gone, his family were suffering enough already and it would only spread panic in the neighbourhood. But from that one decision, everything else sprang. He gave permission for the dying boy to be transferred to a safe place. (Safe for whom?) The step after that was equally easy – turning a blind eye to the unauthorized removal of organs from the boy's body. They weren't *his* hands on the saw and scalpel. *He* wasn't breaching the Human Tissue Act, *he* wasn't breaking a common code of respect for a parent's right to grant or withhold permission. Besides, there was justification, if he needed it: he'd been convinced by Welland of the value of his research and even seen himself as making his own minuscule contribution towards the preservation of human civilization. And then came the next and similarly easy step: the lead-lined coffin and the special funeral arrangements. Having got that far, how could he refuse to collaborate in helping to send Laura and Grace away while the house was checked and cleansed, and then to provide a covering explanation when they returned?

Pragmatism was pernicious: each step might be just a few simple inches, but the cumulative result could be horrific. The root danger lay in basing actions on reason and logic. Most of the world's inhumanities flowed from one small seed of an idea, an assumption often lost too far back in the mists of memory, from which events then marched on by irrevocable logical steps, irreversibly gathering momentum. The only way out was constantly to affirm the truth. Ultimately, his crime was against *truth*.

He knew Father Gregory had been right. He wouldn't have felt truly absolved by a mere word from a priest or the performance of a penance. To reverse the *un*truth, he had to proclaim the truth to those he'd most hurt. And that meant to Laura. He did want to share a life with her, but he couldn't live with her if he didn't tell her. On the other hand, would she live with him if he *did*? That was a risk he'd have to take. Perhaps, in the end, his atonement would be the healing of them both. Perhaps too, in the act itself, he would find some kind of faith to echo hers.

He reached into his desk drawer and took out the small blue exercise-book he'd recovered from Grace's bedroom. For a while he sat reading through it with a growing sense of wonder and humility. For all the bombast of modern medicine, for all his arrogant belief in rational dicourse and scientific method, was there not something here that went beyond all that, something that transcended the confines of the senses and that should perhaps be allowed to remain forever beyond? A resonance shared throughout the family of living things, a tuning-in to a reality that existed on a different plane altogether, beyond the grasp of the mind of man? He shivered. Was this not moving towards a description of God?

He pondered for a while then, refilling his glass, he reached for a thick pad of paper. The hall clock struck two. Outside, in the darkness, an owl hooted; from far off, after a while, came a hoot in reply. He took up his pen, then paused. Where should he begin in making his atonement?

Where it all began.

'*Matthew Francis Holmwood died on 6th March 1981*,' he wrote, '*at the Royal Hospital, Gloucester. He was twelve. He had been admitted three weeks before, complaining of severe*

349

stomach pains. His blood count was catastrophically low and, despite frequent transfusions, it continued to fall . . .'

*

Slipping a glove on his good hand, Tom Welland carefully unscrewed the lid of the cryostat and eased the stainless-steel rod out of the cylinder of liquid nitrogen. He managed to work a pair of insulated tongs into his other hand, despite the splint, and unhooked one of the small polythene sachets from the rod. Taking the sachet over to the bench, he chipped a splinter off the frozen matter with a small sharp chisel and returned the rest to the cylinder. Within a few minutes the tissue would have thawed sufficiently to enable him to begin extracting the DNA.

While he waited he took a couple more painkillers, wincing as the motion of swallowing moved his broken jaw, and glanced with smouldering rage around the desolated room. A sheet of plywood board had been nailed across the isolation chamber panel and makeshift shelving and benches lined the walls, while piled up in one corner lay the debris of broken electronic equipment beyond salvage. His fury and hatred welled up to boiling-point. Somehow he'd find a way of screwing that mad bastard. First, he had to get back on his feet. He'd lost *years*. This unique, unrepeatable experiment, the prize of his life's work, lay literally in ruins around him. But he'd start again. It would mean changing tack, but he hadn't lost absolutely everything. Some things had escaped the ravages.

He turned back to the Petri dish on which the shaving of tissue was already softening and regaining its fleshy pink. It might possess two extra chromosomes, but he could readily eliminate that flaw. Then what would he have? The first human parthenogenetic material. The first human foetal cells composed only of maternal genes. The first natural human clone. The experimental value of the material would be immeasurable. Laboratories across the world would bid against each other for the smallest sample. It would be

350

ideal for mapping the human genome. Some workers might introduce it into mouse and rat lines for research into congenital illnesses. But finally, it could only be a matter of time before someone just wanted to find out *what would happen if* . . . Scientists were like mountaineers: they did things because the things were there to do. Someone was bound to try to introduce this material into a human female ovum and, with its genetic flaw corrected, grow the child that Grace would have had. What might that produce? Science's answer to the Second Coming?

He smothered an ironic chuckle and reached for his surgical gloves. He was a scientist: his job was to do the work, not to worry about the end uses.

Gradually his smile died. With mounting excitement, he turned towards the window and let his gaze stretch far out into the infinite blue sky.

Yes, what *would* happen if . . . ?